ALVAH BESSIE'S SHORT FICTIONS

By Alvah Bessie

Fiction: Alvah Bessie's Short Fictions
One for My Baby
The Symbol
The un-Americans
Bread and a Stone
Dwell in the Wilderness

Non-Fiction: Spain Again
Inquisition in Eden
Men in Battle

Anthology: The Heart of Spain (editor)

Alvah Bessie's Short Fictions

with an introduction by Gabriel Miller
Rutgers University

SOLO FLIGHT

seventeen short stories

&

THE SERPENT WAS MORE SUBTIL

a novella

Chandler & Sharp Publishers, Inc.
Novato, California

Grateful acknowledgement is made to *Esquire* for their permission to re-print "Profession of Pain" and "Man with Wings" in *Solo Flight*.

Library of Congress Cataloging in Publication Data

Bessie, Alvah Cecil, 1904–
  Alvah Bessie's Short Fictions.

  Contents: Solo flight, seventeen short stories —
The serpent was more subtil, a novella.
  I. Title.
PS3503.E778A6 1982   813'.54   82-9739
ISBN 0-88316-546-5

Cover and Title Page design and art: David Sarvis
Book design: Jon Sharp and Alvah Bessie
Composition: FW and Marin Typesetters

To the memory of
Kyle S. Crichton

Contents

Acknowledgments / ix

Introduction, by Gabriel Miller / xi

Solo Flight / 1

Redbird / 3
Only We Are Barren / 8
Horizon / 29
A Little Walk / 39
Pet Crow / 47
Bare Grain / 58
Deer / 72
No Final Word / 82
A Night Call / 93
Profession of Pain / 112
A Personal Issue / 116
Sam's Woman / 126
Solo Flight / 138
Soldier! Soldier! / 145
My Brother, My Son / 153
Man with Wings / 164
Call It Love / 175

The Serpent Was More Subtil—A Novella / 185
Susan Aldridge, *Requiescat* / 187

The Snake Friend / 197
Save the American Eagle! / 216
The Time Now Is . . . MAZOLA! / 232
Bubo virginianus / 246
The Scientific Method / 257
The Serpent Was More Subtil / 269

Publishing History / *Solo Flight* and
The Serpent Was More Subtil / 289

Acknowledgments

It is embarrassing to realize that I have outlived eight of the nine publications that printed these stories, so I am obliged to thank *Esquire* alone for permission to reprint "Profession of Pain" and "Man with Wings."

I am far more deeply obligated to the many sons and lovers, husbands and wives, front-line comrades and writers, actors, artists, directors, lawyers, doctors, editors, publishers and business people whose support and encouragement, whose energy and affection, whose advice, patience and experience helped make the publication of this book a reality.

They know who they are and they know how much I love them.

Alvah Bessie

August 1, 1982

Introduction

ALVAH BESSIE's primary subject, throughout his writing career, has been his own life. In his best work he has projected his personal experience in imaginative constructs that at once evoke and define some special aspects of the contemporary human condition. Early in his career especially, Bessie infused his fiction with a concern for language as a device that could permit the imagination to purify and transform reality.

Bessie the young writer who thus forged a distinctive, impressive voice is the man we meet in this collection, which features stories composed between 1929 and 1941 and a novella written between 1951 and 1956 (never before published). The twelve-year span from which the stories are collected was Bessie's most productive period of artistic achievement, compassing not only these (and other) penetrating and award-winning stories, but also his two most important larger works: his first novel, *Dwell in the Wilderness* (published in 1935), and his account of the Spanish Civil War, *Men in Battle* (1939). This period of efflorescence concluded with another fine novel, *Bread and a Stone*, in 1941. During this time Bessie lived in New York City (where he was born in 1904), in Vermont, and in Spain, where he fought as a member of the Abraham Lincoln Brigade. Prior to 1929, he had spent one winter in Paris.

His literary career came to a hiatus when he accepted an offer to work for Warner Brothers in 1943 and then busied himself accumulating five scriptwriting credits in six years, including an Academy Award nomination (original story) for *Objective Burma* in 1946. Because of his commitment to and participation in radical political causes, however, Bessie was fired shortly thereafter and subsequently blacklisted. He was one of a series of unfriendly witnesses (the group later known as the Hollywood Ten) who refused to cooperate with the House Unamerican Activities Committee's investigations of Communist infiltration in the film industry in 1947. Fined and sentenced to a year in jail, he served his term (1950-51) in the federal prison in Texarkana, Texas.

The aftermath of the hearings, court appearances, and prison left Bessie little time for writing. Most of his energy was spent in looking for work, and that which he found was not the kind that paid very much or spared him the time for creative composition. He held a variety of jobs, including writing for the International Longshoremen's and Warehousemen's Union, stage-managing at the Hungry i nightclub, and writing publicity for film festivals. Inevitably, the books he did write during this period were basically self-defense, as he lashed out at the system that had wronged him. First came a novel, *The unAmericans* (1957), about a writer who fights in Spain, publishes a book about it, becomes a Communist, and is jailed for perjury when a colleague lies to the court trying him, and the jury believes the lie. The novel alternates between the protagonist's present life (as a writer) and his experiences in Spain. Next, Bessie produced *Inquisition in Eden* (1965), a nonfiction account of his days in Hollywood, his experiences with HUAC, and his time in jail. The latter is the superior work because in it he managed to balance his bitterness with humor, particularly in his portraits of various Hollywood personalities, whereas the novel's major weakness is his failure to temper the autobiographical foundation with imaginative recreation. Balance and sympathy, the hallmarks of the earlier fiction, are overthrown here, making *The unAmericans* his weakest novel. (Bessie, however, is convinced that it is his best novel and perhaps the best work he has ever done.) Bessie's more recent fiction, two novels rooted in the world of show business, displays a welcome resurgence of the form and vision that distinguished the early work.

The Symbol (1966), his only commercial success, concerns the private and public forces that destroy a movie star (whose resemblance to Marilyn Monroe made the novel an object of controversy, both profitable and damaging). His most recent book, *One for My Baby*, which was inexplicably ignored by its publisher upon its release in 1980, focuses on the nightclub scene of the 1950s and on the psychic torments of a stand-up comic monologist named Dr. Sour, who turns his private nightmares into material for comedy. It is Bessie's best work in over forty years.

Alvah Bessie's fictional concerns are not those one might expect of a political radical. His first novel was written during the Depression, but it does not focus on the materially dispossessed who found a spiritual home in the Communist party, and it does not conform to any of the dictates of radical cultural commissars as to what proletarian fiction should be. In most of his work, Bessie's criticism of the system is implied, not directly stated. And although Bessie emphasizes (in correspondence and conversation) that his fiction is based on Marxist understanding of economic exploitation and class struggle as played out in contemporary capitalist societies, the thrust of much of his writing, certainly the early fiction, is away from political cures, for the artist in Bessie seems to distrust isms, and he finally does not suggest cures of any kind.

Bessie's protagonists are emotionally, psychologically, and spiritually isolated. Each work concentrates on the interior landscape of (usually) one character, exploring the dark, mysterious aspects of the personality. This emotional isolation of the protagonist, then, is often reflected in the physical environment. His experience of Vermont — Bessie and his family lived there for a few years in the 1930s while he made attempts to live off the land, to do odd jobs for pay, and to write — seems to have provided a useful objective correlative for the inner contours of the human psyche, in a sense releasing his own aesthetic vision.

The Vermont scene served as the basis for most of Bessie's early stories and was clearly the artistic inspiration for *Dwell in*

the Wilderness (though the novel is set in the Midwest). This landscape, while it occasionally teases man with its beauty, remains
brutally indifferent. A man may labor hard and fight the land, but
it yields little to him in the end, and it is always there, immutable,
mocking him by its endurance, power, and sheer expanse. The
people live in ragged shacks which barely stand against the ele-
ments, offering minimal comfort and warmth. Neighbors are far
away, and because of this the people have become stoics, self-re-
liant and introverted.

Many of the protagonists in the stories are Bessie's alter egos, city
people struggling to be at home in this alien environment. They are
articulate, sensitive men in a universe that seems to have no use for
such sensibility. Their isolation, moreover, is not simply a matter of
physical separation, however extreme, for Bessie's protagonists are
alienated not only from their neighbors, but more important, from
their families and from themselves. The countryside thus becomes
an ideal testing ground for the human spirit, where Bessie's characters are made to confront basic anxieties: apprehensions about the
dissolution of marriage and family, imminence of death and extinction, the desperation with which men must deal in order to survive,
and the horror of a world in which nature's design seems all too
often predatory, if not, indeed, utterly random and chaotic.

The best stories in this collection have an almost claustrophobic
feel about them. The protagonists are very poor, have difficulty
finding work, and enjoy little intercourse with the larger world.
Trapped within the maze of their own personalities, they struggle with forces they are unable to understand. In "Only We Are
Barren," an artist who strives to approximate life on canvas is
teased by the nature around him, which in its myriad changing
forms continually frustrates him, and his artistic block is mirrored
by his wife's sterility. The narrative offers glimpses into the minds
of each as they struggle to overcome what separates them from
each other and from active participation in the life around them.
The wife is more successful in this effort, managing at least to re-
spond openly to her surroundings. In her husband's case, however,
Bessie seems to take a Romantic position, building toward his artist's recognition that what he lacks is authentic intuition, a gener-

ous openness to nature – this is why his work lacks that final mysterious quality needed to breathe life and real meaning into his art. He realizes that an authentic relationship with life is sustained only by living it, confronting it on its own terms. Bessie is close to Robert Frost here, and his story approximates Frost's

> Something we were withholding made us weak
> Until we found out that it was ourselves
> We were withholding from our land of living,
> And forthwith found salvation in surrender.
>
> (from "The Gift Outright")

Bessie's story, however, concludes with only a tentative sense of surrender, for its final image is, again, of the enigma of nature's design; total acceptance is withheld.

The concepts of spiritual isolation and the struggle for meaning are reinforced in "Pet Crow" and "No Final Word," wherein the central events are, respectively, a miscarriage and a still birth. The latter, one of Bessie's most exquisite stories, takes place mostly in the consciousness of the protagonist as he waits for his wife to give birth. As this man grapples with a disturbing lack of any feeling at this moment, his thoughts run from the mundane to the philosophical: "No final word may ever be spoken, no image drawn from which the mind may leap as from a springboard, to touch truth and destruction at once." The need for understanding and communion still plagues Bessie, and he is frustrated by the inability of man to achieve true identification with nature or with his loved ones. In the final scene, too poor to buy a coffin for his dead baby, the father prepares a box for the burial. The story concludes as he kisses the "yellow face that was so much his own." Death thus opens up the emotions of this protagonist and presents the possibility that, in reconciling opposites, he may be prepared to surrender himself to life's design.

Death forces two other protagonists to meditate on life in "Bare Grain" and "Sam's Woman." In the first a preacher thinks about the life of a man who has just died, the events of that life forcing him to confront examples of human selfishness and greed, but also to dwell on the mystery of love. Considering how illness and death polarize and then permanently separate us from those we have loved, the preacher is forced by his own recollections, gradually, to accept the frailty of man's essentially selfish nature. During the course of his meditations he remembers his own father's death:

> For five years I watched my father die. I tended him skillfully, I held the basin when the blood flowed in torrents from his mouth, I watched the doctors thrust needles into his chest, I gave my own blood to swell his depleted arteries. But I hated him and the night he died I was elated, for it meant an end of restriction, an end of worriment, an end of sympathizing with a man whose suffering by then made no impression on my mind or heart.

He is finally able to accept his own limitations as well as those of others as he stares into the winter darkness outside.

This same attitude pervades "Sam's Woman," told from the point of view of Ella Carter, who is tending a dying woman. At first the hypocrisy of the various relatives and friends who are waiting for Jennie to die enrages her. But again, the contemplation of, and finally the love of the commonplace bring comfort. Learning, also, that human weakness is occasionally redeemed by a noble impulse, she accepts death and its attendant suffering while at the same time embracing life.

These "Vermont" stories are characterized by a tone of struggle with the nature of things. At times the protagonist is unable to resolve the dilemma facing him, defeated by the inability to surrender himself to nature and open himself up to his fellow man. However, in most of these stories a tone of acceptance dominates, as Bessie seems bound to acknowledge that if life were not a testing ground, "a hard place to save one's soul in," there would be no way to find out if one were very good.

The stories rooted in the Spanish Civil War are remarkable for their restraint. Where one might expect either polemics or excessive didacticism, Bessie neither implies nor invokes any ideology.

The stories concentrate on men under pressure and the psychic wounds left by the war. Although the Spanish war is the specific backdrop, they are in a very general sense war stories, as always the universal experience is emphasized. As is the case in all of Bessie's stories, specific detail is meticulously woven into the fabric of private moments.

In "Solo Flight" the protagonist is alone in an airplane. He has been taking flying lessons and this is his first solo flight. Initially buoyed by the thrill of being outside the customary confines of space and time, he is disturbed by intrusive memories of the war, finally coming to a frightening realization of how truly outside all normal experience he is. Despite the sparing use of details about the war, "Solo Flight" is decidedly a war story because of Bessie's technique of recreating its disorienting psychological and emotional effect by expanding his protagonist's concept of space and time and then suddenly contracting it.

"Soldier! Soldier!" is also about a soldier's personal confrontation with war's destruction. Sent out to find food and supplies for his regiment, the protagonist discovers what he thinks is a deserted dwelling. While exploring the house, he finds an old woman who was obviously considered too old and ill to evacuate with the rest of her family. She is surrounded by her own feces and remnants of food, apparently in a state of incomprehension. The soldier has no time to deal with her, but must quickly gather up supplies before the enemy finds him. When he returns to camp, then, he watches as the house is blown up. The story effectively demonstrates how the innocent are caught up and destroyed in a chaos they barely understand and how the soldiers, more comprehending but no less victims, are sustained by what the dead leave behind.

Perhaps the best of the war stories, and one of the highlights of the collection, is "My Brother, My Son," a tale linked to the others in that death is the catalyst by which its protagonist gains insight. The story takes place after the war, when the protagonist meets the parents of his closest friend, who died in battle. Probing each character's inability to communicate his profound sense of loss, Bessie concentrates on how people busy themselves with social formality and domestic trivia in order to avoid confronting their pain. Again there is precision in the use of detail to capture the small and insignificant gestures that occupy the important moments in life. These characters manage at last in a hesitating way to communicate the deep emotions that silence so effectively punctuates.

Bessie's novels expand on the themes of the stories, but the protagonists they develop are no longer author surrogates, as Bessie learned to distance himself more from his characters. If the protagonists of the stories are mostly artistic and sensitive souls collectively crying out for "design," the protagonists of most of the novels seem overwhelmed by events which they cannot comprehend or even articulate. And if, in the stories, some of the protagonists discover that the earth is a hard place to save one's soul in and accept it as such, the characters in the longer fiction achieve no revelations and are inevitably destroyed.

Bessie's masterpiece, *Dwell in the Wilderness*, is a family chronicle that concentrates on life as a repetitive, boring routine. The novel centers on Eben Morris, who grows up in a backwater Midwestern town after the Civil War, marries the sheltered daughter of a Victorian minister, and sets up a business. Their life is benighted and harsh, a fabric of wearying trivialities. Husband and wife are very different in temperament: he is kind and soft, she hard and possessive. Eventually he is forced to leave her, but not before they have raised four children, each maimed in some way by the parents' mismatch. Roger, the eldest, has much of his father's decency and enough resolution to move away as soon as he can. Manley, the second son, is very much like his mother, displaying no true sensibility but liking to have a directing hand and enjoying the feeling of power and superiority that success in business brings him. Dewey, his mother's favorite, escapes her dominance because of his single-minded and obsessive devotion to his own career in the theater. Neither his family, his financial troubles, nor even his homosexuality shake his purposes — to a degree his mother's dogged nature finds a kind of creative release here. It is in Martha that all the family currents become fixed. She is her mother's target, her father's comfort and her brother Dewey's servant. Married to a man who cannot satisfy her spiritually and in love with a homosexual (her youngest brother's lover) who cannot satisfy her physically, she is not strong enough to find fulfillment in herself, and so must seek it in others. This family comprises thus a highly divergent group, but Bessie emphasizes how much more aware of each other they are because of this, how truly strong are the connections of family despite all attempts to deny or escape. His accomplishment is in probing an institution too often taken for granted or regarded superficially, and, in so doing, exposing the mysterious nature of this most commonplace of situations.

The novel covers the period 1876 to 1925, but Bessie avoids theorizing on the changing American scene or its possible effects on the lives of the family. He deals with his characters exclusively as individual psychological entities, penetrating to the interior life and representing external events only as they affect the thoughts of his characters. The novel is essentially a mosaic of psychological scenes heightened by Bessie's attention to form, structure and sentence rhythm. It is an incisive and penetrating series of portraits, inexorably revealing the dark, isolated, and fragile beings who are mankind.

Bread and a Stone, too, is concerned with personality. The story deals with Ed Sloan, an ex-convict, who marries a schoolteacher and finds that providing for his family is very difficult. After a long internal struggle, he attempts a holdup and accidentally kills his victim; a few days later he is caught and sentenced to death. The novel is similar in its aims to Dreiser's *An American Tragedy* and Richard Wright's *Native Son*, although Bessie avoids the suspense of arrest and trial that would only detract from his intensive investigation of the mind and character of Ed Sloan. (It is so narrow a focus that the novel's other characterizations suffer as a result.) The novel opens with the arrest and moves by slowly uncovering the layers of Sloan's personality: his life has been one of dislocation, his character formed by a cruel stepfather and a series of reform schools. This, however, is not a thesis novel about the effects of environment on character, but a study of Sloan's attempts to achieve integration with life and to find some meaning. His marriage begins to help him, but hope and possibility are then cruelly ended by his crime, leaving Sloan unable to understand why his life has so suddenly simply fallen apart.

Wanda Oliver of *The Symbol* is no more fortunate than Sloan, despite the fact that she has achieved the personal and financial rewards of movie stardom. Her end is to be just as stark, just as brutal. This is clearly a Hollywood novel, although Bessie dispenses with the genre's characteristic exploitation of the Southern California landscape — the brilliant sunshine, the palm trees, the hills, the spectacular beauty that seems to mask and even mock what is going on in its midst — preferring, again, to explore the mind under pressure. Bessie's moral interest displays a psychological, rather than a cultural perspective.

In this novel, then, Hollywood is not so much a place of recognizable boundaries as a state of mind. Wanda's inability to comprehend either her own "magic," or her "star power," or the relationship between her promiscuity and her sexual frigidity, or even her failure to form a lasting love relationship, is quickly established and therefore becomes the controlling tone in the complex narrative investigation of her life story. Wanda is an individual destroyed by extreme tensions, those precipitated by an orphaned childhood and those forced on her by a Hollywood system that she is unable to come to grips with. Moving back and forth in time between 1957 (the present), which is wholly created in monologue and dialogue (with her psychiatrist) formats, and the major incidents of Wanda's past, the physical action of the novel gradually brings the reader up to her psychological collapse and death.

Bessie's most recent novel, *One For My Baby*, examines the mental disintegration of a nightclub comic, Dr. Sour, who struggles to maintain some emotional distance from his difficult past by exorcising it in his monologues. However, he finds himself unable to keep his demons at bay forever. Caught up in the inferno-like atmosphere of The Nightbox, a club in San Francisco, he is surrounded by a series of psychologically maimed grotesques and becomes the centerpiece of a Goyaesque nightmare tableau that finally comes crashing down around him.

Sour shares characteristics of many Bessie protagonists: a childhood in an orphanage (this one, however, run by his mother), a frustrated sex life, a failed marriage. His life is marked by a lack of love and an inability to express it in personal relationships. He is able to temper his frustrations only by exposing them in public. The other characters in the novel are psychological and spiritual orphans as well. Like Sour, they find that their adult lives offer no improvements or solutions, and they are caught in a spiritual maelstrom that sucks them continually downward into depression and despair. The myth of the fifties, outwardly manifesting "the good life" for all, is thus exposed as a sham.

One of the novel's special achievements is its style, which can best be described as a daring combination of the naturalistic and the surreal. The milieu of the nightclub and its environs is described in detail, a portrait precise and revealing, but the book is structured like a reflected dream: episodes dissolve into other episodes, monologues evolve into third-person narratives, history alternates with fiction, personal confrontations are resolved into comic routines. Successive scenes, occasionally violently juxtaposed, reflect upon each other and thus refract upon themselves — the effect is unsettling, and highly dramatic.

In this novel, however, the destruction of the protagonist is not Bessie's final word. Sour is balanced by Dan Noble, a writer who works at The Nightbox. He, too, is seeking to reestablish contact, after a recent divorce. He does succeed in breaking out of his nightmare existence and is able to touch another human being and experience love. In this sense *One for My Baby* is Bessie's most generous novel, firmly linked in tone with some of the early stories whose promise it fulfills.

A word about *The Serpent Was More Subtil*. The first of the interconnected stories that form the novella "Susan Aldridge, *Requiescat*," was written in 1951, while Bessie was in prison; during the next five years he wrote the other six stories. The total work is an autobiographical account of Bessie's young manhood — a coming-of-age story, a portrait of the artist as a budding herpetologist, it is a fiction unique to the Bessie canon because of its breezy, light-hearted tone (something like that in parts of *Inquisition in Eden*, though there it was more hard-edged). Whatever points Bessie wants to make seem secondary to the sheer delight he takes in telling the tale. The story is unusual, too, in its relation to the many narratives of this type published in this century. Bessie has succeeded in distancing himself almost totally from his own story, looking back on his childhood with only a certain fondness and an impulse of forgiveness. He does not use his authorial perspective to comment directly on the action, but simply presents it in a way that implies the relationship between the characters and events that played formative roles in his adolescence. The narrative voice skillfully combines the maturity of the man with the whimsy and wonderment of the boy growing up; the story seems to have happened and to be happening at the same time. The richness of the narration effectively captures the double perspective of the story and provides further evidence of Bessie's ability to use language to create marvelous effects.

Alvah Bessie's public career has overshadowed his literary accomplishment. He is known today primarily for the causes he championed and fought for. However, he has produced as well a body of written work worth reading and discussing. The private Bessie seems to be a much different person from the public one, for when he writes fiction the public world and its struggles seem to fade away. Instead he concentrates on the isolated individual and his attempts to understand himself and to come to grips with death, the mysteries of nature, and the struggle to survive. His characters seem to inhabit a timeless world where history and politics rarely intrude. His fiction usually takes the form of a dream, reverie, or meditation, and his career thus becomes a record of an artist's struggle to come to grips with all of these things. The novels are more often than not records of failure and disappointment, although sometimes there is an epiphany — a breakthrough — a moment of genuine meaning. Many of the stories gathered here offer glimpses into such moments, clearly revealing an artist in full command of his material and his craft. They are well worth reading and discovering again.

Gabriel Miller

Rutgers University

Solo Flight

Redbird

S INCE a whole year of careful tracking and perfect marksmanship had practically wiped out all signs of Indians, The Boy Hunter now decided on bigger prey — the Dinosaurs. He had casually noted their great spoor during his many years' experience in this particular range of wood, but at all times he had been preoccupied by the ideal of finishing the work that the Pioneers had begun so long ago — extermination of the hated Reds. Of course, the Pioneers had had other work to do — the clearing of great woodlots and the cultivation of deserts and swamps, and so it was not to be expected that they could have taken the time or trouble to track down every remaining Indian and slay him in his tracks. Therefore, he, Edward Anderson, The Boy Hunter, had undertaken to pick up the torch where they had let it drop, and he had dedicated all his extra hours to the hunt.

Men knew him now and there was no stigma attached to his appellation of *The Boy Hunter*. It was just because he was still a boy of twelve and at the same time a hunter of renown that the word *Boy* here assumed a special significance; and he would certainly have rather been called *The Boy Hunter* than *The Hunter* or even *The Redkiller*, as he had often seriously considered being called. Men had recognized his prowess, and that very afternoon he had been presented, through the medium of his father, who had served as spokesman for the populace, with a handsome new air rifle engraved, "To Edward Anderson, The Boy Hunter, in grateful token of our gratitude. . . . The People of San Antonio, Texas."

Perhaps it was not altogether by accident that the Anderson house stood on the edge of the Great Cottonwood Forest — a sparse patch of second-growth trees, darkened by great tracts of thickly tangled underbrush and sage. Here it was that Edward Anderson had wrought the daring deeds that made him known. Now, as he swung his brightly polished rifle on his shoulder and patted the light lariat at his belt, he knew that it would take many weeks of hunting to find the slightest trace of a Redskin, and so he finally turned his thoughts to the almost fabulous Dinosaurs, who inhabited the darkest part of the wood. His noted hunter, Rab, stood by his side, impatient for the chase — a hound of purest breed and keenest nose. He bent and gave the beast an indulgent pat upon the brow and said, "No nonsense, now — big game is on the rampage today, and until we have it safely in our bag, no play for you." He had to curb this tendency of Rab's for, great hunter that he was, he had never left his childhood and was almost always ready for a romp, no matter whether serious business was on hand or not.

Entering the wood, Edward unslung his rifle and cocked it cautiously; his eyes narrowed to two steel-sharp points that saw every leaf and twig and blade of grass. No Dinosaur would take him unawares, for it was a noted habit of the beast to appear where it was most unlikely to appear. He knew, for he always spent years of patient research before he took his gun in hand to hunt. He stepped and cautiously took aim at a trembling leaf and pressed the trigger with his forefinger. Pip! said the gun, and "Bang!" he shouted with it, and he saw the leaf tremble end to end. He nodded grimly and pursued the path. Soon the path would end, and he would be in virgin forest, untracked and unsurveyed. But he knew no fear, for he knew the forest leaf by leaf and stone by stone for many hundred miles. Often he had seen himself lying dead there, his insides ripped out by the wild beasts and strewn along the earth, and he had frowned — not so much for himself, for he knew no fear, but out of pity for his family. He knew he could die when the time came, but he knew how hard it would be on Ma and Pa and Sis. They would never survive the sudden shock, and of course it would be a sudden one — no Hunter ever . . . . He stopped and wiped a tear from his eye and laughed aloud.

Rab looked up at him and cocked the little white patch of hairs over his left eye and ran his tongue out and smiled with glee. "No nonsense, sir," said Edward to the beast, and Rab closed his mouth and dropped his ears and prowled forward with his eyes intent and cold. Suddenly Edward stopped and dropped to the earth. His gun came to his shoulder and he aimed and fired at a huge bracket fungus on a fallen tree. "Bang!" A corner of the fungus dropped to earth, and Rab ran forward and retrieved the piece.

Good, thought Edward, placing the fungus in his canvas bag; and he was tempted to pet the dog, but he did not want to spoil him for the hunt; too much praise, he knew, was bad for dogs. He made a small clucking sound in his throat and Rab went on a-head of him, his tail scraping the earth.

An ideal day for the hunt, Edward thought – the air was thick and heavy with the approach of rain, and there was no breeze to carry sound or hinder its approach. He stood silently and listened, enjoying the tenseness of his muscles – those steel springs that he exercised upon the chinning-bar every night before he went to bed. He knew they'd serve him in his need and he was happy in that knowledge.

There was a cardinal that he had noted in the brush. He clucked to Rab, and silently, as though he walked on feathers, he tracked that cardinal. He watched the bird with firm and ice-cold eyes. He felt the power of his sight as it shot its powerful beacons from underneath his brows – nothing missed the eyes of Edward Anderson. He watched the redbird now as it flitted here and there in search of seeds, ignorant of the presence of mankind. He raised his gun and drew a bead at the brilliant scarlet body and followed it with his rifle barrel, round and up and down; then heedlessly, he trod upon a twig. The redbird heard and raised its head, while the Hunter cursed his awkwardness and bit his lips in rage. The redbird cocked its head sidewise at him, and a tiny beacon shot from its brilliant black eye. Edward laughed and lowered his gun, while the bird flitted from tree to tree, cocking its head and watching him from out the corner of its eye. He frowned and followed it, still cursing himself for his poor woodsmanship and whispering, "No man or beast dares withstand the rage of The Boy Hunter."

I'll let you get away with it this time, he thought, because you are so beautiful; and he enjoyed watching the glossy plumage of the artificial bird as it caught the dying beams of the sun through the foliage. Rain was coming up and the air was static and close; odors from the forest floor rose quietly in straight lines from plants and berries growing on the earth.

"Here, beauty," Edward said, "tweet tweet," and the bird flashed its round dark eyes at him and stopped its hunting and was motionless. Rab looked up at Edward. Suddenly he threw his gun to shoulder, cried, "On, men, duty calls!" and fired. "Bang!" said the gun and the shot died down and echoed through the vast and silent wood. The bird fell like a dropped stone, one small white feather from its underwing floating softly earthward after it.

Then The Boy Hunter stood on tiptoe and shouted to the sky. "Bravo!" he cried, and "Hurray!" and his whole body tingled with electricity. He followed Rab forward to the foot of the tree and searched through the fern until he saw the body lying there. Rab nosed it and looked up at Edward, cocking first his left eyebrow and then his right, with a bewildered expression on his face. Edward felt ashamed of the look in Rab's eyes and, ordering him off, he picked up the light, limp body of the bird. Its head rolled idiotically from side to side, and it looked absurdly unlike itself — there was no gloss on its feathers and its eyes were almost closed; the nictitating membrane was thick and half-opaque. He rolled it in his hand and was horrified to find a drop of dark blood on his palm. With a shudder he hurled the body far through the air into the sagebrush and trembled as he thought of its landing with a thump. He bent down and plucked a fern and wiped his palm with it, then scraped his fingers on the sandy earth.

He rose and slung his gun onto his shoulder and marched on, Rab following, back towards home. There were no Dinosaurs a-broad that day — they did not like the rain; they were only human after all. Far off through the wood he could hear the early patter of the rain as it marched through the trees after him. Black round eyes were flashing from behind the thin tall trees — he saw them everywhere, and finally he stood still and cried, his hands hung limply at his sides and his face raised into the light rain.

"Oh, beauty," he sobbed, "oh, beauty" and dug his fists into his eyes and stamped on the earth with first one foot, then another. How would you like to be dead, you big bully, he heard the voice of Edward Anderson; and he saw himself dead in the wood with his insides ripped out by the vengeful animals who sat around and smiled at him with round, dark, flashing eyes and ran their red tongues in and out between their teeth; Sis and Ma and Pa stood by and said, It serves you right.

Unmindful of the lurking Dinosaurs, or the one remaining Redskin, Fallowdeer, who had been seeking vengeance for the murder of his kin, he tramped on homeward in the soft, light rain, trailing his rifle behind him on the earth. Once in his room he hung the rifle on its rack and washed his face; then chinned himself six times upon the bar – the hunter must keep training, he reflected, but then he thought, I'm not a hunter now.

Rab sat upon the floor and watched him out of his deep, sad, darkened eyes. . . . Then Edward dropped to the floor and sobbed again and gathered the great dog into his arms and rocked himself back and forth, hugging the dog and saying, "Poor Rab, poor Rab, poor Rab." Rab licked his face and thrust his nose into his armpit and laid his ears back and rumbled softly in his throat.

"To your corner, sir," Edward said and sat down at the desk and started to write, sucking the end of his fat pencil and making sporadic dabs at the paper. Then he sat and looked at the wall for awhile but finally rose and looped his lariat over the chinning-bar, swung up onto the bar; and, putting his head through the noose, he hanged himself.

The body struggled heavily in air – a heavy weight rocking clumsily on the end of a line, and Rab sat curiously watching it, then started jumping playfully up and about the swinging body and pushing it with his stiffened forelegs and leaping out of its way when it swung back.

"I killed myself on account of shooting a redbird," said the note.

Only We Are Barren

Morning:

T HE little house stood on a meadow fenced all about with a light growth of trees that marched up the low hills to the higher ones, and out of these woods at dawn came the early birdsong and low social quacking of the crows, till group by small group the birds themselves came out, seeking their food and playing in the air. Swallows shot twittering over the house in the early gray light; and in their separate beds the young man and young woman lay listening with a half-attentive ear to the insistent summons of the ovenbird on the wooded hill behind the house, and the slow cawing of the crows flying over the land, and the twittering of the barn swallows, swooping after early-rising insects. Out of half-closed eyes, weary with the pleasant morning semi-sleep, they saw the gray light outside the windows, and the birdsong mingled with their receding dreams to weave a medley that would be forgotten by the time they were fully awake.

She rose always before him, with a mind immediately clear and fresh, and went out into the clean, damp air, doing her morning chores with brisk movements and a light heart. She glanced at the tomato plants and plucked off the leaves that had been riddled by the striped tomato bugs. The dead woodash she sprinkled every day had proved ineffectual, and there was always a heavy beetle to squeeze between reluctant fingertips and throw away.

The woodchuck sat erect among the boards of the torn-down barn, looking this way and that; and she smiled at him as he finally ambled off into the long wet grass, even though he'd eaten the new leaves of the beans and chewed the tender spikes of the sunflowers.

But this morning as she bent beside the rows of springing plants, she thought suddenly of her mother, and she knew that her mother was up too and thinking of her daughter far away — "a pity she never married again and settled down to a happy married life" — and she smiled at what her mother might have thought if she could only know.

She called him for his breakfast, and even as he answered grouchily from the tumbled bed and rose, blinking and groping for his bathrobe and slippers, she shivered from head to foot at the irony of her position — thinking she could never tell her mother of her happiness, or that she was living the sort of life that she really would desire for her daughter. But the sun spilled in the windows and the cool breeze stirred the curtains, beads of dew sparkled on the spider's web across the windowpane, and across the meadow there were already heavy shadows slanting among the old, abandoned farm buildings as he shuffled across the dining room and smiled at her at work over the stove in the kitchen.

"Don't look at me," he said, and went outdoors. There he frowned at his reddened face in the mirror tacked on the back of the house — at his sleep-lined face framed by the dark foliage on the wooded hill behind the house — and he brushed the hair back on his head and turned to look with moist eyes at the hill as he stood brushing his teeth, his legs apart and the breeze flapping his robe. A flicker chattered close above his head and dipped into the wood, its white rump winking among the trees.

It annoyed him that he could not waken easily, as she, his mind immediately bright and regulated — that for at least an hour after rising his head should be clogged and dull and everything he looked at ugly and uninteresting. He remembered the time she'd awakened him at night, saying in a voice hushed with excitement and a certain awe, "Darling, the skunk is out in the yard — I saw his eyes just now!" and he'd refused to sit up in his bed and look out of the window. Troubled and restless, she had taken the flashlight out into the dark to see their nightly visitor while he fell fast asleep immediately. "I've seen a skunk before," he'd said, ruffled that she should have wakened him.

Not that he lacked interest in the deathless prodigality of nature, for of the two he was the naturalist and bored her for hours with minute descriptions of the haunts and habits of the animals — their physical construction and their daily lives. It had come to them both almost at a blow — a dim, as yet uncomprehending glance of the vast design that turned on slow, inexorable wheels about them both. She, led by blind faith in her intuitions, and he by a skeptic curiosity and restless observation, had both arrived at a pathway that they felt might bring them to the field they would explore. For all about them were the surface symbols of life — the myriad, yet quantitatively insignificant, facets of a great, immeasurable scheme. Not that they had never looked at them before, but they had seen them solely with the eyes of the mind.

There were the bright eyes of the skunk at night, and the seasonal songs of frogs and toads in the pond just down the road. All night the small stream rushed through the darkness, singing in its variable scale, and the field was full of fireflies and moths. One night on the road they had seen a dull gleam on the earth, and his flashlight showed a dead firefly being devoured by ants, that even in its death gave forth the light that served its apparently meaningless purpose during life.

"All this is going on about us in the dark," she'd whispered and had shuddered slightly. All day the crows flew back and forth across the meadow and along the wood, cawing in different keys and registers, or conversing in the trees. You met them seeking grubs in the field, or sitting on a fence post down the road, whence they arose crying, and flapped heavily away, drawing up their clumsy feet. A dead porcupine was found in the spring one day and thrown up on the hillside to be forgotten. He pulled a tiny quill out of his finger with much pain. Two days later, a bad smell floated off the hill, and a visit showed the carcass boiling with maggots busily at work, who disappeared again when they had finished their employment.

It was impossible for the young woman and the man not to see these phenomena gathered beneath one universal plan in constant motion; and though he refused to grant a sentient deity or spirit to the plan, his refusal was but the necessary limitation imposed upon him by the exasperating Why?

They talked of that at breakfast. It was good, he felt, to see her long-familiar face across the table and to watch her large, strong hands, serving him with scrambled eggs and coffee, and he wondered at his domesticity. In her presence he felt a powerful yet quiet peace; and though he knew her body intimately and it held no further mystery for his eyes or for his hands, that familiarity itself had built a stable structure that now stood of its own accord and did not totter under contemplation.

It amused her to see him draw a present moral from perfectly fortuitous events — a trace of the pedagogue. Thus, when one of the kittens leaped to his lap, he said, "Perhaps no clearer understanding of the meaning of life — if it has a meaning — can be reached by one of *my* simple intuition than can be drawn from the feel of a cat purring like this under my hand," and he stroked the vibrant little kitten and smiled at its face rubbing against his fingers; and he wondered as of old at the small and stubborn flame of life animating its body to seek its own pleasure and looking out of large, inarticulate eyes at the purveyor of that incomprehensible joy.

He dropped the subject, for it maddened him just then. But she was thinking of what he had just said about the cat, and because she felt much the same way in his arms — for no words would come that might have given some tangible meaning to the quiet moment, and though they both would say that their silence was a more speaking conversation than their speech — she knew that that too was a flight from the faceless wall of unavoidable misunderstanding that circled them about. So she pursued the question again:

"If you don't believe in something besides the physical and the material, what makes you afraid of walking in the woods at night?" And because he could not answer her question, even in his mind, he was angry once again and rose from the table glaring at her long-familiar face and wondering what the devil he was doing there when he should be a few thousand miles away with new friends and new sights and new people to talk to.

So he said, "Well, at least I don't make a vast mystery of things and invent gods of the dark woods and heavens and hells and punishment for sins and hobgoblins and devils." He knew she didn't either, so when she said, "The only devil that exists is inside your own skin," he dropped the cat on the floor and slammed the door and went outside.

In the outhouse he sat looking out the door towards the west, at the tall pines on the hill silhouetted against the pink reflection from the sunrise and the pleasing tall thin birches growing among the darker trees. Insects buzzed and hummed outside the door in the warm morning light and occasionally ventured in, till he waved his arms and chased them out again. Nothing could horrify his flesh so much as a great whizzing beetle, striking against his skin; and if it occurred at night in the dark, his cold flesh shrank and with a cry he frantically whirled his arms. But sitting now, he thought of his recent mental cowardice; and he deplored it as usual, for a moment, dismissing it from mind with a sense of duty done, and he allowed the passionate physical pleasure he derived from her presence and her love and their long-standing relationship to overwhelm his mind once more and he was pleased to think himself "in clover," enjoying the balanced sort of life he'd always sought, his flesh appeased, his mind at work, his body happy and well-kept. Then, when the child came, he would be complete! Thus, when he came out to get the pails to go for water, he actually sang melodies from Strauss' *Heldenleben* and noted that the devil's paintbrush had almost covered the meadow with its rich, scarlet wash. There were clouds in the sky, mottling the sides of the mountain with slowly moving patterns till it almost looked majestic as it raised its meager height against the light sky, easing the eye with its varicolored greens, and capped with gleaming rock.

The spring tumbled down the hillside, slid down its moss-grown slide and cascaded into a little pebbled pool, and he brushed aside the whirling gnats that frequented the pool, stepping over puddles on the ground. A ruffed grouse was drumming on the hillside, and he thought of the carefully hidden nest the grouse would have, roofed over with dry leaves and wisps of grass into which the bird might creep and remain concealed while it brooded on its eggs.

When he came back she was looking in the tall grass beneath the apple tree, and he knew she was hoping to find the young bluebird that had escaped its nest. A surge of shame swept over him as he went to aid her search, for he knew it really was his fault the bluebird had been lost. The parents were still flitting through the tree over their heads, uttering only occasional sharp cries and listening for reply, for the young bird had been lost almost a day. He had insisted on taking it out of the hole in the apple tree — pointing out the primary and secondary feathers growing in their tracts, and they had laughed together over its appearance.

"Do you call that thing a bird!" he'd laughed as he held it on his palm. "The birds, you know, are closely related to the reptile group — it's really more a lizard than a bird."

So day by day they'd inspected the little fledgling while its parents scolded and swooped low over their heads till yesterday it had leaped from his palm and flown. He put it in the nest, but no sooner were they back in the house than the now flight-thirsty youngster leaped again and this time disappeared into the grass. It had interested them to watch the parent-birds wheeling over the grass, until after fifteen minutes he'd said, "They can't put it back — I will," but it was nowhere to be found.

Disheartened and contrite, they searched all afternoon, till they were completely discouraged and unhappy, then they spent the evening sitting miserably side by side in the window behind the spider's web, watching the wretched female hopping from limb to limb, calling and cocking her head, while the male sat in the tree and looked at her. That night it rained, and as they sat reading by the lamp they could catch faint call notes regularly uttered, and they looked at one another and smiled faintly or shook their heads and looked away. It was almost as though they'd lost their only child.

Afternoon:

THEY never spoke about it any more, for though they had a-greed to have a child, there never had been one. The birds were silent in the heat of the early afternoon, with the exception of the bluebirds, who still gave short, sharp cries and listened for an answer. The sun beat down almost painfully, and they lay side by side on blankets in the yard, naked and sweating in the vibrant heat.

Sometimes it saddened her to contemplate her infertility when everything around her was so fecund — the bluebirds on their nest had absorbed her gaze for hours as they made innumerable trips for insect-food to stuff the youngster in the hollow tree. It opened its mouth and raised its feeble head when she had thrust her finger in the hole. There were frogs' and toads' eggs in the small pond early in June — the ants hurried frantically to carry off their great larvae when disturbed; and she herself had planted the lettuce in the kitchen garden and set the tiny radish seeds to grow and daily watered them and measured them with a kindly, vigilant eye; rejoiced to see them flourish and lift their leaves into the sun despite the swarms of predatory insects. She did not feel so sorry for herself, somehow, even though she knew herself to be irrevocably barren — not even during the years of her married life had she missed a period — but she felt sorry for him when she saw him looking at her with that accusing expression she knew so well. She had the conviction that he would never produce a painting that would satisfy either of them, and it was usually after he had sat an afternoon before his canvas and come dejected to her in the evening that she wanted so to be able to say, "Darling — I know you'd like to know — I'm pregnant." Then, though she knew he did not care for children, she knew just as surely that he would not feel so sterile.

She looked at his paintings, and something in her breast began to sink — they were clever, they were often brilliant, but something was missing that could, had it been present, have pulled the whole canvas together and given it authenticity and love. She called it understanding — that was the only word she knew for it. He saw the surfaces of things with an uncannily inclusive eye; he did not miss a thing that could be seen, but the intricate landscapes he painted were cold and had the dead, supine reality of photographs; and the old men's heads, while miracles of line and character and observation, were not instinct with life or age or wisdom. So, when she saw him look at her and silently say as loudly as any tongue could speak, "You're barren — why can't you produce a child?" there was

nothing for her to do but go about her housework and do it as carefully as ever she could, making the house a joy for him to enter
and a shelter for repose. She knew he loved tea in the afternoon,
so tea was always ready when he came in from his work — she built
a fire in the fireplace, and his tea was served in a glass with two
spoonfuls of sugar ready stirred so he no longer had to ask, "Did
you put sugar in?" He merely smoked his cigarette until the glass
had cooled, then threw it in the fire and picked up the glass and
smiled at her and talked.

She turned her head to look at him — he lay upon his back with
his reddened face lifted to the sun; his eyes were closed and sweat
streamed off his cheeks and ran down his neck. His whole body
was damp with perspiration and it gleamed; and although she drew
particular satisfaction to note how the mountains in their contours
seemed to follow the curves of his body, she thought, I would not
care to have him embrace me like that.

The thought startled her for a moment, for she usually was not
conscious of his body in its uglier aspects. He was quite self-con-
scious about his slender arms, but she had not noticed them till he
mentioned it — and, after all, didn't they wash each other in their
outdoor baths, pouring water over each other from the sprinkling
can and rubbing down the places that were difficult to reach? It
was like him to remark at such a moment, "God, if anyone can
love you now! Greater love hath no man than to survive seeing
his girl with her hair screwed up on the back of her head, her face
all soapy and gooseflesh standing out all over her;" but for her
part, she never noticed the soapy, matted hair when he was washed,
and his squinting, soapy face, and the way his toes turned up because the stone slab underfoot was cold — her retina registered
the sight, but her mind made no satiric comment.

Watching his body lying parallel to the distant sunny hills, his
hot red face and heavy breathing, she remembered the various
times he had incited her to make quick sketches of him, determined
that he'd teach her to draw. "Any fool can draw," he used to
say, so he placed his body in grotesque positions and timed her by
his watch until she gained considerable proficiency at catching
lines and postures; and then he became jealous of her success and

stopped his sittings. She remembered the other afternoon at the spring, when she had given him a cold shower, at his request, laughing as she held the sprinkler over him and he howled and wriggled and rubbed his body down. Suddenly it had struck her a terrific, almost physical blow — just as he thrust out his chest against the spray, and she saw the great muscles bulge with the cold and the brown skin tighten across them and the flush of red blood rise to the surface of his body — just as he held his head under the cascade and the water tumbled over his shoulders and down his back to flow between his legs, and he rose with a shout of pleasurable discomfort and grasped the glass and drank a great gulp of the ice-cold water — "inside and out," he'd said, "inside and out"; then it struck her that this fine, sentient body with its gleaming brown skin and hot red blood and firm muscles — that this man standing there erect on his strong legs, gulping down ice water and rubbing his stomach with a large, strong hand, was oh so surely going to die and turn back into the earth he stood upon and rot away into a dry and powdery dust — and she was glad of it! It seemed right to her, and just and beautiful, and she was thrilled with the beauty of the destiny that nature held out to all living, with smiling eyes and firm, implacable lips, as though it were a much desired gift.

He wiped the sweat from his face with a blue bandana lying by his side and said, "Time's up," and turned to look at her. She sat up and smiled and he saw her head and shoulders against the sky and distant hills; and with that relationship he became aware of the heart of his problem — and it struck him that a painting of her head against the sky and the green hills, with those heavy, moving cloud banks in the north, her face smiling down out of the canvas with large, pale eyes, would just about express all he could ever feel or think or know.

"I'm going in now, darling," she said and rose, and folding up her blanket, "I'll have tea for you after work. . . ."

"It's much too hot," he said, "I'll try to work and then go chop some wood."

"Well, then I'll weed the garden; I've left it now a week — so I won't have to wash the dishes till tonight. I think there'll be enough clean ones for supper." She went in, and he watched her naked body walking across the little lawn, swaying slightly at the hips.

"How I have wasted my life!" he said aloud, and lay back again for a moment, clasping his hands behind his head and staring at the sun with eyelids firmly closed. . . .

All during the sunbath he had been looking at the sun, and his eyes had noted the spectra that his eyelids could induce, depending on how tightly they were closed, and he'd been enjoying the flowing of the heavy heat into his flesh. But with the vision of her head against the sky, it was as though all the problems he had ever pondered rose up at last and assumed material form to vex him. He knew he could never get that down on canvas, and he knew deep in his heart that he could never get anything as completely "down on canvas" as he so hotly desired. All the great pattern that seemed to turn about them both — it was too vast a scheme for him to compass. Look at how the morning had been wasted! It was the same thing every single day. He envisaged himself so busily at work, if the ideal could only be attained, that he'd have no time for anything but work. He saw great glowing canvasses rise before his eyes — the progress of the seasons, the program of the day, the weather, faces of men and women from birth to death in beautiful schemata — he would achieve them all! But what could he do about it? All he did was to copy mountains down on prepared cloth — he painted the gnarled and weathered cedar on the hill, in sunlight and in rain and in the moon, thinking thereby to have said at least one thing completely and put it aside forever. But when that had been done, there was still the not-to-be-considered task of painting the naked body in all its possible aspects — or even choosing an aspect which would imply all others from birth to death — and thus truly express his intuition of it.

A child would somehow explain and sanction their socially unrecognized relationship, he knew. Instead of making it a worse offence in nature, they both felt that it would be a final proof of the validity of their love, and yet it never came; and because it never came he felt himself trapped and snared into compliance with her will. The words, "Well, here I am," were ever present in his mind, and he laughed at the irony of his position — had he been married he would have really felt himself enslaved, but still unmarried, he was twice as fettered as before. So he resented the demands of his own flesh, as well as hers, and saw in them a symbol of the senseless repetition of all natural phenomena — dawn and noon and night again; birth and life and death and birth again; spring and summer, autumn, winter and then spring again — and to what end?

Life has meaning, he thought, as he sat before his canvas with the running brook and the hills sketched in, only insofar as we draw our trite conclusions from it for our own guidance and contentment. No child! he thought — no work to survive me; the fruit of love is stifled in the womb and never comes to light. The intuition is smothered in the mind and never can be uttered in its total beauty of completion, no matter how we strive. . . .

Such thoughts as these, which he knew to be invalid to anyone else and he dared not convey for fear they would be scored for puerility — and therein lay his great exasperation, for they were the best that he could do — inevitably brought him to the only bearable conclusion: life had meaning to him only in the living. So he scraped his dirty palette, and he folded up his dirty paint box and took his empty canvas that was to have a mountain and a stream displayed in colors real as life upon its face, and he went to the house and got his axe.

He looked at the spider's web stretched on the windowpane. It had been repaired since last night's rain, and he wondered again if there were not some geometric plan at the basis of all natural processes, until he remembered that, at least as far as the spider's web was concerned and the hexagonal cells constructed by the bees, the line of least resistance was always the easiest to take; and therefore a certain mathematical precision was always to be expected of living tissue at work.

He viewed his woodpile with pride — day by day it grew as he gradually split up the half-rotten boards and beams of the old barn; and he had even established a routine in his chopping, selecting the lighter boards to break up first, and then the heavier, and then the beams, though he often thought it would have been easier to reverse the process and take the hardest work when he was fresher. But it didn't matter so long as he achieved the ultimate sweet agony of fatigue, followed by a cold shower and its miraculous muscular freshening; and the subconcious knowledge that he was building up his body as he worked was a precious secret that he spent many minutes daily contemplating, usually when the fatigue had begun to pile up to its tetanus and his arms ached cruelly. Then he said to himself, "Just one more beam," and dragged it out of the heap of broken boards and scattered shingles and debris; and he rejoiced in the will power he displayed.

The sun was declining in the west, thrusting its fingers through the brisk comb of the pines on the western hill. He looked over to where the kittens were playing among the tall weeds around the hotbed, lying in wait for each other and then, with prodigious leaps and bounds almost vertically in the air, pouncing on each others' backs. Their complete relaxation permits them their apparently unbounded energy, he thought; and then bit his lips and fell to his chopping, for the kittens were a sore spot in his heart. Try as he would, he could not get a sketch of them at rest or sleep or play that caught their gracile forms and nimble spirits. They were constantly eluding him with hitherto unbeheld attitudes, uncatlike in the extreme, and careful study seemed to no avail. Their movements seemed untimed and unrelated — they might spring out of a completely relaxed pose into a grotesque attitude of gymnastic abandon; and yet it was the perfect timing of their actions and the artless articulation of their bodies that baffled his really careful research.

Bending over his woodchopping in the pleasant heat of the setting sun, he glanced over to where she was transplanting from the hotbed to the little plowed area that was her garden. It pleased him to reflect that the garden was entirely her own creation — she had constructed the hotbed herself and covered it with some old windows from the torn-down barn, she had planted the seeds herself and nursed them carefully during the long hot June days. "I like things that grow in the earth better than those that hop on it, I guess," she had said, and he smiled remembering that night they had investigated the great, fat toad with his flashlight. "How perfectly he's constructed, " she had said; and he'd said, "*She* — it's a she — the males of this species have black throats. Too bad she's not a male," he'd added, "for if it were, we could make him sing by picking him up by his two forelegs. They always do, somehow."

Now he enjoyed watching the strong curve of her loins as she crouched at her work, digging the warm earth out with her fingers and placing the tender little plant in the hole and tucking it in firmly.

She fitted perfectly into the landscape, and the curve of her haunches was paralleled from his angle by the greater curve of the quiet hill; and he enjoyed thinking of her pregnant. And if she were, he felt the hill would suffer by the comparison, for she was quick with life and the hill stood lonely and silent forever and would never bring forth so much as a mouse.

He waved his hand before his face — the gnats were torturesome these afternoons — and he bent again to his work, swinging the long axe as powerfully as he could and grunting as it bit into the hard, weathered wood. He enjoyed beyond measure the deep, sharp bite of the blade, and the heavy thud, and the echo of the blow off the wooded hill; and he formulated the words, This is right — this is as it should be; but he could not speak them for the sudden sheer joy that flooded him, and he harbored them in his breast and swung the axe harder and harder, grunting rhythmically and feeling his muscles tire, and shaking the little drops of salty sweat off the end of his nose. The pain of fatigue gradually crept up his arms and sides and back.

The sound of the stream was in his ears from the south, and from the north he heard the sound of the evening wind in the trees, like the roar and insensate rush of a great overhead fire; and as he stood, axe in hand, and watched, there drifted out of the west great banks of lead-colored clouds tinged beneath with salmon, as though the sun in setting had touched the earth to fire and this was the flame-lit, belching smoke of its monstrous conflagration. Slowly and steadily it drifted over the land, casting its shadow upon field and wooded hill, and the swifts wheeled nervously beneath it on crescentic wings, restless from the long day's insect hunt and anxious for their nests.

He carried his axe in his hand over to where she knelt beside her plants. She said, "Hello," but kept to her work and did not look up at him.

"Which are the peas?" he said, and she pointed to the geometrically folded leaves and the curling tendrils, ready now for their supporting sticks and spared by some miracle from the marauding 'chuck. "Christ!" he suddenly said, pointing to the meadow, "look at it all, life all around us!" and he grinned idiotically and slapped her on the back, "millions of blades of grass growing, each one a little life, each one coming out of a little tiny seed, flourishing and growing. . . ."

"Yes," she said, and turned her face up to him, and he stopped dead in the middle of his fervid speech, for he saw there were tears in her eyes, ready to spill out. Her hands were black with the rich soil she had been handling. "Yes," she said again, "only *we* – oh, forgive me!"

Night:

During the day the little river could be heard if you cared to listen for it, but at night it was the night's own sound, superseding all others; and with the cessation of the frog- and toad-song at the end of June, it assumed undisputed sway and rushed over its smooth round stones all night, imperious and yet ghostly in its insistence. So it became their habit, when they paused in their evening conversation before the fire, to sit and listen to the river and allow its restful sibilance to smooth away the slightest remembrance of what they had been talking about. He engaged in this escape more frequently than she, and more completely, for he added the further hypnotic of staring at the fire until he was so far from her and the little house and their main problem, and himself, that he could not recall their recently interrupted talk, when she suddenly spoke to him, and he was for the moment a complete idiot.

She drew a quiet, contemplative sort of peace from watching his face as he sat sucking at his pipe, and trying to read his thoughts. She never could. He was still young enough unconsciously to mirror his slightest feelings and ideas upon his face, in conversation; but with the coming of night and the rush of the river in his ears and the sight of the aspiring flames before his eyes, it was as though his old age came upon him with a rush and a pounce — a mask of age-old weariness fell before his face, and it was impenetrable to her gaze and to her mind.

What a fine face he has, she thought, and she was glad she had sufficient self-restraint to still her tongue and not talk to him when he sat drowned in his mood. She constructed whole realms of ideas for him to wander in, and when by accident his face assumed a momentary expression that tallied with her thought, she felt a slight triumphant thrill within her, as though she had compelled him by the power of her mind to think of what she thought he ought to think.

The firelight cut a slender line on his face silhouetted against the dark wall behind him, and she thought what a pity it was that people's externals were such inadequate symbols of their minds and their hearts. Surely the high white forehead and the long straight nose, the sensitive lips and chin in their sure and steady contour should somehow spell a finer artist than she knew him to be; and she suddenly knew that despite his endless protestations of insignificance in the face of space and eternity and the very earth itself, such an idea in its full implication was as far from his consciousness as he said the nearest star was from the earth. You had only to look at the way he held his pipe and the unconsciously studied seriousness of his posture and expression and his movements when he thought himself "deep in thought" to observe how much he really thought of himself. So she was overwhelmed with a great contempt for him, and she hated the way he held his pipe and the way he crossed his legs and the way he sat with head inclined to the side, looking at the crackling fire and so concerned with thoughts he obviously considered deep and pregnant. But she was immediately flooded with immense maternal pity — he grew young in his chair and was a tired and scared little boy, petulantly sucking at his thumb and pouting at the fire; and she wanted to gather him in her arms and press his face between her breasts and rock his body back and forth until he fell asleep.

The moon mingled its unearthly light with the healthy flame-light, slanting in the windows and cutting pale squares and oblongs on the floor. Once more, as she sat by the table looking at the pages of her book in the steady glow of the oil lamp, she was amazed at the numberless infinitesimal bugs and winged insects that collected round the lamp. If she touched them, they were spots. They hopped, or they fluttered back and forth about the shade, or they flew in idiotic circles round and round until exhausted and then dropped into the chimney and were scorched.

"Say!" he suddenly cried and grasped her hand just as she was about to drop a fair-sized miller in the chimney, "What's the idea? Why, I'm surprised at you!"

She let the miller go and looked abashed. "I am myself," she said, "I can't imagine what made me want to do it." They let the subject drop and sat quietly a while listening to the kittens scampering back and forth across the floors of the little house, chasing one another in the dark. Then he got up and went out of the door.

The field outside was sparkling with so many thousand fireflies which winked so brilliantly and incessantly that for a moment after stepping out he had the impression that he had been dealt a sharp blow across the eyes. The night was cool and full of the rush of the rocky river, and the stars were far off and very cold, and mist was creeping toward the house from the fields about. Then he knew that it would be just as impossible for a musician to "get" the sound of the stream flowing at night as it would be for him, the painter, to get the fire he'd been watching down on canvas; and he decided that painting fire and light and water was just as much a bastardized "program" work as translating into music a rooster crowing, or a brook rattling over its pebbles, or a kitten mewing, or the roaring of a tempest in the trees. Then he knew that his whole approach to his art had been wrong — for why should he want to paint the gnarled mountain cedar in all weathers and all lights, and think thereby he had caught its magic with his brush. And why should he want to catch all the wrinkles in an old man's stupid face, or the minute details of an autumn landscape, or his lady's face against the sky — ridiculous conception!

Empty of feeling and chilled by the night air, he returned to the house. One toad was still singing, out of season, in the pond just down the road, and he had a sudden desire to escape life in all its manifestations and not have to look at the hard and distant stars or the blinking fireflies, or stand in the weird mingled moon- and starlight; and particularly he wanted to get in bed and put his head under a pillow so that he might not hear the inevitable dron- ing of the river.

The one thing he felt constantly glad of was their constant iso- lation — there in the mountains they did not see or speak to more than two or three people a week, and he rejoiced because they were such simple people, and envied them their true simplicity. At Far- mer Brown's, where they went to get their milk, he invariably dis- cussed cows and milking with the dry old man and felt a desperate delight in learning of the effect that various grasses had upon their daily yield, while she went to the barn and bent down to the part- ly Persian cat and stroked her pregnant belly. "She likes to have her kittens stroked," she said and smiled up at him when he came to her.

He took his pipe out of his pocket and knocked its ashes out upon the floor, filled it again, then groped for the box of matches that he knew was on the windowsill. She came out of the sitting room, the lamp, now out, in hand. "I'm going to fill the lamp a- gain," she said. "It looked as though it wanted to go out."

Lighting his pipe, he saw a movement in the spider's web and held the match against the windowpane. "Look!" he cried, "the spider's in its web," and she came to him from the little kitchen after she had filled the reservoir. They sat down on a bench and watched the spider as it adjusted itself to wait for a chance prey. It climbed up to the center of its web, walking delicately like a dan- cing master and, reaching the center, turned upside down and hung there, pulling in its jointed legs. She went to get the flashlight, but in the meanwhile a small ichneumon fly had flown against the web, and he alone saw the spider's lightning slide down to the bottom of the web and its quick, skilled movements as it killed its prey. When she came back with the light, it caught up the now dry body of the fly, dropped it to the ground, climbed aloft again and settled down to wait.

"You should have *seen* it!" he exclaimed. "We'll sit here and just watch till another comes along — the light'll drum up trade for the spider." But nothing answered to the lure of the light in the window of the little house, and they became impatient with delay. "You're good at catching millers," he said. "Why don't you go out and get one and put it in the web?" "I will," she said, and went outdoors to search for a small moth.

The cold air of the mountain night struck her body with its sudden impact and she looked up at the night flowing away from her, leaving her feeling as though she were standing in the doorway of a vast and empty hall. The hills were a dark circle all around, and the mist lay thick and heavy on the meadow. Fireflies darted about, winking and flashing silently, and she was surprised to see how high they sometimes flew. Occasionally one would leave its greenish light burning for a moment as it flew and simulate a tiny meteor. She caught a moth and brought it to the window.

"I hate to do this," she said. "What shall I do?" Inside she saw his strangely pale face behind the pane, and he said, "Just throw it at the web – not too hard, of course." "Gee, I hate to do this," she said, feeling the soft body of the moth in her hands and its ineffectual wings beating against her fingers; but she threw the moth gently at the web and said, "Hurray, I'm glad it got away!" as it fell off the web. Then she said, "Oh!" for the moth in falling was caught by the lower part of the web, and there it hung fluttering and pulling mightily away.

"Look!" he said, and she saw the spider slide down its fireman's pole and seize the moth with all its eight legs at once, and she saw its sharp-pointed legs seemingly thrust into the moth's soft body again and again with the rapid technique of long practice as it turned the miller round and round.

She came into the house to watch with him and said, "I feel perfectly awful doing that – but I suppose spiders have to eat." "Why?" he said. She did not answer, but instead she saw his intent interest in the cruel performance and felt for it the same disgust she felt for the brutal spider and its ways. And then she went inside.

When he came in he found her lying on the couch in the dark – and he stretched himself beside her and took her in his arms and wooed her with the casual tactics born of long habituation. She suffered him to woo her for a while and then turned into his arms and gave him kiss for kiss out of the warmth of her deep love for him. But even while they loved, his mind was far away, and he could remark the softened edges of the moonlit room and the dying coals in the hearth and the fireflies tapping against the windowpane; and he heard the kittens playing on the floor — till their climax, when for a brief moment all of him flowed toward her and into her, despite himself, and he lay helpless and palpitant in her arms, breathing against her face upon the pillow.

Then he rose, and as she watched him her mind assumed a strange relationship to her heart, and for the first time she felt impersonal in his presence and could watch his movements unprejudiced by her affection for him and the long months that were between them and the inception of their love. She saw him pick up his clothes from the floor and turn the legs right-side out again and put his feet in his slippers; and though he stood in the shadow of the fireplace she smiled, for she knew just how he would look in his shirt and no trousers. She saw him pick up her clothes and wondered if he'd shake them out the way he had his own, or throw them carelessly aside upon a chair. She sighed. He lit the lamp, and she wondered if he'd remember the loose piece that came off with the chimney and was pleased to see he did, although she knew he'd seen it only once.

"No wick?" he had said, and his voice was still and pleasant in her ears. "Ah, yes — what's that! — oh, kittens asleep in the chair. . . ." He poked the fire up and laid on more wood, took the kittens in his lap and sat looking at the fire. "Humph!" he said irrelevantly; and she remembered, looking at his chin against the light, that he had said, "I have too much nose and not enough chin," but she found his chin good and reflected that all chins looked weak relaxed, and she had a momentary access of pity for all the poor men who must get tired keeping their chins thrust out to simulate a firm determination, as though they believed their wills could shape their destinies. I wonder if he'll ever understand? she thought — I wonder if he could? and for a moment she played with the idea of killing herself so he might understand. Oh, I would willingly kill myself a thousand times a day if I thought that understanding would descend upon him suddenly and surely. No, I wouldn't, she thought; simply living should make him understand, more than ever death could. God is in every man the same, she thought, and if knowledge comes it must be born of sorrow — oh, she thought, and tears sprang to her eyes, Why must wisdom come sorrowing — wisdom is love and love is wisdom. . . . There is no hope, she thought, for love to come rejoicing — no hope. . . .

Sitting alone now in the armchair by the fire, his body lax and dull and his mind borne down by his body, he was aware that she was lying and looking at his profile in the firelight, and though he felt he looked old and worn and a bit thin about the ribs, and though he was conscious that his profile could have been distinctly improved by a little more chin, still he formulated the conscious yet unspoken challenge — To hell with you — do you think I give a damn if you are looking at me? His feminine mind could hear the criticism her mind was turning over, yet somehow he felt too worn and tired to move an inch to soften criticism; and he felt, Well what of it? let it be all over now, if you like — the thing has gone too far now for me to court you with artlessly assumed advantageous postures, sharp sidewise glances and studied attitudes. You've seen my body in every possible pose at every time of day or night — why should I shrink from this ultimate scrutiny and deprive your prying mind of this opportunity to find fault? If this vision end it all, I am content. So he stayed as he was, his face and thin arms silhouetted in the flickering firelight; and he looked into the fire and listened to the river and coaxed the peace he'd sought so long, until it seeped coyly drop by soporific drop into his mind.

"God!" she said, "I'd like to paint you now!" Then he laughed, and when she asked him why he'd laughed he would not say he was ashamed of the misunderstanding his mind had erected while he sat. He simply said, "I'm tired," and wondered at his strange reply.

"Why don't you go to bed, darling?" she said. "I'll make your bed," and she rose and went into the separate bedroom while he put on his bathrobe and went outdoors again to brush his teeth. He looked into the mirror tacked on the back of the house and saw his pale face framed by the dark green, moonlit foliage on the hill behind the house; and he turned, brushing his teeth, to look at the hill. Two bright eyes looked at him from over near the garbage pit, and the mist had closed down about the house and stirred perceptibly with the cold breeze from the circling hills. He looked once more up at the stars and went indoors, latching the screendoor and, feeling his way through the dark rooms, he bent to kiss her face, then went into his room.

"Goodnight," she said. He felt something touch his foot and, bending down, picked up the little kitten and put it in his bed and climbed inside. Lying quietly, he stroked the kitten, which had crawled under the covers and lay beside his legs. He lay and looked out the window at the fireflies and the moonlight on the birch trees behind the house and heard the quiet rushing of the stream — so he turned over and hid his face in the pillow and lay listening to the beating of his heart and the vibrant, steady purring of the kitten.

She could not close her eyes for quite a while — and even when she did, she saw the spider's web stretched across the dark field of her vision, and the spider in it, moving daintily on dancing-teacher legs. It had bright eyes. So she raised her lids again and lay staring at the ceiling and the moonlight streaming in the screened window, and the silver face of the mist pressed against the pane, looking in. Far off, on the state road, a motorcar was droning rhythmically. . . .

Horizon

for G. J. Petrie

FTER the ninth day at sea he found himself able to write again. Before that, any efforts he made had foundered even before their inception, through disinclination, ennui or sheer disability. Standing at the rail, he tried to image himself writing again and he laughed — there could be no more absurd incongruity than the contrasted images of the sea and a man writing at a desk. So for eight days he stood at the rail or wandered up and down the deck, or paced the bridge of the ship. Here he was most at home, and he buttoned the old army overcoat about his neck and stood with what he enjoyed thinking were steel-cold eyes, gazing over the sea at the circular horizon. Day after day the horizon presented an unbroken line, dim and vaguely beckoning. His eyes were strained to such a pitch that he continually saw puffs of smoke or the funnels of nonexistent vessels, and he called the mate's attention to them.

"I can't see it," the mate would say. "I must have been mistaken," he replied. But when an occasional ship did come in sight, he felt his heart pounding proudly and joyfully in his breast, and he paced the deck more vigorously than before. A symbol, his unheard voice would say to him — here we are, hundreds upon hundreds of miles from any land — two isolated human beings touch hands for a brief moment and are gone. He could hear the thin buzzing of the apparatus in the wireless shack, and when he saw the operator later in the day, in the saloon, he'd say: "What ship was that we spoke to this morning, Sparks?" And Sparks said, "Southern Cross — bound for Baltimore." But most of the time no ships were visible, and he had to content himself with watching the terns floating on curved and rigid wings behind the ship, waiting patiently for the cook to throw the garbage overboard. Occasionally, he could see them turn their sharp heads with a quick movement, and at those times he felt peculiarly close to them in spirit and could almost hear the conversation in which they were undoubtedly engaged: "You watch the portside," said one tern, "and I'll watch the starboard," and they hung absurdly suspended over the ship, rolling in the air on rigid wings, just as the vessel rolled upon the sea.

He picked up his pen and wrote: "The thing that hurt him most was the fact that at the first few dinners aboard, no one spoke to him. He sat at the captain's table with the captain and the other officers and was constantly amazed at the silence that prevailed. Of course, he was used to the stories of the taciturn men who sail the seas in ships, so it was with real astonishment that he encountered a legend that for once seemed true. They all ate with their eyes on their plates and hurried to stow the food away inside; so that when he felt an extreme necessity for butter, it was all he could do to summon courage enough to say in a weak voice, 'Pardon me, may I trouble you for the butter?' "

He paused and dipped his pen, then held it in his mouth. Strange, he thought, how strange that was the first day out — I must be developing an inferiority complex, to have been so abashed by the presence of these men. They had all looked up at him when he spoke and they all looked so far away and alien that he'd felt the hot blood course up his neck and cursed himself for a fool for having spoken. One of them had reached him the butter, then they all looked down again into their plates and resumed eating.

These men do things, he had thought — here are men, silent and mature, men who are as stable and well-oriented as the tested compass in the binnacle. They knew what was what — they knew their business and they knew their lives. They had every single moment of their lives on tap — mapped and charted, ready to consult. Give them a crisis and they were on deck, steady-handed, cool-eyed, tight-mouthed and, above all, in action. While I, he had thought, am a spineless jellyfish. I am a creature of moods and dreams and passions, of impulses and tics. Here are men who are solid and substantial — their feet are planted on the deck, and their eyes too are on the horizon — but not for the same romantic reason as my own, and not with the same focus.

And so he had attempted to cultivate the officers, probe gently into their quietude, and see what pearl of wisdom he might fish out of the depths. Of course, he would reason, they are human beings — their occupation is responsible for their silence — four hours on watch and eight hours off give little time for the amenities of polite society — there is little to say and no time in which to say it. A man who paces the bridge on a rainy night for four hours back and forth in the same tracks, his eyes on the invisible horizon, his ears utterly open and alert, becomes something more and less than human — becomes a machine — a receptive organ of the finest sensitivity, and the darkness of the night and the low soughing of the wind across the sea and the incessant dash of the water along the side, all combine to make him turn inward upon himself, and whatever thoughts he may have remain inarticulate and sealed away. So he stood up on the bridge at night and waited for the mate to speak to him.

The first night as he came up the stairs, the third mate barred his way. "Is it all right," he'd said, "to come up on the bridge? I can't sleep." The third mate turned away and mumbled, "Have to ask the captain, he's in the pilothouse." He felt his way across the bridge to where he knew the pilothouse door stood open. He walked in, straining his eyes to see, and could see nothing but the face of the helmsman, wanly lit by the light from the binnacle in front of him, and hear nothing but the creaking of the wheel as he turned it to and fro, and the ticking of the clock.

"Captain?" he said, in a surprisingly loud voice. "Yes," a voice said almost at his elbow, and with the snap and precision of a shot. "Is it all right to come up on the bridge? I can't sleep." "What seems to be the trouble —" He wondered what the captain looked like — he had not seen him yet. "— seasick?" "Not yet," he'd said, "but I — oh, just the strangeness of it all, the vibration and the noise." "First trip to sea?" "Yes, sir." "Well," the voice replied, "you sure picked a good time o' year. December and February are the worst months on the North Atlantic."

"Yes?" he said alertly, and was silent and stood rigidly, looking out the window of the pilothouse, afraid to say another word. Not that there was anything to be seen; for after his eyes had become accustomed to the darkness, he was only rewarded with a view of a dark, starless sky and a darker sea and two pale wakes where the prow of the freighter pried the sea apart and sped it backwards. Little lines and spots of phosphorescence swelled and glowed amid the wakes, and glowed and disappeared.

He gave up writing for the day and lay back on his bed and stared at the ceiling of the cabin. He was the sole passenger on a freighter, and although he hated to admit it, he was lonesome. Lonesome? Ridiculous, he thought — now I know why men go to sea. It is impossible to be lonely on the sea — the sea is your friend and companion and it whispers in the hollow of your ear. Standing on the bridge at night in utter darkness and detachment, he had failed to note the loneliness he'd felt at night, in the woods, even with a cheerful fire and the homely sound of frogs croaking down by the shore. Here, as he stood with the salt spray whipping across his cheek and mouth and stinging his eyes, with nothing to connect him to the earth or the presence of man but the lonely topmast light and the realization that after all, although there was a man nearby, he might just as well be dead, here he could not be lonely or unhappy, but there was nevertheless a sense of isolation all about — it was so keen and persuasive that he buttoned his coat closer about him and turned his mental eyes within and shut his physical eyes to the night and the topmast light and the fireflies that played among the waves.

The roar of water was in his ears, and the myriad uncatalogued and unidentified sounds that mingled with that roar. Somewhere a bolt was banging against the hull — Clank, it said and was silent for a long time, and then it said clank again when he least expected it. There was an endless high note from amidships — the engines, he thought, and counted the minutes till inside the wheelhouse the brass clock said, Ting-ting. One o'clock, he thought, and then the helmsman pulled the cord of the ship's bell that hung in front of the wheelhouse, and that bell said, Tang-tang. There was an interval which the wind's moan and the water's rush and the vibration of the engines filled, and from the prow came the echo of the bell pulled by the lookout on the forecastlehead. Far away it said Tang-tang and paused, and a voice far away said: "All lights burning brightly, sir." He could barely hear it above the medley of other sounds. "All *right*," the mate inside the wheelroom said.

So after he had gained the master's sanction to visit the bridge whenever the mood seized him, he spent more time up there and finally got on speaking terms with the young third officer, Pearson. Pearson was a tall, red-faced young fellow with a reticent, almost surly air. As he paced the deck the first few times the passenger Perry was there, he scrupulously avoided looking at him. He'd pass in back of Perry, as he leaned against the rail, and turning, look right through him and walk back. This annoyed Perry, so he said, "Fine weather," and the third said, "Yeh," and went back in the wheelhouse and disappeared. But after the first few visits, Perry discovered that Pearson was more than willing to talk — in fact, he did most of the talking, and when he felt that he was running down, Perry would prod him with a leading question and Pearson sailed away again upon another track. He usually talked about women, and his red face grew much redder as he spoke.

"I knew a girl on Telegraph Hill," he said. "God she was a hot baby — funny thing," he said, "she used to play around a lot with me, then one time a girl got ahold of her and by God, if she didn't go and live with her. I've never understood that," Pearson said, "but I dunno — I've sort of got to expecting anything of women." Then he looked puzzled and scratched his head and shook it a few times and resumed his feline pacing back and forth.

Then a curious thing happened — for it shook Perry even more than it did Pearson, and he was jarred enough. They were talking about books, and Perry said, "I've had a little experience with publishing — I once had a book printed — it was illustrated by Rokål." "You don't mean that book called *The Piper*," Pearson gasped, "why, you didn't. . . ." "Yes, that's it. My God, don't tell me that you bought a copy of that thing," Perry said, and Pearson, "Why,

Jesus Christ — now isn't that funny — you didn't — you didn't write that book? Well, I'm damned!" "Don't tell me you bought a — did you like it?" Perry said. "Well, now, if that isn't the best ever," Pearson said. "You bet I bought a copy — in San Francisco — ye-es, I liked it," he said, "but — say, I've got it in my room — will you autograph it for me?" he cried, his face as red as a beet. "Delighted," Perry said, leaning back upon the sliding door and looking worldly. He suddenly wished that he were ten years older. After that Pearson and Perry thought a little more of each other.

II

When they were presumably two days from shore, Perry sat down again and took his pen: "In analyzing the strange behavior of Pearson," he wrote, "I shall only attempt to write as a scientist now — there will be time enough when I've got to Vienna, far from the sea, to sit down and try to acquire a perspective which will permit of a more imaginative treatment of both Pearson and the sea in general. All the seamen on this boat — Pearson corrected me when I said boat — 'Ship,' he said, and looked at me, 'ship.' Then I said ship. 'And also,' Pearson said, 'chart, chart — not map,' and to tantalize him, I said map and boat. . . . However, all the seamen on this — ship, agree that Conrad was a lousy writer. To put it more precisely, what they mean, I gather, is that as far as they're concerned, as a writer of the sea, he fails to touch accurately and illuminatingly upon the very things with which these men are most concerned and should understand. Now, whether Conrad found it necessary to alter the facts of sea life in order to satisfy the sort of audience he catered to, or whether he was just so poor an artist that his creative mind did not select the right details, and when it did, perverted them beyond their importance, I know not, but clinging to the latter supposition, I also feel that a large part of his lack of success was due to the fact that he had the wrong perspective, or worse, no perspective at all . . . being at all times too close to the thing he was attempting to express. Thus, in the case of Pearson . . ." Here Perry paused and laid his pen down and closed his inkbottle. I'll wait till I get to Vienna, he thought, and went up on the bridge.

It was a cold clear day, the sun was low in the south and gave no heat and the ship was rolling, pitching and laboring heavily. Great waves shot up from her bows suddenly, geyserlike, and exhausted their energy in furiously hissing sprays. The fume from the wavetops snapped viciously across the decks and drenched the tarpaulins stretched across the hatches. Perry delighted to stand for a half hour at a time and watch the shipped water wash to and fro across the steel deck and note the multifarious courses it pursued. The great rocking waves sprang and leaped and sank and died away, then leaped the rail and landed bodily on the forward deck with a dull boom that shook the ship from end to end. She shuddered to the surface, dripping from every pore and shaking side to side, her nose pointing twenty degrees above the taut horizon. As the great palls of spray rose from the ocean and drifted across the ship, the sun caught them and flashed momentary rainbows through the mist that died as soon as born.

Alongside, where there was a continual slaver of froth and spray, the rainbow rode triumphantly along, plunging and dipping like a painted veil. Perry conjured the poor dejected shade of Conrad and challenged it to write a single line that could express, however poorly, the beauty that surrounded him on every hand. Conceive of it, he thought, thousands of miles of living, leaping waters, girdling the globe from continent to continent — no mere mud puddle this, but a titanic force, majestic even in repose, terrific and fearful when whipped up by a gale, a force greater than all the other forces put together — an overwhelming hive of energy, unbounded and unharnessed. Even though he felt like Napoleon whenever he stood on the bridge, even though he could not help feeling that somehow he was in control of the great ship that bore him over the sea, it was impossible for him, try as he would, to feel anything but humble in the presence of the only real god whose sanctum he had ever dared invade. "I feel humble," he said aloud into the wind, and the wind tore the very words out of his mouth and flung them down his throat.

III

A fter his sudden burst of confidence, which lasted a week and even permitted him to invite Perry to his room, Pearson had withdrawn into his shell, and his red face expressed the complete inanition that had masked it heretofore. It came on slowly e- nough — he spoke less and less day by day, until within another week he answered once again with grunts and nods and avoided looking at Perry when he passed. There was no explanation. I know what it is, Perry thought, he is afraid of me, afraid of me. His inherently modest mind fought against the idea, but he finally had to admit that the impending silence dated from the revela- tion of the printed book, and that it was the shock of knowing a flesh and blood author that had sealed the springs of Pearson's confidence. Surely that day they had been at their flood — he'd taken Perry to his cabin and shown him the copy of *The Piper*, which Perry signed, "With gratitude and much astonishment, L. Perry," and when Pearson was at his best, Perry had said, "I've al- ways wanted to ask, but was rather timid — we read so much a- bout the fascination of the sea and how it holds men to it — I personally can't see it — it looks the same to me every day, some- times a little rougher — but what is this miraculous lure of the . . ."

"Bull," Pearson said, then, "aw, I don't know. I guess there is something though." (The second mate had said he thought so too, only he'd been a little more particular. With his southern accent, Caverly had said, "Waal, ah don' know — ah guess it's mo' the sea than the life at sea, fo' that ain't so pleasant") . . . "Well, y'know," said Pearson, "I lived ashore for six months this year, down in the Village, with a nice apartment and a sweet girl to love, but I just didn't feel right somehow. Then I got a job and, believe me boy, when we got standing out to sea and I smelt that breeze — boy! You know (he took up a pencil), when you get up late at night and go to the galley to get your coffee, and then go up on the bridge and pace back and forth, and every half hour the clock goes like this (he rapped on the desk), taptap-taptap, and fo'ard another bell goes, taptap-taptap, and the lookout on the foc'sle head says,

'All lights burning bright, sir,' and you say, 'All *right*' — boy! that's it," he said, "I guess that's it."

But day by day Pearson said less and less and Perry felt embarrassed in his presence. He got to coming up on Pearson's watch and only staying long enough to look at the pilot's chart and see how far they'd gone since noon the day before. Then he stood in the pilothouse while Pearson paced and carefully avoided seeing him, and finally he said, "Making good time today," "Uh huh," the third replied, and went into the chartroom. Perry wanted to be able to say, "Look here, old man, how have I offended you, what's the matter?" but somehow he couldn't do it. He knew he hadn't offended him and was completely baffled. He did manage one night at mess to say, "You've crawled back into your shell again, I see," and Pearson grinned and passed the butter to him. He determined to make Pearson talk, so he didn't go up on Pearson's watch again and he didn't talk to Pearson at the table, and Pearson didn't talk to him at all.

I give it up, he thought on deck one night, the last night before the freighter docked at Havre. I'll send him a letter from Vienna and ask for a response. To hell with him, he thought, and remembered how the day he'd come aboard he'd seen Pearson looking at him and talking him over with another mate, with a sly grin on his face. He remembered that he'd hated him that day, so he picked the thread up where it had been broken and hated him again, and stood on the deck in the clear winter night with the stars wheeling back and forth and round and round overhead, and Orion lying on his side far to the south and the Big Dipper almost on its back. Somehow the stars seemed very far away and utterly impersonal and cold at sea; they did not comfort him as they had so many nights in the summer as he lay alone in his blanket in a hayfield, winking merrily and keeping him company. Now they wheeled and soared like terns, miles above, majestic and ironical and cold. . . .

He looked out to sea — the fabric of waves tossed and soared and swayed away and sank, and the cold salt spray flashed back and forth across the deck and swished against the ports and dripped warm phosphorescent lights off the bulkheads. The miracle, he thought, of passing ships at sea . . . one star in Orion went out beneath a bank of low clouds at the dark horizon, and the whole night was tremulous with the high, thin howl of the wind through the cables and the high voice of the engines, and the sibilant hushing of the sea against the steel plates. . . .

A Little Walk

AS he read he could hear the clock ticking in the bedroom, and he recalled that every time the little house was empty the clock suddenly began to tick loudly enough to be heard throughout the first floor. He always listened to the passage of time. In a few minutes — the end of the chapter — he could get up and look at the clock and find out what time it was. Then he would know how long she had been gone. He looked up from the page and out the window. The rain had turned to hail.

"I'm going for a little walk down by the brook," she said, "with the kitten." A fine time for a walk, in weather like this; but he was silent. After all, four years of marriage had sanctified the custom. He sighed. "All right, be careful," and turned to his book. She wore a tan jacket.

Four o'clock. Two hours now. A little walk. Dark clouds soared over the hills and lay over the valley. The sleet rattled on the windowpane, and he watched it bounce on the sill. That was four years ago — the night we were married. She had moved into his furnished room, and as they were too poor to buy a bed, and it was impossible to double up in the narrow cot, he had laid the mattress on the floor, and they slept on that. . . .

. . . At three a.m. he woke with a start to find her gone. Leaping to his feet, he lit the light and looked around. Marriage-night. Her bags and books had not yet come, so all she had brought with her was gone — her coat, hat, purse. He looked frantically about for a note. He looked out the window. The streetlamps were dim in the fog and footsteps echoed on the pavement and reechoed off the walls of the rooming houses. Sitting in the chair, still drugged by sleep, he tried to remember whether he had said anything that might have angered her, caused her to repent their marriage — she had left him.

He fought off the definite knowledge that her walks at night were a habit of long standing, dating from her arrival in New York, lonely and friendless. He fought off that reassuring knowledge and tried — even hoped — to believe she had left him for good. After all, he had not wanted to marry her — he had not wanted to marry anyone. She must have felt that. Yet it happened. Telephone: "I'm sick and tired of this thing. If you want to marry me, come out to Roslyn tomorrow and I'll meet you at the store. If not, so long." Not knowing why, "I'll be there," he said. He sat by the window the rest of the night, fighting off the desire to say, To hell with it, and go to bed and sleep. He tried to feel worried, anxious, decided to call the police in the morning and fell asleep in his chair. At dawn a pebble rattled against the windowpane and there she was, standing in the gray street below, smiling and waving her hand. He was furious. "I felt like going for a walk and didn't want to wake you. That's all." "Where were you?" "I walked up and sat in Grand Central Station and talked to a man." "You sat in Grand Central Station!"

He sat by the window watching the sleet rattle against the pane and bounce off the windowsill. The wind howled around the house and the dark clouds soared behind the hills. The trees were bare and a few dead leaves swirled on the lawn. He listened to the loud passing of time, put down the book and lit a cigarette. He closed his eyes for a moment, then looked out again, staring across the valley to the hills. . . .

. . . she went down the bank, twigs crackling under her feet. kittykittykitty. the cat looked at her and she saw its pale eyes flash,
then turned again and picked her way down, setting her heels into
the rotting leaf-mould. the stream rushed below and swirled on the
stones; the trees across the stream rustled in the light breeze *He
heard a gun* that swept down the stream bed. a nuthatch uttered
its nasal cry, flying from the base of a spruce to the bole of a maple,
where it lay flat against the bark head down, and peered at her. at
the stream edge she turned over a few flat stones, called the kitten
again and stood surveying the way before her. she stepped on a
wet stone, her heel catching the moss *It's 4:15 it's hunting season*
and stripping it from the stone she fell forward and her head struck
a pointed crag. she lay with her face in a pool of water two inches
deep. the kitten mewed, stood still, looked about, mewed again,
then climbed the hill. . . .

It's hunting season now. The woods are full of men with guns
hunting rabbit and partridge. Deer in two weeks. 4:15. What a
fool you are — Russell went rattling past the house in his Ford to
fetch the schoolchildren home — you know she went for a walk
with the kitten. You can set your watch by him: 4:15 down, 4:30
back.

. . . alone, the kitten wandered vaguely up to the house and he
rushed out, looked at it and cursed it for not being able to speak.
for want of a nail the shoe was lost for want of a shoe the horse he
organized a searching party of farmers and all night they beat the
brush up- and downstream before they found her body. the hair
was wet, and when they turned her over, it lay plastered across her
bloody face. he fainted. . . .

Another gun. Paul Svenson came rattling downhill in his old
Buick touring car, careening from side to side; the air hissed with
his passing. *if a tree in the middle of a forest four square miles in
extent falls* (crushing a woman under it) *and no one is near, is there
a sound?* He put out the cigarette and walked up and down the
room. As he walked he felt his heart pounding against his ribs and

was aware of a slight feeling of nausea — sick to the stomach with excitement and anxiety. *all for the want of a horseshoe nail.* The wind howled in the chimney, the leaves were sodden now and plastered to the ground — plastered across her face! He picked up the book, then suddenly flung it against the opposite wall and heard the binding snap, the dry glue crackle.

He put on his hat and coat and gloves and went down the bank, digging his heels into the sodden mould. It was useless to shout against the rushing of the stream, but he called: "Margaret! Margaret!" and uttered the low whistle they used when one or the other was returning to the country house they now inhabited. *there could be no sound, because sound premises an instrument of perception, and if there was no one in the forest there could have been no sound because sound premises an instrument of* Twigs snapped back in his face as he trotted through the brush, peering over and under bushes and calling. He went back, hung up his coat and hat and lit a cigarette. 4:30. Now where could Russell be?

. . . them tracks go into this thicket, jeb said; then he put his hand on the other man's arm and they were both motionless. listen jeb, the man said, what chances are there fer being caught at this? i'm not fixin' to spend no three years in jail up to keene f'r killin' deer outta season. jeb laughed quietly. do as i tell ya, young feller, an' don't yew worry none. look! he pointed into the brush and they saw the tan hide of a buck. . . .

It was no good trying to read. His heart pumped and pumped and the clock ticked and every minute meant one minute more and every minute meant one minute less. He heard a rat working in the walls, and the faint pleasant sound of plaster falling. "Remember," she had said, "just because we're getting married doesn't mean some day I might not get the notion to up and go. It's just like me." Now where could Russell be? Here it was 4:45 and he hadn't come chugging up the hill with the schoolchildren who always waved as they passed the house. . . . i heard yore wife died, mr. blake, so i thought as how i'd come in an' pay my respecks. that's very kind of you, he replied; i appreciate company these days, you know. now w'en *my* wife was took to the horspital in keene, they said as how she'd pull through. but w'en the case was diagnized, it begun to look diff'rent. . . .

. . . he fired and they saw the buck fall and heard it kicking in the leaves and ran forward. *all for the want of a horsehoe nail* my god! jeb said, yew killed a woman! they lifted her, laid her back, then tore open the man's shirt she was wearing and tried to listen to her dead heart. they were abashed by her naked breasts and closed the shirt. it's thet blake woman, jeb said, yew know — them city folk as moved into the old nelson house last summer. they carried her down the bank, across the brook and up the other side emerging on the road, and went slowly up it in the last glow of early sunset. at the window they saw his pale face staring out. . . .

H e stood at the window and watched the crows flying over the Clark house down in the valley. . . . then he saw the two men coming up the road slowly, carrying something between them. he rushed out without his hat and coat and stood there staring at his wife. tears rolled down his tanned cheeks, and the men bowed their heads. it was a accident, mr. blake. i know, he said, i heard your guns. . . .

It was getting dark, so he lit the lamp, carefully turning the little wheel until the flame was at the right height and there was no danger of its smoking. I'll call the Clarks, I'll call the Rogers, I'll call the Murdocks, I'll call the . . . . "My God!" he said aloud, running his fingers through his hair and walking up and down. . . .

. . . coming back from the schoolhouse russell came on the crowd standing around the body on the road and stopped the car. she come out'n them woods an' paul svenson run 'er down. there were tears in the man's eyes as he stood between clark and rogers. i didn't mean t'hit 'er, i was drunk i didn't mean t'hit 'er. . . . He looked at the room into which she never would come again — at the life-sized picture of her hanging on the wall, with its sad, faraway expression. . . . he buried her in the little country churchyard

and lived nearby the rest of his life. people pointed him out on the
roads — that's old mr. blake, they said, he's a city man come here i
guess some thirty year ago. his wife died in a thunderstorm one
day; she was out walkin' early 'n the mornin' an' stood under a
tree durin' a sudden shower.   the tree was struck an' it fell an'
crushed her to death. every afternoon he goes to the churchyard
an' lays some wildflowers on the grave. done it now thirty years.
but you know — he seems so cheerful — you'd never think such a
terrible thing happened to him. always a smile, always a pleasant
word for everyone, gives money to the school every year. oncet i
ast him if he wasn't awful lonely livin' all alone an' he said, no.
margaret — that was his wife's name — margaret is here all the time.
i guess he's a bit cracked, i guess. . . .

Now you're letting your imagination run away with you. He
laughed. Now I must finally look myself squarely in the face, he
thought. All these years I've been avoiding it — it explains a lot.
He realized, without surprise, that he didn't much care whether
she came back or not. The idea had occurred to him before, and
he had glossed it over, allowed it to slip back into the recesses
from which it had arisen. Inertia, I let myself be married — but
my God! what could I *do* without. . . .

     . . . a man came up and knocked on the door. it was old mur-
dock. *5 o'clock!* beyond he could see a rim of pale light on the
hill in the west. the bare chestnuts on the ridge stood stiffly in the
failing light. he could hear the train whistle from across the notch.
That means a cold winter. i know! mr. blake, murdock said, i have
some bad news for yew, an' i'm hopin' yew'll take it like a man.
he smiled. you couldn't have much bad news for me, he replied,
god knows, things are bad enough as they are. he laughed. no, mr.
blake. murdock fingered his hat, then looked up, cleared his
throat and said, mr. blake, yore wife — well, old man, she was
comin' up the hill a w'ile back an' paul svenson — yew know, he's
always drunk — run her down with his car. i'm afraid she's hurt
bad. . . .

He sat down and determined to read again. Oh God! come home for Christ's sake! He was up and putting a piece of wood on the fire, and feeling the palms of his hands sweating, he wiped them on his trousers. Never again! *Just because we're getting married doesn't mean* Where is Russell, where is he, that all our swains — Day after day, week after week, month and year after year, he would be forced to get along without her. He was lost. He looked around him and the glow of satisfaction he felt contemplating the homely objects they had gathered left him, flowed back and out of his life like water recedes from a rock pool on the shore when the tide goes out. Little by little the pool dried, and only a rim of bitter salt remained, caked on the edges. . . . Her clothes hung in the closet, her shoes stood in a row under the dresser, her necklace hung over the door-knob, and there was the little toy razor she used to shave under. . . . Admit it! go ahead and admit it!

He felt his brows contract, his teeth grit. "I don't care!" he said aloud. "See if I care — stay away, you goddamned . . ." Her shoes under the dresser, her necklace over the doorknob, her fountain pen on the table, and all the letters tied with a blue ribbon and all the letters bound with a broad elastic band, lying in the drawer with the picture of her as a little girl, dressed in white, sitting in the swing under the apple tree. . . .

She whistled under the window, the low, three-noted call they used, and she said, "Kittykittykitty!" and came in. He was facing her as she entered, his hands clenched at his sides, his teeth gritted. She smiled at him and he went red in the face and cried:
"Now for Christ's sake, where were you?"
"Why, I went for a little. . ."
"I know, you went for a little walk *down the stream.* That was three hours ago . . ."
"No," she said. "Only two . . ."
"I looked for you down the stream, but . . ."
"I know. I went up the stream for a change."
"Didn't you have sense enough to come back when it hailed? In this weather! Do you want to get pneumonia?" He worked

himself into a frenzy and screamed at her. "Haven't you *any* consideration at all . . ."

She looked puzzled. "Why, I dropped in at old man Murdock's up the stream. He called me from the window and I had a glass of beer with him."

"Can't you understand! *Can't* you see . . ."

"Why, no," she smiled. "I must confess I can't. Though I suppose it *was* inconsiderate of me."

"Hump!" he said, snorting through his nostrils. She came and kissed him and he sniffed again and lit a cigarette with trembling fingers. She went into the kitchen and he heard her poking up the fire and rattling the pots. It was a victory for him, but he felt he'd lost its fruits. Russell's old Ford came slowly chugging up the steep hill, crammed with schoolchildren dressed in bright flannels and mufflers. He stood at the window and waved to them and they waved back eagerly. Russell lifted his hand in greeting. It was a ritual now. It didn't mean a thing. If she hadn't come back? . . . i don't know where i'll get the money for the funeral, he said. mr. blake, we people — the town will be only too glad to help you out till you get on your feet again. it's awfully kind of you. . . .

"Margaret!" he called, "When will dinner be ready?"

Pet Crow

SHE turned on her side and watched her husband sleep. It was light outside and she could hear the crow calling imperiously from his perch beside the front door. Wide beams of clear light fell through the window, and the bee that had been imprisoned in the room so many days was still buzzing feebly against the panes. She marvelled at its tenacity. Watching him sleep, she wondered at the faculty he possessed for complete relaxation — the faculty that enabled him to sleep like a child no matter what had been harassing him the evening before. He could reach depths of depression that invariably frightened her — determined her that some immediate action must be taken, though what form that action would assume she was powerless to conceive. Had not every expedient been thoroughly examined and its empty husk thrown aside among the others? But he could sleep — like a child — and she saw that his mouth was partly open and his lips moist. She listened to his deep breathing.

As she rose from the bed she suddenly remembered, and felt ill. It was almost three months now. She examined her breasts and tenderly pressed the swollen nipples. Three months, and they had done nothing about it — nothing could be done. There was no money and there were no prospects. She had a persistent, symbolic image of the two — three of them; well, two of them anyway — sitting in chairs facing each other across an empty space and twirling their thumbs. That was the way the situation presented itself to her inner eye — unfair as such an image might be to the actuality. They were stuck. They had frantically pulled every string, written letters. He had obtained occasional day labor from the neighboring farmers, but it brought in little, and their bills continued to mount.

So Bert, as he had named the crow, proved a diversion. In him they could forget their daily anxiety, pour into him all the accumulated bitterness born of an unsolvable situation — sit and watch his unconsciously hilarious antics and feel that life was good and sweet and kind. Damn his black hide! He was always hungry. All the livelong day, from morning to night, he called imperiously from his perch — for food. He's young, she thought. Ralph tells me his metabolic rate is high. He must be fed.

She slipped on her dressing gown and looked out the window, down across the stream to the hills beyond. The morning mist was dissolving, and the sun glittered in a thousand facets on the little stream. She saw a trout leap from the water, and the air was washed and clean, the foliage sparkling in late autumn colors. As she watched, a few crows soared out of the forest cawing and circled over the house. Simultaneously, Bert set up a screeching that outdid his usual performance. She could almost see him hopping and dancing on his perch — lifting his clipped wings and flapping them wildly with excitement. His mouth would be open.

"Hey!" she cried to her husband, and shook his shoulder till he opened puffed lids and looked out at her, a frown on his face.

"Hey!" she said. "Your bird of evil omen is yelling for his breakfast." He turned over on his side and pulled the covers over his head. From beneath them she heard his muffled voice. "Feed him," he said.

She flung the door open and Bert turned on his homemade perch. Lifting his wings, he squatted on the stick and let out a piercing shriek. She saw the pink lining of his mouth and the long flat tongue. She laughed. "Shut up, damn you," she said. "I'll feed you when I get good and ready." Bert flapped his wings and croaked hoarsely in his throat and was silent. He cocked his head and watched her through the windowpane as she gathered kindling, lit the fire and started to prepare breakfast. There was no milk. There was one egg, and she set it aside to scramble it for him when he rose. Let him sleep awhile, she thought; he'll be working on the roads today.

She toasted the two pieces of dry bread for herself, warmed the coffee and drank it without sugar or cream. Then she took the small package of cornmeal he had bought with their last dime and stirred some into a half-cup of water. Outside the bird was hopping up and down on his perch and craning his neck. When she approached with the cup and spoon in hand, he flapped his wings, tipped forward and nearly fell off the perch. She laughed at him.

"Well, greedy," she said, "hold your horses." Once only, she tendered the spoon and withdrew it; then, ashamed, she fed the mixture to the bird, laughing as he gripped the hard edge of the spoon in his beak and gulped the cornmeal mush. It slopped over the spoon and oozed from the sides of his mouth, dripping on his breast. He even cawed as he ate, and the result was a strangled and ridiculous gurgle. She remembered the sea lions at the Zoo back home — how they barked as they submerged, and the strange comical sound they made.

After a time Bert seemed to have had enough, and though she knew he'd be crying again within ten minutes, she set the spoon and cup down on the tray Ralph had improvised under the perch and said, "If you get hungry, feed yourself." He cocked his head at her and looked up out of sparkling, slate-gray eyes, and blinked them slowly. She went indoors.

He had washed and was sitting at the table. "Where's the box?" he said, so she brought the cardboard box and he found a butt slightly longer than the others and lit it carefully. After a few deep draughts it was gone, and he put it out. He looked at his wife a-cross the table and said, "How do you feel this morning?" "Fine," she said. "Why lie? I can tell when you're not feeling well." "All right then, I feel rotten." He nodded his head.

"When do you think you'll be back?" Watching his face, she was filled with a sense of great security and ease. It prompted her to smile, but she quickly repressed the temptation, aware that his restless mind would pick her up and ask questions she was in no mood to answer.

"About five," he said.

"I can't make a lunch for you today. There's nothing in the house."

"Have you got a tomato?"

"Yes, I think there is one."

"All right." He sat looking out the side window, reluctant to get up and go to work. Across the stream, a tardy kingfisher was sitting on a limb, and as he watched it rose easily, hovered over the stream, folded its wings and dropped like a stone into the water. It seemed gone for a long moment; the surface of the stream was almost smooth when it arose, bearing a gleaming, flashing fish in its beak, and was gone. He looked at her.

"Listen," he said. "This can't go on much longer."

"I know it," she said brightly. "What do you want me to do?" Now he had found a loophole for his anger.

"Use your brains!" he cried. "You know it can't go on like this. You've got to have proper nourishment – food – enough food. We've got to have money – enough to pay our bills and a margin besides." He stopped. What was the sense of going into that again? He had done his best; there was certainly nothing *she* could do. She was doing her best to stand for the situation as it was, to put up with a husband who could not make a living for them both. *He* had got her into the predicament, and it was up to him to get her out. *He* had insisted on coming to the country, saying food was cheap, rent a minor item, work easy to get. Well, it wasn't.

"Kids have come into the world under worse conditions," she said.

"This kid isn't going to come into the world. It can't be done!"

"Why not?"

"Why not?" Because I said it couldn't – that's why not."

"I'd like to see you stop it," she laughed and wondered why she'd laughed.

He pinched the bridge of his nose and sat there awhile, staring under his hand at the yellow stain on the plate. Then he looked up, his eyes flashing.

"Damn it!" he said. "Why did you give me this egg — the only one in the house! You do it all the time, I'm getting sick of it."

"I didn't want it. You know I don't feel like eating in the morning."

"I don't care whether you feel like it or not. I don't need the egg, and you do!"

"I like toast and you don't."

Bert had started to screech again, and they both listened. She thought she would tease him a little.

"Why did you spend that dime on cornmeal?" she said. He didn't see the joke; that was his way at times.

"Do you want the bird to starve!" he cried.

"What did you want the bird for in the first place? You accepted it when John brought it. You clipped its wings. It's a wild thing and doesn't belong on a perch. Besides, it gets on my nerves with its continual screeching for food."

"Well, wring its neck, then," he said.

"I've a good mind to."

"You do, and I'll break yours!"

"Darling," she said, "you'll be late for work."

He looked at her. "Listen, kid," he said. "Take it easy. You're letting your nerves get the better of you." That made her smile.

"Listen, guy," she said, "I gave you the egg because I don't like eggs, because you're going to work all day and I'm not, etc., etc."

He bent and kissed her face, picked up his coat and went outside. As she watched him up the road, Bert cocked his head and let out a low, throaty squawk. "All right," she said, "in a minute."

W ell, old girl, she thought, you've got yourself into it this time. She sat by the stream watching the kingfisher on his morning hunt, and scratching in the sand with an alder stick. The sun was behind the stiff comb of pines on the hill, and the acrid scent of burning leaves was in the air. When she was tired her mind occasionally toyed with the idea of placing the blame on Ralph's shoulders. It *had* been a freak idea, and she had been seduced by the whimsical conceit that just because it represented a new departure it was bound to turn out all right.

She did not regret leaving the city; she had been as tired of it
as Ralph. With the little money saved, he had come home one
night and said, "Listen, kid, you know what? I'm sick and tired of
the insurance business. I'm tired of following leads and talking
people into parting with their hard-earned cash for a doubtful
benefit to accrue twenty-five years from date. I like — I've always
liked — to work with my hands. One of my prospects told me
about a swell place in the country, where rent was cheap and food
cheaper. I'm a pretty good carpenter. People in the country are
always wanting repairs made, shacks put up. There's room for a
good carpenter any place. Are you game?"

Of course she was game. They burned their bridges; he bought
some new tools. They moved into the country and settled into a
spring and summer of delirious happiness. But he'd reckoned without a few things. Any native could do the little carpentry required
on a frame house. His services were rarely sought out. Early in
the fall he had done a little clapboarding, put up a smithy, painted
some old buildings. And labor was cheap — thirty cents an hour.

Now the fall rains were on them, people were banking their
houses against the winter, the sky was overcast day after day and
the wind howled all night. Bert could have flown away if Ralph
hadn't kept his wings clipped. She was sorry for the bird, but it
afforded him so much entertainment on the idle days he spent at
home, she could not bear to insist on his letting it free.

They sat for hours at a time watching the crow as it capered
on its crossbar or on Ralph's shoulder. "He's shore a comical
jigger," John had said when he brought the fledgling to the house.
"I clumb four trees afore I got 'im. Ef ya split 'is tongue, folks
say as how he'll tawk." They had not split his tonge, but the days
were clamorous with his screeching and squawking, the porch was
filthy from his droppings, and he got into dark holes when he
jumped off his perch. Fearful that he'd be lost, she had crept under the porch time after time to retrieve him.

Now she could hear him calling from the house and hear the
flapping of his wings. It made her sad. But that wasn't the problem. She rose from the bank, threw her stick into the stream and
watched it swirl over the dam Ralph had built. He liked to work

with wood. She could see him now, sitting on the road scraper in the cold, his body bathed in sweat, his face and hands crusted with the dirt kicked from the horses' heels. "This can't go on much longer," he had said. That was true.

She came back to the house and looked for Bert. He had got under the porch again, so she crawled in after him and pulled him out, flapping and screaming, by the left leg. He pecked her viciously, and she launched a cuff that fortunately missed. Plumping him on the perch, she got a spoon and crammed him with meal till it drooled from his bill and splattered her dress when he shook his head. "You're a pest!" she said, "but I like you." He scraped his beak on the wood like a man sharpening a carving knife, then looked up at her and cawed loudly three times.

Sitting on the porch she watched the horses on the hill opposite as they galloped madly back and forth across the slope, playing in the failing light. The mare and the gelding reared and pranced, nipped each other gently, and raced away in opposite directions, only to swerve, rear, and double back. Their manes streamed on the late afternoon wind from the north.

"Krawk!" said Bert.

"Yes, I know it," she said. "But you'll have to wait till your old man comes home. You're going to go hungry soon, my boy, for the cornmeal's almost run out, and I'll be damned if I'll dig worms for you." The earth was hard and cold.

"Kraw-awk!"

She listened for the team that would bring Ralph home — he walked to work, but Carlson brought him back, thank God, for he was generally so tired he went to bed shortly after supper. "This can't go on much longer," he had said. I'll write to mother, she thought. I can't let him go on worrying like this, and it wouldn't do to go back to the city these hard times. Quoth the Raven, Nevermore! Oh, well.

In the woodshed, she searched for kindling in vain. There were some old slabs Ralph had obtained by working on shares, so she took down the axe and swung it as she had seen him, splitting and chopping them into small pieces. It was clumsy work, but she knew he'd be tired when he returned and decided to spare him the effort. It did not occur to her that the earthen floor of the shed was soft with a twenty-year carpet of wood dust and chips and that her work was consequently harder. She swung the axe till she suddenly became so dizzy she had to sit down for a long time, gasping for breath. "That was a foolish thing to do," she said aloud. "What an ass I am!"

She picked up the armful of wood and went indoors. Ralph was there. He had taken off his coat and was washing at the sink. He looked at her. "What have you been doing?" he said. "You look like a ghost."

"Nothing," she said. Then, "Oh, what did you bring?"

"Carlson had no money to pay me, so I took it out in trade. He gave me some potatoes, a loaf of bread, some butter and some milk.

"Bravo!" she said, "we eat!" He smiled. "I forgot to take the tomato for my lunch."

"Gee whiz!" she said, "you poor kid!" He waved his hand. Then he went outdoors to see the crow, and taking his spade, he dug for half an hour till he had a small can of worms.

Dinner was on the table — creamed potatoes, toast, and what was left of the coffee. "Listen," he said, "you don't look at all well."

"I feel fine."

"Can't you ever tell the truth?"

"What do you want me to tell you?" she cried with exasperation. "You seem to get some sort of satisfaction when I tell you I feel rotten. *You* don't come to me about every little pain you have."

"Have you a pain?"

"*No!*" she said. Then, "Forgive me; maybe I'm a bit jumpy. Bert's been shrieking all day long, and there's no cornmeal left."

"I'll shoot him," he said.

"Go ahead!" Then she felt sorry, and reaching across the table laid her hand on his wrist. "Don't be angry with me. Every little thing seems to get on my nerves these days . . . you understand."

"For Christ's sake!" he sneered.

"All right!" But *you* don't have to sit here all day and listen to that damned bird squawking. He's hungry all the time and I think it's a dirty shame to keep him."

"I said I'd shoot him," he replied.

She laughed. "You wouldn't hurt a fly."

"I want to know what you've done today to make you look so pale."

"Nothing, I tell you! Oh, well, if you must know, I –" she hesitated. "I crawled under the porch a couple of times to get your pet."

"What for?"

"Because I didn't want him to get away."

"He'd have come out again."

"Jesus Christ!" she said. "Nothing I do seems to please you." She threw down her napkin and went upstairs.

After he had finished the butt, he took down the .22 and loaded it. Then he went outside and got the crow, folded its wings against its body, and tucked it against his breast. As he crossed the field behind the house the wind was singing through the telephone wires, and he paused to listen to its hum. Dark clouds were scudding across the hills, and an unearthly green light lay over the land. Across the field he sat Bert on a fence post, walked back six feet and drew a bead on him.

"Kraw-awk!" Bert said.

He fired and saw the bird drop from the post. Bending over, he watched its mouth slowly open and the dark blood well up from its throat. His heart beat furiously as he walked back to the house and hung the gun up over the door. Then he took the perch and broke it up, throwing the pieces on the dwindling woodpile. He cut some kindling for the morning fire.

They sat in their chairs across the room from each other and read a while. The wind was howling about the house, and the old building creaked and groaned with strain. The windows rattled. Looking out, he watched the twinkling of the stars in Orion's belt and saw a meteor. In the north the aurora was brilliant – vast streamers of ghastly light reached to the zenith, wavered and faded out. A dazzling streak would suddenly appear high in the sky, glow for a moment, then shift and glow again, fade out and die away. The hills were bathed in its effulgence.

"I haven't heard Bert all evening," she said, looking up from her book. He was silent. "I'm sorry," she said. "My nerves were all on edge. I'm really fond of the little bum. Is he asleep?"

"Yes."

"You didn't really shoot him, then," she said. "I knew you wouldn't." She laughed, came over to him, and standing beside him at the window, kissed the back of his neck.

"I shot him."

"Go on! You know you didn't."

"Have it your own way," he replied.

"You didn't really," she said, turning him to face her and looking sadly in his eyes.

"Yes," he said.

They had not spoken a word for an hour before they went to bed; then they lay side by side, listening to the wind roar around the house, and the creaking of the old beams. She went to sleep, but he could not forget the last flash of Bert's slate-gray eye, nor the dark blood welling from his open mouth. He felt ill and trembled; then finally he too fell asleep. . . .

Late at night she called him faintly, and as he sat up with a start, he saw that she was lying on the floor. Springing from the bed, he closed the window and lifted her back again. He lit the lamp. "My God!" she said. "This is terrible."

"I know," he said, "Lie still. Take it easy." He hurried downstairs and poked up the fire, setting a pot of water on to boil. Then he called the doctor, and till he came rushed up and down stairs frantically, trembling with fright, bringing her a glass of water, pillows to put under her head, extra blankets. There was no ice.

When the doctor came he entered the house, threw off his coat and rolled his sleeves up as he spoke to him.

"I've made some boiling water."

"Good," he said. "How did this happen? Did she fall? Have you been letting her lift anything heavy?"

"I don't know," he said. "I was away all day."

The doctor threw him a contemptuous glance and went upstairs. He held a lamp.

"I won't need you," he said; and as he entered the room, he saw his wife's pale face, turned away from the light. He stood outside the door a long time, listening to the rustling of the bedsprings, the doctor's low voice, and the sound of the lid being placed back on the commode. The floor creaked under the doctor's steps, and he heard a groan. . . .

Bare Grain

AS the cutter drew up before his door, the Reverend Ralph Polk smacked his mittens sharply together, picked up the package, and smiled at the couple who had driven him home. In the north, clouds veiled the dark hills in a white mist that he could see was steadily drifting his way. More snow. "More snow, Bill," he said to the driver and glanced at the steaming horses with compassion. The woman sat in the back and looked at him.

"That was shore a purty talk you give, Reverend," Woodruff replied. "Wot with the flowers an' all I guess it's about the best hand out old Les Burke's had in a month o' Sundays."

The Reverend Polk turned away, his face flushed and a strange constriction in his throat. Bill was still talking. "I ain't much of a hand at funerals," he said. "Can't say as I'll ever go to another, less'n it be my own." He laughed. The Reverend Polk turned to look at the man, an expression of patient forbearance on his face. Anything else to say? Bill Woodruff glanced at him, was embarrassed and flapped his reins. The woman turned her head. "Get up!" Bill shouted and waved his hand to the minister.

"Forgive me, O Lord," the Reverend Polk said to himself, "for my intolerable pride." Inside, he quickly removed his coat and overshoes, tore the muffler from his neck and hung it on the hall rack. With rapid strides he gained his study, poked up the stove, laid another log on the fire, and opened the draft. He unwrapped the package and stood the oblong tank and the cylinder it contained on his desk. From the window he could see the snow drifting slowly over Wilson's mowing; soon it would cross the stream and march up the low hill to . . . .

He sat at his desk, brought out paper and pencils and flung the drawer closed again. The cat rubbed against his leg and mewed, and he automatically reached down to touch the animal.

"Les Burke," his pencil wrote, "in the eightieth year of his age." He hastily crossed it out again and went to the window. It is snowing on his grave, he thought.

"The heavens declare the glory of God," he wrote, "and the firmament sheweth his handiwork." God's handiwork is nowhere so evident and so heartening as it is in these hills. Here He has been lavish; and if He made the stony soil and decreed things so that the season should be short and the farmer's toil unremitting, He also flung up these wooded hills and sowed them with His feathered creatures and planted gleaming fish in the streams. In the Winter the winds howl from the north and the house shakes and man sits by his fire waiting for the Spring, but soon now the earth will melt under the ardor of the mounting sun, and the earth will flow with many streams and be damp underfoot, sap will rise in the maples and man's industry once more enter upon its deathless cycle.

And when the earth's blood is flowing once more, as it has every year of the fourteen I have worked in this parish, I can repeat with the Psalmist, "I will lift up mine eyes unto the hills from whence cometh my help," truly feel that the earth's blood flows in my veins, that every day that brings the grass from the ground and new birds from the south strengthens my weakness, fills me with new courage, and the doubts born of the long hard Winter leave my heart. Now when Spring comes it will not be snowing on Les Burke's grave, but there will be tender new grass and pale violets, testifying to the truth of the life everlasting, even unto the very eyes of unbelieving men. . . .

In a sense I am the only man in this community who can write his story — for old Les Burke was not loved here. Yet

was he any more misused than any other men whose story I do not
know? I loved him. I loved him as a fa—

When I entered the church this afternoon my heart was bitter
with gall at the sight of all those faces. Any understanding of my
fellow man I may be blessed with deserted me as I faced them over
the dead body of our brother, for I could not understand why they
had come. I looked at each face individually in the clear light falling through the big windows — there they sat in their best clothes,
these people who had done the man to death — I felt my eyes
strained to find a face, two faces in particular, and to my utter astonishment they were there — Bill and Betty Woodruff — and I felt
my heart grow cold within me and heavy as lead, and my throat
was dry else I would have stood up in the pulpit and denounced
them both, profaning the holy place.

I looked at the dead face below me and pressed my lips together, but I felt so many hostile eyes upon me that it took all my
strength to say the simple words I had come to say. For there
they sat — Bill and Betty Woodruff — who had literally eaten his substance; old Forsythe, who had doled him out an occasional handful of crackers and mocked the man as he left his door; there were
young Rowley and his mother, who had taken him in two weeks
before his death, in dead of Winter; and there they sat smiling at
me as though awaiting benediction for their kind deed! I hated
them all, and perhaps it was that hatred that saved me, that sealed
my lips with an unworthy rage and so prevented me from dis-
gracing my holy office. I sat there fifteen minutes before I could
open my mouth to pay our last respects to this dead husk that so
resembled — only in the fact that he was dead — my father (who
art in heaven). . . .

Surely you have all lived with a man or woman who was death-
ly ill for a long time and realized with horror when it was too
late for repentance how your feelings underwent several stages —
how you began by wholeheartedly pitying the invalid and did
your best to comfort him; how you became bored by him and
furious with his illness; how at long last you came to hate both
him and his disease with an implacable hatred so that the very

sight of him lying there so patiently enduring his pain threw you into an ungovernable rage when it was all you could do to prevent yourself from shrieking, "I hate you! I hate your being sick! Who cares if you are sick — and your ghastly smile when someone asks how you feel, and the reproach in your eyes for all well people!" Surely you have entertained the idea of killing that person and putting an end to his misery (your own misery!). But no, you have not killed him. Instead, something inside you has died! You have lost the capacity to suffer with your fellow man, and for him. You have continued to perform the same gestures intended to alleviate his suffering, but they have become perfunctory and meaningless. You have come to such a point that you can look upon his affliction with a cold eye, unmoved by his crises, bored by his hysteria in the face of pain, heaving a relieved sigh when you can leave the house and forget him for a moment.

I am not trying to condone my sins. I am trying to understand them. For five years I watched my father die. I tended him skillfully, I held the basin when blood flowed in torrents from his mouth, I watched the doctors thrust needles into his chest, I gave my own blood to swell his depleted arteries. But I hated him and the night he died I was elated, for it meant an end of restriction, an end of worriment, an end of sympathizing with a man whose suffering by then made no impression on my mind or heart. I was young, yes, but my youth was no excuse. I followed him to the grave and I endured the reproachful glances of my relatives with perfect equanimity and a sneer for their hypocrisy. (They never meant a thing to him, nor he to them.) He is lying in his grave, flat on his back, and he is wearing a wing collar with a black bow tie. . . . It is snowing on his grave.

I first saw him in the Spring of 1919, and he was a familiar sight within a week in his bright buggy with the yearling bay mare. He struck me as a kindly man in his late sixties; his beard was already white. I learned soon that the Woodruffs had been living with him for some time; and since he was the wealthiest man in the community, any number of tales were brought to me about him and poured into my ears with an eagerness that seems so universal among folk in the country, where there is little news to be transmitted except the local gossip. They told me he was living in sin with Mrs. Woodruff, even though her husband was present and their nine children lived in the house with him. I closed my ears to this malicious slander, but now I remember it struck me as peculiar at the time that a family of eleven with no visible means of support except the day labor of the husband could so unscrupulously make its home with a solitary man. Les Burke had never married.

They said he was crazy — had been working thirty-five years on an invention that wouldn't work. I praised him for his perseverance and his interest in something aside from his horses and his butter. They said he'd chopped off a toe to avoid being drafted into the Civil War. I commended this action with my whole heart, but the gossips could not understand that there exists a heroism higher than the soldier's. I attributed all this to the jealousy that hangs over the head of any successful man, for Les was wealthy in his way.

I called on him that Spring. He was sugaring and I recall how pleasant it was to stand in the sugar house amid the uprising steam from the pans and listen to the hiss and bubble. Out on the snow his hired men were gathering and pouring sap into the great wooden tank and Les stood at the end of the long line of flat pans, occasionally dipping a scoop into the syrup and waiting for it to be ready to be drawn off. We went into his house for lunch.

I remember that he took great pride in his possessions, for which I gently chided him at the time. I believe I was smiling when I quoted Matthew to him: "Take no thought for your life, what ye shall eat, or what ye shall drink; nor yet for your body, what ye shall put on. Is not the life more than meat . . . ." But I have had occasion to regret those words in the past few years, though God knows it is doubtful that he ever remembered them or held them against me for a moment.

But there was something he did hold against me, and I see now that the wise minister must modify the doctrine to his flock; though this be heresy, I have held to it. It is not well to hurl Scripture at a man's head as though it were a law of nature. . . .

In time there had come to me incontrovertible proof of the man's sinful ways, and in my young zeal and out of my inexperience of life I took occasion to denounce him from the pulpit. Christ was so wise he could encompass contradictions, and though I fulminated from the pulpit against the sin of adultery and tactlessly looked Burke straight in the eye, I was forgetting those other words: "And why beholdest thou the mote that is in thy brother's eye, but considerest not the beam that is in thine own. . . ." He did not speak to me again (until a year ago) nor lift his hand in salutation as he passed my door in his brightly painted buggy. He had once said to me, "I'm not much of a hand for church-goin', but I know the right and wrong of things." He neither smoked nor drank. Now he dropped me, I felt, as though I had offered him a bad bargain. He said nothing, but he went his own way.

He even glanced at me with a superstitious eye, for it was not long after that the break came and he must doubtless have felt I had some hand in it, though God alone knows I was guiltless in that respect. For in the space of seven years the Woodruffs ate him out of house and home. I say that, and I mean it literally. For seven years he had fed eleven ravenous mouths out of his substance, receiving no return. It was a cruel price to pay for mere carnal delight − I cannot believe it was that alone.

I saw the butter churn only recently; it lay rotting in the piles of manure in the yard. One by one the stock was sold, the mowing and the timber land was sold, the farms he owned and rented all were sold. The big house was no longer repaired from season to season, the paint on the buggy was chipped off and the axle broken and mended with cord. He did not sugar in the Spring, for he had no sugar lot. (He sent me a note about two years ago. I could not understand it at first, for it was fully eight years since his home had been broken up. "This is yore doin'," it said. I recall that I wept over that note and went to visit him, but he would not open the door for me that day.) And when he did not have a penny left, when he had sold the house to old Forsythe, keeping only the bay mare, when the stocks of canned meat were gone from the cellar and the barrels of flour and the bins of potatoes, beets and carrots, cabbage, turnips and the pork put down in the brine were gone, they all moved out together, leaving him alone. Bill and Betty Woodruff drove off in the buggy and the nine children tagged along behind.

It was indifference that killed my father, not disease. He had the best medical treatment our means could procure, but it was too late then and the ironical part of it was that the night he died he said he had not felt better in years. He did not know he was going to die — he sat up late that night, talking about the war and how it would destroy the flower of our youth. He shook his head sadly and I was prompted to smile, for he had lost nothing through the war. To the contrary, he had gained immeasurably in worldly means.

It was indifference that had killed Les Burke, not hunger! Old Forsythe said to me, "God 'a' mercy, he was eighty year old. You wouldn't want a man to live longer, would you?" I replied that I would have given my right arm to have had him live till Spring, but he could not understand that. "Ay-eh," he said. "He'd had another colt comin' in, come April."

When he finally opened the door to me I stepped into the shack he inhabited. That was last Winter. Since he'd been forced to give up the old place he'd been living rent free in one of the Forsythes' abandoned hovels.

The house was full of smoke, and with my eyes smarting I looked about for a chair to sit on, but there was only a box, so I offered it to Burke. "Naw," he said smiling, "set down an' rest ya." He sat on a mattress that lay on the floor in the corner, and these two objects and the stove constituted the entire furniture of his house. "The house looks kind o' poorly," Les said. "I hain't had time to fix it up none." He waved his arm in a tentative gesture. "Young Rowley give me a roll o' roofin' paper this Fall, but I'm kind o' scared to climb up on the roof."

"Have you no bedding?" I said. He laughed, and his intense blue eyes lit with a sparkle of divine amusement.

"But!"

"W'en you git as old's I be," he said, "you won't be thinkin' o' things like that. I climb in atween 'em nights." I found it difficult from that point on to avoid mention of all the things he obviously needed. They stared me in the face at every turn and I felt their absence was a personal affront both to me and to the community at large. He had no saw, so he merely thrust the end of a long-quartered log into the stove door and pushed it farther in as it burned down. Piled in the corners were all sorts of odds and ends, broken parts of farm machinery, tools and crockery. The cracks in the walls were plastered over with pages from ancient almanacs and calendars, Montgomery Ward catalogs and newspapers. Old Burke recalled me from my rude inspection.

"Do you know anybody wants a colt?" he said. "Ef I don't find a buyer I'll have to turn him in to Frank Forsythe fer crackers."

"No, Mr. Burke," I said, "I'm sorry, but I don't." He offered me a cup of milk.

"Time was," he said, "w'en I raised the best colts in the country." His eyelids were red, and I turned away, embarrassed. The wind whined through the cracks in the shanty and I pulled my collar up. I was acutely mortified, ashamed of my good clothes, ashamed to think of my comfortable house as I sat in this miserable wreck of a place with the thermometer registering twenty below outside. In the presence of this old man whose hands trembled so he could not hold a cup without spilling its contents, I was ashamed to be only forty years old. With a last attempt to cover my embarrassment by a hypocritical show of an interest I could not somehow feel, I said, "Tell me about your invention. They say you have been working on it all your life. What sort of device is it?"

He smiled at me and set down his cup. It was agonizing to watch how slowly he had to move, for it seemed minutes on end before he reappeared in the room with a small oblong tank containing a cylinder. This he handed to me without a word as I sat shivering on the box, and resumed his seat on the mattress.

"Et's a invention," he said, "to create perpetual motion." He got up again and came toward me, peering anxiously into my eyes to see if I would smile, I believed. Perhaps it was only my sense of guilt that made me feel this, for I should have realized that a man who had spent his entire life on one idea would be impervious to disbelief — would not even have noticed it.

He poked the cylinder with his dry finger and looked up at me. "Of course," he said, "it needs a workin' model to show you. I hain't never had the money to make one."

"How much would it take?"

"Mebbe three thousand dollars, mebbe more."

"I don't understand."

"Well, y'see," he explained, and his voice assumed a singsong intonation, "you fill the tank with water half way. Then half o' the cylinder sticks out o' water. Now the half that's out o' water turns down, because o' the pull o' gravity on it and the half that's in the water turns up 'cause o' the buoyancy o' the water. That keeps the cylinder spinnin'. . . ."

"Just a moment," I said. "You mean the tank must stand on its side, don't you, so . . . "

"Yes," he said.

I sighed, for I thought I had detected a flaw in the idea and I debated for a moment whether to ask the question or not. I asked, "What is to keep the water in the tank when it is turned up on its side? If you put in a partition that would hold the water, it would be too tight to let the cylinder turn."

"That's right," he said, "that's right!" His eyes sparkled. "That's somethin' I got to find out yet. But if I could build a workin' model . . . ."

To my everlasting shame let me confess that when I left Burke's house I did not go straight to young Rowley, the overseer of the poor — I let it slide for an entire year. Instead, I found myself standing stock-still in my tracks, thunderstruck by the fact that during my entire visit not one word had been said of the note Les had sent me only a year before. I felt cheated, for I had built up the illusion that he harbored a grievance against me — had for years, in fact — and here the man had been graciousness itself! He had taken me into his confidence about the most intimate of his concerns.

I realized of course that he was bordering on senility, but at times his mind displayed astonishing vigor for a man eighty years of age. He rambled a good deal in his conversation but would suddenly fish out an incident that occurred anywhere from fifty to sixty-five years before and retell it in a sprightly and vivid manner. He made prophecies concerning the future of mankind and the progress of science, and as usual he deplored the alcohol and tobacco habits.

And as usual I am glossing over my own behavior. I, Ralph Polk, ordained doctor of divinity, allowed that man to go on in his miserable way for another year while I pondered over the ambiguous behavior of men. I knew that he existed on crackers and milk which he procured from Forsythe's store at such times as he could summon the energy to come down from the hill in the rickety buggy he had hammered together.

I knew he was literally starving to death, though he had, of course, become accustomed to his diet, and a consistent regimen of heavier food might have killed him. I thought of that. I also thought of his pride and told myself he was old, he was proud, he had once been a wealthy man and would resent any too-forward attempt at charity.

I said to myself, there are thousands upon thousands of impoverished men and women in the world and you must not look upon him as an exception. What can be done for them? You must realize that ninety-nine out of a hundred of these people do not want to be helped and would probably be grievously injured to have your so-called kindness forced upon them. These were the facile rationalizations of a coward, but they effectively blocked any attempt at action on my part until well into the middle of Winter.

Then four Mondays ago it came on to snow and for three days it snowed incessantly — great lacy flakes that whirled past the pane and blocked out the hills . . . blocked out everything beyond a radius of twenty feet from the house. Toward noon of the third day the wind rose and howled maniacally and despite the excellent banking of my house, the carpet in my study rose an inch or two from the floor and sank back every few minutes. The cold seeped through the walls; then it rained and froze tight and for all the deceptive brilliance of the sun you could not stay outdoors for fifteen minutes. The cold stabbed to the bone, and I thought of Les Burke in his rattletrap hovel on the hill and called young Rowley.

I was suddenly in a fever of anxiety and could barely wait for them to answer the phone. All along the line I could hear the receivers cautiously or boldly lifted, and I knew my words would be addressed to all the people on that wire, so I merely asked Rowley to come over and see me.

"Can't, your Reverence," he said, "till the snow plow comes through." I knew that would not be for at least two days, so I said, "All right," and rang off.

With perspiration on my brow and a strange exultation in my heart, I strapped on my snowshoes and walked over the drifts the four miles to the Rowleys' house. It took me two hours.

"How is Mr. Burke?" I said.

"All right, I guess," Rowley said. "Saw him down at Frank Forsythe's day before the storm, gettin' some potatoes."

"Potatoes!" I snorted, and Rowley stared at me as though I were mad.

"Something must be done about that man," I said. "You are overseer of the poor, and it's up to you to do it."

Rowley licked his lips and twisted his neck. "We made a dicker," he said, "ma and me, to have old Les down here next Summer — board him — for his old mare."

"Next Summer!" I almost shouted. "It isn't in the Summer the man needs to be boarded, he can take care of himself in the Summer. It's right now he needs to be boarded. Have you ever been in his house? He needs food and clothes and warmth. Potatoes and crackers!" I cried. "How dare you take his horse in trade for board? You are supervisor of the poor. The town will pay his board as it has paid in the past year for the wretched quantities of food he's bought. That mare is the last solitary thing he owns!"

"You can't force him to eat more'n he's a mind to," Rowley said, his face flushed.

"You're avoiding the question."

"It was his dicker, not mine," he stubbornly said. "He offered it to me, it wasn't my idea. I can use a horse."

I stamped my foot on the floor like a peevish child and said, "You will bring that old man down here the minute the plow comes through, clothe him, feed him, keep him warm this Winter.

Feed his horse, too, and his cat, for he has one. If the town refuses to pay for good food for a starving man, and adequate shelter, I'll pay for it out of my own pocket."

Every man loves power and it was a source of great satisfaction to me to learn that my peremptory command was being carried out to the letter. They brought him down to the Rowleys' and I heard later with what revulsion Mrs. Rowley succeeded in scouring him of ten years' of accumulated filth. They outfitted him with some of young Rowley's cast-off clothes, and there he sat for two weeks' time with his feet on the stove and the oblong box on his knees. They told me he gazed at it by the hour, occasionally making the cylinder spin in its sockets, and then looked off into space. He ate more than he had eaten in all the time since his home was broken up, and he seemed happy. Then a week ago today he went up to his room and didn't come down. He had a cold and said his chest felt "full of matter." The doctor came over, and they called him again late that night. "I'll be glad to come," he said, "if there's a thing in the world I can do to make the man more comfortable," but as he didn't come, I went myself.

They had him propped up on pillows in the cold attic room, and he smiled at me as I came in. "You're just in time," he said, "t'see me kick over the traces."

"Nonsense," I said.

"Will you keep my invention?" he asked. "Chances are somebody might want t' try their luck at it some day." I promised. Then he suddenly said, "I want t' apolergize to you for the letter I wrote."

My eyes filled with tears and I kissed the man, then abruptly I found myself on my knees beside his bed, shouting at him. "Forgive me!" I cried, "for all the misery I have caused you, father!" I clapped my hand to my mouth and looked at him, startled. But he hadn't heard. . . .

The Reverend Polk put down his pencil and slowly massaged his cramped hand as he walked up and down his study. He made the cylinder in the tank spin and watched it slow down. He put another block in the chunk stove. It is strange, he thought, how little emotion I feel now that it is all over. There only remained a sense of having, in some subtle way, been cheated, and this he resented. He bit his lip and, sitting by the window, watched the swirling of the snow. The great lacy flakes drifted past the pane, but in the distance they seemed to be racing to earth. As always, his mind reverted to the Scriptures: "Blessed are ye, when men shall revile you and persecute you and shall say all manner of evil against you falsely, for my sake," and he rose from his chair mumbling, "To this end was I born, and for this cause came I into the world, that I should bear witness unto the truth. Everyone that is of the truth heareth my voice."

He lit the lamp and set it on the table, and with the pages in hand he sat staring at the lamp. It was a habit of his to think back over the day's events, and now he saw himself standing over the casket with its poor little bouquet of withered carnations, and he heard his voice in the gathering gloom: "But some man will say, How are the dead raised up? And with what body do they come? Thou fool, that which thou sowest thou sowest not that body that shall be, but bare grain . . . but God giveth it a body as it hath pleased Him, and to every seed His own body. . . . All flesh is not the same flesh, but there is one kind of flesh of men, another flesh of beasts. . . ."

It was at this point in the service he had looked over them and seen Mrs. Woodruff in tears; and his heart had been quickened with joy and thanksgiving, for was there not more rejoicing in heaven. . . ?

"So also is the resurrection of the dead. It is sown in corruption, it is raised in incorruption; it is sown in dishonor, it is raised in glory; it is sown in weakness, it is raised in power; it is sown a natural body, it is raised a spiritual body. . . . Behold I shew you a mystery: We shall not all sleep, but we shall all be changed, in a moment, in the twinkling of an eye, at the last trump. . . . So when this corruptible shall have put on incorruption, and this mortal shall have put on immortality, then shall be brought to pass the saying that is written, death is swallowed up in victory."

She continued to weep at the grave as they all stood with uncovered heads in the snow and saw the casket lowered into the raw, hard wound of the earth. But she was cold and hard as the earth when they drove back along the gleaming road cut through high drifts, and the Reverend Polk wondered as he looked at her. She was a fat woman with thick eyeglasses; she was dirty. It was only ten years this Winter past that they had moved away from Les Burke's, and she could not surely have been pretty even then. . . .

It was time for dinner but he stood by the window crumpling the story in his hands and straining his eyes into the moving darkness outside. He wondered if his father's tie had remained in its neat bow — whether the stiff wing collar had not wilted.

Deer

THE season opened with torrential rain that slanted down the east wall of the valley and, crossing the flats in a solid mass, fell for twenty-four hours on the Tapley's house. It was surprisingly warm for the middle of November; there was even thunder (*thunder in November, green winter*) rolling behind the valley walls from south to north and reechoing for minutes after it had passed. The road down past the house was a swift river of interweaving streams that carried off the surface gravel and ate deep ruts in the roadbed, like an acid.

All that first night the rain drummed on the worn shingles and hissed off the pitched roof onto the tangle of dead nasturtiums that bordered the house. They sat in the living room watching dark wet spots form on the ceiling and spread up and down the room, and they listened to the howl of the swollen stream below the house. But after they had gone to bed, trying to lull their empty stomachs with sleep, the rain held off and frost came, and when they looked out late the next morning (one less meal to worry about) they saw that the dry grass was white and the windows were frosted in intricate whorled patterns.

All that morning they lay about the house indulging their persistent lethargy, avoiding activity lest it bring on the imperious nausea that had become so frequent in the past few weeks. Anna sat at the window and scraped at the frost patterns with her scissors, peering down across the meadow toward the heavy stand of spruce on the hillside. "I wish I could see a deer," she said.

"You may see one before you expect to." She turned to him with a smile, saying, "You're not really going hunting today?" He nodded.

"Is Clem coming?"

"He said he would — " Irritated by her smile, he cried, "Why do you think I borrowed the old man's rifle?"

"You wouldn't shoot a fly."

"Self-preservation," he laughed.

"For an educated man, that's a pretty trite remark."

He sighed. "My dear," he said, "if I told you there were more important things in life than its irremediable aspects — money, food and work (of course there's love) — you would answer —"

"— what I always have."

"To wit?"

"To wit: that we have no money, that we have no food, that you prefer not to work."

"True." He sat beside her and grasped her hands in his own, feeling a sudden urge toward her body, a sweet flux of love and pity for her that demanded closer contact, if only to hold her hand. "You have chosen," he said, "to become my wife — do I flatter myself when I say *not* for the little money I had, and in spite of the fact that I never worked when I had it?"

She bowed her head, powerless to answer and feeling a perfect fool for having spoken. As she saw it, it mattered little whether he worked or not, what he was or what he might become. (She felt there was nothing he might not achieve if he felt it worth the trouble.) She asked nothing but to be herself with him, to feel him at her side. Yet, "Money —" she said, and paused.

"We haven't got it. What does it matter where it went? More will come. . . ."

"From heaven, no doubt," she said wildly, tears in her eyes.

"From heaven," he said reverently, and kissed her hand.

"I'm awfully stupid, Bert," she said, "but how can it come if you won't work for it?"

"I have faith," he said, "in the power of virtue — Anna!" he said, "I don't know where I'm going, but I feel that I must wait for something that will be revealed to me — something that is

growing, like a plant in the dark, something I feel always present
wherever I am or whatever I am doing, yet I cannot give it a name."
He looked shyly up from her lap and said, "Would you think me
a fool if I said that what I feel is . . . love?"

"I love *you*," she said, and was bewildered when he rose with
a sigh and said, "My dear, I know. . . ."

They spoke little during lunch, when he devoured the only po-
tato and the bread and peanut butter as rapidly as he could. She
ate slowly, turning the food carefully in her mouth, extracting its
last particle of flavor. Then once more they sat in the living room,
listening to the slow interminable ticking of the clock, waiting for
time to pass. During the meal there had been a light flurry of
snow, and now she sat by the window once more, looking at it and
wondering at the stillness of the earth — watching the snow lie
quietly on the cold ground, and thinking of deer moving about,
nibbling at the slight buds on the dormant trees. With the season
opened yesterday there would already be men in the woods with
pieces of red flannel pinned to their caps, moving quietly among
the trees, their rifles held ready — and she beheld a vision of thousands of men with scraps of red flannel on their caps, advancing in
solid battalions through the brush, moving in one direction, silent
as the figures in a dream, bodiless and sinister. From the corner of
her eye she could see him handling the old rifle with evident satisfaction, and she pondered the paradox of her husband, Bert Tapley, with a rifle in his hands. Hearing him in conversation, she realized that arguments he thought cogent when stated were, whether
he knew it or not, masks for an emotion quite beyond his control;
that when he said he did not *believe* in killing anything that
lived merely for the sake of killing it, the statement should have
read: I am incapable of killing anything that lives. Yet she had
seen him with a target rifle, noted his absorption in the game, felt,
almost as an emanation of some vital heat, the satisfaction he experienced when his bullets reached the mark, the joy he felt that
day with the shotgun, when he riddled a thrown tin can before it
hit the ground.

"I shall put this on the mantelpiece," he declared, holding up
the lacework of twisted metal. And there it stood, over her head,

a curious object to find in your living room. Now she dreaded the potential explosion that the rifle held within, as he turned it in his hands, polishing the stock with an oily rag, sliding the bolt back and pushing it home. She was impressed by the silence of the weapon as it lay across his knees, knowing that a slight pressure on the trigger might release violent noise, death and resounding horror.

Holding it, he knew that if the combination of circumstances were exactly right, he could pull the trigger, release swift (*and* really *painless*) death and watch the buck kick in the dead leaves, see the blood issue slowly and finally from the open mouth, flowing between the teeth, his own eyes wide and tight-feeling, satisfaction leaping through his body, and well-being urging him to dance and shout. Now he amused himself by pulling back the bolt (Clem's coming, she said, up the hill) and thinking about the beautiful inevitability of its action, how each time he pulled back the bolt the cartridge in the chamber leaped out and away from the rifle, how every time he pressed it forward (*a toy, you know, a toy*) the spring of the magazine threw up another shell and the bolt thrust it perfectly home. To his particular type of mind, this mechanism presented an analogy of inevitability — things were, hence they were meant to be. He ignored the corollaries, the interminable arguments that might be deduced from such a lopsided assumption; at the moment, he chose to ignore them. Meat moved through the forest on four legs; meat was lacking in his home: what more perfect, more true or beautiful than that he, with a machine invented by men like himself, should procure that meat, outwitting the outmoded plans of life, leaping the aeons from the beginning of time down to this particular time, when he would walk, rifle in hand — he held the rifle to his shoulder (*a toy*) until Anna turned in her chair and said, "Put that thing down before you shoot yourself, you big kid." Then, suddenly ill, he laid the rifle across his knees, thinking of the raw red meat that would hang in the shed from the crossbeam, and the smell of its blood that would thicken their own blood and replenish the depleted juices of their bodies. He shuddered and stood the rifle in the corner.

There were steps on the porch and Clem Fell stuck his head in the door. "Hi there!" he said, "you all ready fer them side-hill grumpers? I'd a ben here t' wake you at four a.m. this mornin' only last night there come a job o' work t' do this mornin' an' I thought I might earn a honest penny."

"Hello, Clem," Anna said.

"How *do* you do, Mrs. Tapley?" Fell said. "Now, won't you be proud o' this man o' yo'rn w'en he comes home t'night with a quarter o' vinizen t' hang in the shed?"

"I'd have to see it first," she said. "You know, in all the time we've been living in the country, I've never seen a deer."

Till the path narrowed down they walked side by side, their guns resting in the crook of their left arms, fingers on safeties. It was noisy. The frost that came after the night's rain had touched the bed of dead leaves and they lay in curled masses that crackled like crushed glass under foot. "Bad business, bad business," Clem said, "might 's well of stayed t' home." Tapley tightened his grip on the stock and smiled, enjoying the futility of being constantly alert when there was no need, his mind reverting to its childhood and pursuing imaginary Indians, tracking noiselessly as possible through a trackless wilderness infested by lions, tigers, wildcat, dinosaurs. He glanced from left to right, seeing dark forms moving among the trees, soundlessly following.

They sat on a fallen log and lit cigarettes. "Wouldn' smoke ef I 'spected t' see anything," Clem said. "They can smell it?" Clem grunted. "They c'n smell a man in their sleep," he said, "but they're damn nosey too — 'll let you come within a rod an' stand lookin' at you. You move an' they move an' you stop an' they stop. Keep it up all day long. Last buck I shot," he said, looking up at the trees, "twelve-pointer he was, was standin' still as a stump, but I wa'n't takin' no chances; I put the lead right to 'm an' he busted away through the trees head over tea-kittle. Two hours I follered that feller — c'd see 'm ahead o' me an' the blood was somethin' fierce . . . ripped him right up the underside an' his guts spilled out."

"Could he run far that way?" Tapley said, looking at the ground.

"I'm tellin' you," Clem said, "I follered him fer two hours, not two rods behin' — c'd see 'm cross over the hillside, trippin' in his guts an' gettin' up."

"Let's go," Bert said, crushing the cigarette on the wet bark. They followed the trail in silence for some time, and when they reached fresh tracks neither was surprised.

"They're fresh all right; not a half-hour old," Fell said. "Listen, young feller," he said, "c'n I trust you t' foller instructions —" he pointed. "There's a chicken hawk!" he said.

"Red-tailed," Tapley mumbled.

"Eh?" Clem said. "I be'n't as sharp t' hear 's I used to."

"Red-tailed hawk," Tapley said apologetically. "All you country guys can't tell one hawk from another.

"I can't exackly see the color of his *tail*," Clem said, "but ef I c'd put some salt on it, or mebbe some lead, mebbe I c'd tell better."

"Most hawks are harmless," Tapley said,

"I *know* they be."

"But that wouldn't prevent you from taking a shot at it, would it?"

Bert smiled. "Hell, no!"

"What for?"

"F'r the hell of it."

Under his breath Tapley said, "That's what's wrong."

"Huh?" Fell said. "Well — listen, I'm goin' to cut round in a circle an' set down on that deer's trail — this is one o' their reg'lar trails an' it comes out at the foot o' Milburn's sugar-lot. I'll be settin' there w'en you come 'long. Take it slow an' easy an' foller this trail up an' ef you see somethin' put the lead right to it an' don't look too sharp w'ether it's got horns or no." He grinned.

"Oke," Tapley said, and watched him out of sight through the second-growth stuff and over the low hillside.

For a short time he walked cautiously along, leaping from hard bare clump to clump, feeling his body move inside his clothes. He glanced right and left and occasionally stopped to listen, turning his head and staring straight into the spruces about him till he realized that he was seeing nothing, that his fixed glare was focused beyond the trees, on a series of images that existed only in his own mind. He laughed; then he bit his lip, and before his inner eye he could see the buck watching him intently, curiously, and he could feel the muscles of his arm tighten, the gun rise to his shoulder, and he took a short bead and let drive. Meat, fresh meat in the shed . . . Anna.

There was a light wind but it was in his face, so he moved along, picking his way along the sides of the worn trail where there were less leaves and the ground rose slightly. That's what's wrong. Huh? I mean, why shoot something just for the sake of killing it? Why the hell not? Can't you see, can't you feel? You crazy? B'Jesus, Bert, you mus' be plumb crazy . . . all the folks 'round here'bouts says you mus' be off y'r nut the way you don' fish an' you don' hunt an' there ain't nobody ever seen you do a tap o' work an' w'ere does the money come from they says. . . .

He stopped to listen — the wind was sharp on his face and there was the smell of frost and more snow, and through the trees he could see the lavender autumn hills and at his feet were last year's dead weed stalks and dry moss.

You cannot argue with a man like that; you might as well argue with a tree. What for? F'r the hell of it. He could feel his cold toes moving inside the boots, and he contracted them, felt them grip the soles. That's exactly what's wrong; ethically wrong. Huh? I get ya, Bert, you speak of ethics, Bert, an' ya don't know w'at y're talkin' about. How so, Clem? Because, Bert, there is something deeper involved here than you are reckoning with. I don't know, Clem; all I know is that, to me, mind you, to me — he watched a squirrel scale a tree and sit erect on a limb to watch him pass — the root of the problem is this: everything that is alive has, by virtue of the fact that it *is* alive, the right to continue living. *Do you eat meat, do you? Ah there!*

Something brought him up dead in the trail and his eyes resumed a focus ahead of him, staring at nothing. He stood, hearing the crackling of the frozen needles underfoot, the moaning of two boughs against each other, the bark of a crow in the west. . . . The short autumn day would soon be done. He walked on. Anna is hungry.

Now, Bert, I grant you all that, but you'll have to grant me this — I don't like to kill; yet, knowing that, I practically force myself to do it — Do you need meat? Are you hungry, Clem? *Specious, specious!* No. Well, then? *Aha!* That's not the point, Bert, the point is that I recognize in my disinclination to kill, a — call it a trait — that, if followed to its logical conclusion would mean death — (You exaggerate, Clem.) — actual, physical death for the race. It's weak, it's a disease, I recognize it for a disease in myself, so I combat it. It's the direct result of this damned Christian training, turning-the-other-cheek-love-your-neighbor stuff — it's back of the no-more-war agitation, the charity rackets, the bellyaching for more and better anaesthetics, the average man's ambition to found a free hospital for the poor before he dies. . . .

Just fifty feet ahead he saw the buck, its antlers spread like an autumn bush in the path, its wet eyes watching him. Buck fever, he thought, and said to himself, No — this must not be passive, this must be an act of faith. He lifted the rifle slowly, thinking Anna is hungry, saw the buck lift its head and listen. Then, as though he were not within a thousand miles, it lowered its head and nibbled the dry moss, scraping with its hoof. He drew the bead down finer and finer (*defenceless!*) and along the sights he watched, following the animal as it moved slowly along, grazing. There was no sound, the wind died down and his feet were set solidly in the dry grass, rooted like stone. One, two, three. The buck started and lifted its head, saw him and froze where it stood, gazing with great soft eyes, its antlers spread once more as though for centuries they had sprung from that very spot. "Bang!" he said softly, and the beast whirled. He dropped the gun and jumped in the air, flailing his arms and shouting silently, his face contorted with rage and irrepressible excitement. He picked up a stick and flung it, watched the white undertail flapping, magnified till it looked a yard long, through the brush, off the trail and into the east. Then he picked up the gun and strolled slowly and deliberately along, watching to right and left and occasionally stopping to listen. . . .

"Stick 'em up!" a voice said, and Clem rose from the side of the path, his gun extended dramatically, his false teeth protruding from his mouth. "See anything?" he said. "Nothing at all; yet all that is I see." "You're a card," Clem said, "you're the comicallest jigger I ever see." They lit cigarettes and shivered in the failing light.

"This is a good crossin' place," Clem said. "We'll set here aw'ile till it gets dark an' mebbe we'll bring somethin' home t' put in the pot." The wind had sprung up again and they pulled up the collars of their jackets, sitting with their hands in their pockets, their rifles across their knees, shivering. The hills faded from pale lavender to deep purple, and there was a green tinge in the eastern sky. "What's that?" Bert said. "Sounds like a dog barking."

"Geese."

They stared into the east and soon they could see the flock flying south in loose echelon formation, low over the darkening earth. "I'd have sworn that was a dog," Tapley said. "A hell of a cold night to be traveling."

"They'll settle," Clem said, "first open water they hit — w'at the hell are you doin'!" he cried; his mouth hung open, his large eyes protruding from their sockets.

"Something to put in the pot," Tapley said.

"You dumb fool, you couldn't hit one o' them geese at that distance t' save y'r fool neck."

"Nothing like trying," Bert said, and pressed the trigger, exulting in the flash of light in the deepening dusk and the deafening roar that followed. "Let's go home," he said.

All the way down the hard-rutted road Clem said nothing, glanced at Bert Tapley from time to time out of the corner of his eye, and deliberately spat his tobacco juice in the road, scuffing it in with the sole of his shoe. "Come in and smoke a cigarette," Bert said.

"Naw," said Clem, "I'll have to be f'oggin' my li'l jacket down the road or my missus'll have my ears."

"Better luck next time," Tapley said. "I wasn't much help to you, I guess."

"You shore got some dumbed funny notions," Clem said, "them ca'tridges costs seven cents apiece."

He found Anna sitting by the window, looking down at the stand of spruce, and suddenly he was ashamed.

"See a deer?" he said.

She turned with a smile and said, "Did you?"

"Yes."

"I thought I heard a shot," she said, "and I wondered whether you'd finally managed to shoot yourself."

"It was Clem," he said, "he missed."

"I'm glad." With astonishment, he saw that her eyes were wet, and he moved to take her in his arms.

"My dear," he said, stroking her hair, "I *do* love you – you know I really do. . . ."

No Final Word

URING the pauses in the game, while Dr. Rogers went into the trance so familiar to those who play at chess, knowing nothing but the way the pieces move, Blake looked over the doctor's shoulder at the windowpanes, streaming with rain, and listened to the hiss of the water against the glass. Like a sleeping dog, he listened over his own shoulder, anticipating that sound from the bedroom, regular as the ticking clock. There was no sound, only the dripping of the rain from the eaves and the creak of the floor under their feet when they shifted in their chairs, and an occasional sigh from the woman, already dressed in her starched white dress, sitting behind him in the corner, and the rustle of the magazine she was reading, waiting for the thing they were all awaiting. Watching the doctor's sleepy face, Blake thought, This is like waiting for a guest at a party — everyone ill at ease and anxious to be enjoying himself, only the expected guest has not arrived. Enjoy!

The doctor cleared his throat and Blake sat forward in his chair. That was the signal, he was going to move now; and rising from his own trance he quickly surveyed the board, glancing up and down the files, wondering whether the doctor would move his queen's pawn again and lose his other knight. "Now," said the doctor, looking up, "if I move that pawn, you'll eat my horse, won't you?" Blake frowned and the doctor hastened to explain: "That's what the Chinese say — they say a man is eaten, not taken.

They have a lot more pieces to this game, too. I used to play it a lot when I was —"

When you were in China, yes, I know about that. *Old Doctor Rogers,* old Mrs. Murdock said, *spent ten years missionatin' in Chiny. He's a good doctor* minister too, *heart o' gold, 'll go anywheres any time o' day or night. 'Member when Miz Taylor was sick, there was four feet o' snow on the roads, in the middle of the night it was, way up to hell an' gone in the woods.* . . . Yes, yes, it's an old story . . . his car got stuck, he got pulled out, stuck again, he got a cutter but the horse went up to its rump in the soft snow, snowshoes, walked, floundered, seven miles up and over the drifts all night like a horse he worked, and what did he bring into the world? — an idiot, a hydrocephalic idiot now the butt of the town's jokes; not one but speaking of poor Simey imitates poor Simey's speech: I-don't-reckon-I-could-do-tha-a-t-nohow (slobber). It was a great pity, old Mrs. Murdock said, it was a visitation o' God in His infinite mercy. Praise the Lord, let us glorify Him for His ways are inscrutable.

The doctor lifted his brows, sudden glee lit in his dull eyes; and, pouncing with delight on David Blake's king's pawn, he said, "Check and *gardez!*" Blake sat back in his chair and bit his lip. I should have foreseen that, I can get out of that — like fencing with a poor fencer, the good fencer can easily be beaten by a poor fencer, he doesn't fence according to Hoyle. Instead, he listened to the rain, and then, yes, now, there was an unmistakable groan from the bedroom, and he moved his chair back. The woman in white, Mrs. Pfeiffer, German, rose saying, "Yes?" and went into the bedroom, and a low voice came from the bedroom, his wife's voice, saying, "Don't mind me. Finish your game. It's nothing at all yet."

"Check and *gardez,*" the doctor said, rubbing his hands. "When I was in Hankow I used to play this game a lot . . . out of practice now. Smart little fellows, these Chinks, can see a move before —"

"Resign," David Blake said, resting wearily back in the chair. The doctor's face fell. "Well, now," he said, "that's no way to play chess. Of course, you're bound to lose your queen, but you can easily get out of that hole — you've got two rooks, two horses and a bishop to my queen and horse."

Mrs. Pfeiffer came to the door and said, "Dr. Rogers, it's time."
The doctor rubbed his hands. "Well," he said, "we'll finish this
game some other time, Mr. Blake. I'd sort of like to see you get
out of that pickle. You didn't have your mind on the game, I'll
reckon." He saw Blake standing before him, his face white, and
said, "Better look to that kitchen stove, young fellow, and see if
my glove's boiled up."

Watching the red glove flutter in the steaming water, like a
bloated, severed hand, he — This is common as the dirt we spring
of. This is to be expected, what we have all expected, waiting these
long dull months, nervous at night and springing awake at the
slightest touch, eyes awake to the night at the windowpane, the
feel of cool air through the room, the ticking of the clock. Now?
is it, darling, now? No, not yet. . . . *You sure picked a time to call
me, Mrs. Blake; brought a baby last night, night before a pneumonia patient, baby the night before . . . three nights now. I bring
'em and I see 'em go. Never sleep.* This is his third night up. *We
Work While You Sleep.* It is a miracle, he decided, unexplainable
by the laws of physiology. He lifted the iron lid and slid a birch
stick into the firebox, removed the pan with its glove to one side
of the stove and lifted the lid on the basin of gleaming instruments
. . . needles, gut, hemostats, syringe; bubbles jeweled the steel and
the bottom of the basin. *You studied medicine, didn't you, Mr.
Blake? I prepared for it. Thought I'd heard you use the terminology.* Dilatation cervix foetus placenta amnion.

I could have avoided that, he thought, by moving that pawn
two moves before. Finish your game! she said, the guest has not
arrived. The Wedding Guest. Mrs. Pfeiffer came into the kitchen
and he whirled on his heel to face her. The gaunt face, the broken
teeth, good nurse, the thin lined hands, large, veined. "It's beginning now," she said, "she's making real progress now." From the
bedroom there arose a sound — unlike all other sounds — a rising
tide (I bring 'em and I see 'em go) of sound, singing and wavering
in the now quiet night, no rain, no sounding wind, no water on
the glass, only a fresh breeze that stirred the curtains in the kitchen and was cool on his face through the open door. Quietly, he
stepped onto the porch (hearing the Sound), and closed the screen

door softly behind him. You'll wake the dead, he thought, you'll
wake the dead in the valley, listening to his own feet on the sagging loose boards, seeing the night fall away before him . . . childbed, deathbed, childbed, deathbed. . . . Swiftly he slapped his own
face and reached into his pocket for a cigarette. . . . You can walk
around the house and climb the bank where the nasturtiums are
blooming and look into the window. *He* would have his back to
the window, *she* would have her back to the window, *you* could
see. . . . He dragged on the cigarette, watching the receding darkness over the hills, the dark trees, a wan moon scudding swiftly
behind black clouds, moving swiftly and staying in the same place,
like the moon through the windows of a train.

The brook down the bank roared in the quiet night, hissing
on its stones, and down the valley a fox barked. He looked to the
east, but glanced immediately away. Twelve o'clock. Six o'clock
it was. *We've got a long night ahead of us, Mr. Blake. I'll drop
off if you don't find something to amuse me. Can you play chess?
Why sure, I used to play it a lot when I was in* . . . . Even asleep he
beat you . . . you could easily walk around the house and climb
the bank where . . . . He stepped off the porch, then, overcome by
a sensation of shame and fear, stepped back on it again. It is now
the very witching hour of night when . . . . Standing on tiptoe, he
looked down into the valley, where in the intermittently flashing
moon the stones gleamed in the churchyard, on and off . . . mist
rose from the wet earth and floated off the land and the fox barked
again. From inside the house, deep in the secret womb of the
house, a sound arose, singing and wavering, higher than before,
strangely melodious, and he felt that once more he had clenched
his fists and felt his palms wet with perspiration. Why don't I
feel anything?

Indoors, he put another chunk in the stove, saw there was a
long oblong tank standing on it and lifted the lid. That was what I
was afraid of, looking impersonally at the large instruments in the
still cold water, their broad blades, their gleaming black handles.
That is to be expected — complicated history. Through the kitchen he walked quietly, but she heard him, and she said, "Poor
David," from the room, "I hear him walking up and down," and

immediately he was ashamed . . . one *who by the art of known and feeling sorrows, Am pregnant to good pity.* That she should feel sorry for *him* affected him immediately with a desire to laugh and he put his hand over his mouth, clinging with the other hand to the upright doorjamb, leaning forward into the room where the chessmen stood on the little table, silhouetted in the yellow light from the bedroom. Then he became aware that, sitting in the chair behind the table was the doctor, asleep, his arms on the chair arms, his heavy head resting back. TEND TO YOUR PATIENT TEND.

There was a murmur of voices from the lighted doorway, and immediately the doctor was awake, with a muttered phrase, and crossed into the room. He dodged back guiltily, like a small boy found in the jam closet, and heard her say, "Poor David, I can hear him," cautiously tiptoeing away into the kitchen as her voice rose to a wail, saying, "It's coming again, oh dear me, it's com-ing a-gain, *doctor!*" "Yes, Mrs. Blake," the doctor said, "that's right, everything is all right —" and through his voice speaking there rose the other voice, passing from an understandable and human sound (help me, doctor) imperceptibly to a wail that hung high in the house and lingered in his ears like a popular song and then, decrescendo, easily, inevitably soared down: "Oh," it said, "dear me, dear me, dear me, dear me."

He sat, clenching his hands, on the sofa in the living room, looking at the lighted doorway and the shadows crossing it, seen in a static dream state that would endure forever, hearing the low voice of the doctor and the nurse, and then silence. The moon, free of the clouds, lay in the window of the dark room, making pale squares on the carpet, and remembering, he leaped up and went into the kitchen, lifted the lid and laid another stick as the nurse entered the room. "It has red hair, Mr. Blake," she said. "Is it — born?" "No . . . oh, no," she said, "only the pains (she blushed) you know, we can . . . see. When the pains go away . . . ."

She prepared a basin of hot water, poured into it a dark-brown viscid fluid that sent up waves of sharp odor into the room, and left. "Very difficult," she said, over her shoulder. He tiptoed back again to the living room, standing at the door and leaning in, aware of a sensation of being sealed in concrete, fixed for life in an unalterable posture, muscles rigid and confined to that doorway and kept from that bedroom as inexorably as though he had been chained to the wall. This must stop, this must stop; this cannot go on any longer.

"Yes, Helen," the doctor was saying, "yes, of course, it helped, of course, Helen, it helped. You are a fine brave girl." "I'm sorry," she said in her everyday voice (he lifted his brows to hear it) "to cut up such a fuss." "Don't think of it, you are coming along fine." Childbed, deathbed, childbed. He rapped his knuckles sharply on the frame of the door, hearing the wind rising again outside the house and the ticking of the clock. . . . Time flies; you cannot, their flight is too irregular, he said to himself, his lips moving. Three o'clock. On an impulse, he went to the kitchen door and looked into the east, but there was no faint glow . . . the matin to be nigh. It was dark in the east and the moon was standing in the heavens, and lo! if you listened, you could hear the earth rolling on its axis. The glowworm shows the matin to be nigh— no, near, and 'gins to pale his uneffectual fire. No . . . but suppose I had moved that pawn, there is the barest possibility he might have advanced his queen's bishop and . . . .

This must not be; this simply must not be. All over the world — well, not all over, but over a range of perhaps two thousand miles, men and women are asleep, unaware that this is happening, sweetly oblivious of the fact that I, my wife and I, are caught in this snare like the grinding of a mill. I cannot walk into that room and say, This must stop; you cannot let this thing go on; it is obscene . . . you can walk around the house and up the bank where the nasturtiums are blooming . . . last year's pleasures on wheels, ah no . . . (The Sound).

In the kitchen he looked into the pack of cigarettes and was astonished to discover that he had only smoked six (why can't I feel something), and heard the voices conversing in low tones, heard them speaking of inconsequential matters — how the pneumonia patient had died: "No," Dr. Rogers said, "there was nothing to be done. Oxygen was out of the question and too expensive." "Yes," Mrs. Pfeiffer said. "We have movies now over our way, every

Thursday evening in the Grange Hall." Even Helen, yes Helen
said, "We sometimes feel we'd like to see a movie, but then we
have no car and so — oh, oh dear me oh dear me now it's going to
begin again, oh dear —" He pushed his fingers in his ears and opened his mouth *cannon's roar* thinking, If she screams I will go in
there! I will go in there and tell them to stop this thing. "Now, all
right, dear," the doctor said (dear!) now all right dear, everything
is all right, that's right dear, that's right, yes, yes."

When the sound had tapered off and (you'll wake the dead,
rising in the mist in the valley from their graves, floating off the
land like mist) the house was still, he lay back on the couch in the
living room, smelling the hot oil of the kerosene lamps in the bedroom, thinking this is proper *obscene* to the night, night-born,
this can very well go on at night but I will not let the glowworm
show the matin. . . .

No final word may ever be spoken, no image drawn from which
the mind may leap as from a springboard, to touch truth and destruction at once. A man (Dr. Rogers) in all the fullness of his intuition TEND YOUR PATIENT all the grasp of his sympathy (dear,
yes dear) may sit by the laboring woman (Helen, my wife Helen)
and hear with terror the first cry of the newborn (when); he may
sit and hold the hand of the moribund (dying of pneumonia) and
take her last breath into his own lungs and watch with astonishment and envy the relaxation of the features (childbed) and the
decrescendo of expression, till what lies before him is an effigy
that could never have lived — all these things (dear me dear me dear
me) *this will have to stop* he may apprehend with his bowels and
touch with his hands, yet he remains an individual (thousands of
them, sleeping on their backs from here to Omaha, snoring) incapable except in the remotest fashion of personal identification
with the rest. He sleeps snoring and as he sleeps multitudes die
and are reborn — true identification would remove the possibility
of sleep oh let me pray, sweet Jesus, let me pray! while a single
man or woman was agonizing. It is only in the sound of the (4 o'
clock) telephone wires, or on star-filled nights or moon-filled nights
that we may, for an infinitesimal flash of time feel a sense of immediate identification with the earth — through some inner vibra-

tion that stirs the wind in the wires, through an awareness beyond knowledge that the earth is rolling through space, that its motion *can* at moments be physically apprehended. Only the dead may be loved.

He pressed his face into the couch and carefully enunciated the words: "This-cannot-go-on; I-will-not-permit-this-to-go-on; I have sinned . . . I have sinned . . . We do not want this;" she, my wife, laboring to rid her womb, helping (yes, dear, that helped a lot — very soon now, very soon) to bring into the world — what? A hydrocephalic idiot, a whore, a fool, a professor of political economy?

At such times there comes an exultation too deep for overt laughter tears you fool, tears too innately religious to permit of movement. A rationalization from the facts. A man were a fool or a woman were a fool were he not aware that these perceptions are capable of "rational" explanation (undernourishment? neurosis?) more a fool if **he/she** accepted them — for it would entail a sacrifice of something more precious than the bread we eat, more sweet to the thirsting body than clear water.

Through the small dark rooms there came a breath of fresh air *Crescendo* that stirred the curtains in the living room, making the **oil lamp flicker this must stop I will put a stop to this**, and he tiptoed back into the kitchen, put wood in the stove and hearing the fox bark in the valley went again onto the porch, where standing on his toes he saw the sickly light of dawn, the paling stars, then to the west, the moon wallowing drunk through the swift clouds, the dark trees on the mountainside. A cock crowed, and he opened the screen door to be met physically by a *shriek* that rent the quiet night, rising and rising (someone will come up the road! someone will call the state police!), pausing for breath then rising again until silence choked it off in mid-utterance, and the voice, normal and human as even day after day he had heard it between the coffee and the toast, said, "What a cur-ious thing, what a curious thing."

The mind, he said quietly under his breath, returns to the dust from which it sprang, and with the disappointment of inarticulateness, there returns the closed cycle of aspiration and yearning for self-knowledge. (Let me pray, sweet Jesus, let me pray.) This is the climax of the story, this is the climax.

Boldly he walked into the living room, making his feet resound on the hollow flooring, hearing a mouse working in the hard plaster, feeling his teeth on edge. "I'm all right, David," she said from the lighted room, "don't worry about me." "I'm not," he replied, embarrassed to have to answer. Why can't I feel anything; why don't I feel something? The doctor came out, and on the table by the little lamp he had lit, he drew into his syringe a mixture that lay in the shallow bowl of a spoon. *Look at me!* Bent over the lamp, his heavy sleepy face (*J'accuse!*) lay in shallow folds, as though melting *look at me damn you look at me, I can beat you at chess any day of the week.* From outside, the growing light poured (Sunday morning, the Sabbath day) through the misty windows into the room, and he rose from the sofa and placing both hands on the doorjamb, stood there poised as though to run. He lifted himself on his toes, all his muscles taut for the nowcoming sound, and when it burst suddenly from out of the square paling lamplight, he rose higher on his toes, grasping the wood till his knuckles ached and opening his mouth, "I know she will not die," he said aloud, "I know she will not die!" He paused, but the sound continued, mounting and swelling crescendo to a torrent of insane and beastly noise, frank and unrepressed and glorying in its tumultuous, echoing horror. Quickly he opened his mouth, crying over and over again, "Stop! stop! *stop!* STOP!" and then clapped his hand over his mouth as silence closed down on them all, and left them suspended, dangling, ridiculous. . . . There was a hoarse male voice that said with sudden astonishment, "God Almighty!" and sweat rose on his flesh. There was a hoarse female voice speaking in the growing sickly light, "God help you and us, to deliver this child into the world, healthy and well, through Jesus Christ our Lord, amen. . . ."

He rose from his knees (where is the cry?) and walked boldly to the bedroom door (where is the cry!). "All right, Mr. Blake," the doctor said, "you may come in now if you wish." Where is the cry! He saw his wife's pale face smiling at him from the tumbled bed and intuitively he avoided looking at the small gray figure that lay at the foot of the bed, wrapped tentatively in an immaculate piece of white flannel. He knelt beside the bed and his eyes blurred, but he could not cry, he could not feel like crying. "It's all right," Helen said, "it's all right, darling. Do you care much, my darling, do you?" And he knew her face was wet too. "No," he said, "no, no . . . ."

The kerosene lamp was still lit, and he put it out. The doctor and the nurse were in the kitchen washing their hands, washing their instruments. "Too bad," the doctor said, "but these things happen. It was a fine baby. Too long coming." He took a piece of paper and rapidly sketched something on it, and as Blake looked at him he saw his mouth moving rapidly, but no sound came. His pencil indicated things on the design. Good Christ! Do you think you can make it up to me by praising the kid? What the hell do I care about the kid? He said, "What am I to do?"

The doctor turned to glance at him, his face yellow and dead, melting. "That's your problem, Mr. Blake," he said. "My job is over." He was tired.

"I mean," he said, "what am I to do?" The doctor smiled. "It will have to be buried," he said, "the sooner the better. You can come with me to the town clerk while I fill out the death certificate, get his advice."

"Yes," he said. "You two must be dead. Would you like breakfast?"

"I could do with some eggs," the doctor said and the nurse smiled wanly.

He put on the pan, put butter in the pan, pleased to see the heavy meat drop neatly from the shell, turn white, feeling the cool new morning breeze from through the screen door, blowing on his back. All through the night thousands slept while this was going on, thousands slept innocently *the dead alone are lovable and I am a fool even to think they ought not to have slept. Man must abide . . . .*

They ate their eggs with relish, and the doctor hastened to pack his bag — "Bad typhoid case other side of the mountain."

. . . his going hence, even as his coming hither: "I have no money for a coffin," Blake said.

"Haven't you got a box?"

"I couldn't —"

"A cardboard box?

"Why, yes."

"Well, that will do."

He went into the shed and got the carton and lined it with newspaper and a clean blanket, then went into the living room where, hearing his wife speaking in calm pleasant tones to Mrs. Pfeiffer, he lifted the light form in the flannel and looked at it, his eyes dry, his heart light and measured in his breast, fighting a desire to say to himself, This is right; this is sweet and true. You are my son, he thought. He glanced around to see no one was looking, then hastily bent to kiss the yellow face that was so much like his own.

A Night Call

WITH the first jingle of the phone the doctor automatically rose from his deep sleep to a state of awareness that instantly absorbed every dim detail of the bedroom. He noticed the rectangle of pale light on the ceiling, felt Anne stir at his side and mumble, heard the children in the room across the hall utter a low, whimpering sound.

"Yes?"

The low, familiar voice spoke in his ear.

"Yes, what is it?" He listened, his mind absorbed by what he heard, alert, leaping ahead to details he could foresee. "Did you try to pass a woven catheter?" he asked. He listened, bit his lip, went on. "All right, doctor," he said. "Set up for a suprapubic, probably under local, I'll be down within an hour."

He hung up and jiggled the hook, turning to glance about the room. "Pullman 2-1742," he answered.

Every sense awake, he lay on his side impatiently waiting, hearing in his other ear the muffled, everlasting hum of the sleeping city, that seemed clearer, more intensified at night. There came the irrelevant recollection that it was his forty-fifth birthday, the definite farewell to his youth; he felt his body heavy in the bed, felt that his skin was slightly damp with perspiration; ran his hand through his hair.

"Karl? Doctor Morton speaking. Can you bring my car around?"

He hung up, lay back for a moment and sighed, reflecting with mild bitterness for the necessity to break a refreshing sleep, hurry the length of the Island to perform this little piece of plumbing. Then slowly, as always, the image of the seventy-four-year-old patient rose to his mind and he sprang from the bed, revelling in his state of wakefulness, his head clear, his body refreshed. The children had gone back to sleep and only Anne stirred restlessly in the bed. A dog was barking some blocks away. There came a screech of brakes, suddenly applied.

He spoke in a low voice as he dressed, knowing she was half-awake, would want to know. "Claney at the hospital," he said. "Emergency."

"What time is it?"

"Two ten."

She turned in bed, drawing the covers up about her face, and he heard the car roll to a stop at the curb below, the single honk Karl always gave to let him know. He drew on his coat and hurried out the bedroom door.

"Don't forget to take the gun," she said.

"My people write me frequently," Karl was saying. "Tings are not so bad dere as der papers say. But I am toroughly in favor of der change." (It was amusing, Morton thought, listening to the man's formalized, slightly pedantic speech.) *"Der Führer* has der right idee; der Jews must be put in deir place. Don't you tink so, doktor?"

There it is again, my dear, the doctor thought; he knows I am a Jew. "I can't say," he said. "It's not my line."

Karl leaned toward him and touched his arm. "I vill explain," he said. "Id iss really very simple to understand. . . ." The voice droned on, low and deferential, with the occasional rising inflection that denotes a question, followed by a pause. Morton nodded his head and offered noncommittal phrases, reluctant to be drawn into serious consideration of anything but the immediate work in hand: generalized arteriosclerosis, age, myocardial degeneration; he thought of surgical shock and wondered, and smiled at the man as he stopped before the garage and Karl raised his finger to his cap. "See you later, doktor," he said. "I have many idees on der subject dat might possibly inter*est* you?"

"Yes," he said, and turned the corner, turned the next and drove crosstown to West End Avenue, his eyes on the lighted expanse of asphalt before him, his mind momentarily clean of all thought. At Seventy-second Street he remembered with a smile that he had forgotten the damned thing again, and his lips formed words: But my dear wife, no one will hold me up; no one in the seventeen years of my practice, in all the years I have driven up dark side streets late at night (suspicious of dark shadows, expecting at any moment to hear the roar of a pursuing car) has ever held me up. He had stopped carrying the gun for good. He listened now to the satisfying hum of the motor, the rumble of tires on the cobbles of Eleventh Avenue, and he was gradually lulled into that hypnotic state that comes with hours of night driving, when the mind is dead asleep, the body reduced to an automatic device that registers the objects of perception and judges for the mind.

Into his semi-sleeping mind there rose images of the past, images of things that had never occurred at all but were recorded there with all the sharp definition of acts that have been performed a thousand times. He had never fired it and he knew he never would. It was a lovely thing to lie in the hand, it had a compact beauty even Anne had seen, *shuddering as you thought of the dreadful wound it can make. You recall the Italian with the gunshot wound, you remember that night at the theatre when we heard a voice speaking the familiar words that are so seldom heard: Is there a doctor in the house? You remember the garish backstage lights; the Italian stagehand lying on the canvas.* He sighed. He had often wished Anne had the constitution of a nurse; often, at the table, he had wished she were standing at his shoulder instead of some young probationer who had come in to watch. *Then you could wipe my forehead, dear, when I sweat under the lights and I would not have to wipe it on someone else's shoulder, or have some strange woman wipe it for me.*

If she could only watch me work some day, he thought, I might be able to convey to her the sense of many things inexplicable, of intuitions that keep me always in a world apart; that sentiment that comes over me when I sit in my office with the shades drawn, the table lamp on, seeing the glint of the light on the instruments in the glass case, turning over the case histories, writing up my notes. Philadelphia. I could say: You remember the Humphries woman — she died. Did I do right there? Did I? Was it my fault?

He rounded the Island, turned up South Street to Clinton, silent now with the stranger desolation that night brings to populous districts. No groups of exasperating kids to run before the car, to stand until he almost knocked them down, cursing and cold with sweat, his hands gripping the wheel, his legs thrown out. *In moments of extremity, my dear, such as come to every rational human being, I have even thought of firing the automatic; at myself, at you. . . .* This thing we have all felt, a loathing of the trap that holds us where we momentarily, irrationally would not be; a trap all the more ineluctable for being nonphysical in form, for being woven of the evanescent bonds spun of years of close association, of common interests, likes and dislikes, activities and thoughts.

But he could not fire it, for though death was a common enough thing to him, it could never be too common. So he had been able, sincerely, with emotion, to bow his head at innumerable deathbeds, to listen with patience and compassion to sentimental tears, hysteria, the expression of that blind insanity that visits those to whom death is not the common thing it was to him.

He drew up before the hospital and locked the car, nodded to the operator at the switchboard and checked his name in on the board. In the anesthesia room, the patient, an elderly bearded Jew, was lying, prepared for the operation, his head wrapped in a towel; he opened his eyes and groaned. Two of the younger men were leaning against the wheel-table, talking in loud voices, and Morton looked at them and bit his lip. "Please," he said to one, "this patient is fully conscious, doctor." He examined his man, noted the distended abdomen, the pulse, covered him and turned into the doctors' dressing room where he removed his clothes and dressed, thrusting his wallet into the top of his sock, making sure the garter was secure. Claney, the house surgeon, came in.

"Good evening, Doctor Morton."

"Evening, doctor."

Eagerly, Claney resumed the history he had repeated over the phone and Morton listened. He had the chart and Morton took it from him, read it, then drew his fountain pen, glanced at his watch and wrote after the last entry on the sheet: "2:45 a.m. Patient bad surgical risk. Emaciated, undernourished. Fibrillating badly. Heart completely decompensated. General arteriosclerosis. Bladder distended almost to umbilicus. Signed: R. Morton."

I t was a routine affair. He dressed again, discussed the prognosis with Claney and with him went to the ward to have a look at his man. "If he pulls through this and you can lower his blood chemistry sufficiently, we'll hazard a second stage," he said; then, seeing the patient in the bed, aware of the old man's eyes, he turned to him. "Wie geht's?"

"Schwer, schwer, Doktor," he replied. "Weh ist mir." He gazed at Morton, his eyes wide and liquid; his long hand came from the covers and grasped the doctor's hand, and drawing it to his bearded mouth, he kissed it several times. "Ach, Doktor, 'bist gut, 'bist gut," he said, tears in his dark eyes. Silent, Morton patted the hand and turned away. When I was younger, he thought, I was moved to tears myself by such a demonstration, *but now, you see my dear, the so-called scientific mind comes to the rescue, and while the analysis of such emotion explains nothing, it is a placebo for the mind, my dear, it does pacify the mind. . . .*

He glanced at his watch — 3:45 — and automatically set the car in motion, retracing his way around the Island's tip, back across to Eleventh Avenue, where the warehouses loomed in two-dimensional bulk against the dark void of the river. When the body is at its lowest ebb, he thought, the mind is often at its flood. *This is such a night, my dear.* He was aware then that the time had come again to set aright in his mind certain matters that had so long disturbed him ("City of Brotherly"— you were mad), and he was immediately tempted to seek some rationalization for an act that was totally alien to his makeup. *I have never held any definite convictions, my dear, and you have often smiled at the spectacle of my*

vacillating mind, ready at any moment to leap to the defense of
ideas diametrically opposed to those I held a little time before.

This is a night like many another night, he thought. From the
elevated highway he glanced up the straighter side streets, could
see the glow in the sky of false dawn, and he knew that another
day was coming to find him pursuing his routine tasks with a com-
placency and a sense of fitness that, on sporadic reconsideration,
seemed almost desperately criminal. *Yet what else could I do, my*
dear? Eleventh Avenue was desolate, the streetlamps threw dark
shadows between the warehouses *(now is the time for that holdup*
of yours!) and there was no sound but the drone of the motor, the
rumble of the tires on the cobbles. No traffic lights were lit, yet
suddenly he found that he had thrown the clutch and shifted into
neutral, and as the car rolled to a stop in the shadow between two
posts he sat back, wondering at what he had done, when it came
to him — suddenly, with an abrupt flux of well-being, exuberance
all the more startling for the utter fatigue that had overwhelmed
him. He shook his head and thought of that. No, that was all.
Then it came again, that everything was clear as crystal, light, trans-
parent, *singing*. He knew that, given an instrument of music, he
could play as man had never played before; that given a pen, he
could write with a lucidity, a penetration that would lay bare
the very heart of life; that given an hour alone in his chair, he could
think through to an ultimate conclusion every riddle that had ever
puzzled man, unravel the knot of introspective thought, take the
strands in his hands and weave a fabric that would be bright with
explicit truth and revelation. His body was light; it shed itself; his
spirit *(a fine word for a general practitioner, my dear!)* sloughed
off its carnal residue and was, for a flash of time, free of all that
had ever hampered it.

Then it went, it was gone, and automatically he started the car,
ran his hand across his face and felt ashamed. But it *was* there! he
thought; I had it, it was present with all the actuality of physical
pain. Anne would surely understand the experience, an experience
he had often heard her describe as an "illumination of the spirit,"
a "spiritual exaltation" — an experience that had brought with it
the concrete knowledge, based on nothing, that its moment repre-

sented the sum of all unheeded moments of the past, a crystalization of all we have ever felt but not recorded consciously, of all we
have thought but left uncriticized.

At Sixty-ninth Street the cobbles ended and the tires hissed on
the wet asphalt. Morton was aware of a double shame — the shame
of one who has traduced the very principles he lives by — and he
knew that he was strapped and bound, felt his face warm with rage
because he was doomed to silence now forever, on this as well as
on that other matter ("Love;" you were mad), for somehow the two
seemed inextricably linked together. Anne would smile. *You
would smile, my dear, and recall that in our past discussions of the
subject of suprasensual experience I have been inclined to make
mock of you, yet you have understood (?) that such mockery was
but the voice of my scientific training speaking through me — a
training that, ideally, takes no cognizance of the tenuous, the evanescent, except to renew its assaults in an effort to explain the particular phenomena away.*

Yet there was no explaining the etiology of the experience, for
he still held to his previous convictions, and he decided that he
would not drive back to the garage for Karl, but since dawn was
near, park the car before the door. His face flushed with anger as
the image of that smug, complacent face came before him on the
windshield, as the echo of those bland, pedantic words sounded in
his ears. He knew he could not face the man again that night, that
he might make himself ridiculous with impotent rage *(why must
he say those things, my dear? he knows I am a Jew)* and then there
was the other guilt, that other thing, to be reconsidered once again
in the light of the night's findings. With the tingling excitation of
a child who harbors a secret he is wild to reveal, he parked the car
and locked it, and with his secret (Philadelphia) hugged to his
breast, bent over slightly, he unlocked his door. Anne!

II

He threw the latch and walked quietly and surely through the
dark foyer into his office, where, with audibly pounding heart,
he closed the door behind him and switched on the desk lamp.

The guilt was sweet and aching in his chest, and as the sequence of familiar images clamored in his mind, he held them off impatiently until the ritual had been performed again that justified one more indulgence in his memories of that week in Philadelphia, one more hour of cowardly abandon. (Onanism! he thought bitterly.) So he put down his bag and sat at his desk, gripping the arms of his chair, and brought into his mind first the image of his wife (*one* Anne) as he had left her earlier that night, as he had left her many a night in the past eleven years: her body hot beneath the covers, ever so slightly moist with perspiration. He could hear again her audible breathing, could see, as though a light played upon her, her mouth sagging open, moisture gathered in its corners, that expression of death-alive that sits upon the face of every sleeping human being, and he permitted himself to be filled with horror at the thought of returning to bed with her. And tonight there was another reason, more cogent, for that horror: for there was still present in him to some degree, that passing intuition of immortality, that cruellest of all illusions, that for a moment of time he had escaped the common lot of flesh.

The excitation mounted, and to hold it off a moment more — five years ago, it was — he looked about his office, noted the microscope under the bell jar, the cold-seeming instruments behind the glass panes, and he took a fresh card from the filing cabinet, uncapped his fountain pen. *(When will you wake again, my dear, dimly aware that you heard me coming in, that I'm not in bed beside you?)* "Isaac Semansky," he wrote, "143 Rivington Street," and in the appropriate places, "74. Previous history: arterial sclerosis, hypertension, chronic retention, 'dribbling' for past ten years. Present illness: Unable to void for past 18 hrs." He looked up. *When will you call, my dear?* Roland, come to bed! He was filled with momentary, hysterical resentment (cometobed, cometobed, cometobed), and laid his card aside without completing it. He stared at the rows of books across the room and for the thousandth time wondered why they had ever married, driven to a union that simply could not be. He recalled, with still another smile for the ambiguities of which the so-called scientific mind was capable, that she (one Anne) had once been his patient — that

when she had first come to his office he had had occasion to examine her and feel no stirring of the flesh. It was not until, leaving
his office together, he had offered to drive her in whatever direction she was going, that he noticed she was a rarely lovely woman,
felt his blood rise in a senseless torrent of lust that convinced him
on the spot that she was his, and the memory of that youthful excitation saddened him again, as it had saddened him on many an
occasion in the past six years — for the passion had lasted five years
at the least — when he had been forced, by its rebirth in her, to a
sober consideration of its loss and the obligations that loss imposed
on him. *For it is lost now my dear, and what we still retain is but
a poor reflection of its flame,* which he could neither accept as the
ultimate lot of man, nor as the expected, sanctioned and acknowledged end of youth and love. For there was *Anne* (ultimate irony!)
. . . one moment more, he thought, one moment more!

There was still the final ritual to complete before he could let
go, for since he had sketched in certain unattractive aspects of his
married life in justification of his treachery, there still remained to
erect the sophistry by whose aid he sought to expiate the mute de-
sertion of his responsibilities, the cruelty of this silent, ruthless criticism that his wife (one Anne) was powerless to answer. He had
watched with dismay her figure lose the lovely lines of youth, her
skin lose its texture, her teeth grow dull and her hair lose its sheen,
but he was not unaware of how he must appear in her own eyes,
with his thinning hair, the adipose deposits on his body, his lax
gait and dulling eyes, the coarsening of his pores. *What we have,
my dear, is no better than what brought us together in the beginning, nor is it any worse.* It was enriched by the existence of their
children, who had brought him at moments to the brink of joyous
tears when, out of the nonentity of their experience as human beings they had repeated a gesture, an expression that was hers or
his. Such items, in their daily repetition could, he knew, bring
them closer together in the end than passion ever had; it was the
only security, the only earnest of immortality they had, and there
was only this — that they had built, together, a sounder life than
many couples he had had occasion, in his practice, to observe, and
it had had its reward, for him, if only in his ability not to laugh

at the spectacle he presented in his own eyes, when he was asked, in sober seriousness, for advice by his patients on affairs that did not properly come within the scope of medicine or surgery. He could give such advice with a straight face, in all sincerity, *but perhaps you could not keep a straight face if you heard me!* They had built this life together on foundations which, examined, would prove unsubstantial, *and so have all the rest, my dear, so have all the rest!*

So the scene returned in all its least significant details – the anteroom of the Association's temporary quarters the day before the conference was opened – the broad, velvet-carpeted room with its competent but uninspired etchings on the stuccoed walls, the half hour he had passed largely in staring at the young girl at the receptionist's desk. Twice he spoke to her: "When will Doctor Anderson see me?" She smiled, and he stared at her jet hair, her pale skin and large dark eyes, and when she rose to stand for a few moments at the window looking down on Walnut Street, he saw her small and supple figure, the wide hips and the small firm breasts. (You thought of Anne's great, flabby bosom, coward!) He went into the inner office, where he exchanged platitudes with the chairman, and left, returning to the anteroom.

There, his mind empty of thought, his heart beating wildly, Morton found himself standing before the receptionist's desk, heard himself saying in a low voice, "What time will you meet me tonight? What street?" He did not look at her, but as she did not answer he looked up, prepared to accept the rebuke in her eyes, acknowledge her justifiable resentment. She was looking at him calmly, her eyes wide. "At eight o'clock," she said, "on Locust Street, in front of the Sylvania." His mouth dry, his lips pressed together, Morton ran his hand over his face, nodded, put on his hat and left, pausing for a moment on the sidewalk when he remembered that he was registered at the Sylvania for the week. You are mad, he thought; Parker is there; Neilson and Ahrens are there!

Until six o'clock he wandered through the streets, losing himself, looking in shopwindows, recalling little when he found himself back at the entrance to the hotel, except the smell of Negro shanties he had passed, the sight of small, isolated brick houses that stood back from the streets and wore an air of antiquity amid the city's modern squalor, the sight of some frowsy women standing among a group of jeering men at the stage door of a cheap burlesque house as the matinée was letting out. Silent, they held aloft a peeling oilcloth banner on which were printed the words: WHAT SHALL IT PROFIT A MAN IF HE GAIN THE WHOLE WORLD BUT LOSE HIS OWN SOUL?

He entered the lobby and spoke to the room clerk (she will not come, you fool, she will not come!). "Doctor Morton," he said, "Room ten-o-three." He wet his lips. "I'm expecting my wife on the eight o'clock," he said. "Can you change my room for a double room?"

The clerk looked at him, his eyes blank and deferential. (You *know*, you swine! Morton thought, you *know*!) "Certainly, Doctor, Front!" he said. "Move Doctor Morton's things to ten-o-nine."

Morton left the lobby, hailed a cab, said "Bookbinder's" and lay back on the cushions, his mind in revolt at what he'd done, at the commitments he had made. WHOSEVER LOOKETH ON A WOMAN TO LUST AFTER HER . . . but she will not come; he hoped she would not come. Parker, Neilson and Ahrens.

He ate his bluefish without relish, staring at the large, old-fashioned beer glass filled with oyster crackers that stood in the center of the cloth, then he left the restaurant and started walking back. At a cheap luggage store he purchased a small suitcase; at a florist's he bought a dozen roses which he put inside the bag; at a delicatessen store he bought some sandwiches (smoked tuna fish, his favorite), some salted crackers, mixed pickles, sweet crackers. He bought some cigarettes, although he did not smoke; perhaps she did. Then, at the hotel he asked for his key and rode up to his new room, knowing that the room clerk's eyes, the bellhop's eyes, the elevator operator's eyes were on the unexplainable suitcase he was carrying. Parker . . . Neilson . . . Ahrens.

In the room he pulled the shades, wondered whether he should turn down the beds or leave them made. "Room service? Please send up a vase — a vase," he repeated, then impatiently, *"a vayce* if you must, for *flowers*! And two wineglasses. Ten-o-nine."

The bellhop said, "Certainly, Doctor," accepted the exorbitant tip and returned in fifteen minutes with two quarts of bad white wine which Morton placed under the tap in the washbasin. He placed the roses on the dressing table, arranged them in the vase; one rose he put in a glass of water on the bed table between the beds. He arranged the sandwiches on the paper dish, placed it on the dresser with the cigarettes, which he opened, the pickles and the crackers. He experimented with the lighting arrangement, noting the effect when the ceiling lights were on or off, the desk lamp on or off, the bed light on in conjunction with the reading lamp beside the armchair. This satisfied him (dimlights and softmusic; roses and dimlights) and he undressed, took a bath, changed into clean underwear and socks and dressed again, careful to straighten up the bathroom. It was only seven o'clock. She would not come.

Until seven-thirty he sat in the semidarkened room, looking out the window, watching for the light in the tower of the *Inquirer* building, staring at the sky, resolutely trying to keep from his mind's eye any image of the scene that might unfold within this hotel room, any image of his wife at home with the children; trying to cut himself loose from the entanglement he saw himself already involved in. At seven-thirty he left the hotel with the empty suitcase, moving swiftly through the swinging doors, his room key in his pocket. He glanced up and down the street, walked to the Russian Inn and sat for another half hour sipping a glass of tea too hot to drink, wondering if the water flowing in the bathroom basin would overflow or whether he had calculated the drain correctly. Then, numb with premonition, he left the Inn and walked slowly back to the hotel, careful that the doorman should not see him. She was there!

Suddenly, all the trepidation left him; he was calm, jubilant and flooded with a sense of well-being that stripped him of fifteen years of life. He took her arm and started to walk her away from the hotel, saying, "Mind if we walk a little; it's pleasant out."

"Not at all," she said, and smiled up at him.

"Are you hungry?"

"No. I just had dinner."

"I didn't catch the name."

"Anne Cassidy," she said.

For a moment he fought a sensation of panic, of wild desire to drop her arm and run; then, "How strange," he said. "That's my wife's name too . . . Anne, I mean."

"Really." Then, side by side, silently they walked the streets, Morton carrying the handbag, glancing at her when he thought she wasn't looking, hoping to see in her face something that would spur him on, turn mild curiosity to passion, titillation to a driving urge. They looked in the window at Wanamaker's, commenting on the articles displayed. She told him she held only a part-time job as receptionist. He said he had never visited Philadelphia before, did not care much for what he'd seen.

He glanced at his watch, found it was eight-fifteen and grasping her arm, turned her around to face the other way. "Where are we going?" she said. "Where would you like to go?" "Nowhere in particular." "Let's go." They laughed like children, and still laughing, crossed the hotel lobby, Morton carefully avoiding the eyes of the room clerk, doorman, bellhops, elevator man, knowing their eyes were on him with cynical amusement, prurient curiosity. Parker . . . Neilson . . . Ahrens.

"It was nice of you to get the roses."

"Do you like them?"

"My favorite flower."

"*You* are like a flower," Morton said. She looked at him and did not smile and he was grateful. She saw that he was staring at her, and she saw in his eyes a loneliness she felt that she could match.

"Anne," he said.

"Yes?"

"Stand up." She stood and he looked at her, then turning and finding the bottle in the bathroom, noting with satisfaction that the basin had not overflowed, he poured the glasses full and gave her one.

"You think of everything," she said.

"I was lonesome."

"Yes," she said, "I know." She sat in the armchair under the reading lamp and he sat on the bed, trying to understand why she was there, but he had to give it up. The wine warmed him and he could not take his eyes from her, noting her youth, the texture of her skin, the firm sweet contours of her body beneath the simple gray woolen dress she wore. They looked at each other and smiled as they sipped the wine, and Morton felt his blood stirring, felt that he was shaking, knew he had lost control and relished the strange sensation.

"Drink your wine," he said.

She smiled at him, said, "Bottoms up," drained the glass and set it on the windowsill. "Anne, come here." Simply, with a smile she came to him, and she smiled as he plucked with trembling fingers at her dress, lifting it over her head and dropping it un-heeding on the floor. She did not try to hide her body with her hands, and for a moment he was abashed.

"You're immodest, Anne."

"No," she said. "I'm modest, really."

He tore at her chemise till it dropped from her body and lay around her feet. She stepped out of it, her eyes on his face, grave and wide. He put his hands out and touched her body gently, pass-ing his fingertips over the small firm breasts, the wide sweet hips; he stepped back and noticed that her legs were short, a trifle heavy; then blind with lust he grasped her in both arms and clung to her.

III

Morton glanced at his watch — 4:45, and leaning back in the chair (it squeaked, and he listened for a moment), he lifted the shade and glanced into the street. A taxi sped by, going north, and after it had passed, a cat crossed the avenue with a determined lope, looking neither left nor right, and vanished into a basement across the way. The streetlamps cast wide empty pools of light upon the gleaming asphalt and the effulgence of dawn lay faintly on the houses facing him; he dropped the window shade and turn-ing to his desk passed his hand across his face, ran it through his hair. Nothing was settled — *nothing settled, dear* — and automati-cally he reached for his keys, unlocked the bottom drawer, drew out the leather folder and pressed its catch. There was a letter there, and the letter was the last act of the ritual. He listened, then spread it on the glass-topped table, took out his glasses and perched them on his nose.

> *1721 Spring Garden St.,*
> *Philadelphia, Pa.*
> *October 23rd, 1928*

Dear Roland,

Thirty minutes ago you were here and now you've gone and I'll never see you again. I can't believe that thirty minutes could make such a difference. You were tender, you were kind and understanding. I felt very close to you, you spoke to me and kissed me. I could feel your face against my face only thirty minutes ago. You said, "It was lovely; don't be soft and don't be hard — be honest." I can still smell the odor I will always remember you by — a clean odor of disinfectant of some kind or other. Now you are gone — I shall never see you again — you are probably at the North Phila station by now and I am here all alone and feel so near to you and yet it is terribly hard to imagine I shall never see your face again, never watch your slow, measured walk, hear your low voice.

But I want you to know it was grand. I know you are gone but as yet I can't accept it I don't believe it's true — you are very real to me now. I feel such an awful sense of loss; I want to look at you, to touch you, to hear your voice but you are not here. You are riding away out of Phila where you came by pure chance and will probably never come again. You are gone; it's true; I know it's true. I feel as though someone died and I am overcome with grief but I'll get over it. Each day the pain will grow duller, it will lose its agony and gradually it will ebb away. I know that day will come but now I only feel this awful loneliness, a despairing loneliness, but it won't last. Nothing so intense could last.

I want you to know it was grand knowing you. I want you to know that you meant a lot to me — in many ways. You took me out of my inertia. You made me live. You made me want to keep on living; to fight for life if necessary but above all to want to live. Yes, eventually I shall forget you — you have gone back and will

*forget me and I will grow and expand, take on and discard new
ideas, new people, and you will recede. But in a sense I won't forget you because you were the first person to show me how men
and women should react as God meant them to (or did he?) or if
he didn't, nature certainly meant them to. You broke down the
web that was around my mind and I feel as though I understood
and shall always understand more fully the poor weak hungry lives
that most of us lead. I know now that I shall never fall into the
depths of despair so overpowering but still so negative that I won't
give a damn. I feel, since knowing you, that I have received great
strength and with that strength I shall be able to build up within
myself the ability to grow serene. Because I have had this week I
shall not become indifferent. I shall not compromise. I shall not
have any relations with anyone who doesn't mean something to
me. I shall remain remote, happy, secure in the knowledge that I
have received something from you which will remain with me and
be a source of happiness — a well from which I can always draw.
I shall be honest.*

Anne

Anne, you put this letter on my desk the morning I returned!
The old shame of that morning five years past returned to him,
when he had felt, unopened letter in his hand, that there was something strange about the thing, and reading it, known with the impact of a shock that it had been given to Anne to strike, unconsciously, this final blow at the security she cherished. The shame
receded from his mind with the rapidity of long habituation, and
as on that first morning his eyes were moist again with commisera-
tion and another sort of shame — of having thoughtlessly started
something he could not finish, provoked a thirst that he could
never quench. There could be no question of wanton spoliation,
of having blasted a life or poisoned it at its source, for when he
looked at it with the eyes of his maturity he could see (he felt it,
knew it intuitively) that it would ripen her, it would not kill. But
this was specious reasoning, for *she* could not look at it with the
eyes of his maturity, being still painfully immature herself. (Where
are you now? What are you doing now?) And there was the still

persisting nostalgia of curiosity unsatisfied, of his own frank thirst for her, still quite unslaked.

Nothing had brought him home from Philadelphia but the innate knowledge that he must come home. There had been no conflict in his mind; it had never occurred to him that there was any alternative to face. And home, he took up life with Anne (one Anne) where it had been dropped a week before. Only as the months went by and no further letters came (and the urge to answer died more easily under each separate practical act of self-control) the need to go to Anne and tell his story grew to almost ungovernable proportions. Night after night he checked himself upon the very brink of telling her; hated himself for remaining silent; hated himself for wanting the confirmation of a smile, a touch, the words: I know, my dear, I understand; it's all right; there is nothing here — no need for self-reproach, yet his certainty (?) that Anne would understand, condone, still somehow balanced his certainty of the pain she'd suffer should he come, innocent of such intent to wound, saying, *Read this, my dear; isn't this beautiful? can you see how beautiful this letter is? can you see what this means, in its true perspective? can you see what it means to me? and that it cannot touch our life together? and yet can you see what this has meant to me?*

So he was silent because he could not tell her he had wounded her; could not say that he had failed her and she did not know it; could not reveal that he had, from a sense of misguided responsibility and pity, driven himself to her arms with the whips of memory and speculation; and his hatred for himself, his vacillation, mounted as he caught himself increasingly compensating for his defection by more frequent attentions, little acts of sacrifice, consideration. To his horror he even observed a recrudescence of passion for his wife, born partly of pity for the unfelt blow she had sustained, but mostly of forces touched to life again by Anne, the other Anne. And he sighed with the satisfaction of the knowledge that these forces were not dead, as he had thought.

Slowly, deliberately he placed the letter in a drawer and took up the card when he heard Anne come to the head of the stairs and clear her throat. He listened.

"Roland? Are you there?"

"Yes."

"Are you coming to bed? It's after five o'clock."

"Right away, my dear."

She turned and he heard her enter the children's room, could see her touch their blankets with solicitous fingers, listen to their quiet breathing, smile. She returned to bed and he took the card and wrote: "Patient admitted October 17th, 1922, to emergency room, with acute retention of 18 hrs. duration. General condition very poor. Fibrillating, marked pulse deficit, cyanotic and dypsnoeic. Blood pressure 240/80. Long prostatic hypertrophy history. Complicated by generalized arteriosclerosis, hypertension, probable chronic nephritis, myocardial degeneration, and auricular fibrillation. Catheterization by Dr. E. Claney unsuccessful. Called at 2 a.m. Performed emergency suprapubic under 1^0 novocaine. 1000 c.c. of foul-smelling septic urine evacuated through cystotomy opening. Removed to male surgical ward with slight improvement in heart condition. Resting well in Fowler's position. Tinct. digitalis Mxxx, every four hours, prescribed."

He filed the card and took the letter from the drawer again, waving it gently in his fingers as though the ink were wet. Just as he had been unable to show this thing to Anne, so had he been unable to destroy it. He had a superstitious dread of destroying it, for it represented to him more than a vulgar trophy or memento. It was the only tangible evidence that the events which prompted it had actually taken place; it was a crystalization of those events and it was at the same time the expression and the essence of a revelation that was precious to him — so precious that he could not reveal it in his turn, though constantly tormented by the need to cry aloud: *This thing has happened to me — this thing is beautiful and of enduring value!* It had been (the week with Anne, with its sweet meetings at night and its partings in the morning), a forerunner of the exaltation that had come to him tonight, and that he now remembered with a pang of regret for its evanescent nature, for the knowledge that he could never reproduce it in the future, never reveal it even to his wife, whom he truly loved. It was both an omen and a part of the night's discoveries, and as such indestructible even though its tangible expression, the letter in which it had been crystalized, were destroyed. So he knew that he could now destroy the letter without danger of destroying more than the outward symbol of a part of him that never could be touched. He could part with this letter because he no longer required a springboard from which to leap into the contemplation of a new and "ideal" life with the twenty-three year old girl who'd written it. The experience, receding though it had been with the years, drawing with it the very memory of her features and her voice, would still remain with him, as would the gentle melancholy imposed on him by silence.

He folded the letter and tore it down the center, hesitated, then ripped it rapidly twice more, experiencing once the sheets were torn, a pang for the irretrievable, the irreplaceable. It was only momentary, but of long enough duration for him to reproach himself still one time more for the vacillation and timidity that characterized his least significant activities. *(Why must he say these things, my dear? He knows I am a Jew.)*

From the head of the stairs Anne called. "Roland, aren't you ever going to come to bed? It's almost morning." Morton sighed. "My dear," he said, "I'm *coming!*"

Profession of Pain

WHEN my brother cleared his throat I looked reluctantly up from my book, for I knew I'd have no peace until he finished what he had to say. "Did I ever tell you about the fellow who came into the accident-room when I was at Gouverneur?" "No," I said, suppressing the remark that he'd told me about so many "fellows who came into the accident-room" when he was an interne at the hospital. He bowed his head a moment and bit his lower lip, clasping his large hands and twining the long fingers. I have always been fascinated by my brother's hands – they are not handsome – they almost look crude, with their abruptly blunt fingertips, but there is a paradoxical appearance of sensitivity and nervous strength about them – preeminently the hands of a surgeon, and a good one, for I've seen him operate.

"The history of this case was pitiful," my brother said, and when he said that I pricked up my ears for the first time, for it was a phrase he hardly ever used. He knew I noticed it, for he smiled at his intertwined fingers and looked up. "No, seriously," he said, and shook his head as though to apologize for an unconscious error, "this fellow came into the accident-room one day when I was on duty, and one look at him convinced me that the man was in great pain – excruciating pain, I should say, for his face was absolutely ashen and he was bent almost double. He tried hard to stand erect, but it was obviously impossible, so I had him lie on the table – you remember," he said, and smiled again.

Could I ever forget! His reference caused my memory to execute a "flashback" of that hot day in August when I'd ridden on the ambulance with him for the first — and last — time. In one vividly moving sequence I heard the bell rattle in the corridor, saw us both running down the hall, my brother grasping the huge black surgical bag, and jumping onto the back of the "bus," slipping our arms through the leather loops that hung on either side of the padded seat. We shot rattling over the cobbles down through the jammed streets of the lower East Side, while the unbroken crowd was cut like a stream and formed a bipartite closing wake behind us. There was what appears to me now to have been one composite photograph of the endless mob that opened and then swallowed us as we stopped before the tenement on Rivington Street, and my brother ran up the stoop and into the house, looking strangely small in his neat white suit. Inquiries among the surrounding morbid crowd drew diagnoses of "man shot," "man's leg cut off," "man fell off roof," or "man killed himself." It seemed an hour till my brother reappeared, white and competent, heading a small procession of policemen, who carried a man sitting in a chair. He was wrapped in a blanket and his gray face jogged from side to side as they came down the steps. His eyes were wide and alive — in violent contrast to the strangely impersonal cries he uttered. "You'll have to step on it, Mike; don't want to bring in a stiff." Then I remember the passage back, easily twice as swift as our arrival, with the patient shouting in mixed English and Italian and my brother urging the driver to greater speed despite the patient's protests. He shot strychnine into his arm and talked to me. "Got to get this guy in before he croaks," he muttered, "worst laceration I've ever seen. He fell off a roof and got caught on a projecting hook." Unconsciously, I followed them into the accident-room, where the man was tumbled onto the table, his clothes were cut from him and three doctors worked packing a wound which to my eyes seemed easily a square foot deep. They put everything back in place and stuck adhesive plaster over the edges of the great angular tear. "Take my shoes off — take my shoes off!" the man shouted in Italian, and I removed his bloody shoes. Then, "Take off my socks — take off my socks!" he cried, but before I could, they wheeled him out and up to the emergency ward, where they pumped him full of saline and waited to see if he would die. He went home three weeks later.

"Have a cigarette," my brother said, and then continued, "Well, I asked him what the matter was and he whispered, quite intelligently, too, 'nephritis, Doc — I've already had one kidney removed — shrapnel wound during the war — and part of the other, but it's still affected. Lightning pains radiating from my groin, right up to the small of my back. I know the thing's come back again, because my water's smoky.' I was surprised," my brother said, "to hear him use those terms, for only a person acquainted with medical nomenclature would ever think of them. I asked him if he was a doctor —"

"What terms?" I said.

" 'Radiating' — and particularly 'smoky,' " my brother said. "He wasn't a doctor, but he told me that he'd had occasion to read the subject up, and I agreed that he certainly had. The morphine and atropine I gave him had no more effect than so much water, and I gave him a terrific dose at that, and then repeated it. By God, I felt sorry for the chap — after his pain had gone a little, he told me his story — I'd had him put to bed — a young chap, too, war record — was wounded in the war and had to have a kidney removed. Then when he got back to the States, his other one started to kick up trouble, and he had to have a part of that removed. Now this remaining bit was up to mischief. I told him definitely that it looked bad for him, since a man can't live without any kidneys at all, and he told me he was resigned to it — he'd spent all his money on treatments to no effect, and he had to come to clinics to keep himself going. Wife and child to support. His pain came back, so I gave him another shot. 'I'm a bit habituated to the dope, doc,' he said and smiled. 'I've had to take so much of it in my time.' "

"When I was making the rounds the next day with Dr. Rogers, the Visiting, I mentioned the case to him, after we had passed through the ward. 'A rather pathetic case in there,' I said. 'What case, Doctor?' Rogers said. 'A likeable young chap — one kidney gone and part of the other — and now he's having trouble with the bit that's left — I may be funny, but I can't help feeling sorry for the kid.' Rogers stopped dead in his tracks and looked at me. 'I know that case,' he said, 'name's Wilson? Injured in the war — shrapnel? Knows all the terminology?' 'Yes,' I said, and by God, Rogers turned on his heel and literally ran back to the ward. Naturally, I followed him. Wilson was asleep, and I could scarcely believe my eyes when I saw Dr. Rogers shake him violently and slap his face! 'What the hell are *you* doing here?' he shouted; 'your name's Phillips, isn't it?' 'No,' Wilson said in a faint voice, 'Wils—' 'Don't lie to *me!*' Rogers screamed, 'weren't you in Roosevelt Hospital last week? Got kidney trouble, have you? You're a hophead, aren't you?' He shook Wilson again, and suddenly Wilson started to cry and admitted it all —"

"What!" I said.

"Can you beat it," my brother said — "a dope malingerer — he'd cooked up all the story himself. I mean about the war and the disease — he'd actually had the operations, of course, but it was the craving for dope that led him to have them, and then when he couldn't have any more, he went from hospital to hospital for over three years in various cities, doubled up with pain, and got them to give him the stuff. He'd read it all up in the books, and so he knew what he was talking about — imagine it! He was so badly addicted to the dope that he had one complete kidney removed and a portion of the other. . . ."

"But what about the operations?" I said, exulting in the thought that I'd finally caught my brother in one of his medical whoppers; "surely the doctors could see there was nothing the matter with the man's kidney when they opened him up —"

"Of course they could," my brother smiled, "of course they could — but what were they to do? When a man comes in and gives you a beautiful clinical picture of acute nephrolithiasis, and is obviously in excruciating agony, you open him up, and even if there doesn't *appear* to be anything the matter with his kidney, you take it out anyhow."

"Oh," I said.

A Personal Issue

A ND as day followed monotonous day across the endless land,
Gisela Wilkerson knew in her heart that they would come
back to New Hampshire, and that thought filled her heart
and made it big; that emotion of homesickness and of love of home
grew in her till it was all she could do to contain herself, prevent
herself from crying out as they crossed the Illinois farmland, flat
and deadly and neat: Let us go home, my darling; darling, let's go
back to Woodvine; for great as was the disappointment of finding
the vast country depressing, so slow to change, so uninspiring, they
had determined for so many years to make this trip that made it
must be, even at the expense of their long dreams of America.

So the life they had left behind in Woodvine grew larger in them
as they left it farther behind, and they knew that the farther behind
it was, the nearer it was becoming; and every day that the car
climbed over the southern end of the Sierras into California, they
knew was one day nearer home. One day nearer home, where life
was calm and measured, where the seasons moved majestically by
their windows; the people who lived in the Notch were there to be
seen; she recalled them now with tenderness and heartwarming
affection. She thought of the activities that had grown up during
the past ten years among the wealthy settlers of the Notch and
the North Road; the church activity and the socials; the school
meetings; the teas and the Woodvine Country Club with its fine
golf course; the Society for the Protection of Dumb Animals; the

Red Cross; the Grange; the meetings and discussions of books and art and the theater; the concerts of visiting musicians and – gem of them all – the Garden Club. They had a rustic greenhouse nestled in the woods just outside the village, and there they grew the rarest flowers of all countries and all climes. There, too, they had a little auditorium where they could discuss the problems they encountered.

Yet strange to say, she and Samuel had at first resented these strange people and their wealth, who had come in and bought up all the old places and driven off the good families, so that no native representatives of Woodvine remained but the shiftless. And at first they had held themselves aloof, until gradually it had dawned on them that they were – in all modesty – the living, beating heart of Woodvine – they, Samuel Wilkerson and his wife Gisela Parker; for money was nothing to them, yet they were accepted by these new people; they had no money but their little crumb, and though the wealthy residents gave the money for the country club and built the greenhouse and inaugurated the social life that flourished all summer among the younger people – they, the Wilkersons, remained at the center of it all, and could, if they had not been so modest, have taken the credit for the reconstruction of this place – since they had given out the inspiration, Sam by his commercially unappreciated hand-bookbinding and Gisela by her little known, but widely loved, book of verse – for the questing folk who came to Woodvine, searching for the quiet and the peace the city could not give –

–May and June and most of July; it was an endless torment for them as their slow car, driven carefully by Samuel, was now pointed eastward over the monstrous continent: San Francisco, Reno, Salt Lake; Cheyenne, and Omaha; Peoria, Fort Wayne, and Pittsburgh; Harrisburg and Philadelphia and New York. . . . Why, by contrast, the last three hundred and fifty miles to home literally flew; like a hired saddle horse that knows to a minute the length of time it must work, their eagerness grew in them as the more familiar scenery passed, and they felt that with their growing eagerness the speed of the car mounted proportionately. Their nostrils expanded, their hearts swelled in their breasts as they caught the first glimpse of the Old Man of the Mountains and the tumbled green hills stretching to the north, and far in the clear air, that bare cleft on the western slope of Lafayette, that was prominent at every time of the year.

The season was at its height, and though they had been gone but a little less than three months, they felt that heart-thrilling elation of a return that takes place after many years; peace and security flowed back into them as they passed the Woodvine House and their eyes feasted on its clean white pillars and the clean people strolling or sitting in front, the expensive foreign cars drawn up at the curb. The nightmare of the transcontinental tour faded from their minds; the dusty roads, the baked and fissured earth of the drought area, the starving beasts, and the sullen red-eyed people, and it was with an emotion of contentment that was almost unbearable that they came up the Woodvine road, passed the old quarry on their right, passed the camouflaged trench mortar the Legion boys had mounted on the roadside and turned up the Notch road once more as they had done so many thousand times in the past. Not to mar the elation of the homecoming, not to admit even once more into her mind the wretched thought of the ugly people and the places they had seen — the interminable road with its thousands upon thousands of advertising signs that proclaimed a preoccupation with the material that she could never understand — she closed her eyes as Samuel drove up the entrance of the Notch, closed her eyes to the miserable hovels of the indigent, the shiftless, whose presence was like a scab on the healthy flesh of the valley, who persisted in living their sordid lives in the presence of the graciousness and dignity that was all about them. And so she did not see that beside "Bud" Fillmore's gas pump there was a newly constructed cage, and in the cage there was a large black bear. Samuel told her and she opened her eyes with a start, but they had rounded the turn and were climbing toward the converging hills, passing The Studio with its copper bowl gleaming in the sun, passing Milton Bellows' English home with its exposed beams, standing in its serenity on the slope of Bleak Hill, passing the long stone wall that skirted the Mowbray's place, crossing the bridge and turning and passing the last hovel on the road . . . they could see the roof! they could see the gate!

II

Gisela stopped the car, her lips set, her hands clenched at her sides, stepped out onto the filthy ground. As the man came toward her smiling, his broken teeth showing in a dirty grin, she felt a shudder of revulsion come over her; his unshaven face, his dirty overalls, smeared with grease; the odor of his body.

" 'Mornin', Mis' Wilk'son," he said, "Have a good visit out West? What'll it be today, five?"

"I —" she said, and was momentarily angered by his obtuseness; if the man had any eyes in his head, he could certainly see that she didn't want gasoline; she hadn't stopped anywhere near the pump.

"Reckon it's good t' be t' home agin," he said.

"I've come to see you about that bear," she said, nodding her head in the direction of the cage; she could not trust herself to look at it.

"Want t' see the b'ar?" he said. "Fine crittur; the Watson boys cotched it up on the mounting, month ago. Name's Rebecca."

"I should think you'd be ashamed of yourself," she said. "I should think you'd have more decency than to coop up a poor dumb beast like that."

He scratched his head and showed his ragged teeth. "Got a permit," he said.

"That doesn't make a particle of difference —" She was infuriated by the fact that he was grinning; that he refused to take her obvious vexation seriously; *she* knew; she had overheard them say she was a "character" in the neighborhood; she'd show them that she was, indeed! "—permit or no permit," she said, "it's cruelty to animals to keep —"

"I feed 'er."

"I want you to get rid of it immediately; I want you to let it go immediately," she said, her eyes avoiding the man's person, but glancing in a wide circle she tormented herself with the vision of the ugliness that surrounded them as they stood there talking; the old yard strewn with tin cans and discarded auto parts, old tires cracked and rotting in the sun and rain; tools and scraps of rusting wire; the hovels of the Woodvine "poor whites," as Milton Bellows had so amusingly said.

"That critter already cost me a-plenty, Mis' Wilk'son," he said. "She attracts the trade. I won't get rid o' she. . . ."

. . . She stood on the stage of the rustic auditorium and looked down on the people at the meeting; she nervously fiddled with the scarf at her throat and then, as she had seen experienced speakers do, she focused her eyes on a distant point behind the people attending this meeting of the directors of the Garden Club, and said, "On our trip out West, we saw, on many occasions, similar manifestations of the sordid spirit of commercialism. There must be, my friends and neighbors, thousands — yes, thousands of poor beasts enchained all over this country of ours, and for just such identically sordid purposes — to catch pennies; suffering the torments of imprisonment and semistarvation, fed on refuse and vile concoctions that were never meant to feed swine — soda pop and Cracker Jack" (she pronounced the words with ineffable contempt), subject at all hours of the day and night to the tantalizing of vulgar, unfeeling people." (She looked into their great collective eye.) "This, my neighbors, is a situation that, near Los Angeles, I swore we would never tolerate in Woodvine. Woodvine must not allow — cannot *afford* to allow such exemplifications of the sordid, corrupting scramble for the Almighty Dollar to take place within her fair domain. I have lived here all my life, and I shall die here (she heard her voice quaver, and was strangely proud); all my life I have been proud of Woodvine, but now, my friends, I am ashamed — *ashamed* (she gently pounded her dry bosom) of what has been permitted to take place here! I call upon you all to join me in protesting this degrading spectacle of a helpless, harmless dumb brute's subjection to cruelty and starvation — for the sake of a coarse, degenerate individual's personal aggrandizement." She stepped down from the stage and the chairman said, with a half-smile, "Any comments?"

Milton Bellows stood up on the floor in his neat gray flannel suit and ran his hand through his gray distinguished hair. He glanced down at his feet and cleared his throat.

"With all due respect for Mrs. Wilkerson's sincerity," he said in a high-pitched voice, "and mind you, I am in complete agreement with her on the matter — it's a crying shame, and something should be done about it — I scarcely feel that this is an issue which concerns this meeting in any way, or falls by any chance under the heading of new or unfinished business of the governing board of the Woodvine Garden Club — "

—"Well, then, I will *buy* it from you," she said.

He put his foot on the running board of the car and she felt contaminated.

"Where'll you keep it? You can't turn it loose; b'ars is dangerous when you get 'em riled."

"Never you mind that," she said. "I'll take care of that. What do you want?"

"Well, Mis' Wilk'son," he said, "I ain't much minded to sell Rebecca; she means a lot o' money t' me an' I —"

"How much?"

"An' I've growed right fond of the crittur; the kids like her too —" he nodded at his five undernourished children, who stood in front of the door of the shack; his wife sat in the window with a baby at her breast. "I tuck good care of she, an' she's —"

"How much?"

He scratched his head. "Two hunerd dollars," he said, and Gisela gasped.

"Why —" she said, "why you're trying to *rob* me, as well as insult me and the entire community!"

"Ain' nobody let a peep but you."

"I'll give you fifty dollars," she said, "in *cash.*"

He laughed and started to turn away, scratching his head. He shrugged his shoulders at the dirty, ragged children in the yard and made an impertinent gesture with his finger at his temple.

"Listen," she said, raising her voice, feeling tears come to her eyes. "I will give you seventy-five dollars and not another cent."

"Two hunerd dollars, lady, f'r the b'ar. That's my price; she

cost me that much in trouble an' her vittles. But I tell you what —
make it a hunerd seven'y-five an' she's yourn."

"A hundred."

"Hunerd seven'y-five."

"A hundred twenty-five."

"Hunerd fifty."

"A hundred twenty-five."

"Mis' Wilk'son —."

"A hundred twenty-five."

"All right," he said. "A hunerd twen'y-five, an' you come fetch
she when you want she; I can't deliver she f'r no sech figger —"

— It was all part of the same thing, she thought, and experienced
a slight thrill of elation to recognize that she could relate this dreadful experience to the many other glimpses she had caught of aspects
of American life she did not really care to think about. Over the
whole country, it seemed, people had been caught up in a rising fever of covetousness; they had grown mean, petty; they were willing
to sacrifice their neighbors or themselves for the sake of grasping a
few pennies. (This ability to recognize universal human trends was,
she realized, what had given her modest little book of verse such
wide appeal!) Thousands upon thousands of signs competed with
each other across the great expanse of the land, to attract the pass-
erby.   Merchants, small and large, cheated you on the slightest
provocation; on that side trip to the Painted Desert, they had been
forced to pay twenty-seven dollars for a tire that was worth only
fourteen; crossing the Great Divide they had paid exorbitant prices
for gasoline, because the road-stand men knew the next gas pump
would be many miles away and were at pains to tell you so; people
in the grimy little towns of Pennsylvania, people on the farmlands
of Illinois, all looked as though they would cut each other's throat
for a scrap of bread; people along the roadside in Kansas, Colorado,
Utah, and Arizona glared at them as they passed (one disgusting
tramp actually threw a stone when they refused to pick him up!),
envying them the comfort of their comfortable car, envying them
their freedom to move about and the diversion they had anticipated
for so many years, sacrificed for, sweated for.

And Woodvine, Woodvine itself was changing! Woodvine, lulled in its ease and comfort, had allowed the world to slip up on it unawares; had allowed the ugliest qualities of life to slip in unawares and poison its beauty, destroying its seclusion and its calm retreat. And so she had known that she would have to do something about that bear; the Garden Club would give her no support; the Society for the Protection of Dumb Beasts had protested with her, but the man was obdurate, and so she had been forced to spend their little money to purchase the poor creature, and then, as Samuel had so accurately foreseen, her troubles would begin. They had. She had a cage built for the animal until she could think of something to do; the carpenter had charged her fifty dollars. The truckmen who had brought the creature charged her ten. Food for the bear cost more than they could possibly afford; it was ill, obviously as the result of the wretched treatment it had received; in the two months of its captivity it had faded, it pined for its freedom; its small red eyes watered constantly and its fur fell out in patches. It paced the restricted space of the generous cage she had had built, up and down, up and back all day and night, rubbing against the heavy wire till it wore its coat away on one side; walking backwards to the other end, rolling its head on its heavy neck and then starting forward again. It stood for minutes at a time on its hind legs, grasping the wire in its claws, staring into space, snuffling the air; it grunted and uttered soft moans from time to time. It smelled. Then one morning she had found it really ill, lying in the shelter that had been built inside the cage, and there, staring her full in the face with the effrontery that inanimate objects can occasionally display, were fifteen empty Cracker Jack boxes and a dozen empty soda bottles that some vandal had brought up during the night and fed to the wretched animal.

So she had written to the game warden, but before he answered she heard of a man in Lincoln who owned a private zoo, and she called him on the phone. "Yes," a charming voice replied, "I can take good care of it; I'll send a man this afternoon." She sighed with relief, and she wept a little on her husband's shoulder.

"Well," Samuel had said, "I guess your troubles are all over, darling. But you shouldn't take such things so much to heart."

"Oh, Samuel," she said, "the world is such a cruel place. I never knew that people could be so despicable."

"We'll forget it," he had said. "We'll try to forget it. We're home again now, darling, and everything will be the way it was before."

So she was relieved of her burden; they had called for the creature with a truck and carried it to Lincoln a week ago, and now as she sat at the window, watching the early September leaves falling to the ground, she knew that she had done the right thing; she knew that she had done her bit to preserve the beauty and seclusion of Woodvine from invasion and she had done her best to right one of the world's injustices, for it was a personal issue with her; she could not bear to see anything that lived suffer, for it made her physically ill; she gave the most she could at the yearly bazaars for the poor; she baked cakes and donated their discarded clothing and subscribed to the Red Cross really more than they could easily afford. And surely it was more than you could ask of one lonely person that she should take the world's troubles on her shoulders and set them all to rights. You could only do the best that you could do. But it was a matter of some concern to her that the rest of the world could not be like Woodvine; that people could not live always surrounded by the beauty that was Woodvine, in fine houses set on fine grounds, engaged in those activities which lifted the human spirit to its heights, which set it apart from the spirit of other animals that was now so widespread in the world — the spirit of crass materialism, of personal gain that set men, like wild beasts, at each other's throat and stultified human potentialities. So it came back to her again — she rose now, hearing the telephone — that day in May so many years gone by, when she and Samuel had plighted their troth on the other side of The Flume, standing under the old crab-apple tree, and she murmured, I *dare* any one to show me a better life, a cleaner and more sacred life than we have lived (the phone was ringing), to show me where we have gone astray by remaining aloof from the world, growing old together and sedulously cultivating the little garden that is ours — our love and our mutual understanding; to show me a place on God's green earth that He has looked upon with greater favor or benignity than Woodvine —

"I'm coming," she said to the phone, and picked it up.

There was a harsh voice in her ear. "This is Bud Fillmore," said the voice, and she said, "Yes, what do you want?"

"That b'ar," she heard him say, "you bought offn me —"

"Yes, what about it?"

"I thought you'd kinda like to know," he said and chuckled. "You sent it down Lincoln-way, didn' you?"

"I did," she said. "What is your business with me, Mr. Fillmore?"

"I was down thataway yesterday," he said. "That man, he didn't have no per*mit* t'keep it."

"Oh, dear," she said.

"So the State men come f'r it yesterday, but when they was takin' it outta the cage, it run away.

"Mercy!" she said, "did they catch it?"

She heard him laughing into the phone, and then he was suddenly serious. "I thought you'd kinda like t'know," he said. "Ay-eh. Yeh, they cotched it agin."

"Thank you," she said, "for telling me."

"On'y," he said, "they hadda shoot it."

"Shoot it!"

She heard his harsh voice chuckling and sputtering with laughter over the wire. "Ay-eh," he said. "I thought you'd kinda want t'know. I bought me the hide f'r a dollar. I got me a buyer who'll give ten."

Sam's Woman

THEY had taken out the window in the bedroom and on the sharp air — the tang of receding Winter reluctant to leave the land — there rose from the barnyard the stench of drain water, chickens, old garbage left to rot. As she cleaned the sickroom Ella Carter felt a recrudescence of her old resentment — the lazy shiftless loafers — there they sat in the sitting room, gathered from a hundred and fifty miles around to wait for old Jennie to die, glum as at a funeral, looking at each other, saying nothing. The paper was peeling off the walls, old pans and buckets that had been set out to catch last night's rain were still at their feet in the middle of the floor and around the sides of the room, the water standing rusty in them, speckled with dust. There wasn't a man among them with the gumption to get up on the roof and stop those leaks; old Sam would say, "W'at it needs 's a new roof, but I hain' got the money f'r the roofin' paper." His excuse was age — he couldn't climb up on the roof at his age; he was seventy now and exempt from poll taxes. But Will Salter, who married Jennie's granddaughter, Emma — he was just plain shiftless; at twenty-five his shoulders were permanently bowed and he sat sucking his dead pipe, too lazy to light it again, looking fifteen years older than his age — and Emma, her teeth gone at twenty-one, waiting till her gums shrank so she could get her new teeth; too lazy to brush their teeth, Ella thought, too shiftless to raise enough vegetables to get the proper nourishment. Salt pork and potatoes!

126

She lifted the slop jar that had not been emptied in two days, carried it to the shed, emptied and scoured it with soap suds and an old brush, dropping in a few drops of the antiseptic she had brought from her own house down the road. "What good'll it do for you to wear yourself out sitting up all night with the old woman?" her husband, Ed, had said; "it won't do any good." The blind fool, she thought, he couldn't understand I wouldn't do it for Murdock's folks; they're only too glad to have a neighbor woman in to do the dirty work; "I'm doing it for old Jennie," she had said. "She'll never know it — you said she's in a coma." "Do people have to know the good you do?"

"I want Ella Carter," Jennie'd said that afternoon. "She's a good neighbor; her an' me been neighborin' now f'r two years; she'll take right holt."

"Do you want me to stay with you tonight, Jennie? Would you like for me to stay here with you?"

"Yes," she said, "my folks ain' no hand t' take care o' the sick." She heaved her great bulk over in the bed with a moan, pulling the dirty pillow under her sweating head. "Yore a good girl, Ella," she said and sighed. "I ain't a mind t' go yet; it's Spring. I ain't a mind t' go yet f'r a w'ile, but I guess it's time."

"Don't be silly, Jennie. Your time hasn't come yet by a hell of a sight. Why, you'll live to see my little Ed's grandchildren."

Jennie sighed and threw the blanket off peevishly. "Ain't nathin' I'd ruther see," she said, and was asleep. Ella pulled up the blanket, tucked it around her neck, laid a clean towel by her mouth in case she should vomit again. The intermittent coma had returned; there was nothing more to do. She went into the sitting room where they all sat staring at their feet — Will and Emma Salter, old Sam Murdock, Jennie's brother Philo Allen, Al O'Brien who had married Jennie's only daughter, Netta, even a niece from some town fifty miles north — Dorothy Aldrich, a wan, bedraggled female whose stringy hair hung low on her forehead, whose eyes were permanently red with easy tears.

"Now folks," she said, "you'd all better go to bed and get some rest. You've been up four nights running. Jennie's asleep — I'll call you if I need you." She laid her hand on old Sam's shoulder as he sat hunched in his chair. "Get to sleep, Sam," she said.

"No sleep f'r me t'night," he said. "I got t' be t' hand 'f Jennie calls."

"If Jennie calls I'll get you right away," she said. "Can't you trust me?"

"Like enough I c'n trust you all right," he said, "on'y I won' get no sleep nohow." He lowered his face into his hands and sobbed. "If anything happens t' my woman," he cried, "I'll go out 'n the woods with my gun."

"You'll do nothing of the kind, Pa," Netta said. She clasped her three-year-old between her knees; her nose reddened.

"That's w'at you say," Sam mumbled, his voice rising hysterically in grief. "Don' seem I just c'd get along without Jennie," he sobbed. "Don' seem I just c'd go on livin'." He rose from the lopsided chair and went into the shed, and as though at a signal they all sprang to their feet, their eyes wide with terror, and rummaged the house high and low collecting all the many guns and pistols that hung over the doorways, dangled from nails. They ransacked the drawers for extra cartridges, even took down the old Civil War bayonet that hung over the mantelpiece of the blocked-up fireplace. "Give 'em here," said Al O'Brien, standing in the middle of the room. A short, stocky man with a pipe between his battered teeth, he stood, his arms bristling with rifles, pistols sticking out of the pockets of his lumber jacket. "I'll put 'em in the car," he said; "I'm goin' home t' look after the kids an' I'll take 'em home with me." He left the room.

Old Phil Allen looked up at Ella, standing by his chair, and his eyes twinkled. "Sam allus was a great hunter," he said. He carefully eased off his Congress boots and rubbed his feet. "Don' think I ever had the pleasure o' meetin' you b'fore," he said. "I'm Jennie's brother — folks allus says we look exactly alike."

"You do."

"Bunions I got," he said, "they never give me a minute's peace." He rubbed his feet. "I come sixty miles with my ol' mare t' be here," he said, "— wore out two women I did, an' three housekeepers." The corners of his eyes folded up, a twinkle shone from between his heavy lids.

"You looking for another housekeeper?" said Ella, her hand upon his shoulder.

"W'at's that? I don't hear ' good's I used to —" he cupped his long ear with a hairy hand.

"I said, if my man didn't mind, I wouldn't mind keeping house for you." She smiled. "You looking for another?"

"Can't say I'd exactly mind," he said, "ef'n you'd rub my feet o' evenings. All my housekeepers has gotta rub my feet." Embarrassed, Ella laughed, controlling the urge to bend down right then and there and pull his socks away from his toes; she knew how nice it felt.

They all came into the sickroom and stood around the bed silent. They looked at one another (this may be the last time we see dear mother-Jennie-grandmamma-auntie alive), then one by one they left, Ella and Dorothy Aldrich remaining, the niece the arrogant custodian of the unconscious woman lying on the pillow over her. She stroked her damp forehead, smoothed back the white hair Jennie'd had ever since she was a girl — silky white hair that Netta O'Brien had at forty-three, that even Emma, Netta's daughter out of wedlock had at twenty-one. "Poor Aunt Jennie," she said, her wan face hanging over the pillow, "d' you think she un'erstands w'at we're sayin'?"

Ella shook her head.

"W'en my son was took from me," Dorothy Aldrich said, "seems like I couldn' never get over it." She dropped her head and sobbed quietly. "Why don't you go to bed, Dorothy?" Ella said, "you've been up four nights."

"My place is here," she said and smiled her thin pathetic smile. She looked down at her aunt, then shyly at Miz Carter and said, "Do you believe in prayer?" Ella Carter sat up in her chair, thinking what her husband, Ed, would have said to that question. "When you're dead you're dead." Why, that man couldn't sit in a room where there was a clock without his eyes went into a trance and he sat listening; clocks somehow fascinated him. He'd sit and every once in a while he'd nod his head, and then she had no need to say, "A penny for your thoughts," for any number of times in the past he'd sat just like that and nodded, "One minute less," he used to say. "One minute less for what?" she'd asked him once, then with a smile that could never conceal from her his real anxiety, he'd said, "One minute less to live." An infidel afraid to die! she thought.

Free for once in her own mind, Ella Carter spoke for herself and him — he couldn't stop her if he wanted to; he was down home minding little Ed, probably listening to that devilish clock right now. "Yes," she said, "I do."

"Let us pray," Dorothy lay face downward over the head of the old woman, who had slipped down in the bed again, and was silent for a while. Why do they make so much of this? Ella thought; why can't they see — why, Ed is right! she thought, or is he right? What good will it do?

Dorothy looked up. "I don' believe in prayer," she said. "I don' think it does no good at all. W'en my son was took from me I prayed f'r days on end but he was took jus' the same. I guess his time had come." She smiled, her stringy hair falling over her forehead as she stroked Jennie's hand. "But it don' do no hurt t' pray; I just wouldn' feel right in my mind again about Aunt Jennie's goin'," she sobbed, "less'n I said a prayer f'r her."

"You go to bed," Ella Carter said. "You'll have to have some rest or you won't be good for anything at all."

"I'll go in the settin' room, but I won' sleep."

"No, you go to bed in the front room with Netta. Now you get right undressed and go to bed."

"I'll go but I won' sleep."

Yes, Ella thought, he was a great hunter all right, and that's about all he ever was. She remembered when they'd moved next to the Murdocks, two years before, in the Fall — old Jennie was carrying the scholars then, had carried them in fact for seven years, a privilege granted by the town at meeting years ago, a job the Murdocks might do competently, and as it was their only source of income it was better they should earn two dollars a day than have them on the town.

Old Sam would sit all day by the kitchen stove, smoking and spitting into the grate till it was time to go to bed the horses down or milk the cow. Not until last Winter, that was it, when Jennie'd come down with the grippe, did he get his old Ford out and carry the scholars himself. He fished a bit, he set out traps, he hunted through the woods, but mostly his activities were confined to killing vermin — skunk and weasel, coon and crow and hawk; he hadn't shot a deer in seven years. So every morning old Jennie set out in the surrey, the fringe on the top flapping in the breeze, and after she'd delivered the scholars at the school she went right on, calling on folks along the road for fifteen miles around, selling her cottage cheese at five cents a ball, done up in waxed paper, trying to induce the farm wives to buy the cheap hats she got from a mailorder house in York State, figuring her time so she could pick up the scholars on her way back. She unhitched the mare herself and put her in the barn.

"He's a great old guy," Ed said, "you can't dislike the old cocker, but he riles me up something fierce. You know, Ella, I went up there to get some help with the wagon — Christ, it got me sore, no way of doing things is right but his; no one can do anything but him; he wouldn't even let me unscrew a nut — said I was doing it wrong! He's like a mule —" Yes, he's like a mule but then he's like a magpie too, she thought. Every piece of junk he's ever owned in the seventy years of his life he's kept, stowed in the ramshackle garage or in the spare bedrooms upstairs — piles of trash you have to climb over to get across the room: old Ford engines, parts, broken harness traces, boxes upon boxes of assorted nuts and bolts, rusty screws and bent nails, cartridges he was going to reload some day, broken buckles, old tobacco tins he might want to use again for bait, piles of magazines and pieces of farm machinery that had been smashed ten years before, cracked windowpanes, dull tools, old boots and rubbers, bottles, sweaters, clothes eaten to shreds by moths and rats, rusty traps, pieces of crockery and worn-out furniture. He said he knew where every single solitary thing he'd ever had was kept, but not one could he find. ("That's funny, I had my hand on that not a month ago, it was right here an' now it ain' now'ere.")

Fifty years Jennie supported him, Miz Carter thought, and what's she got for her pains — no, that's the sort of thing that Ed might say — I know what she's got. She listened to the old woman's

breath rasp through the dark hole of her mouth, over her purple
tongue, her cracked lips – the one black fang she'd saved for thirty
years Sam pulled out for her not a week ago; it bothered her so
long she thought she might as well have it out as not. Slowly,
quietly, her rank breath came into the room, then it died and Ella
reached to feel the pulse. Under the fat flesh of her wrist it beat
feebly, fluttering, then just as suddenly as it had waned, it throbbed
again against her fingertips with all the healthy power of the well.
The old kitchen clock (I must wind that clock) rattled and rang out
the half-hour (11:30), ticked noisily in the quiet house. Ed. Sam
lay back snoring on the couch she had made up for him in the kitchen, and she smiled. In the sitting room she could hear old Philo
stir and cough, strike a match for his pipe; then the house was silent once again and the breeze whined through the gaping window;
a hound howled over in the valley, the hens stirred restlessly inside
their coop.

So despite them all, she decided to lift old Jennie in the bed,
wondered if she should get the niece to help, decided not to. Feeling the ache in her back before she even tried to move the great
corrupting body, she stood astride the woman in the bed, gathered
the sheet in her hands on either side, then tugging desperately,
shifted her an inch or so. From the rumpled covers there rose a fet-
id, nauseating odor. Jennie moaned, opened her glaucous eyes
and murmured, "Sam." Ella bent over her. "Do you want Sam,
Jennie dear; shall I call Sam?" "Sam," Jennie said.

He woke at the touch of her hand, said: "W'at is it – is she
gone?" then understanding, groped in the half-dark room as though
he were blind, his legs sagging at the knees. "Yes, Jennie, darlin';
this is Sam, darlin'."

"I always loved Sam more than all the rest," she breathed,
"more than even Netta." "Yes, darlin' Jennie," he said, his head
bowed over her hand, kissing it, "this is Sam; Sam is here." She
was silent, so he left the room again. "Is there any wood, Sam?"
Ella Carter said, "I want to keep the fire all night."

"Naw." He wiped his eyes.

"Well –"

"Well, I guess I'll hadda split some," he said, pulled on his boots and lit the blackened lantern. She heard him in the shed, splitting with slow, regular strokes, grunting as he split. He brought in a small armload of wood, thumped it in the kitchen woodbox and, lowering himself onto the old couch with a sigh, snored again.

In the silent house, Miz Carter sat at the bedside, the lamp turned low in the room, her husband's sweater thrown around her shoulders. For comfort she held old Jennie's hand, thinking: Soon, will it be soon — it's almost midnight, or maybe with the rising of the sun. She tried to think if there was anything she had forgotten — she had scrubbed the floors, washed the dinner plates, washed out the rags and towels they'd let the dying woman use, then left to smell under the bed. She made a fan out of a calendar and fanned the air. Before the image itself rose into her mind, she felt her blood go hot again with resentment for the treatment this woman had received in the house where she was born; in the house where she was going to pass on. Like a sick dog they'd let her lie in her own wallow, making the feeblest efforts to relieve her discomfort, upset themselves by the violent odor in the room. Like dogs with scarce life enough to live they lived themselves — scratching the earth enough to raise potatoes that went with their salt pork all Winter. They worked on the roads once in a while, and the little money they earned — where did it go? It went to license an old motorcar; they'd rather starve, and starve they often did before they'd let the car go unlicensed for the year — they let their children go barefoot to school, the houses go unroofed, unpainted, unrepaired, just so they'd have an automobile to go — where did they go? They really never went anywhere at all!

A pretense, the old lady, the mother, the grandmother, the aunt — she lay dying in her bed to furnish a pretense for a reunion when for once they overate — pie and cake and doughnuts; yet they all loved her in their way. They spooned milk into her when she was unconscious, watched with superstitious dismay as it drooled out of her mouth; they said, "We gotta get some nourishment in her or she'll go!" They came into the filthy room and wept — Will Salter, what was he to the old lady? He married Jennie's daughter's ill-got brat; he came into the room and bent down to hold old Jennie's hand, tears dropping from his weak red eyes, saying, "Gran'ma, Gran'ma, don't go way, don' leave us, Gran'ma!" Why, Ella thought, it was enough to make me cry myself! Now in the dark house they all lay sleeping except old Philo in the sitting room, scratching another match for his old pipe, while outside Spring stirred in the dying tang of Winter; daylight would come sooner than you'd think. Daylight would come and Jennie would be gone — the slovenly old woman whose spirit was decaying even as her body would decay. But did the spirit decay? Ella could not believe it did — I have no thought, she felt with some concern, that is not the reflection of my husband's — for it was only ten years ago, before I married him, when I was still a girl, that Frances died!

She recalled the nights she sat with Frances Turner, her girlhood friend, watching her die, watching the wretched body shrink upon itself till there lay under the covers the mere simulacrum of a human being, a design of bones covered with skin; thinking, I will come to this, even I— here is the least common denominator of our earthly life; and strange to say, the more hideous death manifested itself as it slowly claimed the body of her friend, the more abject the features, the more sunken the flesh, protruding bones that seemed to burst the skin, the greater Ella's exaltation, the purer, more unconfined her spirit. She sat night after night, day after day, closer to her friend (no words!) than life had ever granted her to be, firm in the knowledge she could sit and watch over this body till its spirit left — that it would be granted her, out of her great love, out of her great faith, granted her of all the people living in the world, to see that spirit leave! She knew then there was no death, but a continuing; there was no grief when she closed her friend's eyes, knowing with disappointment that the breath had flown the flesh and given no sign. Yet her sense of rightness had remained, the love that bound her to her friend had not dissipated with that friend's body into nothingness — it had watched over her, it continued in her, it extended to all other flesh, it was with her at this other bedside, beside this woman who in health would have made four of poor Frances, who in approaching death was as heavy as Frances had been light.

She no longer hoped to grasp the moment as it fled, she knew the line was too imperceptible for human witness, she saw only the bluing hands, the parched appearance of the skin, the stiffening fingers, the open mouth, the tongue blackened as by the passage of a flame. Yet the sense of rightness remained without the exaltation, only the weariness of long watching, a weariness of long living that precluded now any faith in a continuation, that made her feel (with joy!) her husband's bitter words were true (When you're dead you're dead) and took away the bitterness, leaving only a resignation that the truth lay there, that it was right and just and, yes — healthy. There was no sickness in it; it was rich, and she longed for words that might convey her sense of fitness, her knowledge, born strangely of the flesh and not the mind, that it was only just the others should lie sleeping in their beds, waiting till the earth should have rolled around again to bring another day — that in the mere continuity of the days there lay the answer to what had so long terrified the race.

So in the light of this revelation — for she felt it as such — the shiftlessness of the Murdock family shrank to the insignificance of rolled dust in the corner of a room. They loved her. Their love could transcend and did transcend the facts of their neglect, and perhaps there was a deeper wisdom working through them, that stripped them to the essential bone — their grief. That they did not change the sheets, that they did not scrub the floor, that the milk they offered the dying woman was turned and specked with dust, that the rain leaked in the sitting room, that they were content to sit and wait till life had worked its will, was as little an indictment of them as Jennie's slovenly ways was of her. Ella recalled the first time she had met her neighbor — she was the younger; it was her place to pay the first call. The kitchen was hot as an oven, the windows nailed shut, the panes so dirty you could barely see through them, the cracked and dirty oilcloth on the table was smeared with the oily residue of many a forgotten meal and soiled uncovered pans of milk stood on the table collecting dust and flies that swam about in them until they drowned. Jennie, barefoot, sitting in the broken rocker, nervously fingering a cheap string of imitation pearls that hung around her fat neck; her cane propped up beside her; her feet unwashed, her nails black, her chin covered with a heavy growth of long hair. From outside the shed door came the stench of old manure, old garbage, drain water from the sink; and in this place they sat and passed the time of day, exchanging commonplaces, sizing each other up.

Jennie made a cup of tea that she offered in a stained, chipped cup — it was strong as poison — the flies buzzed around the greasy rags of meat left from last night's supper and Ella felt her stomach rise and turn. Yet as the minutes ticked past on the rusty kitchen clock everything disappeared from sight and smell and hearing — the unwashed floor and table, the reek of putrid vegetable and animal decay between the kitchen and the barn, the buzzing of the flies that swarmed on the sticky tablecover, the steamy smell of half-washed clothes drying over the stove, and there remained only a sense of sweetness she could feel in her flesh with a poignancy unparalleled by any past experience of human beings — repose, wisdom unbacked by formal knowledge, the kindliness of final resignation. What matter that her man sat by the stove, spitting into the grate from dawn to dusk; what matter that the house went unrepaired, the grounds untended, strewn with rusting cans, old tires, splintered boards and chicken coops; what matter that they were content to sit and let their lives move on, happy so long as they had something to fill their bellies, no matter what it was; what matter that her folks left her to die untended except by their bitter grief, their desolation? Yet you could do no less than sit and wait until the body had ended its long struggle — men had done no less for other animals, squatting all night in cold barns or in the fields, shivering, to help a cow bring her calf into the world, to nurse a sick horse, to sit with a hand on the forehead of an old dog, moved to something close to anguish by the perplexity in their soft eyes, the cruel fact of their inability to realize what was happening to them.

The weariness that comes at four o'clock when you have been awake all night came over her as she held the warm hand in her hand, widening her eyes from time to time to ward off sleep, shaking her head. She heard a twig snap outside the bedroom window and looked out — in the east the gray light of dawn flushed the sky, and under the window, muffled in her old overcoat, stood Ed, his cap pulled down, looking up at her. She felt like laughing, but frowned and put a finger to her lips, answering the question in his face. "Just the same; asleep; go home and sleep. Don't leave little Ed."

"Little Ed's all right; I couldn't sleep," he whispered, "thought I'd come up the hill." He turned to go, smiling, and she watched him disappear behind the budding bushes at the corner of the house.

The air was washed with dew and the chill of a new day was in the air as she turned back into the close dark room, saw Jennie in the bed, huddled under the clothes, the lamp with its smoky chimney burning, throwing wide reflections on the peeling walls, the bottles on the little bureau, the yellow light from the kitchen. She listened to the ticking of the clock, hearing old Philo in the sitting room scratch a match for his pipe, grunt as he rubbed his feet, hearing old Sam snoring in the kitchen, thinking, Now, praise God, let it be soon.

Solo Flight

THE plane rolled to a stop, my instructor released his safety-belt, stood up in the front cockpit and stepped out onto the wing. My God, I thought, it's come! (Twenty years ago I wrote a letter.) He bent down over me in a confidential manner, as though he were about to impart a piece of information intended for my ear alone, and he said: "O.K. You can go alone now." He stepped down off the wing onto the ground. "I'll be right here when you get back," he said.

"Hey, wait a minute," I said. "I don't feel at all confident about this."

"Nuts," he said. "Remember what I told you. There's a stiff breeze; you'll probably need the engine till you're most of the way down. Don't level off the way you've been doing. Bring it right down to the ground. Go ahead." Tachometer, I thought; climb at 1,600, turn at 1,550, cruise at 1,500. Five hundred feet.

I looked at him, but he turned away. I jerked the throttle open and snapped it closed again. I turned to him (he'd swung on his heel toward me with an angry expression), and I said, "I'm sorry." I wanted to get off the ground; I wanted to get away from there before I lost — (Twenty years ago . . . .)

The plane rolled; I made a special effort with the throttle, pushing it forward slowly, infinitely slowly and with a steady pressure. The grass moved by swiftly, the engine was roaring, I held the stick forward, enjoying the pressure necessary to hold it against the air-stream. The nose was down now and I eased back a bit on the stick, gently, gently. We were rolling fast now and I eased the stick a tri-fle farther back toward me, felt the excitement of the life in the wings, held the stick toward me, my left hand on the throttle, my feet against the rudder pedals. I felt it lift, it was lifting now, it was off the ground, the ground was slipping by under me; it was dropping away. I enjoyed, for a second, the memory of many hours of maddening self-disgust, when I had had to fight the ship, fight my fear, fight my body to keep the plane running in a straight line across the ground. It had been impossible. But now I was climbing steadily; the earth was fifty feet below; the Coast Guard's squat military planes were beneath me, warming their engines on the ground; I shot a swift glimpse ahead, above, to both sides; there were no other planes in sight. I was rising diagonally across Flatbush Avenue, saw the toy cars going through the toll gate at the bridge, saw the green piers of the new bridge I had used so many times as a guide when I was trying to fly straight and level. A straight line is the shortest distance . . . (Twenty years ago . . . .) *The fascists, the flight commander said, are sixteen miles due south.*

I remembered and glanced at the tachometer; it was at 1,800 r.p.m. and with a feeling of deep regret I eased the throttle back a little till it fell to 1,600. ("*Listen* to the goddam engine!" he had said at least a hundred times. *Listen* to it; don't fly so mechani-cal.") It made me sore that I had not heard the difference between 1,800 and 1,600. But I hated to ease it off; I hated to lose those 200 r.p.m. on the climb.

The bay was below me now, the shoal waters and the clean rip-pling surface, like watered silk. I could see the hundreds of parked cars in Riis Park, and on the far side, the beach, black with people safely on the earth. *Sixteen miles due south, under the baking sun, the enemy. Do you love peace? Do you love freedom? Do you love human dignity?* There was a small steamer far out on the horizon, and I suddenly recalled with a shock entirely unwarranted by the im-portance of the phenomenon, the fact that there really was no hori-zon; that was mist. That meant that when I got to the top, I would have to hold the nose above the point that looked like the horizon.

Exhausted, I reached the top of the climb (the altimeter on the underside of the upper wing read 500) and cautiously, as though I were handling eggs, reaching down a box from a high shelf, I pulled the stick slightly toward me and brought the throttle back a trifle. I leaned out to the left and looked at the tachometer in the front cockpit — 1,550 — and nodded my head. Slowly, cautiously, I brought the stick a trifle to the left and pressed gently on the left rudder pedal, saw the horizon tip, and then remembered that I had forgotten to look to the left before I turned. I cursed. The nose was swinging slowly around, and when the field came into sight on my left, I brought the controls back to neutral again, brought the r.p.m. to 1,500, felt myself shaking as though I had the ague, and consciously relaxed. My legs ached; my knuckles were white with the grip I'd had upon the stick; I relaxed my throttle hand, took it off the lever for an instant, and then hurriedly put it back again.

"By Christ!" I said aloud, "that's funny." I laughed. I said, "Ha! ha!" as loud as I could say it, and then consciously relaxed again. My flesh was wet; there were beads of perspiration on the backs of my hands; my back ached and my neck was stiff. I said aloud, "Well, you're flying." I said, *"Well, you're flying!"* I shot a swift glance down at the field, but I couldn't see him; I looked for him anxiously for a moment, felt the left wing go down, and hurriedly, my heart in my throat, looked forward and corrected the unintentional bank. The shadow of the plane moved under me across the earth, a dark cloud scudding, man's shadow on the earth he'd left behind.

Wind rising. A gust of wind struck us and the plane rose ten feet, dropped five, fell off on the left wing, and righted itself before my mind got round to directing my hand to correct the error. I could feel that I was tightening up again and relaxed. "Relax!" I said aloud, *"Relax, you damned fool, relax!"* ('You'll either fly it yourself," he said, "or it'll fly *you*. I want *you* to do the flying, not the ship.") Twenty years ago I wrote a letter. . . .

There was something in my mind trying to get my attention, but I rejected it, I held it off without too much effort; I knew it would worry me. Time enough. Across the field I could see long lines of cars parked, and a thin edge of people standing at the wire fence before the concrete apron. There were three people there I couldn't see. My wife was there, and my two small sons: one four and a half years old, one two years and three months. Maybe they're having a cocoamalt, I thought, not watching at all. How would they know he'd got out of the plane; they couldn't see a-cross the field. The thought of them sitting calmly on the veranda of the restaurant, the kids having a cocoamalt, not watching, an-noyed me. Don't they know? Can't they tell? Don't they feel it. . . . No, my mind said; it doesn't matter. I want this for you all; I want you to handle this, not the enemy. (Twenty years ago:

TO: Master Alvah C. Bessie
From: Chief of the Signal Corps
In Re: Riding in Government Airplanes

   1.   Your recent letter to the President has been referred to me.
   2.   I regret to say that it will not be possible for the President to grant you permission to ride in a government airplane.
   3.   If we gave permission to all boys your age to ride in government air-planes, there would be no planes available to train pilots for France.
   4.   If you wish to see an airplane, you may go to the nearest army flying field and ask for the commanding officer; and he will be willing to show you an airplane.)

This is no place for you, my mind said. This is no place to be; what are you doing here? The kids . . . the older boy has been up five times now; it doesn't mean a thing to him. "Poppy," he said, "if I jumped out of the airplane, would it hurt me?" "Yes," I said, "I suppose it would." "Poppy," he said, "if I jumped out of the airplane with a parachute, would it hurt me very much?" Four and a half; thirty-three. What did I say, the kid? Dear President Wilson, did I say? Honorable Sir, did I say? I am a young boy thir-teen years of age, and I would like to ride in an army airplane twenty years ago. Now, now.

Suddenly I knew I was in the air, that I was flying, that the earth was below me, that the water was down there on my right, the field on my left, and millions were walking the earth, in Brooklyn, in Manhattan, in Chicago, and in Spain. The front cockpit looked empty for the first time, and I fought off the thing my mind wanted to tell me; just a little while longer now, just a little longer. Let them all fly; let all of them soar on stiff wings above the earth. Man made this thing for all, this was made for man and who is keeping it from him; who is keeping the shattering joy of flight from the multitudes of the earthbound? Who will give it to them? I put my left hand out and felt the solid rush of the airstream. I looked to the left, and with my heart pounding, my body awake for the first time in my life, I eased the stick off to the left, gave it left rudder, felt the seat tip under me, saw the horizon tip. There were wings over the earth, moving swiftly from point to point, seeking out the distant places of the earth. Over the North Pole, the broad Atlantic, bringing peace and happiness and the exultation of accomplishment.

Below me there were some fishermen's huts on the edge of the swampy land; there were rivulets running out into the bay. *Basque.* There was a rowboat moored a few feet offshore, its shadow on the water. There were gulls below me, wheeling over the surface. The nose swung gently across the slanted horizon, Flatbush Avenue came into my field of vision, and the cars moving slowly on it, crawling like army ants on the march. There was a ship coming into the field ahead of me, and I banked to keep an eye on him and let him have all the time he needed. I remembered my instructor in the front cockpit; his goggled profile, pointing at his own eye, then at another plane in the air, then at his eye, then at the plane. Below me, the fishermen's huts; poor people. *Suddenly I released the bombs, saw them melting away below as they fell, twisting, saw the soundless detonation and the flash, the smoke, and the geyser of earth and broken wood and broken water. I thought of Guernica, of Durango, of Bilbao, and shut the sight out of my mind, the hate out of my heart. . . .* Who is keeping them all (the poor) upon the ground? Why can't they soar, why can't they stretch their wings? There are wings over the earth, moving swiftly, point to point, bringing death and grief and pain and the horror of man's ingenuity.

I leveled the wings with the horizon and looked down. The wind sock on the little signal tower was plain, and as I watched

I could see him, he was standing there, just where I had left him. My heart rose into my throat and my mind acknowledged the thought that it had been shunting off as a football player stiff-arms interference. I banked to the left again and slowly pulled the throttle toward me, heard the engine idle down, shoved the nose down, and waited. It was *now*.

"Do it!" I said aloud, and was astonished by the sound of my own voice. The wires were whistling and the plane rocked and rolled under me. I corrected a bit for the wind, gave it a little right rudder and brought it into the breeze. *For a brief moment, the machine guns rattled, two through the propellor, one on either wing, and the fascist troops threw themselves flat on the road, rolled into the ditches, their hands above their heads.* I could see him now, he was waving his arms to show me where he was. The wires were screaming and I pulled the nose up a trifle. I could feel I was undershooting the field, opened the gun for a few seconds, closed it again. There was nothing to do but wait — "Don't sit there like a *dummy*; keep your wits about you; you can't fall asleep in an airplane," he said. "What the hell do you want to do, dive it into the ground!"

The earth was rising, the soft green field was swelling under me, I corrected for the gusts of air nearer the ground, keeping the wings level, holding the nose along the line I had determined to land on, parallel to the concrete runway. My voice was in my ears.

"Wait. Wait. All right now, soon; all right now, soon. Don't level off too soon.

"Don't level off too soon. Bring it right in.

"Now," my voice said, and I eased back on the stick. He was standing to my left, his hands at his sides, watching. His goggles gleamed on his forehead and I had a momentary image of my own serious face, the sinister face of the pilot, helmeted and goggled, like some monster, like an insect under a microscope, the clean sweep of the skull, the enormous eyes, the firm mouth with the lips in a thin line; watching, alert, the eyes moving behind the lenses. *Machine guns rattle for the poor.*

"Now," my voice said again, "take it easy; take it easy take it easy take it easy."

The ground was rushing past me; the individual grass blades could be seen; I felt like bursting.

"Now!" I shouted, pulled the stick into my lap, and felt the ship sit down, felt the dull shock of the solid earth vibrate through the fuselage, kicked the rudder right and left to keep the plane rolling straight across the grass, my chest aching with the desolation, the joy, and the agony of flight.

He was running to me and I could feel my face cracking with the smile, my jaws aching from the pressure of my teeth against each other. I wanted a drink of water; my throat was bone-dry; my eyes felt as though they were bursting from their sockets; my head ached. The strap of the goggles cut into my scalp. (Twenty years ago I wrote a letter.)

"That was *ridiculous!*" he shouted. "The whole thing was *ridiculous*! Your takeoff stank, you climbed too fast — do you want to stall and crash! You yanked it through the turns, the approach was absolutely absurd, you bounced when you landed! Didn't I *tell* you not to dive the wings off it! Do I have to *teach* you to glide all over again? Do I —"

"I don't remember bouncing," I said.

He put his hands on his hips. "You don't remember?" he said gently, as though he were talking to a four-year-old. "Do you want me to hold your hand? I'm perfectly willing to hold your hand. I say it *stank*!"

He turned away from the plane, and without looking back at me he said, "Go ahead; do it again, and stop *dreaming.*"

Soldier! Soldier!

WE were on the run. Ever since they retook Belchite we had been on the run, and it was a mighty uncomfortable feeling. Either they were damned clever or we were damned stupid, or something. Probably a little of both, for every time we took up a position, dug in and prepared to meet their attacks, we'd learn, a bit too late for comfort, that we had been outflanked again. (There might have been some sabotage as well.) Word would come that the flanks had given way; that battalions to left or right had retreated without the formality of informing us, and so we had to fight our way out of the position we had taken up, run again, then take up another stand. That happened three days running; exhaustion and its poisons had set in; the men got to such a point that even while they were digging in, they'd say, "What the hell's the use of this; in a couple of hours we'll find out we've been cut off again." They had four-day beards; their faces were dirty, their clothes were in rags; their rifles and machine guns were dirty; they had lost their gear — blankets, packsacks, canteens, shovels — days ago.

But we did it again. We dug in below this little town along a slightly wooded ridge of hills, and we prepared to face them. We knew they would be coming soon; we could hear their avion bombing and bombing, banging the roads to pieces behind us so we couldn't bring up reinforcements, ammunition, food. There *was* no food; there had been no food for three days, and you know how you get to feel after a couple days' hard work on top of an empty belly.

You feel disembodied; you feel as though you were floating two feet off the ground, you can't feel your legs walking or running, but they have a way of going on. It isn't so bad in your belly; after the first day or so the pains wear off and you only have a dull ache to think of, with attendant dizziness from time to time. You want to sleep, badly; you want to sleep, and I remembered the days when I used to live in Philadelphia and there was no work and no food, and I used to sleep twelve, fourteen hours a day, because when you sleep you don't mind not eating so much. The body has a way of taking care of you. Any working stiff can tell you how it feels. Only now there was no possibility of sleep. We could hear them coming.

The battalion was dug into this hill; the sun (even in early March) was hot as all hell and the men were improving the little time they had, cleaning their rifles, stripping the machine guns, even wiping off each cartridge with a bit of rag. There was no oil for the guns, for the rifles. There was no water on the hill for the men, but we had decided to hunt for some. Then they began; they began to feel us out with their artillery; light stuff at first, antitank and such, and then they opened up with mortars and their equivalent of the French 75's. It got hotter on the hill, and the guys who had been griping began to wish they had saved their breath and strength and dug in deeper instead. Those flying ash-cans came over, rushing through the air like the Bronx express and banging behind us, on the left, on the right. Our observers said they had tanks in reserve, but the tanks weren't coming on just then. Then they lifted the artillery and a flock of Messerschmidts came over and put on a lovely show. Like the Indians in Custer's Last Stand, they wheeled overhead, round and round in a pretty perfect circle; then the leader sideslipped off and down out of the formation and came diving longitudinally at the hill. He combed it from one end to the other with his machine guns, tatatatat, tatat, tatatata, his propeller screaming like a ghost, and then he zoomed up off the end of the hill as though he had a fly under his tail. The rest of them followed, one at a time, one after the other, spilling out of the formation, diving and howling at us, opening their guns, climbing, hanging on their props, winging over and around again.

Planes don't do much damage in the line, but they scare the living daylights out of you.

That was when the commander said to me, "Take Fred and go organize some grub. If we get out of here tonight we'll need some."

"But we haven't got a kitchen any more," I said.

"Get something we won't need a kitchen for."

"O. K.," I said, and I got Fred and we started back from the lines. I don't think either of us wanted very much to leave the lines just then; it was safer there than it was further back, for the planes weren't doing much damage — they hadn't hit anybody yet — and the artillery didn't have the angle. It was landing behind the lines, about five hundred meters away, and the shells were landing behind the lines, near a little lime-washed stone house we'd noticed when we came in early that morning. This house stood in the valley behind the lines, about five hundred meters away, and the shells were landing all around it. It looked abandoned.

We ran down the back of our hill, hopped down the terraces and crossed through the vine field without saying anything to each other. I know what we were both thinking, though; we were just hoping that we wouldn't connect with one of the shells, and we were hoping the planes overhead would mind their own business and not take it into their heads to chase us across the field as they had a couple days before. I couldn't feel my feet on the ground, but as I kept on moving, I figured it was all right, and we headed for the house in the distance. We were both thinking of something we had often said: that there's relatively little chance of a small house being hit, one chance out of — well, we'd never figured out the percentage, but it rarely happened.

Besides, we were looking for grub, and the first place you look for it is in a house, where it's most likely to be. It was still winter; nothing was growing, nothing was on the trees, and the only things you could find on the ground were a few of last year's almonds and *avellanas*, and those nuts were just as likely to be empty. So we kept on running, dropping onto our faces at regular intervals when we heard the shells whiffling through the air; then we lay down and counted one . . . two . . . three as the shells

landed, waited till the shrapnel stopped screeching overhead, got
up and ran again. I got to laughing; I was remembering running
through Caspe a day or so before, hotfooting it through the empty
streets and seeing a wooden box on the pavement. It was outside
a store that had been looted, and everything in the store was tumbled onto the sidewalk, where the Fascist soldiers had taken what
they wanted, and we had taken what we wanted later. Now there
was this big wooden box of that lousy Spanish chocolate lying
there, that chocolate that comes in long rolls, wrapped in paper;
and as I ran, I scooped up a handful of the paper rolls on the fly.
I stuffed them in my pockets and inside my shirt, and kept on running. Then I took one out, still running, stripped off half the paper and stuck it in my mouth. It tasted funny. It was dynamite.

The dooryard of the house was piled with junk; there was a
donkey cart with a broken wheel, there were bedsteads and springs
and mattresses lying around; cooking utensils and children's toys.
The place had obviously just been evacuated, and we felt pretty
good, for in those houses you can usually find some chow; especially when they've been abandoned in a hurry — there's a lot of
stuff they can't take along. We'd seen lots of these houses; in
fact, that spring, when the Fascists were on the march through the
Aragón, driving to the sea, the countryside was full of empty
houses and the roads were so jammed with people running away
from General Franco's offers of peace, bread, and plenty, that it
was hard for the troop trucks to go where they were going. The
people didn't seem to want to wait for General Franco to come
and give them peace and bread and plenty; they had their own
idea of what they'd get.

The door was closed but it opened at our touch, and we both
dodged inside with a sigh of relief. There is something about a
stone-walled house, even when it's in the line of fire, that gives
you a feeling of security. But the minute we got inside, into that
dirt-packed downstairs room that the Spanish peasants have to use
for their livestock (they live upstairs), we looked at each other and
we whistled. The floor was alive with food — there were rabbits
hopping frantically around in the semidarkness, there were chickens fluttering and screeching, there was a pig, there were huge

earthen jars of pickled olives, sacks of last year's hazelnuts and walnuts, piles of potatoes, dried figs, casks of olive oil. We looked at each other, dropped the gunnysacks we'd brought and got to work, laughing.

A rabbit doesn't make much noise when you kill it, but the dumb chickens were fierce. They were zooming through the dark air all around us, blundering into our faces, getting in our hair. They screeched and squawked and yelped; we had to kick them out of our way. We wrung a bunch of their necks and couldn't decide whether to pluck them then and there or stuff them in the bags, so we did both. "We'll have to make a couple of trips," Fred said. And I said, "Yeh."

"Look," I said, "you keep up the good work and I'll take a look around." I figured that I ought to see what was upstairs, if anything. The artillery was sounding outside, but it was reassuringly muffled by the heavy walls and as we used to say, "You're safe from anything but a direct hit, and if there's a direct hit you won't mind it." So I started up the curving staircase, tripping over a wooden rake that someone had left on the steps. Upstairs it was lighter, and you could really see how fast these people had got out when they heard the Fascists were coming.

All the doors upstairs but one were open, and the rooms looked as though they'd been hit by a cyclone. There were pictures of Mom and Pop when they were first married, and a family picture with the little kids dressed in their peasant Sunday best. But the bureau drawers were all pulled out and lying around the floors, half-ransacked. Clothing of all sorts was strewn over the floor and the chairs, rags and lengths of materials were draped all around; there was a box of buttons sitting on a little table and a piece of embroidery work lying on the bed. You could see that the folks hadn't been able to decide what to take and what to leave, and they'd probably remember a lot of things they wanted when they got to wherever they were going. A chamber pot had been taken out of the bedside cabinet, and then left on the floor; a crucifix had been taken from the wall; you could see where the paper was faded. There were children's toys lying all around, there was a cradle in the corner, but nothing in it. There were some good blankets (and I thought of taking one, but it was a brilliant white with a brilliant scarlet stripe, so I decided against it. It could have been seen for miles).

I poked around in the drawers (but I really wasn't looking for anything); examined a pipe the old man had left, a package of letters tied up with a faded pink ribbon and written in an illiterate hand. There was a corset hanging on a nail in the wall, and I thought again what a hideous thing a corset was. There was some crockery, white with wide gold edges, on the table, and I could just hear the housewife, who had brought it in from the kitchen, saying, "Should I take this, Juan?" And Juan would say, "Don't be a damned fool, woman," and maybe she cried a little. I felt a little like crying myself; and that was when I heard the small voice calling.

It sounded far away but I knew, with a leaping heart, that it was in the room with the closed door, so I went into the hall and knocked on the door and opened it. The voice was saying over and over, *"Miliciano, miliciano!"* and it belonged to a little old woman, as little a woman and as old a one as I have ever seen. She was lying in a big bed in the far corner of the room, and the room stank. The smell of that room was enough to knock you over, and part of it came from the garbage that was lying on the floor, and part of it from the filthy bed itself.

"Miliciano," she said, "don't kill the animals."

I didn't know what to say, what to do. I stood there staring at the ancient dark face in the filthy bed; it had practically no hair; but it was a quiet face, a kind one. It had big eyes that looked at me standing there, and the body to which it was attached scarcely showed beneath the ragged coverlet. On the bed, next to the body, there were a couple of eggs; on the floor there were broken eggshells, a broken dish with scraps of what had once been a green vegetable, some rotten oranges. I felt sick to my stomach.

"Miliciano, miliciano!" said the little old woman. "Don't kill the animals."

"No, madre, no," I said, and even though I could hear the chickens squawking downstairs as Fred wrung their necks, I couldn't say anything else. "Don't worry," I said. "We won't kill the animals."

Then I heard Fred calling, and I went out the door into the
hall and said, "What?"

"Joe," he said, "I'm going to get some of this stuff down behind the other hill and cache it; you bring some too."

"O.K.," I said.

"What the hell are you doing up there, looting?"

"Nothing," I said. "I'll be right along."

I heard him go out the door, and the chickens got quiet in a
minute or two, and then I went back into the bedroom and stood
there, just as stupid, just as spellbound, as before.

"Qué dices?" she said.

"Nada, nada."

The old woman looked at me and I wanted to cry. I could hear
the artillery banging outside; the walls shook when it landed; I
could hear the Messerschmidts tattattatting and a lower, deeper
rumble and a sickening vibration as they dropped their small bombs
on the hungry men in the lines. I wanted to get the old woman out
of there, but I knew I couldn't. I wanted at least to clean the room
up for her, but it wouldn't have done any good.

"Miliciano," she said, "will the war be over soon?"

"Sí, madre, sí," I said, and then I walked backward to the door
and softly closed it behind me, opened it again and said, "We won't
kill the animals, *madre*, I promise you." It was all that I could say
that would give her any comfort. I closed the door and went on
down the stairs.

The chickens set up their squawking and I groped around in
the semidarkness, cursing the damned beasts because the old lady
would think I had broken my promise. I found my gunnysack
and filled it, indiscriminately, with hazelnuts and pickled olives
and raw potatoes. You could gnaw on them in the line at any rate.
I didn't want to go out of that house, but I soon found myself running with the bag over my shoulder, felt it vaguely bumping me
from behind. I had to fall on my face every few yards when I would
hear the shells coming, rushing, then whistling, then howling, then
crashing; and then I got up and ran again. The machine-gun bullets
from the planes plunked into the dirt, kicked it up in little spurts.
I heard the men yelling as I got back up the hill: "Tanks!" they

were shouting. "Tanks!" and then everything was quiet for a moment and you could hear the Italian tanks rattling and banging their way along toward our flanks.

"What you got?" the commander said, sticking his head out of the dugout.

"Potatoes, olives, *avellanas.*"

"Is *that* all?"

"No," I said, "Fred's got chicken, rabbit, pork, dried figs. I'm going back now," I said. "We'll stow the stuff behind the hill behind that house, and get it and cook it up tonight. There's enough for the whole battalion, almost.

"Muy bien," he said. "We can't get this stuff out to the men now anyhow." We were sitting in the mouth of the dugout, our backs to the lines, and we both saw it together.

"Wow!" the commander said, but I said nothing.

We had both been looking at the little house, and we both saw the shell hit it and the stone fly in a great cloud of dark dust, and we saw the flames sprout and curl and climb, curling and licking till the house was all consumed. It crackled like brush fire, like machine-gun fire. We could feel the heat of it on our faces; the barrels of olive oil in the downstairs room were blazing too, I guess, and I was thinking, I only hope she got it before the flames reached her.

"That where you got the stuff?" he said.

"Sí, sí."

My Brother, My Son

LONG before we sailed back home from France I knew I would have to see him. I did not want to think about it, and as the ship beat a stormy passage across the winter sea, I distracted myself with drinking, attending the movies in the salon, playing poker with the other men. And every time the image of his face rose in my mind (I knew he would look like his son), I resolutely put it out. But when we docked in New York I felt him in the crowd, and I knew Ben's father would be looking for me, and I avoided him (he would only have had a bad photograph to go by), for I did not feel up to seeing him, and it was some time before I did, and even when I did I didn't want to.

Nowadays I know that I was only defending myself against pain; at first I used to think I was defending him. The letter that I wrote to Ben's girl friend must have reached the old man. I told her Ben had died in action, for once he had said that if it happened she would tell his Dad. I realized even then that the old man was hungry to see anyone who had known his son; I felt that he would fasten upon me, fix his eyes (which would be like his son's) upon my face, and release me only with reluctance. I should have understood this better than I did; now I understand it. But I should have understood it even then, for I have a son of my own. (Ben used to say, "Stop telling me about your kid; I'm sick of hearing about him; I don't like kids anyhow." He knew it riled me.)

For that matter he did everything he could to rile me, because

153

he knew that, being older than he by ten years, I felt in some ways inferior to him. He was my Company Commander; I obeyed his orders. And though he hardly said a kind word to me in all the time I knew him — which was short enough — well, you cannot sleep with a man for months without coming to love him or to hate him. He shamed me before the other men; he ridiculed me to my face; he said he wished I would transfer into another company before we went into action again; he said, "I'll be glad to get rid of you; you're no good anyhow." (I was his adjutant, and I knew I was no good.) "Can't you take it, Papa?" he used to say when the going got pretty tough. And I used to say, "Relax, baby; you're not old enough to do that yet." It was a queer relationship.

(When we made that attack, he had said, "I want you to stay behind."

"Is that an order?"

"It's an order."

We attacked and he went over, and I couldn't stay behind; but the fire was so hot I couldn't get very far. I dropped into a depression behind a tree, where the smell of the dead lay thick and sickly over the baking land, and I fired from behind the tree. He was gone but he came back, loping rapidly up the hill, his pistol in his hand, dodging among the machine-gun bullets. He saw me and dropped beside me, and he said with a sigh of exhaustion, "Did *you* have to get mixed up in this mess too?")

Somehow the old man found out where I lived and had his daughter call me. I made an appointment; then I broke it. I pleaded illness and I was thoroughly ashamed. I avoided making any other appointment, although the daughter called at least once a week; I always had something else to do. I was ashamed, but I was afraid too; and that was when I began to realize that I was not protecting him, but just myself. That made me more ashamed, but it was easy to avoid the issue of my shame; I had a lot to do; I was looking for a job and I started working. Weeks passed in this way until I got the letter. And it was the dignity, and not the pathos of the letter that decided me.

"I have tried many times to get in touch with you," the letter said, "and each time I have failed. I would like you to have dinner with my family and me this Sunday evening, and I hope that you will come, because my patience is nearly exhausted. I know you are busy, but I trust you will find time to keep this appointment. I cannot wait much longer."

So I went reluctantly, afraid of what I would meet, afraid of what I would feel. It was a long ride into the Bronx, and I had a lot of time to think. But I determined I would give as much as I could; I knew they hoped to resurrect the dead; I knew they couldn't, but I'd try to help.

In the long weeks between the retreat and the offensive, Ben had told me about his parents; about his father, who was a brave man and a strong one; about his mother who thought he was working in a factory; about his married sister and her husband; about his older brother, who was tubercular. When he spoke of them, he spoke with love, and I realized exactly what I had missed in my own life, for my father died when I was young, and I never cared much for my mother, and my brother had made a body servant of me. So it was something of a novelty to meet a man who loved his family and really felt they were his flesh and blood — the phrase is used so loosely.

He spoke with modesty of his own part in the family life, but what he did not say I could supply. I knew he had left school where he was studying to become an engineer, because his father could no longer send him; he went on the road. He did not need to tell me that he felt separate and apart from other men; I saw how much he disliked the job he held, commanding men in action in a war, and how determined he was to do that job. And I noticed how little part he took in any conversation, and how much he enjoyed singing in his small but mellow voice, when he had been coaxed enough. The songs he used to sing would bring us home again, and the whole man found expression in the hackneyed songs. Watching his face at such times, a face that was both ugly and curiously handsome, you would note an inner illumination, a gentleness that shone through the hardness he had so carefully assumed, a strong and generalized love of people and a tortured lack of confidence. You knew the reasons he had come to Spain and you could not help but wonder at the apparent discrepancy between the motives and emotions that had brought him, and the stolidity he displayed in the performance of his job. Inside, he was a man in pieces; lonely, disillusioned, lacking confidence. Outwardly, he was a man of action who could make rapid and intelligent decisions and carry them out with inflexible determination. Self-tormented and unstable in his personal life, he inspired absolute confidence in his leadership. He was only twenty-four.

The apartment house in the Bronx was like thousands of others, shoddy-modern, new and glaring, the hallway full of cheaply manufactured ornaments in bad taste. I rang the bell of the apartment and it was opened by a young girl I thought at first was Ben's sister who took me into the kitchen. Here there was an oldish woman, a short, stout woman who might have been the studied archetype of the Jewish mother. I was immediately afraid of her as she turned to look at me, her face a mask of ageless melancholy.

"I —" I said, and she said,

"You are —" with a rising inflection, and I nodded. She came to me and put her arms around me; her head rested on my shoulder and I could feel her heavy body shake for a moment; then she rapidly turned away and went back to the preparation of her dinner.

Behind me I heard a man cough, nervously, and I turned around. Yes, those were the eyes, but the face was altogether different. He looked at me, obviously holding himself in check, and he said quietly, "Ben's friend." And then, without knowing how it had happened, we were in each other's arms, clasping each other, and I heard myself say, "Father," and he said, "Son," and we held each other tightly, for we were lonely at that moment. His eyes were shining, but there was no moisture in them, and he took my hand and held it in both of his and we looked at one another. "Come inside," he said.

The first thing I saw in the living room was an enormous photograph of Ben. It was the one we had taken together, but only my shoulder showed in this enlargement, and the picture had been blown up to such an extent that it had lost what little definition it possessed. I felt a momentary, idiotic twinge, that I had been excluded from it; and I felt it was right, somehow, that the image should have been blurred; it was as though there were a veil over him, tangible evidence of his departure. He was gone from the place; he was no more.

"It's not a good picture," the old man said. "We had it made for the memorial meeting." He looked at me and wet his fine, thin lips, and I began to realize how closely Ben resembled him, although there was little enough correspondence in their features. "Listen," he said. "We can't talk tonight, because of Mother. But I want to know," he said. "I can take it; you can tell me . . . sometime."

"Yes," I said. "I'll tell you all I know. It's not much."

"He died in the hospital?"

"Yes."

"How long?"

"A week or so, I think. I tried to get there, but we were in action; they wouldn't let me go."

"In the head, they said."

"Yes."

He nodded his head and smiled, offering me a cigarette. I wanted to say, Your son was a hero, Father; I wanted to say, He *was* a hero, you can be proud; if ever there was a hero, he was. I couldn't say a thing. We lit our cigarettes and sat looking at each other; he kept smiling.

"How are you feeling?" he said.

"Tired, but otherwise all right."

"I tried to get hold of you," he said, then thought better of it. And so I found myself apologizing. I said I was sorry; I said I had been afraid to come, that he would understand. He nodded his head and smiled again. There had only been a brief glance of doubt, and he had understood.

"I know," he said. "You were his best friend over there."

"I think so," I said. "I loved him." And then I started talking. I told him that everybody loved him; everyone respected him; the Battalion Commander said he was the best of the company commanders; he was trusted with the toughest jobs; he could be relied on.

"He was a good shot with a rifle," the old man said. "I saw him shoot."

"Yes," I said. "With a pistol too."

"I never knew he could shoot a pistol." He seemed, somehow, childishly proud of Ben's achievements as a marksman. "He always liked firearms," he said. "But I never thought he would use them in a war." We were silent again; he saw me looking at the books on the shelves. There was a set of London, a set of Dumas; there was *The Boy's Book of Model Airplanes*; there were some school-books, geometry, astronomy, biology. There was a copy of Bellamy's *Looking Backward*, a copy of Veblen's *Theory of the Leisure Class*, some volumes of Conrad, Melville, Anatole France, a text on short-story writing. It was a hodgepodge collection, and the sort of books every young man reads at a certain period of his life.

"Those are his books," the old man said, and his lips smiled with pride. He held his slender body erect as he stood and looked at me. He was taller than his son. I thought perhaps I ought to say something, but there wasn't anything to say. So I looked at him again and wondered why there was so great a resemblance between this father and his son, when actually there was no single point of similarity, except the eyes. It was the way he held his head; it was the way he used his hands; it was a feeling that he gave me, rather than a point of reference.

"Have you anything of his?" he said.

"I have a notebook; there's nothing in it but a few notes about running the company; things like that. I'll send it to you if you like."

"Please," he said, and looked at the end of his cigarette. His fingers were very slender, very sensitive. He cleared his throat. "You know Ben was a writer," he said. "He left a whole box of things here, manuscripts and stories. Would you believe that, since I've known about this, I haven't been able to touch these things? I haven't opened it. I can take it," he said. "I know Ben's loss is a small thing; I can see it in relation to the whole struggle; but somehow I haven't been able to touch these things." He smiled.

"I know," I said. "I'll send you the notebook."

Without my noticing it, the old lady had set the table, and the room had filled with people. I was introduced to them: Ben's married sister, a poised young matron who moved in the assurance of success; her husband, who was a dynamo of nervous energy, talked continuously and made poor wisecracks (he did not wear the pants, but she let him think he did); the elder brother, whose face was a replica of Ben's, except that he was blond — he was silent; a younger brother, who looked like no one in the family, said nothing. The young girl who had opened the door for me, and another young girl with a bird's bright eyes and the sharp beak of a bird — they were next-door neighbors, I gathered.

We were sitting at the table and the old lady served a great meal: noodle soup with *matzoh* balls, *gefülte* fish, creamed onions, salad, mocha tarts. The old man brought out a bottle of good rye and poured a drink for everyone. We looked at each other and I touched my glass to his, said in a voice that no one else could hear, "To Ben," and he nodded gravely.

The folks were too busy eating to talk, except for Mother. She was serving; she paid no attention to anyone's request to sit down, that her food was getting cold; but she did sit down and she did not eat. Instead, she kept looking at me. I was aware that her eyes were on me all the time, and her face was sad but otherwise inscrutable. I was distinctly uncomfortable under her eyes; I wished she would either serve or eat, not look at me. I felt that perhaps she was not terribly intelligent, that this thing filled her life and had destroyed it for her; and then I knew immediately that her intelligence was not of the mind, but of the heart. I felt she knew me through and through, and was sorry for me. I knew that she wanted to talk, but was afraid of talking about Ben for fear I would be hurt and uncomfortable. There was something monumental about her as she sat there; she was a presence and a staple; she was a mother, there is no other way to say this. I remember, looking at her, the loss of my first son, who was stillborn, and I knew how much more deeply this must affect her, for *my* son had not lived long enough to win my love and Ben had lived and grown to young manhood and gone away and died, and she had nothing left of him. ("You ought to eat some of my Mom's cooking," he had said. "She can make *blintzes* like nobody's business.")

I paid attention to my plate, and I could not refuse any of the food they heaped upon it. "You're not eating," his mother said to me. "You don't eat enough to keep a bird alive," and she took my plate and filled it up again. I tried to eat; I bent to hear what the old man was saying; I nodded and smiled, aware that the smile was forced and genial, not genuine. The voices at the table grew louder as the meal ended and the coffee was served; I was suddenly aware that they were very loud and I listened. Ben's married sister was talking; her voice had assumed a tone of utter self-righteousness.

"– and so I fired her," she said. "These colored maids don't want to work. I sent for her, sent her fare from South Carolina, and she soldiered on the job; and so I fired her. And then, to our surprise, we got a letter from the Home Relief Bureau, saying she had applied for relief, and asking about her. I wrote them right back and said she didn't deserve relief; she wasn't even a resident."

"That was cruel of you," the young girl with the bird's eyes said, and she glanced at me for approval.

"Not at all," the young matron said, holding herself erect in her chair. "These colored girls don't *want* to work; running around all hours of the night; she had a boyfriend; sometimes she didn't come home at all."

"There's something else here," the young girl said. "Race prejudice." She forced a smile and looked at me.

"Nonsense!" said the husband. "It's a matter of principle with us. There're thousands of people out of work who deserve relief more. We merely said she didn't deserve it."

"Race prejudice," the young girl said.

"Utter nonsense!" he said. "People like you are always seeing race prejudice where there isn't any; it's like you."

"How much did you pay her, may I ask?" the girl said.

"Eight dollars and board; good pay these days."

The young girl sat back in her chair; as one would say, The prosecution rests.

The old man looked at me and smiled. "These arguments," he said. "They're always arguing." He rose from table and the table was cleared and put away in the corner. Ben's older brother was talking vehemently, and I was startled by his voice; it was Ben's voice speaking; it was Ben's face (except that this man was fair), but he gave me nothing of his brother; they were nothing alike, in the way that he and his father were alike.

"My older son has been very ill," the old man said. "He must go to a sanitarium soon again. It's very difficult to find the money."

The old woman was standing in front of me. She held a small and cleverly made model airplane propellor in her hand. "Ben made this," she said. "He used to make a lot of airplanes when he was a boy. This is all that we have left." (Suddenly I heard the planes; diving, screaming at us; their four machine guns tatting. I heard Ben shout, *"Abajo! todos abajo!"* And to me, "Get down you dope or your kid will have to find another papa. *Debajo de los arboles!"* We dived for the shadow of the trees.)

The old lady walked toward the kitchen, leaving the polished propellor in my hands; it was a clever piece of work; I would have liked to keep it; one blade was slightly broken. I looked up and saw her looking at me; they were all looking at me, and I thought, I can't help it! I wanted to say, It's not my fault I'm still alive; it's not *my* fault!

The older brother and the younger brother left; they had not said a word about Ben the entire evening; I could not tell whether it was because they did not want to talk about him, or because they were only there out of filial consideration; were tired of hearing him talked about. The sister and her husband left; they had a long way to go, and the two young girls helped Mother with the dishes. I sat smoking with the old man, and we did not speak. I was thinking of my firstborn, stillborn son, and of my father, who like this father sitting opposite me was thin and erect, possessed inherent gentility. I was thinking of my brother, who had always been a stranger to me. I was thinking of my living son, who just as Ben and his father resembled each other, resembles me, not so much in his features as in his temperament, his gestures, his personal idiosyncrasies — even at the age of five.

"Ben was her favorite," the old man said. "I guess he was mine as well. He always went alone; he would never let anyone do anything for him; he had to figure things out for himself and he never consulted with us. He was very clever with his hands."

The mother returned again, still in her apron, and she had a pair of cast-iron bookends; they were very ordinary bookends, a head of Lincoln in bas-relief against a block of metal. "Ben made these when he was in school," she said, deposited them in my hands and left again. I looked at them and put them on the table at my side. The old man smiled. "She takes it very hard," he said. "She doesn't understand too well. *I* understand," he said.

It is impossible to resurrect the dead, I thought. I was full of bitterness as I thought of this; I felt with what high hopes the two of them, the mother and the father (but especially the mother), had looked forward to this meeting. How could they have thought that anything would rise from it to soothe their grief? How could they have hoped that I would have been able to restore their son to them, even for a moment? I was a stranger in this place; a strange man who walked into their home, bringing only pain and no relief. She must have known that there was nothing I could do; but she came forward to this meeting with her eyes closed, hoping. . . .

It was time to go; I did not know how to go, but when the old man saw I wanted to, he made it easier for me. "I'd like to see your boy, some day," he said. "I have a little grandson about the same age." "I want you to," I said. (I really did.) "They're devils at that age," he said. "They're a trial."

We walked toward the door and at one room off the narrow hall he stopped and said, "There's something I want to say to you, and I don't know how to say it." He lit the bulb in the room and asked me to step in. "Mother and I," he said, "have been thinking. We don't know what your plans are; what you'd think. We did think that if you'd like to, we'd like you to live with us."

"I —"

"It would save you money," he said.

The mother came in and said, "This was Ben's room. This is his desk, where he used to work. You could use it."

"It's terribly kind of you," I said. "It would be impossible."

"I didn't think you would," he said. "But if you want to, we'd love to have you."

"I have to be near the center of town," I said. "I'm living near my boy now; he's with his mother."

"It's only fifteen minutes to Times Square," the mother said. Then she suddenly said, "I want to know. I'm a mother; I have a right to know." She did not cry (I almost wished she would). But she went on talking in a low tone of voice, as though she were taking one step after another, placing one foot before another, and would not stop until she got where she was going.

"If you could only give me a date," she said. "I don't even know the date."

"I wish I could. I didn't learn about it for two weeks; we were in action; I can't be sure; I'll try to find out if there's any way."

"I heard his face was disfigured," she stated.

I didn't answer.

"I want to know a date," she said, looking warily ahead, avoiding my eyes.

He put his arm about her shoulders; spoke softly. "There's no way of knowing, Mother," he said.

"He didn't even say good-bye," she said.

"Yes, he did, Mother," the old man said. "Only you didn't know what it meant."

"He was always saying good-bye; he was always going away."

I held my hat in my hands, turning it slowly. I looked at the old man and at the narrow hallway outside the room, and he nodded his head and said, "Remember that if your plans change, you're always welcome here. Come any time you want to."

"You could use his desk," she said. "His books."

"Thank you," I said. "Thank you. I wish it were possible."

"Nothing's impossible if you want," she said, and looked at me for the first time since she had come into the room. It was hard to look at what I saw: bitterness, resentment, emptiness — I was a stranger here. She held out her hand.

"Well," she said. "I'm sorry I can't say "Pleased to meet you.""

Man with Wings

F ROM five thousand feet the land was flat and measured into
patterns cut in endless and divergent shapes, and he could
close his eyes for minutes at a time, feeling the ship roll under him, rise and fall and gently reassume its wonderful stability.
And opening his eyes see the same pattern below, the thousands of
small fields in tones of gray and green and brown, the deeper, soft-
er green of the woodlands, the lines of hedges and the tiny boxes
that denoted human habitation. The roads were fine threads binding the small scab-like towns, but tenuously; there seemed no real
connection between them. The sky above had broken clouds that
cast small shadows on the fields below, and he would watch the
solid outline of his plane, moving slowly across the farm land of
Ohio. Behind, on the smoky horizon there was Cleveland, and beyond it the now invisible lake that he had crossed from Detroit,
its many wide islands that could have been stepping-stones or emergency landing fields if necessary.

As always, he was impressed by the total absence of a sensation of speed; by the timeless suspension in which he hung; waiting as it were for the earth to roll slowly beneath him and the airport to appear finally beneath the nose of the ship, as if by magic.
People who did not fly thought of flying as an activity of immense
excitement; he knew better. It was an extension of the human ego;
he could find no words to express this thought, though occasionally he could visualize it for himself by the image of his helmeted

head and goggled eyes, looking casually over the side of the cockpit at the human earth so far below. When you flew, you left the earth behind, and though you never left it for very long, it was long gone, remote; its problems and the problems of the unseen people who lived in the infinitesimal houses that lay below did not vanish, but like the man soaring on his wings, hung suspended for the moment, waiting to reassume their respective urgencies. It was difficult, but not impossible, to think that only that morning he had been worried by the imminence of hunger; the small purse he had won at the local air race in Detroit would be gone almost before he landed in Pennsylvania to make the visit that he contemplated. Three years now! It did not seem quite possible.

In those three years so many things had happened; and so many things in the years before. But never during those long years had he been more than a few short hours away from that small town in Pennsylvania, a few hours by air. So many things are possible for the airman; time contracts as well as space, and he wondered again why he had postponed the visit for so long. For many times, flying east or west to participate in the races that provided his meager living, he had passed over the house; it was there far below him, and he had wondered, Do they know that this is me? Do they hear the propeller hum so many thousand feet above them, and do they think, I wonder where he is and what he's doing? Does the kid say, Mom, there's an airplane, is it Pop? He could not think that *she* could hear an airplane without remembering those days, those few short years when —

He listened carefully to the engine; he looked over the nose at the pushrods, dancing their endless jig; the oil pressure was all right; the temperature; the r.p.m. He gently goosed the throttle with his left hand, watched the instruments, saw the pressure rise and sink, the tachometer needle move gently and then return to 1800. It was all right . . . So many things had happened. (The kid would be six.)

"Sam Falk," she'd said (so many times), "I want you to stop racing."

"I like to race," he'd said. It was a lie; he was afraid of it; he knew he was afraid of it, and that was one of the reasons he did it.

He could not stand to be afraid of anything. (Remember the machine gun!)

"I don't want you to race, Sam. I'm afraid."

"Nonsense," he said. "Flying's easier than walking."

"Not racing."

"I don't intend to stop," he said.

"Not for me — not for the baby?"

"Not for you; not for the baby. It's my job. I can do it; I can do it easy. It doesn't bother me."

"You've got thousands of hours," she said. "You're known all over." (I was better known then than I am now, he thought: Sam Falk, the famous racing pilot, the daredevil, the Man with Wings. Humph! he thought, fame!) "You could easily get a job with the airlines; it's safe; it pays well; we could have a home; you could be in it."

"I'm not a chauffeur," he said with derision, suppressing once again the information he could not give her, but that she must intuitively know. They never spoke of it; he was too old; he drank too much; the air was full of youngsters now, but a chauffeur! a truck driver! That was the rub, he thought; that was the point. A man must pit his strength against the living and the dead . . . so many were gone; so many dead, crashed and scattered to the winds, their blood spilled on the earth they'd thought to leave. They were gone, washed out, wrapped up, but they were still entries; he felt them with him in the ship; in the air that howled past the cockpit; in the screaming of the propellers; they called to him but he fled from them, whipping around the pylons with the field, feeling the centrifugal pull in the seat of his pants, in his guts. They were there all right and he could lick them as he'd licked them in the past. . . . Frank Alberts, who had crashed and burned in the Army primary flying school (have you ever turned a hose on the burning body of your friend?); Kate Allen, who had shed a wing in Akron back in '32, tried to jump while she was running out of altitude; Sam White, who had been decapitated . . . and he remembered the blind rage and the raging homicidal madness when the undertaker, hat in hand, said, "You were a friend of Mr Albert's; if you could persuade the family to throw the job my way, there'd be something in it for you"; when the crowd piled out of the stands and tore shreds from Kate's remaining wing; when the bald little man tried to steal the helmet and goggles from Sam's decapitated head . . . a souvenir!

"You're always fighting," she had said. (I'm going to see my kid!) "Every time you get drunk you pick a fight; you always fight with your boss every time you've had a private job; why must you always fight?"

"The bastards," he said. "The sons of bitches; they want a Roman carnival; they come to see the crashes; that's what they *want!* The more crashes the more money for the Racing Association."

"Why do you drink?"

"I don't drink when I fly."

"You drink when you're not flying."

"Damned right," he said. "I like to drink."

"If you touch another drop, Sam Falk, I'm going to divorce you." He walked deliberately to the cupboard and brought out the bottle, pouring the glass half-full. . . .

The ceiling was falling as he approached the first ridges of the Alleghenies, and he wondered if he would get over them in time. The old crate he'd rented couldn't do better than eighty-five at cruising speed, and he began to grow impatient. The ground rose under him, the wooded hills, and he smiled bitterly thinking that if he had a passenger along, he would have kicked the thing up to at least eight thousand feet, or better still, sat down and waited for the weather to improve. Now, as always, he knew he had no intention of gaining altitude, and less inclination to make a landing. He held the altimeter needle at five thousand, ample to clear the peaks on the course that he was following, but not really safe. Not if the ceiling kept on falling; not if the visibility became more limited. There was a light mist over the ragged mountains, there was lightning in those clouds ahead. He felt the ship heave and correct itself; he deliberately took his hands and feet off the controls, let it ride the air alone. He laughed. ("If you keep on drinking like this," she said, "you're bound to crack up." "The cemeteries are full of people who thought the world couldn't get along without them," he replied. "You'll crash, you crazy fool!" she said. "Can't you think of *anybody* but yourself? Can't you think of the baby?" Sure, he could and did. "I've been flying fifteen years," he said. "I'm more at home in the air than on the ground.")

Now he had to reassert control over the ship, and he took the stick in his hand, the rudder pedals under the balls of his feet, with a feeling of relaxation and assurance. The plane rolled and pitched like a small boat in rough water; the leather seat spanked him although the safety strap was pulled tight, and he was kicking rudder and hauling the stick around all the time. He glanced at the wings; they seemed sound enough; he listened to the wires, watched the instruments. The thunderhead was just in front of him, and he went for it, a smile on his face. There was something in him that made him head straight for a storm area when he saw one, and now the small plane entered the cloud and trembled as though it were being beaten. The air caught and lifted it; the altimeter said 6000, 6150, 6300, 6550. Then there was a strong downdraft and he hauled the stick back into his lap, cracked the throttle wide open, fighting instinctively for altitude. There was nothing to see; the damp mist wet his face, streamed over the lenses of his goggles, and he couldn't see the nose of his ship, watch the pushrods jumping on the cylinders. The pressure gauge said that everything was all right; the r.p.m.'s were steady at 1850, so he relaxed and fought the ship, struggling against the involuntary slips and skids, the pitching and the tossing. The wires groaned and he laughed out loud. (I'm going to see my kid!) There was noise now; the lightning in the cloud crackled and blinded him and he couldn't hear the groaning propeller any more. He thought, This would be a hot joke on me, all right, and he felt lonely as he had so many times before. Automatically, his hands and feet corrected for the more violent maneuvers of the plane, and his mind kept going back and forth over time and the earth, picking up memory and sensation at random.

Sure, you remember the machine gun. Sure, you remember the old man saying, "Sam Falk, you're a mighty uppity youngster and I'm going to tar the living daylights out of you." He was almost as big as his old man then, and surely (he thought) as strong, but the old man sailed into him and larruped him within an inch of his life. And so what did you do? he thought; you lit out that night and said to yourself, I'll *show* the old bastard that he can't do a thing like that to me. I'll show them all; I'll *be* somebody; I'll be a big shot, rake in the coconuts, shake down the shekels. He put himself through college and he boxed at county fairs and walked the slack rope. He walked wings when barnstorming pilots came around, made parachute jumps and joined the Army Air Corps. They busted him out, long after he had graduated, for insubordination; there was rebellion in him always, and he joined an unofficial war in South America and was assigned to a machine gun. You didn't know what it was all about, he thought; you were still wet behind the ears. You hated what they were doing with airplanes, and you still hate it, and you go to a war and work a gun and that's all right too. It's all right when they're coming at you, but when they started to run he took his finger off the trigger. "Work the gun," the officer said, and he said, "I'll shoot men down when they're attacking me, but I'm damned if I'll shoot them down when they're running." The officer pointed the pistol at him and said, "Work that gun." He did. That was one for the books all right; that was something to remember when you were drunk and disorderly in a bar and couldn't stop yourself from talking to strangers, saying, Ever hear of a racing pilot? Sure. Ever hear of Sam Falk who won the International Derby back in '33? No. That's me, you'd say and you couldn't stand the look on their faces, the look of amused pity. So you said, Bottoms up, the answer is Nerts and you left a five-dollar bill on the bar and walked out. That was long ago, or was it? But when you were in the air you didn't have to think of that; you could look down; they can't get at you from there. . . .

But if she'd been alone she wouldn't have done it, he thought. If it hadn't been for her mother, she never would have done it. She thought you were a bum. You'll never make a decent living for your wife or for your child, she said. Racing around the country in an airplane. Trying to kill yourself. Drinking like a fish; if you *have* to race airplanes can't you at least stay sober? "I can fly anything, drunk or sober," he said. "I could fly a barn door if you'd rig a motor onto it," he said. So she did it (she was so goddam beautiful, he thought; she is so goddam beautiful and I loved her, love her) but she did it, and between the two of them they fixed it up; they got the kid because he was unfit to care for it and the kid was all that mattered. A father who drinks; a father who won't make a decent living for his child, refuses the sort of life that would make it possible, a bum, a has-been, a crazy fool who plays with airplanes like a baby with its doll. And what the hell did they know anyhow? Did they know he was putting money in the bank for the kid, where they could never touch it? What the hell did they know of the loneliness and the isolation and the altitude, the heights and the silence except for the propeller whose noise was part of the silence anyhow? How did they know what was inside a man? What did they know of the good guys and the gals who were gone, washed out, wrapped up, scattered, and when you heard about it, you said, "Too bad." What else is there to say?

He was out of the storm now, he had licked it, coming out high from the soaring clouds, but the layer of fog was still below him, with only an occasional rift by which to hunt for landmarks. That would have been a hot joke on me, he thought, remembering that he didn't have a parachute. ("Don't like the things," he'd say.) But he searched for holes now; he was over the worst of the Alleghenies where so many good guys had piled up in the old days, and he kept an eye peeled on the fog below. Despite the fumes of gasoline that always drift about an airplane, he reached for a cigarette and lit it under cover of the windshield, and sat back in his seat. He smiled. Maybe they would know, he thought, if they were here; maybe all of them would know. He took the cigarette out of his mouth and said aloud," I'm going to see my kid!" With the fog below and heavy clouds above, he hung suspended in utter space; now there was not even the sensation of movement, unless he put his hand into the slipstream, felt the rushing air. He was sitting there, gently rocked from time to time, waiting for that moment that would come, he would know when; when something inside would tell him, You are there! It never failed. "I'm going to see my kid," he said, feeling the cigarette waggle between his lips, thinking, He won't know me after all this time, or will he?

Maybe I won't manage it this time, he thought, but there was a hole in the fog layer and he dropped through it, looked around swiftly and smiled again. There below him and slightly to the left lay the river with the little island in it, the airport on the island. It made him feel good, and he remembered the other times when he had flown the soup for hours on end, felt the time had come and eased down through it to hit his destination square on the nose. It was like being a bird, he thought. He opened the throttle, pulled up and snapped it shut, kicked rudder and spun twice to the left, pulled out and spun twice to the right, pulled out. He felt like horsing the old junk around; he was feeling his oats. Christ, he thought, that kid will be surprised to see me! He was over the river now, and idling the motor, he described a lazy seven-twenty, dropped onto the tiny airport as onto a dime, dug in his tail skid first (a habit from flying ships that landed hot) and taxied up to the wooden hangar. There was a youngster there, managing the place.

"Gas it up, brother," he said. "Check the oil and tires. I'll be pulling out tonight or tomorrow."

"Where you from?" the young fellow asked. "My name's Vesey."

"Out West."

"Say, you're Sam Falk, ain't you?" the kid said. "I seen your picture. Won the Special out at Detroit yesterday."

"Always the same," Sam said, smiling. "Never change." He saw the car and said, "I'd like to rent your jaloppy for a few hours, brother; I'll leave this old crate in hock for it."

The boy smiled and said, "That's a fair bargain; your ship's worth more than that old T-model. I'll take good care of it, Mr. Falk," he said. "Was it tough going out there — hot competition?"

"Like rolling off a log," said Sam, climbing into the old car.

"Happy landings," the kid said and waved his hand, then turned to look at the airplane with a smile. He touched it gently.

Why tonight? Sam thought; why tomorrow? Tomorrow is another day; it's been a long time; three years *is* a long time. May-

be it's all changed; I'm on the make again. Small-time stuff in Detroit, but there's better stuff coming up in a month or so, and with
the showing I made with that old crock I'll easy find a sponsor.
Time flies, he thought, as the old car chugged along the rutted
road, the springs squeaking. You cannot; their flight is too irregular. Time flies and lots of water has flowed under lots of bridges.
God. She was so goddam beautiful, he thought, three years ago.

He deliberately parked the Model-T at the outskirts of the little town, started to walk. He wiped his shoes on the back of his
trouser leg, straightened his clothes, took the cap out of his pocket. He took the cap off and wiped his face with his handkerchief,
put the handkerchief back in his pocket and then started to walk
more slowly. The house was near at hand.

There was a neat white picket fence around it, and there were
flowers growing in little regular plots in the yard. It's a good thing
her folks got a little money, he thought; they'd have had tough going with me all this time. He felt somewhat bitter about that; security, he thought, humph! Women and children first. He saw the
boy and started to walk more slowly, almost on tiptoe. His throat
was dry and he wished he'd had the sense to take a drink of water
at the hangar. He cleared his throat and leaned over the picket
fence, watching the small boy playing on the grass. The boy had
a toy airplane in his hand, and his mouth was going "Brr-r-r-r!"
He lifted the toy plane off the grass, whirled his arm about his
head and let the plane down to the ground.

"You leveled off too high that time," Sam said, his face cracking with a smile. The boy hadn't heard him, so he cleared his
throat and said, "Hello, little boy."

The child turned to look at him, still squatting on the grass,
and Sam was startled to see himself repeated so minutely in the
small round face. There was the same towhead, the same deep
grave eyes, the same shaped face.

"Hello," the boy said and turned back to his toy.

"You got a lot of airplanes, son?" Sam said.

The boy looked at him again, and then stood up, he looked
back at the shingled house, then took one timid step toward the
man at the fence. He was painfully shy, Sam noticed, and bit his

lip, remembering. The boy looked at him again and said, "Seven."

"Seven!" Sam said. "You gonna operate a fleet?"

"What?" said the child, coming closer.

"What you gonna be when you grow up, son?" His hands at his sides, his grave eyes on the man, the boy said,

"A naviator, like my Dad."

Sam swallowed, cleared his throat, said, "Where's *he?*"

"I don't know," the child said. "He's dead." The boy fell silent, looked back at the house, and Sam saw the old woman standing there. There was a scowl on her face; she knows me, Sam thought. She would.

"Samuel," the woman said. "Come in."

"Aw," said the boy, "I'm busy, Gram."

"You come right in the house this minute, Samuel." The boy looked back at the man as he walked; Sam noticed he had left the toy airplane on the lawn. He watched the boy. The old woman took the child's arm and shook it gently.

He heard her say, "I've *told* you not to talk to strangers," before she slammed the screen door on them both.

"I —" Sam said and shut his mouth.

He felt his face and neck grow hot, spun on his heel, turned back and glared at the house. He saw himself walking up the path, opening the door, shouting at the top of his lungs. He clenched his fists; then put one hand on top of the picket fence and vaulted it. He stood there, helpless, strapped and bound and put one hand into his pocket. He withdrew his hand and looked at the crumpled five-dollar bill, started to put it in his pocket and then bent and stuffed it into the toy plane. Samuel! he thought, Christ alive. Where's his goddam mother? he thought; what's she up to? where's she gone? He vaulted the fence onto the pavement, strode rapidly away, his throat working. The Model-T wouldn't start on the magneto, so he had to crank it, and he ran crazily back to the airport, piled out and hopped into the ship.

"Gimme a hand with this prop," he said. And when the boy said, "Back so soon, Mr. Falk?" he answered, "Never stay long in one place. Switch off."

"Switch off."

"Switch off," Sam repeated.

"Contact!" the youngster said.

"Contact!" Sam said, and Vesey took the blade in both hands, balanced on one foot, swung the other leg forward and hauled down with both hands. The blade spun, slowed, the motor caught, coughed and roared. He glanced at the pressure, the temperature came up rapidly. He nodded his head and Vesey walked the wing around. Then he jammed the throttle wide open and running crosswind he yanked the ship viciously off the ground, climbed it almost past the stalling point. The prop groaned, the plane vibrated, but he piled the stuff to it and it climbed steadily. He didn't look down or level off, his hands and feet were rigid on the controls. Then he started a steep climbing spiral, seeing the land fall away, the river narrow under him, the low hills flatten gradually till they looked like gentle billows in a mild sea. The earth was growing shadowed with the rising dusk. He climbed till he was at eight thousand feet and the sun was bright on his wings; then he circled, banked. He wondered which way to go; it didn't seem to make much difference. He bent an eye down at the town, saw the house plain as day, saw himself diving at it, wide open, the propeller screaming the way it had in practice combat maneuvers back in the old days. He saw himself diving, zooming over the house, pulling up, stalling it, rolling it, snapping it around, spinning. I'll show you, he thought; I'll *show* you who I am and what I can do. I'll scare the living daylights out of you!

There was no place to go and he was lonesome. He throttled down and listened; the wind hummed gently through the flying wires and the air was full of life; he could almost soar the plane. He relaxed in the seat, gently drawing the stick toward him, feeling the ship mush down slowly, feeling the emptiness and the space and the separation soak into his body once again. It was a long way down, and were they watching? Did the kid say, Look, Mom, there's an airplane? *He'll* show them, he thought; they can't tie *him* the way they tried with me. And he smiled. I'd like to see that kid's face, he thought, when he finds that five-spot tucked in his toy ship.

He smiled gently, pushed the throttle forward and winging over, headed for the West.

Call It Love

THE bags were heavy and the late afternoon sun beat upon the street. He could feel the sweat running down his neck, feel the weight of the sun on his back and shoulders, the heat on his face, reflected from the pavement. He shifted the bags, aware that he was tired and uncomfortable, that the bags were a burden he would gladly have tossed aside. It would have been more pleasant (pleasant!) to have taken a cab, but there would have been no address to give the driver.

On Seventh Avenue and 29th he saw a sign – *Furnished Rooms,* set the bags down, wiped his face and neck with his handkerchief and rang the bell. He stood at the bottom of the three steps that led to the door and looked back into the street, thinking is this where I will live? Will I come out of this doorway every morning on the way to work? Across the avenue a sign said *Elite Laundry* and another *Cafeteria.*

The door opened and a heavy woman with dirty eyeglasses said, "Yes?" in the everlasting hypocritical voice of landladies.

"Have you a single room?" he said.

"This way."

He set the bags inside the door and followed her heavy body up the dark stairs, smelling that smell again (after ten years), the smell of dust and used air and cheap cooking from the downstairs apartment. Without a word, they climbed two flights, the landlady breathing heavily, a slight odor of perspiration coming to him behind her on the stairs.

On the third floor she stepped into a narrow hallway, crossed a dark alcove into a space where two doors faced each other at a wide angle, and opened one.

"Now this is a very nice room," she said, turning at the door for him to walk in front. He took a step into the room and his heart sank, for there it was again: the small narrow room with the white enameled bed, the worn table and the worn chair, the dusty white curtains opening on an areaway — all that he had escaped so many years ago and so nearly forgotten. The ten years of marriage, in New York, in New Jersey, in Connecticut, were as a day, and the personality of those many rooms he had inhabited so many years ago returned to him. In their essentials they were all alike; in the very fact of their existence, they were unfit for human habitation: homes for the homeless, four walls for the lonely, shelter for the poor — sitting in shirtsleeves in the evening reading the newspaper, walking up and down over the worn scrap of carpet, leaning out the window, the ledge hard on your elbows.

For something to say that would conceal what he was feeling, he said, "How much?"

"Six dollars," the landlady said, and he turned and walked past her out the door, saying, "It's awfully small." He was embarrassed by her presence, by the intimation that perhaps she understood some of what he felt, that perhaps she thought him strange.

"I have a larger room," she said, "for eight."

His foot was on the stair; his hand was on the banister. He was overcome by a curious sense of helplessness, a frantic desire to escape from the place and not enter another place like it, an urge to go back home and say to her, "What the hell, Jane; let's call the whole thing off," and she would laugh, and they would hold each other and laugh like hell. He sighed with the relief of that expectation, almost as though he actually believed it could happen that way.

"No, thanks," he said.

"Don't you even want to *see* it?" the landlady said in a querulous voice. It was an effort for him to turn in his rapid flight down the stairs and say politely, "Thank you, no. I think I know where I'm going to stay." And the moment he said it he knew what an absurd thing it was to say.

On the street, the bags were heavy in his hands; there was a blister in one palm and he smiled, thinking how, during the three years they had lived in the country, in New Jersey, in Connecticut, his hands had been hard, calloused from the ax handle, the saw, from carrying the stone to build a garden walk. He knew as he walked that he could not take a furnished room, and he said to himself, "Look for a hotel," even though he knew it was more than he could afford, that a time was coming, not so distant now, when — why *now* it would be necessary to earn even more than he was earning, to support the kid, to support himself, to help till Jane could find work to do. This is ridiculous, he thought; this has not happened; in a day or so I'll go home, shove the bags through the door and say, Hi there, as though I were returning from a trip, and she will say, Hi there, stranger, and they would laugh and buy a bottle of Irish whiskey and get some ice cubes out of the Frigidaire and sit down and have a good laugh at themselves.

It had happened to others; perhaps it would even happen again. For you cannot tear out of your life the roots of ten years' living, ten years of living in the same rooms, the same houses, the same beds, thinking the same thoughts, worrying over the same bills, sharing the few small triumphs of a meager life. Ten years had put some gray hairs in her head; some wrinkles in his face. And the kid was five. He walked now, shifting the bags from hand to hand every three blocks; and he made a point of that — three blocks, no more, no less. It was a routine; it was something to do.

There was a hotel down the block, at Seventh and 19th, with a blue banner hanging on a flagpole from the second floor. *Rooms, With Bath, $1.50 and $2.00.* He was displeased by that banner; the mark of cheapness, sleaziness. A hotel that hung a banner out — it was a worn, converted apartment house; red brick with ornamentation and fire escapes on the avenue. The lobby was worn, the desk had an electrical sign that said *Room Clerk*, and there was an effeminate young man behind the desk, wearing a gray linen coat, his hair slicked down and parted in the middle.

"How much is a single room with bath?" he said, and the clerk said, "I can give you a very nice room for ten dollars on the eleventh floor. For one?"

He put the bags down and said, "For one. I'll take a look at it," and went up in the elevator with the porter. There was a husky young woman in a nurse's uniform in the elevator; her hair was bright and her cheeks were rouged.

"Afternoon, Miss Reilly," said the porter. "Nice afternoon."

"Too hot," Miss Reilly said, and got off on the ninth.

The elevator creaked and rattled and jarred from side to side as though it were loose in its tracks; it was slow. Down the carpeted hall the porter opened a room and drew a shade. There were warped French windows looking east over the city; there was a yellow bedspread on the double bed and a battered dresser with a red velvet throw. The walls were a faded yellow and cracked; the bathroom was dark, the equipment old and worn. He went downstairs and said, "I'll take it," and signed his name, John A. Field.

"I'm sorry, Mr. Field," the clerk said. "I quoted that room wrong to you. It's eleven dollars, not ten."

"Well," he said.

"I'm new here," the clerk said. "I'm sorry, sir," and suddenly Field was overcome with exhaustion. He said, "O.K.," and the porter took his bags and they were riding up again.

"That fellow's a fag," the porter said, turning from the lever that controlled the car. "He's a fag and he makes a lot of trouble around here."

Field wondered with faint interest what the clerk had done or did that made trouble, but all he said was "Is that so?" and they stopped short of the eleventh floor. The porter started the car again, stopped it a good foot and a half above the landing, then brought it down.

"That was a good guess," Field said with a smile, and the operator gave him a dirty look, picked up the bags, and took them to the room; he opened the windows, patted the bed, looked in the bathroom, and came out again and stood there.

"Can you send me up a drink?"

"We ain't got a bar," the porter said, "but I can git you a bottle."

"Make it a quart of Bushmill's Irish," he said, and gave the man the money. "And some ice."

The door closed and he threw the two bags on the bed, opened them and stood looking at them. Then, methodically, he brought out the things he had packed, trying not to think what he was doing, feeling all the time that any moment the phone would ring and she would say, "What the hell, Jack, come on home and —" but how could she know where he was staying? He laughed and tugged at the dresser drawers. They stuck.

He took out the underwear and put it in the top right-hand drawer; he took the four books and laid them on the dresser top. He frowned to see that the shirts were wrinkled and shook them, laid them in the second drawer, took out the toilet articles and brought them into the bathroom, stowed them in the cabinet. There was a small hook in the doorway on which he hung the razor strop.

In the pocket of the grip there was a snapshot of the kid, and he found the four thumbtacks he'd put in the bag and tacked the snapshot on the wall, next to the mirror in the dresser. He looked at the kid squatting there in her short dress, grinning at the camera, the kitten squirming in her hands. He winked at it and said, "Hi, there," then turned on his heel and opened the larger bag, the Gladstone, took out the two light suits and shook them out, hung them in the closet. There was a pair of slippers, and he stood them side by side under the bed; then he sat on the bed and took off his shoes, slipped his feet into the slippers. The armchair was fairly comfortable; he sat in it and lit a cigarette, frowned at the ashtray, which was pink, and made a mental note to buy another.

The elevator man knocked on the door with a bottle wrapped in paper and a pitcher of cracked ice. "Thanks," Field said, tipped him, and waited for the man to go before he poured.

"Frankly," she had said, "there's no point in going on; don't you think so? Why not call the whole thing off?" It was all very friendly, very amicable.

"I'm satisfied," he had said. "There's nothing more I want," but as he said it, he had cursed himself for a coward, determined to speak, then held his tongue.

She had looked at him with her kindest smile, and it didn't matter whether she said anything more or not, because he knew that she had spoken the truth and was still speaking it. It was a washout; it was a bore; it was no good to make a pretense of living in the same old way, the two of them going opposite directions, meeting politely for dinner, politely between the sheets on rare occasions. Call it love or call it habit; he knew, sitting there before her, that there was no way of getting along without her, but the sense of cowardice still remained. Don't you know whether you love the woman? he said to himself; after ten years, can't you tell whether you want a wife or a housekeeper? There was some relief in the idea of going away for good, and there was something else again.

"This is not a moving picture," he had said.

She smiled and lifted her hands, then shrugged her shoulders.

"Call it anything you like," she said. "It's been dead a long time now; we can't bring it back to life again."

Then he knew that he would have to go, and in order to go he had to play a trick on himself. He gripped the arms of the chair and shouted, "Damn it all, you talk like a melodrama! I'll *go!*"

He rose and dashed for the bedroom, dragged out the bags and hastily packed them, aware that she was standing behind him in the room, watching him with those wide, deep eyes, that firm, sad mouth. She spoke.

"You don't have to go right now," she said. (It was ten o'clock at night.) "You might as well stay and think it over. Where will you go tonight?"

"To a hotel," he said viciously; then sadly, "I'll look for another place after work tomorrow."

"Take it easy, brother," she said, but he jammed the suitcase shut and flung into his raincoat and started for the door.

"Have a nice time," he said, and saw her turn away. Then he was gone.

The whiskey was moving in his body and it was growing dark over the city. He had called from the office that day; his voice dry and meticulous. He said he would come over to see the kid regularly, to bring money, and she had said to come whenever he wanted to, come for dinner any time you're feeling low. I'll let you know where I am, he said.

He went to the window and looked down the eleven stories to the street; the cars had switched on their lights, and over the city was the low continuous murmur that may be heard all day and night if you are listening. In how many rooms, in how many windows, behind how many doors? he thought, and stared back into the darkened room. He moved into and around it drunkenly; he stumbled a couple of times, aware that he was behaving as though he were actually drunk. Into the darkened room he said aloud, "Is there anything genuine about you, Mr. Field?" He lifted the house phone, called her number, and before she answered, hung it up again. He could imagine her wondering who it was, whether it was he, what had possessed him to hang up. He took another drink.

The loneliness in him coiled and congealed; the emptiness ached. He picked up the phone again and said to the clerk, "Connect me with Miss Reilly." The receiver wobbled in his hand, and he put his lips closer to the mouthpiece, swallowed once or twice, thinking. You can't do it; you never did it in your life, but you've wanted to do it in your life, but you've never done it. Come speak to me, come talk to me, come be with me.

"Hello," the voice said pleasantly, and he swallowed.

"Miss Reilly," he said, "how are you?"

"I'm fine," she said.

"That's good," he said. "That's very good, You don't know me."

"What?"

"I said you don't know me, but I'm the gent in 1107."

"Oh?" she said.

"Are you Irish?"

"Yes."

"Well, I'm not Irish, but I have some Irish whiskey, and I thought seeing as how you were Irish you might like to come up here and have a drink of Irish whiskey with me."

"I'm not dressed yet," she said.

"Take your time," he said. "Take all the time you want, but I think it would be nice if you came up here and had a drink of Irish whiskey. This is not a moving picture."

"All rightie," said the voice. And he said, "See you later."

"All rightie," the voice said, and he sat there, another drink in his hand, gulping it fast and swishing the ice around in the glass.

Now what is going to happen? he thought, and what is going to happen? And could you do a thing like that if you were in love with your wife and so forth? He lit the floor lamp and straightened up the room with exaggerated care, brushing at the ashes he had spilled on the carpet. He went into the bathroom and washed his hands and face and combed his hair, and wondered how it would happen when it began to happen, and what it would be like.

"Miss Reilly," he said into the mirror, "are you lonely, Miss Reilly; please, Miss Reilly, don't be lonely; you are not alone in the world and there are a lot of people in the world who are lonely too and they are not alone in the world either."

Then he sat in the armchair again, feeling slightly dizzy with expectation and something that approached happiness. He listened carefully for a knock on the door. It was silent in the carpeted hall-way outside, but he could hear the elevator running, clanking and wheezing on its tracks, but it did not stop at his floor. He lit a cig-arette, and then opened the window so the room would not be smoky when she came; he started to pour a drink, but poured it back into the bottle so he would be in full possession of his senses. He thought of Miss Reilly as he had seen her that once in the ele-vator, sweet in her cleanliness and dazzling in her white starched uniform, and he wondered if she would still be wearing it; it looked so antiseptic, so healthy. You would never know, he thought, looking at a person's face, smiling, radiant, that inside they were all alone and waiting in a room for the telephone to ring, and that must be the reason she said all rightie.

He became aware that he was tapping with his foot, and he consciously stopped tapping. Behind how many doors, waiting? In how many darkened rooms? You must not lose touch, he thought; you must keep contact; and even if that was the end, this might well be the beginning, or if not the beginning, *a* beginning, a reestablishment of contact, the first painful knitting of the wound.

His toe was tapping all by itself, so he picked up the telephone again and said, "Connect me with Miss Reilly." It was some time before she answered, and then he said, "I thought you were coming up to have a drink of Irish whiskey with me, Miss Reilly."

"Who is this anyhow?" she said.

"My name is Field and I'm in 1107, and I thought you'd like —"

"Oh," she said, "I'm so sorry. I thought you were my friend who's waiting downstairs for me."

"Who?"

"I'm going out," she said. "My friend is waiting downstairs."

"O.K.," he said. "Think nothing of it."

"I'm sorry," she said.

"Think nothing of it," he said, and hung up. You must not be afraid of me, he thought; I would not harm you for the world. He moved to the door and went into the hall, rang the elevator bell. I'll go right down there, he thought, and bang on the door. I'll hammer on it till she opens it.

The car came and he went down. At the ninth floor the car stopped again and Miss Reilly got in, wearing a metallic blue satin dress and a red fox fur, and looking nothing like a nurse. She glanced at him, but said nothing, and he said nothing, standing in the back of the car. She doesn't know I — he thought; she doesn't know it's me.

At the ground floor she was met by a tall, broad-shouldered young man, wearing a light tan jacket, who took off his hat and kissed her on the mouth. It was surprising how little she looked like a nurse, now that she had changed her clothes. She took the young man's arm and walked out of the lobby with him, laughing.

"That good whiskey, boss?" the porter said, grinning at him.

"The best," he said.

The Serpent Was More Subtil

A Novella

To the memory of
Ben Tabenhouse

Susan Aldridge, *Requiescat*

I used to spend a good deal of time hanging around the Natural History Museum before it was discovered that I did not have a scientific mind. It was R. Maple Foss who made this finding when I was seventeen years old, and it was this discovery that turned me from natural science to literature.

Dr. R. Maple Foss was curator of herpetology at the Museum. He was well over six feet tall, looked more like a Yale stroke oar than a scientist and had a nervous giggle quite incompatible with his stature and bearing. I held him — giggle and all — in the most extreme awe.

Foss, as curator, had been preceded in the job by Susan Anthony Aldridge, and from the time I was fourteen years old her monograph on the *Batrachia of North America* had been in my library. It was a standard work, comparable in its field to Edward Drinker Cope's monumental study of North American *reptilia*. (*Batrachia*, the phylum name for frogs and toads.)

Miss Aldridge had left the Museum only three years before I made my inauspicious appearance there, and if I had not had considerable admiration for the lady, I would have acquired it at the Museum. There were classic stories of her indefatigable devotion to her work. She rarely left the place. It was told how, when the staff of the Museum had gone home for the night, Miss Aldridge continued her labors, sometimes in her office but more often in the basement where the study collection of her department was housed. In the morning she was frequently found asleep — having worked the clock around among the *batrachia*, the *reptilia* and the salamanders.

Of course, I did not think of my activities at the Museum as "hanging around." I was extremely serious about science and had been so since first looking into a heavy book on astronomy at the age of nine. (But since I never could master even elementary arithmetic, astronomy was obviously out of the question.)

My duties as apprentice (unpaid) herpetologist at the Natural History Museum were never distinctly defined. After classes at high school (and later at college) I appeared in the three tiny rooms occupied by the department on the top floor of the old granite building where I invariably found Dr. Foss gazing enraptured through a microscope at the *gastrocnemius* muscle of some species of *Hyla* (tree frog) or counting the ventral scales on any one of several thousand preserved specimens of *Thamnophis* (garter snake).

Since I was a volunteer I was not obliged to do anything except observe and learn. Occasionally I washed jars and bottles (until I dropped and smashed an enormous aquarium), dusted shelves and arranged study specimens of *Bufo fowleri* (one of Dr. Foss' favorite beasts, commonly called Fowler's toad). I dusted books and arranged them alphabetically and I asked questions that occasionally got answered.

R. Maple Foss held out to me the hope that I might at some time in the indefinite future receive an appointment in his department, though I doubt if I could have sustained a cause at law on the basis of his promises. Everything was contingent on my manifesting, in some substantial manner, what Dr. Foss lovingly called "the scientific mind." He did indicate that I should enroll in every undergraduate and graduate course in college biology, zoology and physiology, and that I would find useful, if not indispensible, advanced courses in botany, chemistry (organic, inorganic and qualitative analysis) and (I shuddered) mathematics.

On one or two occasions I was set to tasks to test my scientific mettle and, most especially, my patience. I spent an entire week injecting formaldehyde into living specimens of *Chrysemys picta picta* (the painted turtle). The turtles promptly died, which was the purpose of the injection. (Some actually whistled when injected, which was somewhat disconcerting, and my reaction to this phenomenon no doubt could have been considered early evidence of the fact that I really did *not* have a scientific mind.)

I also counted – from one jar of formaldehyde into another – seven thousand eight hundred and twenty-six specimens of *Hyla crucifer* (the spring peeper) which Dr. Foss had collected in the Hackensack Meadows with the use of a jacklight. This was, no doubt, unsporting of him, but it is the only way you can see the beasts, let alone catch them. I carefully – and scientifically – wrote this number on a square of white paper and deposited it on Dr. Foss' desk thus: *Hyla crucifer*, 4,512 ♂ (male), 3,314 ♀ (female), plus the date and place of collection.

On another occasion I was set to work for one full month, every afternoon except Sundays – total time involved: twenty-six days times two hours a day, equals fifty-two hours – on the following problem:

In twenty-seven separate jars of formaldehyde there reposed the mortal remains of six hundred and seventy-five individual small snakes, which shall be nameless here. They had been in these jars a good long time and whatever coloration they may have had during their salad days had long since been bleached out. This fact, plus the fact that the jars were not labeled, made immediate, on-the-spot, at-a-glance identification of the beasts impossible. My scientific problem, said Dr. Foss, was to identify them.

Now, this is the procedure: you provide yourself with a metal pan, a pair of tweezers (if you are squeamish), a pencil-like stylus in the end of which is inserted a long, sharp pin, and a magnifying glass. Also indispensible are a pad of paper (large), a pencil (sharp), a ruler and an ability to count.

You then count. Snakes (among other *reptilia*) are identified and classified by reference to their scalation. You must therefore count all the ventral plates (on the belly), the smaller plates (sometimes a single row, sometimes double) to be found to the aft of the *cloaca*. You number each specimen as you examine it, then you jot down the various data under the appropriately itemized categories: ventral plates, 101; caudal plates (2 rows), 11-12.

Then you turn the beast over and, using the pin in order not to lose your place, you count again, jotting down the following items: dorsal scales, so many rows, so many scales in each row; then, on the head, the number of frontal plates, parietal plates, occipital plates; then, on the lips, so many supralabials, so many infralabials. (If I have omitted any categories, put it down to loss of memory, the reason for which any competent psychoanalyst will tell you in ten seconds flat.)

I went through this procedure for a total of fifty-two hours and six hundred and seventy-five specimens. There were moments (each day) when I wished to hell I had never started the job, never wanted to be a herpetologist or any kind of scientist. It was *dull*. But there were also moments, at least once a week, when I experienced a tiny thrill, a rosy glow. Not only would I identify this particular beast (whose name Dr. Foss no doubt knew), but I would demonstrate to the good Curator (who lived on inherited income) that I was worthy to be appointed to his staff when I came of age, and to receive the opulent emolument that went with so august a position. ($1,200 a year at that time.) I would demonstrate that I had the dedication of Susan Aldridge who, in the last year of her curatorship, was said never to have left the Museum at all. I would prove that I had "a scientific mind," which was something I was beginning to doubt myself. (Certainly I did not have a scientific back or eyes – they ached.)

Swimming out of a fog of formaldehyde fumes, headache, eyestrain and backache, having popped all the beasts back into their respective jars, I then examined the long tables of figures I had evolved and made a breakdown. This involved averaging all the figures down to a set that could be readily examined and which stated, in effect, that . . . . (unknown ophidian) had so and so many ventral plates, dorsal scales, infra- and supralabials, etc., etc., *ad nauseam*. You were then ready for the final step.

The final step involved "running down" the key to the North American snakes (*that* much, that it *was* North American, Dr. Foss had told me). The author of this magnificently cogent digest was none other than – R. Maple Foss. And it was no trouble at all to discover, by examining the various scalation patterns, that my six

hundred and seventy-five little beasts were, manifestly and indis-
putably, *Diadophis regalis*, 342 ♂ (male), 333 ♀ (female), habitat
Arizona.   This information I wrote down, most scientifically, on
a square of white paper, and marching into R. Maple Foss' office,
I presented it to him with an appropriate flourish.

He looked up from a paper he was writing for *Copeia* (the
monthly publication of what must have been, I suppose, the Society of American Herpetologists) and said, "What's this?"

"The beast," I said. (Beast was Foss' favorite word for his little charges, whatever their size.)

"What beast?" he asked. He had forgotten. After all, a month
had passed since he had set me to this problem and no doubt, as
he had not seen me in that length of time, he had forgotten the
problem, if not the youth he had set to it.

"The one you asked me to identify," I said with a broad smile
and the inner glow of having done a hard job well. In time, I was
certain, I would make my own contribution to human knowledge
in the field of herpetology (like Foss and Susan Aldridge), perhaps
even write a paper for *Copeia* (named after Edward Drinker Cope,
of course).

"Oh," he said. He cleared his throat. Then he said, "No."

"What do you mean — no?" (I guess that's what I said.)

"I *knew* you'd come out with that," he said, and he giggled.
"You'll have to do it over."

"Oh, no," I said, less in refusal than amazement.

"To be a scientist," he said, "one must work slowly, patiently
and — accurately. Obviously, you've slipped up somewhere. The
beast does come from Arizona, but it is definitely not *Diadophis
regalis*. It is not even related to *Diadophis*. Slow, patient, accurate
work makes the scientist," he said. "There's no glamor in it."

I got the point. I was stunned. It was this episode (and my ultimate refusal to rework the problem) that was the immediate cause
of Dr. Foss' discovery that I did not have a scientific mind. (There
were other causes, as well, but they probably have no place in this
particular story.)

Actually, however, the interlude with the Arizonian beasts was
merely a hiatus in my regular job at the Museum. Perhaps this par-

ticular job was also designed to develop in me that indispensible scientific attribute (patience) in which I found myself manifestly lacking during my month-long examination of the beast that remains nameless to this day. It was this:

O ne of the glories of the Museum and particularly of its department of herpetology, was the study collection that had been established by Susan Aldridge during the twenty-odd years of her tenure as curator. This collection comprised over nine thousand jars of alcohol and formalin in which swam several thousand preserved specimens of frogs, toads, salamanders, snakes, lizards, turtles, etc.

The collection was housed in the basement of the Museum, on endless steel shelves that ran from floor to ceiling for half a city block. The staff of the department used this collection in its long-range work and visiting herpetologists from as far away as Tokyo and Cairo (in opposite directions) made regular pilgrimages to utilize the material it provided. If it was the glory of the department, it was even more especially the glory of Susan Anthony Aldridge, who spent the last year of her tenure at the Museum in nightly research among those nine thousand jars.

During the three years I devoted all my after-high-school-and-college hours to the Museum, I spent at least one hour a day in the basement helping Mr. Pildyke (Dr. Foss' assistant) to stick new labels on those thousands of jars. He provided me with endless lists of nomenclature, which I typed neatly on a portable machine, including all the relevant data: name, date collected, place collected, donor, number of specimens in each jar, and their sex. A typical label read as follows: *Pipa americana* (British Guiana, July 4, 1909, Snr. Teopisto Colón, 24 ♂ , 16 ♀ . (This is, of course, the fabulous Surinam toad which lays its eggs on its own back and hatches them out of tiny pockets in the skin.)

To demonstrate, once and for all time, exactly *how* unscientific my mind was, it took me all of two years before I got around to asking why all these labels were being replaced. I assumed at first (a normal supposition) that many labels had faded; many others had been spoiled by spilled formaldehyde, or had been damaged or torn by handling. This was partly true.

But actually this was not the reason for replacing these labels. For, after two years of typing, I discovered, quite by accident, for example, that a jar containing fifty pale and ghostlike serpents labelled *Boa constrictor* (young), etc., was being relabelled *Eunectes murinus* (young), etc.

"How come?" I asked inelegantly and Mr. Pildyke smiled in a crooked sort of way. I must admit at this point that I was somewhat jealous of Mr. Pildyke; for he was a *bona fide* herpetologist, actually on the staff of the Museum, actually earning $1,200 a year and bound to greater glory in the days to come as assistant curator of herpetology at the Field Museum in Chicago.

Mr. Pildyke relished my jealousy and he adopted various condescending attitudes toward me. At this particular moment he said, "Obviously, because it's not *Boa constrictor*. It's *Eunectes*."

I suppose a young man with a scientific mind (even in embryo) would have asked the next question: "Then why were they labelled *Boa*?" I didn't. I don't know why I didn't. Perhaps I was intimidated by Mr. Pildyke's eminence as a genuine, dyed-in-the-formaldehyde herpetologist; A.B., A.M., Sc.D., Ph.D. (I was only a college freshman.)

So I returned to my typing, but when Mr. Pildyke went upstairs I made a further, appalling discovery. Along one entire shelf he had laid out twenty-five of my newly retyped labels, preparatory to soaking the old ones off and affixing the new. Simple comparison of the new with the old revealed (to use scientific jargon) that *in every instance the jars were being relabelled with different generic and species names!* I could not understand this at all.

I was silent as Mr. Pildyke reappeared. But the same analyst who could tell you (in ten seconds flat) why I have forgotten so much about the scalation of *Ophidia*, could also tell you that the unconscious mind works in obvious ways its wonders to perform. For I suddenly heard myself say, "Whatever became of Miss Aldridge?"

There was a long silence before Mr. Pildyke replied. Then he said, quite simply, "She retired." I suppose I should have accepted that reasonable explanation. But perhaps it was the penultimate flicker of my feeble scientific mind (what there was of it) that now convinced me there was something mysterious about Miss Susan Anthony Aldridge.

I recalled the fact that she was rarely, if ever, mentioned in the department — except in the most generalized terms of approval for her great accomplishments — despite her twenty years as Curator of Herpetology. Dr. R. Maple Foss always giggled (nervously) when she was mentioned. No memento of her, such as a framed, autographed photograph, or even a discarded, nineteenth-century hairpin, existed in the department; nothing. She had sunk without a trace, and my mind (not the scientific vestige, surely) suddenly pictured her seated decorously and dressed in nineteenth-century costume, at the bottom of a vast jar of formaldehyde.

This image (possibly the first glimmering of my *literary* mind) determined me to seek out the answer to my question. I boldly asked R. Maple Foss. Again — a long, psychiatric silence. Again — the quietly spoken words, "She retired."

Perhaps she really had. Perhaps, after she retired, she simply died. Many people do. But the identical nature of the pause, the identical reply, staggered me. Could this be a conspiracy? Had the Doctors Foss and Pildyke quietly done away with Miss Aldridge and (no, no!) preserved her?

From this point on I became a considerable nuisance to the staff of the Natural History Museum. I asked everyone I knew about Miss Aldridge. I asked Dr. Pike, Curator of Ichthyology. He looked like a fish all right, but not a pike; a sturgeon (*Acipenser rubicundus, ♂*). Pause. "She retired." I asked Dr. Holmes, Curator of *Lepidoptera*. He did not look like a butterfly (or even a moth); he looked like a woodchuck (*Marmota monax ♂*) and he was a chainsmoker. Pause. "She retired." It *is* a conspiracy! I decided. This was something for the Homicide Squad!

At this point the last guttering of my scientific caution lit up my mind. I went to the morgue — of a newspaper — and looked up the yellowed clips that detailed the obscure life of Dr. Susan Anthony Aldridge, former Curator, etc. She *had* died, sure enough; and she was buried, decorously, in Woodlawn Cemetery. But behold! She had died in a private sanatorium, the Goldenglow Home. It took very little scientific research to determine that this innocuously named institution was a sanctuary for the insane.

I could have obviated this piece of research if I had only turned over a few more clippings before rushing out to find out what kind of a sanitorium was the Goldenglow. For when I came back to the clips, there it was, in less than a stick of type:

"Dr. Susan Anthony Aldridge, Curator of Reptiles and Amphibians at the Natural History Museum, was yesterday morning removed from that institution, under restraint. According to Leslie O'Brien, a night watchman, she had spent the night in the basement of the museum and —"

Leslie O'Brien was still the night watchman at the museum. I knew him well. He must have been over eighty years old and perhaps he too had been injected with formaldehyde by some earlier embryo herpetologist, for he was remarkably well preserved and he looked not at all unlike a *chelonian*; but not the painted turtle (*Chrysemys p. picta*); rather the box tortoise (*Terrapene carolina,♂)*.

He was also reluctant to talk. He said, "That's a skillikin in our closet." He laughed. "We got lots of them," he said. "We don't talk about that at the Museum." I had gathered as much during my frustrated interrogation of Drs. Pildyke, Foss, Pike and Holmes. But if O'Brien resembed an ancient tortoise, he was still a sucker for a pint of Bushmill's. So I plied him with Bushmill's. And while it did not take much plying, I did not get many words out of him. But those few were enough.

Susan Anthony Aldridge, maiden lady of sixty-seven, had indeed been removed under restraint. In a straitjacket, in fact. For she had resisted removal, clinging wildly to the edges of steel shelving, chairs, tables, and other movable and immovable objects.

"My life work!" she had screamed. *"You're taking me away from my life work!"* They pried her loose and wrapped her in the whacky-sack. "Help!" she screamed. "Police! *My life work!* I'm reclassifying the collection," she shouted, one arm swinging wildly, indicating the nine thousand bottles on the half-a-city-block of shelves.

That was precisely what she was doing. For one solid year, the last year of her curatorship, she had spent every night in the basement, roaming up and down the study collection. Slowly, patiently, accurately, like a true scientist, she had been soaking the labels off the jars, one at a time, and then pasting them back on different jars whose pale floating specimens bore no relation to their new nomenclature, except that they *were* reptiles and/or amphibians. She had switched labels on over five thousand of the jars. Even more interesting, she had switched specimens, too, making certain that in every jar there were, for example, fifteen males (♂) and fifteen females (♀); or, as the case may be, four males and four females, eighty-one males and eighty-one females.

My mind was racing. I wondered if she had laughed fiendishly as she affixed a label announcing that *Ambystoma maculatum,* 94 ♂ , 22 ♀ (the spotted salamander) was really *Triturus viridescens* (the common newt), 58 ♂ , 58 ♀ . Did she rub and "wash" her hands as John Barrymore had done when he had metamorphosed from Dr. Jekyll into Mr. Hyde? Did she giggle (nervously) like R. Maple Foss? What made her *do* it? What had made her, after twenty years of bringing order out of chaos, reverse the field and try to scramble everything, except for the sedulous pairing of the sexes?

I asked O'Brien. He shrugged his shoulders and took another sip of Bushmill's. Then he rubbed his nose with the bowl of his pipe. "A wonderful lady she was," he said. "Lonely. Never married. Never had no kids." He paused, nodded his head. "Of course," he added. "How could she?"

He bowed his head; perhaps in prayer. I am not a praying man, myself, but I joined him in a silent prayer for the repose of Susan Aldridge (*Homo sapiens,* ♀). Nor did I remain much longer with the Museum. But that's another story.

The Snake Friend

Another story? True. But the story of my departure from the Natural History Museum at the advanced age of seventeen cannot be told until it is understood how I got there in the first place. A story, I was taught, must have a beginning, a middle and an end.

In the beginning was the family: my father Nathaniel Leonard, my mother Helen (née Schwarzkopf — a name whose translation haunted me in years to come, not to mention the coincidence that I ultimately consulted a psychiatrist with the same name), my older brother Adrian and me — Julian.

Father did and did not wear the pants. His marriage was a running battle, the muted sounds of which I often heard at night in the bedroom I shared with my brother (we also shared the bed).

There were voices — loud voices my parents tried vainly to modulate. The voices were followed by a sinister silence during which the scrape of a suitcase being hauled out of the closet was heard; then the banging of bureau drawers opening and closing, the sound of soft weeping (my mother's), the slamming of the apartment door.

After that I generally went to sleep, to be awakened near dawn by the sound of the door opening again, the suitcase being dropped on the bedroom floor, the muffled voices and the muffled weeping. This went on for years and decades later when I had occasion to remind my mother that she and my father never got along with each other, she looked at me in astonishment and said, "How could you have known? You were sound asleep."

That, too, is another story and is scarcely germane to this one. Or is it? But when I say my father Nathaniel wore the pants, I mean that he gave orders and we obeyed: my brother and I.

When I was six and my brother eleven he decided, for example, that Adrian would play the piano and I the violin. *I* wanted to play the piano. Adrian did not want to play anything. But for six years I studied the violin and played it badly and Adrian studied the piano and played it badly and our command performances in duet may have pleased our parents but they scarcely pleased their sons.

When we were approaching college my father decided that Adrian would be a doctor and I would be a lawyer. *He*, my father, had started his curious career as a lawyer, being graduated from the University of Michigan. He never hung up his shingle.

It is a family legend how, having married my mother and moved to Brooklyn, he applied for a job as a lawyer on Wall Street and was offered one – at $15 a week.

"Why," said my future father, "that won't pay for my carfare and lunches!"

"Where do you live?"

"In Brooklyn."

"Move closer to the office," he was told.

He didn't. Instead, he found a job with the American Tobacco Company and for about a year he roamed the New York countryside tacking up tin signs on barns with a long-handled magnetic hammer. He also sold soap.

Being of an inventive mind and having a first child on the way, he contrived a folding paper box that was waxed (to make it waterproof) and somehow he found the capital to have it manufactured. He manufactured it for years. He made a lot of money with it and my earliest schoolboy memories revolve around that waxed paper box in which my mother packed my lunch. (He also invented an "automatic" toilet, a prototype of which was actually installed in the Great Northern Hotel in New York City. It was supposed to flush when anyone urinated in it – chemical reaction – and our father claimed it would make him a millionaire, but only the pilot toilet was installed; I don't know why.)

When I was living in Vermont in the worst of The Depression, I entered a store in Manchester to buy a pound of butter — and was given it in my father's "butter-box."

"Where did you get this thing?" I asked the storekeeper, and he said, "Twenty years ago a smart Jew came into the store and sold me a million."

"A *million*!?"

"That's right," the storeman said. "I've still got a couple hundred thousand."

"That smart Jew," I said most undiplomatically, for in Vermont in 1935 Jews were alien creatures who wore black beards and lived in Boston (a neighbor's son assured me), "that smart Jew," I said, "was my father."

"*No!*" said the storekeeper, looking at me with added distaste (I owed him about $76 at the time).

I turned the box over and showed him the names on the back: *Leonard & Cohn.* New York. *Patent Pending.*

"Well, I be dog," he said.

My brother Adrian dutifully became a doctor but I did not become a lawyer. Our father died dramatically in 1921, of his first and only heart attack, when Adrian was in medical school and I was in college on Morningside Heights. He was only fifty-one.

The attack had been preceded by a painful spell of grastric ulcers which resulted in a frightful hemorrhage during which my brother held a basin and my father filled it, twice.

This was followed by an operation known as gastroenterostomy, during which the major portion of the stomach is removed and the esophagus is connected to what's left.

This was followed by my father's determination to become a millionaire, again. The folding-paper-box business was slowly folding, priced out of the market by automatic packaging of butter, lard and margarine.

Father was a stockbroker then — on the very same Wall Street that had offered to reward him so poorly for his LLB. He made small killings and he lost small sums. Then he began to make *real* money for he had met another smart Jew, a very young one who was married to a very rich girl, and who had taken a liking to my old man.

One day this young man advised my father to take everything he could beg, borrow or steal and buy cotton futures. "I promise you, Nate," he said, "that by the end of the week you'll be a millionaire."

This my father did, for every tip this young man had given him had paid off handsomely. He even tried to persuade his brother-in-law Art Cohn (the other half of Leonard & Cohn Patent Pending) to do the same, but Uncle Art was either too cagey or too cautious. (He *was* a cautious man. He was *so* cautious that he wore both suspenders and a belt and when he had a sniffle he went to bed and would not come to the office.)

My father was cautious enough, however, not to touch his insurance, of which he carried about thirty thousand dollars. But he withdrew his savings, liquidated his other stocks and bonds, and he borrowed money from his good friend Israel Collins, a fellow poker player who despite his name was Irish, was a two-fisted rye-whiskey drinker who — at every poker game — said he did not like Jews but he liked my father because "Nate is a white Jew." But Nate did not steal; it would have been against his nature.

On Tuesday of that week he had five hundred thousand dollars — on paper. On Thursday he had seven hundred and fifty thousand. On Friday the bottom fell out of cotton futures and Nathaniel Leonard was wiped out. On Saturday morning at three a.m. he awoke with violent pains in his chest that ran down his left arm to the tips of his fingers.

My brother the medical student listened to his chest with his brand-new stethoscope, then called our Uncle Sidney, the doctor, who arrived shortly after in his pajamas and an overcoat and gave his older brother an injection.

We sat and watched. Our father seemed slightly out of his head and started to talk. "The flower of our young manhood . . . the war killed off the flower of our young manhood," he said. Tears came into his eyes. He started to sing, "The old oaken bucket. . . . the iron-bound bucket . . . the moss-covered bucket . . . that hung in the well. . . ."

He resumed enough consciousness and presence of mind to notice my snickering and said, "You don't like my singing." I denied the allegation but he insisted. "You laughed at me. You don't like the way I sing. . . ." Then he turned to Uncle Sidney and said, "That injection's worn off. What was it, water? Give me another."

"Now, Nate," said our uncle, "it hasn't had a chance to work. Give it time."

My father closed his eyes. Then he opened them wide and took a deep breath. His mouth stayed open. We watched him and Uncle Sidney said, "Stop holding your breath, Nate. Let your breath out."

Dutifully, Nathaniel Leonard let out his breath and was still. Uncle Sidney sat looking at him for a few moments, then he applied his own stethoscope. He glanced at my brother and my brother got the signal and ran downstairs, returning almost immediately with a neighbor, Dr. Weidenbaum, in *his* pajamas.

Weidenbaum listened too, took the stethoscope from his ears and said, "I'm sorry. He's gone."

"But doctor," said our Uncle Sidney. "I just heard his heart beating."

"You heard your own heart," Dr. Weidenbaum replied.

N ot even the psychiatrist named Dr. Schwarzkopf was able to pinpoint the inception of my lifelong interest in natural science. He did agree with me that it could have had something to do with the fact that *I* wanted to be a doctor and my brother did not and my father had said, "No, Adrian will be the doctor."

It could have started much earlier because I felt my father had always favored Adrian against me and therefore I started to dislike my father and everything he believed in and to like everything of which he disapproved. I not only rejected him but I developed a schoolboy crush on my Uncle Sid.

Even in public school I used to visit Uncle Sid on Morningside Avenue every Saturday and Sunday and spend both days going on house calls with him. I just sat in the car and when he came out I asked about the patient and he told me what was wrong with him — or her. And how it was treated.

I absolutely adored my Uncle Sid, whose bedside manner was permanent and even extended to my endless questions and his tireless answers. When I was ten years old he talked to me as though I were a grown-up. He took seriously what I asked and answered seriously. He gave me leaflets, pamphlets and even books to read that he thought I might be capable of understanding.

Maybe it had started even earlier, when at the age of thirteen and nine my brother and I had been sent to a very expensive boys' camp in Maine: Camp Mesalonskee. It was not too far from Monmouth, took its name from Lake Mesalonskee and was the sort of camp where you wore name labels on every article of clothing, inside and out, and every outside article bore the red felt initials CM inside a shield.

All I can remember of this camp resolves itself into fragmented images of Chief Moran (*Moran!* At the time I wished his name had been Rain-in-the-Face or something equally glamorous), who was a genuine Mohawk and was our swimming instructor.

He used to make tomahawks for the kids. He showed us how the Indians swam under water (on their side!). He took us on overnight hikes and when we were sitting around the campfire he would disappear. Then we were terrified by a series of sounds: in sequence, he was an owl, a lynx, a mountain lion screaming in the pitchblack night.

It was on these overnight hikes that I used to gaze at the stars spread overhead in their incredible multitudes and vaguely wish I knew something about them; they were so beautiful. When I came home from camp I mentioned my fascination and my father came home one day with a book.

Why he imagined that a boy of nine could understand a technical work on astronomy I never knew. Perhaps he hadn't cracked the cover. In any event, my fascination rapidly faded (like a star of the sixth magnitude) when I discovered that the book was filled with mathematical formulae and diagrams that meant absolutely nothing.

This did not prevent my father — when he thought I was not within hearing — from telling Izzy Collins, the rye drinker, "My son Julian is brilliant. He reads technical books on astronomy."

"Is that so?" said Izzy. "Pass."

That damned book lay around the house for over a decade and after 1913 the bottom must have begun to fall out of the paper-box business, for the next two summer camps were relatively poverty-stricken compared to Mesalonskee.

The first was Camp Okapoket and we attended for three years: 1914-1916. It was on a lake in Pennsylvania. The second (1917-1918) was in Wingdale, New York, which was much later to become famous — or infamous — for Camp Unity, which was attended by members of the Young Communist League and other similarly subversive groups.

At both camps my primary absorption was in athletics — so long as I could win. At Mesalonskee I had run away with every track event in my "midget" class. But when I came out for track at Okapoket there was a kid my age named Clarence Prager who ran the pants off me and left me crying.

So I went out for swimming and was so good at it that they had to handicap me. I still won. (This pattern was later repeated at Columbia College when I tried out for the swimming team — and was left at the starting end of the pool. So I went out for — and made — the fencing team.)

Be that as it may, it was at Wingdale that astronomy was finally replaced by herpetology — a switch that interested Dr. Schwarzkopf some decades later but did not interest me at all. A snake is a penis symbol, no? NO! (Well, maybe it is, for women.)

With no Uncle Sid to adore in the summer time my adolescent homoerotic impulses had been transferred to a young fellow named Abraham Pinsky, whom I had met at the Young Men's Hebrew Association in New York and whose *biceps, triceps, pectoralis major, trapezius* and *deltoid* muscles were the envy of my adolescence. (In later years I restricted my fetishism to the pectoral and gluteal regions of the human female and am faithful to them to this day.)

A group of us were on an afternoon hike with Pinsky when we heard a whirring noise near our feet. Our counsellor shouted, "Get back! *Rattlesnake!*"

I saw the serpent and it enchanted me instantly. I was fascinated by the yellow skin tones, the almost black markings, the triangular head drawn back on an s-shaped loop of neck, the sight of its blurred tail and the sound of its rattle like dry bones in a desert.

Pinsky picked up a fallen branch and warning the kids to stand back, he proceeded to beat the rattlesnake into a bloody pulp. It kept on writhing for an astonishing length of time and I was sickened by his brutality and what seemed to me an unbearable example of injustice. After all, it was such a *small* rattlesnake.

I was still sore at Pinsky a week later when he introduced me to a dark and youngish man with piercing brown eyes who he said was a friend.

The friend told me that Pinsky had called him in New York City and told him we had seen a rattlesnake. He wanted to know whether I would take him to the place it had been "observed." *Observed!* I thought with indignation — *murdered!*

I was delighted to escape the afternoon routine of the camp — after several years it becomes rather boring — so we set out and a new hero figure rose over the horizon to replace Uncle Sid and Pinsky — Aaron Vogelsang.

His penetrating eyes were not only good for looking into *me*, I rapidly discovered: they saw *everything*. We had not been walking down the road ten minutes before he stopped and pointed at a tree fifty feet away.

"What do you see on that tree trunk?" he asked.

I looked at it, looked at him. "Bark?"

He shook his head, walked to the tree and picked something off the trunk, held it carefully in his hand and returned to me. He opened his hand and there, sitting on his palm, was the most beautiful small frog I had ever seen. It was no more than an inch and a half long; it was the color of the bark and had long, delicate fingers and toes with suckers at each tip.

"Tree frog," Aaron said. "*Hyla versicolor.*" He turned to me. "You study Latin?"

"*Cum esset Caesar in citeriore Gallia —*" I said.

"Then you know that *versicolor* means changing colors. It changes color to match its habitat. Camouflage."

I looked at him with amazement, then looked at the tree frog, which chose that moment to leap recklessly into the air and onto the ground beside the road where it was immediately invisible again.

Aaron laughed and we continued to walk. Then he cut cross-lots in the direction I had pointed and without breaking his stride, picked up a dead branch from the ground. He brought out a pocket-knife and as we continued to walk he cut the forked end of the branch into a very short fork with tines no more than three-quarters of an inch long. He trimmed off the shorter branches and excess twigs.

We had reached the hillside and the rocky ledge where the rattlesnake had been "observed" and I noticed that when he walked, although he was wearing heavy high-laced boots, he made no more sound than Chief Moran had made in his genuine Mohawk moccasins. He told me to stay at least three paces behind him and we started to climb the easy slope. The sun was hot and heavy.

Not more than ten feet from where the first rattler had been destroyed we heard the sound and Aaron froze. I did the same. He pointed with his left hand and I saw the snake. It was coiled and rattling furiously and he stood watching it for a moment.

Then he reached the forked stick out toward the reptile and it struck at it twice, hitting it both times. It started to move off into the low brush and with one movement Aaron reached out and pinned it to the earth, right behind its arrow-shaped head.

He reached into the left pocket of his loose jacket and brought out a white, folded object which he handed to me and said, "Open it and *hold* it open."

To my surprise it was a common pillowcase. I held it open, trembling from head to foot, and he calmly bent down, grasped the rattler, placing his thumb and one finger on either side of its neck and his index finger on top of its head and let the stick fall to the ground.

He lifted the snake — it was a good four feet long — and held it out to me. It was still rattling and was trying to twist out of his hands, for with his left hand he was holding it in mid-body.

"A beauty," he said. "Look at it."

I looked. My blood thickened and I shuddered. "I'd never dare do a thing like that!" I said.

"It's easy," he said. "When I drop it in the bag, close the bag fast and hand it to me."

I felt the snake's heavy body as it hit the bottom of the pillowcase, closed the neck — certain it would strike me through the linen — and handed it to him. He swung the bag swiftly in a circle, twisting the neck closed, brought a cord out of his side pocket and tied the neck with a square knot. He grinned.

"How did you learn to do that?" I asked.

"By doing it."

When I looked puzzled he said, "Practice on harmless snakes." He handed me the stick and said, "Keep it." With trembling hands I brought out a pack of cigarettes and offered it to him, for I had been smoking since I was twelve years old.

He shook his head. "Never smoke," he said. "It's poison. Never drink either. You pickle snakes in alcohol — or formalin — you know. No point in pickling my intestines."

"Are you a scientist?" I asked in awe. He grinned again and said, "Amateur. That's a hobby with me."

"What're you going to do with it?"

"Keep it at home awhile, then give it to Roland Martin."

"Who's that?"

"Curator of reptiles at the Bronx Zoo."

Aaron Vogelsang handed me a card when he left camp on Sunday after we had spent two more days in a fruitless search for more rattlers, and I puzzled over it in my tent.

There was a woman's name on the card: *Mrs. Rosa Vogelsang, Jewish Orphan Asylum*, and an address on Amsterdam Avenue. The words Mrs. and Rosa had been crossed out and the name Aaron written in. Who was *she*?

Abe Pinsky said, "His mother. She's the matron there. He lives there."

"Is he an orphan *too*? With a *mother*?"

"No, it's just convenient for him. Costs no rent."

"What does he *do*?"

"For a living? I don't know. I think he's in Wall Street."

My father was in Wall Street but if you were in Wall Street you were rich, weren't you? Well, at least as rich as my father, who could sometimes afford — well, once upon a time — to bring my mother a box of candy and say, "Here's a new brand I found. See if you like it." When she opened the box she found a piece of diamond jewelry in it. That had happened twice.

Certainly if you were in Wall Street you didn't need to live in a free room in an orphan asylum, did you? Or were there poor people on Wall Street, too?

I was shocked by the room in the Jewish Orphan Asylum that Mrs. Vogelsang took me to, saying Aaron would be back in a little while; he had had to go to the corner for something.

It was smaller than the maid's room in our apartment on Riverside Drive that stood empty because we no longer had a maid. There was a wardrobe and a desk, an army cot such as we'd had at camp, a small armchair and a row of books.

The books seemed very odd. One was titled: *Building a Dynamic Personality*. Another was called *Effective Public Speaking*. Still another, *Selling the Difficult Customer*. (Selling him what? I wondered.) There was a 1917 *World Almanac*, a worn-out copy of Edward Drinker Cope's *The Crocodiles, Lizards and Snakes of North America*, a *Collegiate Dictionary* and another book mysteriously titled *You Are What You Think*. (What did I think I was? I was a fourteen-year-old boy.)

Aaron came in while I was looking at his books and said, "How are you, Julian?"

I didn't know how I was so I didn't answer. He opened the wardrobe, hung his raincoat on a hanger and I heard an angry rattling sound and said, "What's that?"

Of course I knew what it was but I didn't believe what I had heard. He gave me his wide grin and poked something on the floor of the wardrobe with his toe. I saw it was a pillowcase, tied at the neck. It was lying among some shoes, a pair of worn sneakers and some dirty underwear. In fact, there were two or three pillowcases and I could see movement inside one of them and looked up at him.

"Rattlesnakes," he said. "*Crotalus horridus.* Have seven. Went down to Pike County, Pennsylvania, the week after I saw you at camp and they've been here ever since."

"That was a month ago! Don't they have to eat?"

"Not often."

"What do you feed them?"

"Don't. Matter of fact, taking them up to Roland Martin this afternoon. Like to come along?"

Over the next two years we went on many expeditions together, but we never went to the Zoo again. He introduced me to Martin, a cool man with a brown mustache who was wearing a brown suit (he *always* wore a brown suit, I discovered later), and the snakes were placed with other timber rattlesnakes in one of the glass-fronted cages in the Snake House.

We spent two hours there that afternoon and we visited some of the other animals on exhibition, too. Aaron seemed to know all there was to know about every one of them but since I didn't know anything, that was only natural.

He didn't talk too much, however, merely imparting what information he felt was essential, just as he generally answered all questions with a "Yes" or "No" or "Look that up yourself."

If I asked where I should look it up, he told me. He told me that if I wanted to be a scientist I should start working in my "field" immediately, depend on no one, hunt down all the necessary books, documents and papers and study them all the time. He said I should take every course in biology, zoology, botany (the very idea made me sick to my stomach), geology, anatomy and physiology. Embryology, too, he said. And we should go on field trips together. He went whenever he had time off from his work.

What kind of work did he do? I asked and he said, "Stocks and bonds." *(Selling the Difficult Customer?)* Did he sell a lot of them? "Not too many." I told him my father was a stockbroker but he didn't seem very interested in that fact.

My father however was interested in Aaron Vogelsang and questioned me about him after our first field trip. I had asked if I could go some Saturday or Sunday and my father had said, off-handedly, "If you want. But that stuff — science — is a rich man's hobby."

I didn't tell him how the expedition worked. It worked this

way: That first fall — it was September and still very warm — the
phone would ring about five a.m. and I, expecting it, would leap
out of bed next to my brother Adrian and dash down the long
bowling alley of a hall and answer it.

The voice said, "Julian?"

"Yes."

"Aaron. Can you meet me in half an hour?"

"Where?"

He told me. It was generally a subway station and before it
was light we were on our way. We went to places in New Jersey
by train (he always paid my fare) or to Ramapo, New York, or
Pike County, Pennsylvania. We were generally back in town by
dark or shortly after.

We caught pine snakes in the Jersey pinewoods (*Pituophis melanoleucus melanoleucus*). Rattlers were never found there but we
found a snake that seemed much fiercer: when you came upon it
it blew itself up and hissed like a red-hot iron in cold water. It
flattened out. It struck at your feet and ankles. It lashed around
and would have terrified a mountain lion.

If you paid no attention to it or merely stood and watched it
for awhile and it perceived (how I would never know) that it
couldn't get away, it promptly turned over on its back and played
dead!

"Hog-nosed snake," said Aaron. *"Heterodon platyrhinos.* Farmers call them puff adders. Watch."

He picked the "dead" snake up by its tail and hung it over a
split-rail fence. It lay there absolutely dead to the world and motionless, totally obedient to the law of gravitation.

"Come on," Aaron said and we walked a few feet, then stopped and watched the snake.

It lay draped over the fence rail, motionless, its tongue hanging out, for a good five minutes. Then it cautiously lifted its head,
seemed to look around and started to glide off onto the ground.
We tried it several times. If we came back before it had started to
escape, it dropped its head again, its tongue hung out and it would
lie there indefinitely.

"A comedian," said Aaron. "Never bites. Its behavior is another form of camouflage. You can tease it and it never bites." I teased it — and many others in the years to come. They struck at me — with their mouths closed! They never bit.

My father nearly bit my head off, however, the first time I came home from a field trip after dark (it was our second trip).

"Who *is* this man you go out with?"

"Aaron Vogelsang."

"Where did you meet him?"

"I told you — at camp."

"What does he do for a living?"

"I don't know. Something on Wall Street."

"Wall Street!" My father seemed baffled but after a pause, he continued. "What do you *do* on these trips?"

"Look for snakes." I held up the pillowcase I still held in my hand and opened it for him. He peeked in. My brother Adrian peeked in, said nothing. My mother peeked — and screamed.

"What's *that*?" said my father.

"*Pituophis melanoleucus melanoleucus.* Pine snake. It's harmless. Aaron gave it to me."

"I don't want it in the house," my mother said.

"What're you going to *do* with it?"

"Study it. It's beautiful, isn't it?"

My father looked at me as though I were demented. "Study it," he said. A statement, not a question. Then his face grew dark and he said, "When you go out with this . . . this Vogel . . . does he . . . *touch* you?"

"What do you mean?" I said, knowing very well what he meant.

"*You* know what I mean," my father said. I surely did. In spite of the dream my father had had one night when I was twelve, and which he related at the dinner table, I was still "touching" myself. I couldn't help it. He had dreamed that I was kidnapped by "a fiend," that the police searched for me for a week. That at the end of the week I was deposited on the doorstep of the apartment, a twelve-year-old boy who had been "abused all day long for a week," my father said, "till he was a driveling idiot."

That dream was the contradictory horror of my young life. I not only couldn't help "abusing" myself; I even enjoyed it.

Decades later the dream interested Dr. Schwarzkopf quite a bit. "That tells me quite a lot about your father," he said.

Finally, in answer to my father's question, I said, "No."

"I should *hope* not," he said.

"Vogelsang," said my mother. "That means birdsong. In German."

"*Your* name means blackhead," I said.

"What's that?"

"Schwarzkopf, your maiden name."

"Blockheads," my mother called us all when I insisted I had a "right" to keep the snake and my father and my brother backed me up. "I don't want the thing around the house."

"*Father* sent me a baby alligator when he was traveling on the road in Florida," I said plaintively. "Selling butter-boxes."

"You think I don't remember?" cried my mother. "It got out and I stepped on it in the dark in my bare feet."

"You squashed it dead," I said accusingly. (Maybe it was that alligator — *Alligator mississippiensis* — that sparked my original interest in *reptilia* after all!)

But she got used to my having snakes around the house. She got used to my taking the books out of the glass-fronted *Globe-Wernecke* bookcases and filling them with assorted ophidians. She did no more than scream when a five-foot *Boa constrictor* I had purchased for one dollar a foot vanished — and appeared again a week later, hanging from a mantle over the dining-room door, covered with dust. She even got used to shelves stocked with rattlesnakes (*Crotalus*) and copperheads (*Agkistrodon contortrix*). That was after my father had died, of course, and I occasionally borrowed such specimens from Roland Martin at the Snake House in order to give lectures all over Manhattan, the Bronx and Brooklyn to other high-school kids.

The relationship with Aaron Vogelsang continued until my last year in high school. During the summer months he would call every other week or so long before dawn and say, "Can you meet me?" He taught me everything I learned at the time about reptiles and amphibians, about mammals, insects, *crustacea*, plants, trees and rocks, birds and fish.

He never taught me anything about himself. He never talked about himself. If I asked him what he was doing, he said, "Stocks and bonds." I got the feeling that he was the loneliest human being I had ever known.

It was not that he was not personable; he was. His deep brown eyes saw everything that went on around us and everything that went on inside of me. He would suddenly say, "You don't study enough." He was absolutely right. He would suddenly say, "You're really lazy; you'll never make a scientist; don't enjoy research." How true!

What research he expected a boy of fourteen to sixteen to do, he never said, but I knew somehow that when he accused me of these lapses in character he was really saying that he himself was not doing what he should have done with his life — what he said *I* would eventually be doing: working at the Natural History Museum. Who could *want* to sell stocks and bonds?

Like my father, Aaron went on trips "out of town" and like my father, one time, he sent me something. It was not an alligator, for the package came from Texas. It was in a small box, tightly sealed, and I sat under the lighted chandelier at the dinner table the day it arrived and unpacked the box.

There was a layer of cotton on top of whatever was inside and I lifted it off and saw what looked like a stuffed horned lizard (called horned toad in the Southwest — *Phrynosoma cornutum*), and carefully lifted it out onto the table.

It felt strangely soft for a stuffed specimen. I thought that it was dead for lack of air and cursed Aaron for his stupidity. I sat looking at it until suddenly it lifted its tiny dinosaur head, opened its eyes, glanced left and right — and ran right off the table. Mother screamed.

But basically she had accepted my preoccupation and she was faithful about giving me messages when Aaron called.

"Your 'snake friend' called," she would say, and tell me where I was to meet him.

One day he asked me to meet him near Orange, New Jersey, of all places, where herpetological *fauna* was as scarce as the *Pterodactyl*. Oh, you could find spring peepers (in the spring — *Hyla cru-*

cifer) and occasional garter snakes (*Thamnophis surtalis*) and a few leopard frogs (*Rana pipiens*) or toads (*Bufo*), but nothing that could possibly excite a pair of sophisticated herpetologists like Vogelsang and Leonard.

I was thinking that it would be wonderful if we could discover a new species some day, or if not a new species, at least a true color variation. It would be named after us, although I had never seen any scientific tag that bore a double name. They were generally along the lines of *Lyodytes alleni* or *Storeria dekayi*, but why couldn't there be a *Crotalus vogelsangi-leonardi?*

Outside of Orange, New Jersey, there was a great meadow surrounded by a barbed-wire fence and, in the distance, a heavy wood. A dilapidated farmhouse stood at the edge of the forest and was abandoned, and I reached the rendezvous point and saw no sign of Aaron, so I sat on the sagging porch.

I brought out my cigarettes — I was sixteen then and a senior in high school and Lucky Strikes were now my brand and I had been sedulously buying the ten-cent pack that held ten butts, smoking them and then cutting the front of the pack off with a pair of scissors and placing it under the glass top of my bureau. There were thirty-five of them there now; this one, when it was empty, would be thirty-six.

I thought of Aaron and was feeling sorry for him. He did not smoke or drink (did he engage in "self-abuse"?). He lived alone in a crummy little room in a gloomy orphan asylum run by his mother. He sold stocks and bonds (not very many) and sometimes traveled to other cities. So far as I knew he did not have a friend his own age; at least, I had never seen one except Abe Pinsky who told me he was only a casual acquaintance. He had met Aaron at the Y.M.H.A., too, and had prescribed a set of muscle-building exercises for him. That's right; I remembered the other book on his desk: *Building a Strong Body*.

It seemed strange to me that he would voluntarily spend so much time with a kid like me; that he went out of his way to encourage me to become a natural scientist. That he would personally *train* me till I was ready for my job in the herpetology department at the Natural History Museum. Yet my father's suspicions had been all wrong: he never "touched" me, never put an arm around me or a finger on me; never indicated in any way that his interest in me was anything but friendly.

Then I saw him. He was coming cross-lots, cutting across the meadow, but he wasn't alone. There was a *woman* with him! She was wearing a bright dress splashed with colored flowers and there was a blue ribbon tied around her reddish hair.

I stood up (as I had been taught to do) and when Aaron and the woman reached me, he said, "Hazel, this is Julie." Not Julian, Julie.

Hazel smiled at me; she was holding Aaron's arm and he did not seem to mind. Aaron unslung a pair of binoculars he had around his neck and handed them to me.

"We're watching birds today," he said. "Last time I was here I saw a Swainson's warbler."

That was an uncommon bird, I knew, but somehow the information did not interest me. I was looking at Hazel's "knockers," which were quite prominent, and I felt terribly sad.

Aaron and Hazel started to walk and he said, "You go on ahead, Julie. See what you can see."

I walked disconsolately along shuffling my feet and occasionally stopping and pretending to look into the middle distance with the binoculars. Aaron would call, "What do you see?" and I would say, "Nothing."

"You go on," he said. "We'll catch up to you."

I could hear him talking to the woman in a low voice and occasionally I would hear her giggle — a ridiculous sound, it seemed to me. My heart was heavy in my chest and I seemed to have lost all interest in natural science.

Once in a while I would hold the binoculars up to my eyes, then swivel on one foot as though I were following a bird, in order to see where Aaron and the woman were. They fell farther and farther behind and on one occasion when I was pretending to track a bird in the field of my binoculars, I saw them step into the woods alongside the dirt road.

Something very strange happened then: I was at one and the same time immensely excited — and slightly sick to my stomach. I knew what men and women did when they went into the woods together — or the underbrush. I had even *seen* them doing it in Van Cortlandt Park, or — parting the underbrush — I would come upon a flattened place in the grass, covered with old newspapers.

I waited for them a long time at the bend in the road but when Aaron called me the next time to go on a field trip I told him I was busy. He was not a hero to me any more. I would have to get into the Natural History Museum — *without* his training.

Save the American Eagle!

THERE was a war going on in 1918 and my brother Adrian was in the ROTC at Columbia and I used to watch in fascination as he skillfully rolled the puttees around his long legs every morning.

Somewhere or other I had found a live cartridge that fit the bolt-action Springfield he drilled with at college. I wrapped it carefully and placed it, with a note, inside a small cylindrical wooden box. The note said: "Do not use this bullet until you are at the front. Bring me the helmet of the Hun you kill with it."

Generally, I was not so bloodthirsty. In fact, I resented the killing of any living creature, even an ant, and my very first effort at verse, written at about this time and springing directly from personal observation, read as follows:

> The red-tailed hawk does fly unheard
> And sail and soar and hover;
> A shot rings out . . . oh! noble bird!
> Some wretch has shot from cover!
>
> Man, to continue, must destroy,
> That is a tale well-known;
> But he who kills for savage joy
> Ne'er will earn his golden crown!

216

Granted it could not have been much worse, it did spring from genuine emotion, which proves that the man who said "I blow in so sweet but it comes out so sour" was expressing a genuine dilemma.

Actually, the war did not mean anything to me at all and actually it is not entirely true that I was opposed to the murder of any living creature. I had thought briefly about vegetarianism — after our father had described a visit he had made to the Chicago stockyards and slaughterhouses — but I knew it had no future for me.

There was also one animal that had earned my enmity and provoked me to throw rocks at it: that was the cat (*Felis domestica*). It killed birds, so there were times when I killed cats, and even found a form of satisfaction in their demise in spite of the fact that as a putative natural historian I *knew* it was not the cat's fault it was a predator; it was merely a vestige of the balance of nature manifesting itself in a domesticated beast. (My eventual psychiatrist, Dr. Schwarzkopf, would have understood this contradiction in me. I wonder why I never raised the question.)

The association with my older "snake friend," Aaron Vogelsang, had created a genuine passion in me for reptiles and amphibians. His advice to an aspiring naturalist bore immediate fruit. I not only badgered my parents for books like Susan Anthony Aldridge's *Batrachia of North America* and Roland Martin's more popularized *The Snake Book*, but I took biology and botany in high school. Biology was fine but botany, as I had suspected, proved to be a bore and I dropped out after one week.

I also discovered that DeWitt Clinton High School, located in what my father called "Hell's Kitchen," had its own Biology Field Club. I joined it immediately.

It was presided over by a large, damp boy my own age who wore glasses and whose name was Isidore Stein. It was populated — to the extent of six members when I joined — by other boys, most of whom also wore glasses and who were, if not damp, pretty dry. That is to say, they were outside the general run of highschool kids who played baseball in the yard during recess and went out for other athletic activities after school.

While I was still interested in swimming, having abandoned

track at Camp Okapoket because Clarence Prager always beat me, Clinton had no swimming pool. Baseball and basketball did not interest me and most of the classroom teachers, if you except two, were even damper than the students. ("All wet" was the phrase we used.)

The two exceptions were a Latin teacher named Mr. Rogin who had done a hitch in the Marine Corps, it appears, and who enjoyed making a reciting pupil stand like a ramrod and "Suck up your *guts!*"

The other was Mademoiselle Nahon, our recently immigrated French teacher who had a tiny, fuzzy mustache and with whom I fell madly in love. I begged her to let me carry her books to the subway station at Fifty-Ninth Street and Columbus Circle every afternoon and she ultimately broke my heart in several pieces, but as Cicero was fond of saying, "I will pass over that." (Of course when Cicero said that, he never passed over it at all; he went right into it, whatever it was that was on his mind. But I *will* pass over it.)

Isidore Stein was so delighted to have a member who actually seemed to be enthusiastically interested in the club that he immediately and quite undemocratically appointed me its treasurer. The dues were twenty-five cents a month and they kept piling up in the treasury because they served no purpose whatsoever. The bulletins the club put out – for meetings, lectures, information, field trips – cost us nothing because we had free access to the school's mimeograph machine and paper.

Right after I joined the field trips boiled down to expeditions by only two members of the club: the President and his Treasurer. Izzy was mad for birds and had picked up a pair of four-power opera glasses in a pawnshop. I could not interest him in my specialty: *reptilia* and *amphibia*. So, when we went on field trips to Van Cortlandt Park (generally), there was a point at which we invariably separated, making an appointment to meet at five o'clock at the subway station at 242nd Street. He went off with his opera glasses and I went off with my snake stick and a pillowcase.

The herpetological *fauna* of Van Cortlandt Park was almost nil: a few frogs, a rare garter snake and one pond in which one might, if he were lucky, observe, if fail to catch, the painted turtle (*Chrysemys picta picta*).

Therefore I improved my time by observing, whenever possible, other forms of *fauna*, and practicing another form of activity — the observation was confined to tracking mating specimens of *Homo sapiens*, ♂ and ♀ , into the underbrush and watching the procedure with my own three-power opera glasses, borrowed from my mother and inlaid with mother-of-pearl. The alternate activity: after watching the mating of my species, engaging in what my father called "self-abuse."

Izzy Stein therefore had a much more productive day in the field: Invariably, he reported that he had seen a species of bird that was practically nonexistent that far north or east, and one day he announced that he had seen a Wilson's warbler, a prothonotary warbler and a cerulean warbler, each of which was a very *rara avis* indeed.

He took me home with him one day and I met his family: that is, his mother and his father, both of whom were as large and as damp as he was himself.

I called home and got permission to have dinner with the Steins and they fed me lox and bagels, *gefülte fische* and stuffed cabbage and even a small glass of very sweet wine that made me slightly sick to my stomach.

Izzy did not partake of the wine; he was a stern teetotaller. Like Aaron Vogelsang, neither did he smoke. He was going to be a doctor, he announced, and everybody knew that alcohol and tobacco were lethal poisons.

"In moderation, no," said Mr. Stein, lifting his glass, and Izzy looked at him with contempt.

" 'Drink no longer water, but use a little wine for thy stomach's sake,' " said Mr. Stein. "It says so in the *goyim's* Bible."

"*That's* a reason? There *is* no such thing as a moderate poison," Izzy announced with finality.

"You should excuse me, doctor," said his father, "if I beg respectfully to differ with you."

"It's not a question of a difference of opinion," said Izzy, as though he were already lecturing on pharmacology from the podium at the College of Physicians and Surgeons, which was only a few blocks from DeWitt Clinton High School. "It is a question of scientific *fact*."

"You should excuse your father," said Mr. Stein. "He's a greenhorn. He's only a pants presser from Lithuania."

His son the physician ignored the remark but I could not help comparing him to my doctor-Uncle Sid. Uncle Sid was *so* charming, *so* personable, *so* modest in speech and manner that I could not see how a fellow like Isidore Stein could ever develop into a doctor that anyone would engage to treat a sick cat. Why, he had told me, he did not even like *girls*, who were beginning to fascinate me, thanks to Mademoiselle Nahon of Montpellier. I was beginning to decide that Izzy was really a cluck.

He had his uses, however. He took me downtown one day to the office of the Audubon Society, induced me to join, pinned a button on my lapel himself (the colored picture of a robin – *Turdus migratorius*), and even introduced me to the President, Mr. S. Robert Stevenson.

Mr. S. Robert Stevenson was a short, plump and avuncular man who wore *pince-nez* glasses like my father's, and he seemed delighted to have another member even if he was only fifteen years old.

The Audubon Society was, of course, devoted to the study and preservation of our native birdlife (it still is), and before we left the office Mr. Stevenson loaded us down with leaflets, pamphlets and brochures published by the Society and full of important information.

Then Izzy took me to the New York Public Library on 42nd Street and Fifth Avenue, where – in a locked room and watched over by a uniformed guard – we were permitted to inspect the original folio volumes of Audubon's hand-colored lithographs of *The Birds of America*.

This gave me quite a thrill and sparked a greater interest in ornithology, although it never replaced or diminished my passion for the beast of whom the Lord God Himself had said:

Because thou hast done this, thou art cursed above all cattle . . . upon thy belly shalt thou go, and dust shalt thou eat all the days of thy life:/And I will put enmity between thee and the woman, and between thy seed and her seed; it shall bruise thy head and thou shalt bruise his heel. . . .

If the Lord God had cursed him, that was enough for me; I was on his side.

The Lord God had apparently cursed John James Audubon as well, according to what Izzy told me. He sweated for decades trying to raise money to publish his great lifework and had had to go to England to find patrons. He had also had to teach drawing and do portraits of "important" people and his wife had had to teach school to support *him*.

His house, Izzy said, was still standing and we went to look at it. You could see it from the viaduct that ran into Riverside Drive and enclosed it in a curve; you could look down on the roof. When you climbed down to sea level there it was, a crumbling house the artist-naturalist moved into in 1839, inhabited now, we were told, by section hands who worked on the railroad that ran along the Hudson shore. In the old days it had stood in a magnificent park of towering trees, and when Audubon looked across the river and to the north, he could see the Palisades.

If Izzy was a dumb cluck who neither smoked nor drank and had no interest in *Homo sapiens* ♀ , I knew that I − at fifteen − was a sink of vice and corruption. I smoked. I practiced "self-abuse." I occasionally stole a bottle of rye whiskey from the case my father always kept in his bedroom closet. I took a sip of it once in a while, mixed with ginger ale − and hated it. I hid the bottle behind the books in the *Globe-Wernecke* bookcase when there were no snakes to harbor.

Of course I stole candy from the store next to the John Bunny Theater on Broadway, those nights I was permitted to go to a movie by myself. I used to ask for ten cents worth of broken chocolate, and while the storekeeper was busy at the other end of the shop, breaking and weighing it, I slipped several packaged chocolate bars into my pocket.

Between the stolen sweets and the Lord Salisbury or *Melachrino* cigarettes I had stolen elsewhere (my father's brand was *Mela-chrino),* and which I sat consuming in the balcony of the Bunny, I got very sick indeed.

This was surely punishment for sin, but I did worse things than that. My father, when he took a bath (two or three times a day) always hung his trousers inside his bedroom closet and I lay in wait for moments such as that. I sneaked into the bedroom, found his wallet in his back pocket and deftly exchanged a one-dollar bill he had given me for a two- or a five-dollar bill, and once even for a ten.

I never stole from my mother — well, at least nothing more than a quarter or half-dollar — and no doubt that would have told Dr. Schwarzkopf my future psychiatrist something about *me* if I had ever told it to him. But the thing that disturbed me more than anything else at that time of my life was the fact that my father *never* said a word about this larceny, although I am relatively certain he must have missed the money and even the occasional bottle of rye.

Why was he silent, Dr. Schwarzkopf? Could it have had something to do with the fact that he was obviously a guilty man himself? He was a case, Doctor, right out of the Freudian casebooks. He not only took three baths a day when he was home, but he changed his underwear three times a day and washed his hands (at home or in the office) at least fifteen times a day.

It was said that he had had to leave a small town in North Dakota when he was in his late teens because he had got a servant girl in a family way. It was said he was a lady's man and certainly he tipped his hat to pregnant women on the streets, whether they knew him or not. Once I asked him why he did this and he replied, "She's going to be a mother."

He not only brought home expensive pieces of diamond jewelry in candy boxes (one cost five thousand dollars) but he insisted on buying all my mother's clothes and sending them home to her. They always fit. He brought home a box of candy or a dozen long-stemmed American Beauty roses every Saturday night for as long as he lived. He brought roses and candy to three of his sisters every Sunday. He was a paragon of virtue and I, sink of evil that I was, figured out in time that the loud scenes in the next bedroom at night that culminated in his regular departure (and return before dawn) *must* have had their origin in the fact that my mother refused to let him mate with her.

I figured this out, brilliantly, when I was thirty-three years old and was separating from my first wife. My mother expressed her sorrow, saying, "I've always loved Anne," and then added, gratuitously, "Of course you never knew it but I thought of leaving your father many times. I never cared for . . . sex. I went to my cousin Emily — she was in the original Floradora Sextette, you know — and talked to her and she told me, she said, 'You mustn't leave Nathaniel. He's a good provider, a good father and a good husband. Men are *like* that,' she said."

"I knew you never got along," I said, and that was when she turned to me in astonishment and said, "How *could* you have known? You were sound asleep."

Of course my mother lied when she said she never cared about sex, and I told Dr. Schwarzkopf all about it, but I never told *her* what I knew, and as Cicero used to say . . . .

But if I was an evil, cigarette-smoking, whiskey-drinking, thieving, self-abusing young man, I had other attributes that may or may not have conferred some grace upon my adolescence and young manhood.

I remember bursting into tears one day in 1916, my last month in Public School 43, when our teacher pinned a newspaper clipping on the bulletin board that announced the death of Jack London.

"He was only forty years old," she said sadly.

By that time I had read nearly everything London ever wrote including *The Call of the Wild* and *White Fang, Martin Eden, Burning Daylight, The Sea Wolf, Jerry, Michael, Brother of Jerry* and *The Iron Heel*, not one word of which I understood.

More than that, and either born with or having developed a premature sense of outrage against injustice, I had joined a Jack London Club, the purpose of which was to protest against trained-animal acts because as everybody knew and London had exposed for those who did not know it, animals were trained for circuses and vaudeville by cruel means.

We members of the Jack London Clubs took a pledge never to attend the circus or witness any trained-animal act. This was very difficult for us to do because everybody *loves* trained-animal acts. It was easier to refuse to go to Barnum and Bailey's Circus, however, than it was to rise in high dudgeon in B. F. Keith's Alhambra vaudeville house, to which our parents took us regularly, and march indignantly up the aisle to the manager's office and lodge the protest we had pledged to make. But I did it and received in turn either an indulgent smile from the manager or a firm, "Beat it, kid."

My sense of burning outrage was revived again the night I came home from meeting Mr. S. Robert Stevenson, and sitting in my room (which was formerly the maid's room and had been given to me only to study in, not to sleep in), I leafed through the publications of the Audubon Society which Stevenson had given me.

I discovered immediately that the Society was up in arms because of the slaughter of songbirds that was going on around the major cities of the East Coast.

Men — generally Italian or French immigrants, it seems — were hunting songbirds with shotguns and . . . *eating* them! Songbirds were of course protected by law but the massacre of these lovely, innocent, beautiful and useful creatures who kept the insect population down was appalling according to the Society and Something Must Be Done About It. Fast!

I knew precisely what *I* would do — the moment I saw one of these vicious Italian immigrants. They might be so ignorant that they did not know songbirds were protected by the law and they might, in their foreign country where they couldn't even speak English, be used to hunting and *eating* them (ugh!) but they couldn't be allowed to get away with that in the good old U.S.A.!

I would immediately find a game warden and report to him. I would lead him directly to the man with the gun and he would be arrested. Of course, it was harder to find a game warden in Van Cortlandt Park or on the Palisades than it was to find a cerulean warbler (*Dendroica cerulea*) but one would *have* to be found, no matter what. Or could a fifteen-year-old boy make what was called "a citizen's arrest" of the foreign barbarian? Suppose he refused to be arrested? Or he beat you up or even took a shot at *you*? What could you do then?

The printed material S. Robert Stevenson had given me contained another horrifying bulletin: *The American Eagle Is In Danger!*

I was reading this bulletin sedulously when my father entered the "maid's" room — without knocking, naturally — and said, "Julie, I have something to show you."

In his hand he held a metal cylinder made of painted brass with a huge cork in one end and a ring through the cork.

"What's that?" I asked. And he said, "A fire extinguisher. I invented it."

I knew my father was something of an inventor. He had invented the folding paper butter-boxes in which I was still taking my lunch to school, even though the butter-box business was no longer in existence. (There were piles of them, folded flat, in the closet of my room.)

I knew he had also invented an automatic toilet that was supposed to flush itself by chemical reaction when someone urinated in the bowl. *That* had been a failure.

Holding the new invention in my hands, I said, "But it has no . . . what do you call it?"

"Plunger?" he said. "Of course not. That's the beauty of it."

"I don't get it."

"Eliminating the plunger eliminates all moving parts and makes it cost about one-fifth of what ordinary extinguishers sell for."

"Then how does it work?"

He took it from my hand and said, "You put a hook in the wall." He took the hook out of his pocket and showed it to me. "The extinguisher hangs on the hook — with this ring." He pointed at the ring. "When there's a fire you simply pull *down* on the extinguisher, the cork comes out — and you pour the contents on the fire."

I looked at him openmouthed. It didn't seem like much of an invention to me and the idea of *squirting* the fire from a distance seemed much more fun — certainly safer.

"This will put all the other extinguishers out of business," he said. "It will make us rich!" (He seemed to believe it.)

Then he brought out of his pocket a leaflet printed in three colors, which he handed to me.

"Read this," he said. "I've had fifty thousand printed as a starter. I have a *Saturday Evening Post* bag for you and every day after school I want you to distribute these leaflets."

"How?"

"You'll take a block and starting at the first apartment house on the corner go to the top floor and put one leaflet under every door. Then you'll go to the next . . . ."

I must have been sitting there with my mouth open because he said something my brother Adrian usually said to me: "Close your mouth. You'll swallow a fly." Then he smiled and said, "I'll pay you. Did you think I wouldn't? I'll pay you fifty cents a day. That will teach you the value of a dollar."

He was always trying to teach me the value of a dollar but I never learned. The last year of his life, when I was a freshman at Columbia, he tried to get me to go to work in Wall Street during summer vacation – for the brokerage firm of Shearson Hammill. I would post Stock Market quotations on The Big Board.

I outfoxed him. I got a job as a counsellor at a settlement-house camp in New York State, as a combination swimming instructor, teacher of natural history and – of all things – drama coach.

But I got the point all right when he loaded me down with the *Saturday Evening Post* bag jammed with leaflets. It must have weighed fifty pounds and I was dead before I started.

However, I did start. I walked two blocks and went into the first house on the corner, staggered to the top floor (there was no elevator) and bending down, slipped a leaflet under every door.

!REVOLUTIONARY INVENTION!
Now!
An *Inexpensive* Fire-Extinguisher
No plunger! No moving parts!
Nothing to get out of order! No time wasted!
No Home Should Be Without Two or Three!

On the back of the illustrated flier there were instructions about how to buy one. You wrote to Leonard Enterprises, 48 Wall Street, New York, N. Y. and you enclosed a check or money order for $3.75 and your extinguisher would be sent to you *immediately,* postage prepaid! Money Back If Not Satisfied.

What were people supposed to do, I wondered, *start* a fire and try to put it out — to find out if they were satisfied? Or wait two years till a fire started and their house burned down — and *then* demand a refund?

Actually, I didn't ponder these questions very long. I had too much else on my mind, matters that were far more urgent. The fate of the bald or American eagle (*Haliaeetus leucocephalus*)!

Attached to the bulletin about the eagle there was a printed petition. The petition reminded the reader that the bald eagle was the Official Symbol of the United States of America.

In the Territory of Alaska and elsewhere local authorities had actually set a bounty on its head — of fifty cents! Imagine that! Their argument was that the eagle was a predatory bird; it caught chickens, ducks and even small goats, lambs and pigs. It had been known to carry off small children from their parents' farmyards and drop them from dizzy heights to their dreadful death!

None of these things, said the Audubon Society's bulletin, was true. No eagle was big enough to carry off a child. But what was more important, this majestic bird, the very symbol of America which appeared on all our currency with an olive branch in one talon and a sheaf of arrows in the other — symbolizing our peaceful intentions in the world *and* our readiness always to defend ourselves and the right — was in serious danger of extermination!

The petition was addressed to the legislature of the Territory of Alaska — and to those of several states. So, I promptly went down to the office of the Society, saw Mr. S. Robert Stevenson again and obtained a stack of them.

Then — since I was now the President of the Biology Field Club and Izzy Stein was my Secretary-Treasurer — we got together and laid our battle plans.

First, we called the club together. Thanks to my energetic efforts at publicity we now had fifteen members instead of six, so we gave petitions to each one. Their job was to cover the school.

Then we called on the Principal, Mr. Henle, and asked permission to address the weekly assembly on the matter. He was impressed and one week later Izzy and I put on a show: specifically, he ran a stereopticon and showed slides of the majestic American Symbol in color while I, speaking part of the time in the darkness, addressed the one thousand captive pupils of DeWitt Clinton High School.

"This noble bird," I said in ringing peroration, my nasal voice reaching the farthest rows of seats in the auditorium, "is Our National Emblem: it is the symbol of courage, strength, independence, yes — even *beauty*. We cannot tolerate, we cannot sit idly by and allow evil-minded men anxious to collect a few paltry dollars to wipe this symbol of our American independence, our American strength, our American courage from the skies and forests of this continent. What will *you* do to save our National Bird? Will *you* sit idly by? Or will you rise to the defense of a noble creature whose very image strikes terror to the hearts of all our enemies?" (Long pause for dramatic effect.) "The answer is in *your* heart and mind — *today*!"

We gave out all the rest of our petitions after the assembly and we urged our fellow students to circulate them in their neighborhoods. Izzy went to the Society to get some more.

Then we started a letter-writing campaign to the newspapers and one letter got published — mine. It was the first letter I ever had published in *The New York Times* — and probably one of the last.

The publication of this letter caused quite a stir — at least in my own family. My father suddenly began to see some virtue in my determination to be a naturalist, whereas he had discouraged my early interest in astronomy and my current activities by saying that these were rich men's hobbies. If I wouldn't be lawyer, at least I could go into business. If I wouldn't go into business, he had an excellent *entrée* into Shearson Hamill & Company, stockbrokers, and by starting out posting quotations and making myself "agreeable" I would soon get tips on the Market and who knows. . . ?

My Uncle Sid the doctor called up and congratulated me on the letter. So did my cousins Cheryl, Lena and Carrie. So did Mr. S. Robert Stevenson. Even Mr. Suck-Up-Your-Guts Rodin and Mademoiselle Nahon commented on the letter, saying it was very well-composed and quite eloquent, in fact. (I gave them both petitions to circulate.)

Then I conceived the brilliant idea of combining my circulation of the petition with the distribution of my father's advertising brochure for the fire extinguisher. Every day after school I went out with the *Saturday Evening Post* bag loaded with leaflets, and with a score of petitions in my side pocket.

First I slipped the leaflet under the door. Then I rang the bell. Sometimes the door was opened and a harassed-looking woman or old man said, "*Nu?*" Or even, "What're you selling?"

They held the leaflet in their hand and looked at me. I brought out the petition and said, "The American eagle is in danger! In Alaska they have put a bounty on it — of fifty cents a head! No patriotic American citizen —"

They looked at the leaflet about the extinguisher, then they looked at me — blankly. Some of them said, "What's that you say?" Others said, "What're you *talking* about?" Others said, "Don't want any." Some merely slammed the door in my face after I had started my spiel. I got about seven signatures the first week.

This was discouraging. The bag of advertising folders grew very heavy within ten minutes after I had started out and it did no good to shift it from one shoulder to the other. Besides, I was getting nowhere with my petition. A decision had to be made and I faced it: Which was more important? My father's dopey fire extinguisher or the American eagle?

I walked down to the Hudson River, under the viaduct, near the nineteenth-century home of John James Audubon, and out onto a pier. I remembered that particular pier vividly, for when I had gone to P. S. 157, years before, I used to bring my butter-box with my lunch in it and sit and eat it on the pier. I stopped doing that one day after a city motorboat came coasting up to the pier towing a dead man behind it and lifted the stiff, mutilated corpse out of the water with a small derrick!

Now I went to the end of the pier and started floating the leaflets down the Hudson River, together with all the other debris that polluted it even in 1919: tin cans and bottles, garbage, human feces and rubber things we called "cundrums."

To my delight the leaflets did not float very long: they were on heavy, coated stock and they sank rapidly. I could dispose of five hundred of them in less than twenty minutes! The rest of the afternoon before supper I concentrated on the petitions and I came home exhausted with the canvas bag under one arm.

My father, who suffered from ulcers, was invariably lying on his back on the sofa, one hand thrust into his unbuttoned pants, tenderly holding his belly. He would look up and say, "How did it go?"

"O.K.," I said, displaying the empty bag.

He looked at me and made a decision of his own. I must have looked exhausted for he took his hand out of his trousers and fished in his pocket and handed me a dollar bill.

"I don't have change," I said. And he shook his head and said, "I'm giving you a raise."

Guilt must have flushed my face with crimson, for he looked at me and said, "You don't need to be embarrassed. It takes a lot of work to earn a dollar."

I gulped and went back to my "maid's" room where I brought the petitions out of my pocket and counted the signatures. I was supposed to ask for a twenty-five cent contribution to defray the cost of further publicity and advertisements the Audubon Society was planning, but I was so happy to get a signature that I didn't dare risk the danger of asking for a quarter for fear my client would change his mind. I decided to contribute one dollar a day to the Society.

The petition to Save the American Eagle *and* my father's misbegotten fire extinguisher both died an early death. I must have collected two hundred and thirteen signatures before I gave up; and the fire extinguisher, despite fifty thousand three-color brochures and my father's personal attempts to introduce it in hardware and department stores, simply did not "catch on." I wonder why.

At that time I was a fan of the nature books written by a man named Ernest Thompson Seton, who wrote about birds and animals and illustrated his books with clever pen-and-ink drawings.

I concealed this fact — my reading, that is — from my "snake friend" Aaron Vogelsang after he had told me that Seton was a "nature-faker," scientifically inaccurate and a man who engaged in what Aaron called *anthropomorphism*. This sounded much worse than the doctor-word for self-abuse.

I kept on reading his books, anyhow. In fact, I *loved* them. In one of his stories he made out a case for changing the American Symbol (Seton was originally British) from the bald eagle to the skunk (*Mephitis mephitis*).

His reasoning, I thought at fifteen, was excellent. Nature-faker or no nature-faker, the skunk *was* a brave and independent creature. It was the only small animal in the world that would saunter casually across an open field, utterly unafraid of any enemies. Other mammals (large and small) scuttled across as fast as they could, when they did not stay in the underbrush and circle the open space.

The skunk was also beautiful and bigger beasts, even the bear and mountain lion, were afraid of it. Whereas the bald eagle, Seton said (and I found out he was right, anthropomorphism or no anthropomorphism) was a bully, a thief and primarily a scavenger. It pursued other birds like smaller hawks and kingfishers and frightened them into dropping their prey. Thereupon it *stole* the dead fish and devoured it!

Of course in my letter to *The New York Times*, in my assembly speech and in my spiels with the petition I carefully refrained from mentioning these disgraceful facts, and any guilt I might have felt about abandoning the campaign to Save the American Eagle has long since dissolved into the mists of time.

The bullying, thieving and scavenging eagle is still in danger of extinction. (And so am I.)

The Time Now Is ... MAZOLA!

SOMEWHERE around 1687 Sir Isaac Newton propounded a law claiming that if you set an object in motion it would keep right on going until something stopped it. Seems reasonable enough. It also seems to apply in the realm of human activity and personality and the events that determine them.

Aaron Vogelsang, my grown-up "snake friend" who occupied a free room in the Jewish Orphan Asylum when I was in high school, first propelled me into the field of herpetology by catching a live rattlesnake (*Crotalus horridus*) right under my very nose in the summer of 1918.

The thrust of that spectacular event kept me moving in a straight line for several years: I too became a collector of living reptiles and amphibians and while I no longer engage in such arcane pursuits, my interest in these anachronistic beasts, these vestigial creatures from the prehistoric past, has never waned.

I made expeditions "into the field" in Van Cortlandt Park, Palisades Park in New Jersey, the Ramapo range near Suffern, New York, and as far as Pike County, Pennsylvania. At first I made them with Aaron Vogelsang, my mentor; then with Izzy Stein, the President of the Biology Field Club at DeWitt Clinton High School. Then I made them alone.

It was lonelier that way but it was also more rewarding. For it was possible, in fact it was impossible *not* to feel closer to the earth, the mystery of its existence and the almost infinite number of

232

forms that life assumes on this terraqueous sphere when you were
totally alone.

You can go to the Bronx Zoo, which I did regularly, and look
at an elephant which, next to the whale, is the largest creature living on this globe. You can also lie prone in any meadow and stare
into the grass-blades and observe forms of life so small you cannot
pick them up, but which are enormously complicated organisms
that still live perfectly and ingeniously within their particular environment.

Usually I started out before dawn on a Saturday or Sunday. If
I were going to Van Cortlandt Park I walked over to Broadway to
take the subway. If I were going to the Hackensack marshes in
New Jersey or into the Ramapos or even Pennsylvania I had to
take the subway anyhow — to start with.

The night before — and every night before I went to sleep —
I sat hypnotized in my bedroom window watching the electric ad-
vertising sign on the Jersey shore that said: THE . . . TIME . . .
NOW . . . IS . . . 9:05. (*Blackout*) Then: MAZOLA. Then it said:
THE . . . TIME . . . NOW . . . IS . . . 9:07. (*Blackout*) LINIT.

In the early morning before the sun came up that sign was still announcing the time and dropping into the minds of those who watched it the names of those sterling products: *Mazola*, the corn oil, and
Linit, the starch my mother bought at the drugstore or the grocery.

Riverside Drive was a constant in my life: the *Linit-Mazola*
clock; the sailors picking up girls; the strolling crowds; the boats
going up or down river; the ferry that went to Hoboken; the floating corpse that was picked up one day by a city motorboat when I
was eating lunch out of one of my father's butter-boxes — a great
invention that was superseded by automatic packaging.

There was an even earlier memory of the Drive that revolved
around the Wright brothers themselves: or, at least one of them.

In 1609 an Englishman named Henry Hudson, still seeking a
northwest passage to the Orient, sailed into New York Bay and
discovered the river that is still named after him although an Italian
named Verrazano had discovered it eighty-five years earlier.

In 1909 there was a Hudson-Fulton Celebration — complete
with reproductions of Hudson's *Half-Moon* and Robert Fulton's

steamboat — and my father took my brother Adrian and me to Riverside Drive to watch one of the most spectacular and dangerous achievements of that year.

Wilbur Wright flew twenty-one miles from Governor's Island in the Bay to a point a little beyond where we were standing, Grant's Tomb, and back to his starting point, with a red canoe strapped to his frail flying machine in case he and it should fall into the river. He died in bed four years later — of typhoid fever.

It was a cool and pleasant day but I remember mostly the child's peevish boredom of waiting hours for the flying machine to appear — and a peddler moving through the crowd shouting, "Hooshey's chocolate! Get it here! Get your Hooshey's chocolate!" (Even at the age of five I knew it was pronounced Hershey.)

Then it appeared — the flying machine — dipping and rocking perilously above the boats and ferries on the river that were hooting their horns like mad.

This experience, I am certain, sparked my first major life passion: to be an "aviator," something I finally achieved — at the age of forty-one. I never became a herpetologist at all.

In 1920, however, I was convinced that I was on the threshold of my scientific career. My father was still alive and still insisting that natural history was "a rich man's hobby," but he got nowhere in his persistent efforts to introduce me into the world of what was then called business and is called free enterprise today because businessmen know that capitalism is a dirty word.

I was a member of the Audubon Society but that carried no scientific *cachet*. Aaron Vogelsang, however, had introduced me to the Curator of Reptiles at the Bronx Zoo and while I privately scorned him as a "popularizer" of scientific data (like Ernest Thompson Seton), he had a certain standing in his field.

Long before educational or even scientific films were popular, Roland Martin of the Snake House had staged a battle between an Indian cobra (*Naja naja*) and its traditional enemy, the mongoose *(Herpestes edwardsii)*. He also filmed it. It achieved a certain distribution in the movie houses and any child or grown-up reader of Rudyard Kipling's story *Riki-Tiki-Tavi* knew the outcome in advance and cheered lustily for the furry little creature in its really unequal battle with the venomous serpent that killed so many brothers of Kipling's other famous character, Gunga Din. (The cobra never really stood a chance.)

Martin staged and filmed an even more spectacular battle but it never reached the movie houses. I saw it at a private showing at the Zoo and the actual battle – nay, the war – had gone on for several weeks.

It was a war between two colonies of mutually inimical ants who were first established in separate boxes of earth for several weeks, until they felt at home. Then a series of strings was laid out, bridging the two boxes.

It took some hours before one of the ants, exploring the terrain at the horizons of his world, discovered the strings, crossed one to the other box and disappeared into a tiny tunnel.

He soon came scuttling out, crossed a string like a tightrope walker, back to his home nest, disappeared – and then reappeared, followed by hundreds of his kinsmen.

Meantime, the ants in the other box had been alerted by the presence of the first intruder and came swarming to the defense – or the assault of the enemy tribe.

The war that ensued was filmed for minutes at a time over the next few weeks under magnifying lenses. No bloodier or more brutal conflict has ever been so minutely recorded by the camera, not even the war in Vietnam. The tiny warriors swayed back and forth across the bridges; their sharp jaws could be seen decapitating their enemies, lopping off their limbs. The wounded fell to the ground between the boxes, when they were not recovered by their fellow combatants and carried back to the safety of their respective quarters.

I was an invited spectator at this special screening because I was a regular contributor of reptile and amphibian specimens to the Zoo. Each time I made such a contribution I would receive in the mail a handsome engraved and inscribed document which read, typically, as follows:

The New York Zoological Society
acknowledges with gratitude
the donation by
Mr. Julian Leonard
of
5 Garter Snakes
12 Spotted Turtles
1 Ring-necked Snake
9 Leopard Frogs
1 Wood Frog

and the document was signed: Roland Martin, Curator.

As I grew more experienced — and bolder — the documents began to read:

One Timber Rattlesnake
One Copperhead Snake

It was at this private screening that I was formally introduced to a young lady I had seen often in the office of the Curator: Miss Betsy Martin, the fifteen-year-old daughter of the man with the brown mustache, the brown hair, who always wore a brown suit.

I had conceived one of my periodic violent passions the first time I ever set eyes on her and I must have stared at her nubile charms with more intensity than *savoir-faire*, for she had noticed it and quite literally turned up her snub nose at me.

At the screening her father had said quite clearly, "You know Julian Leonard, Betsy," and she had nodded perceptibly and walked away. He had not observed this calculated snub but it cut me to the heart.

It might have had something to do with the way I had looked at her the first time; or it might (I suspected) have had more to do with the way I had vainly tried to conceal my adolescent acne with *Mennen's Talcum for Men* (a light, tan powder). Or it might have had something to do with the fact that even without the acne I would have been a most unappetizing young man.

Whatever the unjust and naturally unjustified reason for her obvious distaste for me — and I had had such wonderful fantasies about marrying her, marrying into the world of herpetology – I decided then and there that I did not love her at all: I hated her and in time I would, like Hamlet in another context, ". . . *with wings as swift / As meditation or the thoughts of love /* (Ah, Betsy!). . . *sweep to my revenge.*"

What form that revenge would take I could not imagine, although the next time we met I snubbed *her*, having read somewhere that if you ignored women they immediately started to chase *you*. (It was not true.)

But her brusque rejection did not prevent my having dreams of, if not marrying into the New York Zoological Society, at least growing into it.

I visited the Zoo weekly. During the summer I regularly brought specimens. During the winter I borrowed them back in order to illustrate – with living snakes – lectures at various high schools in Manhattan, the Bronx and Brooklyn. I could clearly see my future. There would come a day when Roland Martin, noticing at last that I was a man grown and a dedicated and even brilliant herpetologist, would casually suggest that I accompany him on one of his highly publicized expeditions to gather specimens in Central or South America, in Africa or even in the Orient.

I recognized, nevertheless, that the man in the brown suit, while invariably pleasant when I appeared and always willing to answer questions, treated me as what I was: a high-school kid.

Patience, Julian, patience. And, as Aaron Vogelsang had counseled: dogged, scientific work, study, research, study. I was at the Zoo at all hours of the day and night when I had free time. If I arrived after hours to deposit new specimens, I entered through what was called The Buffalo Gate, some blocks from the entrance for the general public that was near the subway station.

This conferred a special privilege: I was a scientist, attached to the staff. I also left that way when closing time had come and gone and every time I came or went that way the gatekeeper, a heavy-set man named Mr. Schlachter, raised his hand in patent deference to my exalted status.

One day I stopped to say hello to him as he was standing in the doorway of the little shack he inhabited. It was cold and rainy and I could see he had a small electric heater inside that made it very cosy. He gestured me inside and I thought, why not? You should be friendly to everyone, my father said. You never could tell when they might be *useful* to you — even a gatekeeper at the Zoo.

He closed the door and made some remark about the weather. I looked around the shack and he indicated a comfortable armchair. It might not be such a bad job, I was thinking, though it must get awfully boring sitting here all day long with nobody to talk to and nothing else to do.

"Are you a member of the staff?" Schlachter asked. And I hesitated a moment before saying, "Well, not exactly. But I collect snakes and things for Martin."

"I've seen you coming and going. That must be fascinating work."

"It's not bad."

"I probably know a lot more about you than you know about me," he said. He had disconcerting eyes — pale blue.

"That so?"

"I know you got a bad crush on Betsy."

"Who?"

"Betsy Martin," he grinned. "I hear everything that goes on around here."

I said nothing. He sat on a hard chair facing me and said, "She's too young for you." His steady blue gaze was *most* disturbing.

I didn't know what to say to that, so I said nothing.

"What you need," he said, "is a real woman. A grown-up woman." *Me!* I thought, I'm only sixteen years old. Then I thought, Why not? He was right, of course.

He reached back to the drawer of a built-in desk and pulled it open. Out of it he took a thick envelope and handed it to me.

"Like that, I mean," he said and nodded. "Open it. Take a look."

I took a thick pack of photographs out of the envelope and my heart immediately rose into my throat. The very first picture showed a naked woman and a naked man and the woman was doing something to the man I had heard about but never believed that anybody really did.

I glanced up at Schlachter and he was sitting there, smiling, saying, "You like that? There's a lot of them. I'll give them to you if you want."

I didn't say anything but continued to look at the photographs one at a time. "You want a woman, I can get you one," I heard him say. "Friend of mine. She'd like you."

I grew hot all over and my throat hurt. There they were, doing all the things I had dreamed about or heard about and imagined doing, if not with Betsy Martin, at least with the servant girl who lived across the courtyard from my "maid's" room. She liked to tease me once in a while by starting to undress with the shade up — then coyly pulling it down. I had thought a lot about that girl (woman) and had even tried to talk to her in the hallway one afternoon but she had smiled and run down the stairs instead of waiting for the elevator.

Of course I was aware that the man's hand was on me, and of what he was doing with his hand but I kept my eyes glued to the photographs, staring at them one at a time and placing them one behind the other, the way I had seen poker players handle cards.

What he was doing was what I had done not six months before to my cousin Cheryl who had done exactly what *I* was doing — but with a difference because at the time she was lying on the couch in her living room pretending to be asleep.

I heard his voice say, "Do you mind? I've never done this before and I want to." I glanced down briefly at him and then continued to stare blindly now at the photographs until a point was reached where I couldn't see any more and dropped them on the floor and he kept on doing what the woman in the first photograph had been doing to the man and suddenly I was faint and dizzy; the room was reeling around me and I felt myself falling sideways and knew — to my distress — that I was vomiting all over the floor.

I never went through the Buffalo Gate again but that experience stimulated my day and night dreams about the servant girl in the room across the courtyard.

When she was dressed to go out she wore a round, red patent-leather hat and she had a broad, Slavic face. I lay in wait for her in *my* "maid's" room every day after school and she regularly appeared in her own room and as regularly smiled coquettishly at me.

On such occasions I would hold up a dollar bill and she would shake her head slowly from side to side, still smiling. Then I held up two dollar bills. She smiled and shook her head. On one occasion I even held up a five-dollar bill and lifted my other hand displaying five fingers so she could not misunderstand what the single bill represented. She smiled and shook her head.

That was during my last year in high school. The episode with Mr. Schlachter had taken place during the winter and spring was around the corner. I had never had a girl friend unless you could consider Cousin Cheryl in that category. She *had* permitted that exploratory session one afternoon when her mother and older sister were out and she even went to a Masonic dance with me for which my father provided tickets, dressed in an orange organdy dress that stuck to my sweaty fingers, but she permitted no further liberties beyond a chaste kiss with lips so firmly closed they felt like wood.

So, without any knowledge of the meaning of the word – or of its existence – I sublimated my crescent erotic drive by plunging into the work of the Biology Field Club at DeWitt Clinton High School and, come spring, by making a series of weekend field trips all over the landscape.

The most successful expedition of my entire career as a putative herpetologist took place late in April of that year, in the Ramapo range near Suffern, New York.

On the rocky ledge on the south side of the highest hill at three-fifteen in the afternoon I came upon a nest of baby rattlesnakes and copperheads. There were *hundreds* of them, obviously newborn (both species are viviparous), and they were drowsing in the sun.

In a frenzy of activity and without the slightest regard for my personal safety (but with the subconscious knowledge that vipers as small as these were barely poisonous, for the quantity of venom they could inject with their tiny fangs was miniscule), I scooped them up into my pillowcase by the handful, my heart pounding even more vigorously than it had in the gatekeeper's shack near the Buffalo Gate.

That night, with greater care, I sorted them out into two shelves of the *Globe-Wernecke* bookcase and found that I had a hundred and thirteen baby *Crotalus horridus* and seventy-four infant *Agkistrodon contortrix*, the latter with lovely, sulphur-yellow tails.

The following Saturday I put them in separate pillowcases with tags identifying them and waited at the Snake House for two and a half hours until Roland Martin finally appeared. Then I handed them to him.

He looked into each bag and said, "Very good, Julian. Very good indeed. Where did you find them?"

I told him and he nodded solemnly and said, "A good day's work" and actually touched my shoulder with approval.

The duly-inscribed certificate arrived on Thursday of that week but I knew that something better was in store. I knew that when I went to the Zoo on Saturday I would see them displayed in two glass-fronted boxes, side by side, with little metal nameplates identifying them and adding:

Donated by Julian Leonard
New York

When I arrived at the Snake House Saturday morning at nine I saw no sign of them nor was Roland Martin in his office. The head keeper said he did not know whether the Curator would be in that day or not, but since I had the run of the place he let me explore backstage, behind the huge glass cages that held the python and the *Boa constrictors* and anacondas, the king cobra and all the other beasts. There was always a warm, damp and jungly odor in that place.

I found no baby snakes in any of the storage rooms and I hung around until three that afternoon when the Curator himself appeared.

"Hello, Julian," he said, "what did you bring today?"

"Nothing," I said and came right to the point. "I don't see the baby rattlers and copperheads."

There was a long pause – a pause that I learned later in Psychology I at Columbia, when we were studying free association, was an almost infallibale index of guilt. Then he said, "I'm sorry. They died."

"They died!" I cried in astonishment. "In a *week!*"

That was the second time he touched me on the shoulder – out of sympathy, I knew – and said, "They don't thrive very well in captivity, you know. Too young. Won't eat."

It never occurred to me to ask why he had not told me that the day I brought them in. With grief I accepted the death of my darling baby snakes and started away.

"I'm sorry," he said again and I nodded my head and left the Snake House.

What a waste of life! What a loss! One hundred and thirteen baby *Crotalus* and seventy-four infant *Agkistrodon* – one hundred and eighty-seven tiny lives snuffed out and not even in the interest of science. And *I* had been responsible! For if I had only left them in their native habitat on the ledge they would have lived and grown and multiplied and replenished the earth – with the exception of the very few who would fall victim to their natural enemies, both animal and human.

The next Saturday I returned to Suffern on the interurban train, certain that if there had been one nest there must be others. If there were I would certainly not disturb them and my conscience would at least be somewhat assuaged by knowing there were more.

There was a man on the platform of the interurban train whose face was familiar, though at first I could not place it. It became even more familiar when I noticed he was carrying a "snake stick" in one hand and a pillowcase tied at the neck, in the other.

Suddenly I knew who he was and decided to speak to him. His name was Willits and he was the self-appointed president of a phony organization called The Serpent Study Society of America.

Regularly, twice a year, the S. S. S. of A. got a great deal of publicity; in between, it collected dues of five dollars a year from a considerable number of middle-aged and elderly crackpots who joined it for reasons that were scarcely scientific: they liked to be photographed with snakes around their necks.

Once a year, in the spring, the S.S.S. of A. had an annual snake hunt (five dollars, registration fee), when many of these eccentrics ventured forth *en masse* with Willits at their head, to hunt snakes and presumably study them. Naturally, every self-respecting serpent within miles felt the earth tremble with the thunder of their passage and made itself scarce.

Oh, they caught a snake or two. That is, Willits caught one which he had probably planted in advance and was duly photographed on page fifteen of *The New York Times,* surrounded by a bunch of ancient crocks who were beaming at him in awe and with delight.

Then, every winter it held an annual banquet in a respectable New York hotel (ten dollars a ticket) to which the press was invited, and there was a goodly display of various species of snake and Willits made a speech about the fascination of serpents and (correctly, at least) how even the venomous varieties contributed to the balance of nature and therefore were worthy of protection.

A lot of the old biddies got themselves photographed for the *Times* holding snakes in their hands or draped around their necks. Old ladies with blue hair and bombazine gowns with lace collars beamed idiotically at the camera and qualified, for the moment, as "students" of the serpent that the Bible had most unscientifically said was *"more subtil than any beast of the field which the Lord God had made."* (Actually, it is intellectually impoverished.)

I approached Mr. Willits and said, "Are you collecting snakes?"

"How did you know?"

I nodded at his pillowcase and said, "I collect them myself."

"Then you'll be interested in this," he said and untied the string that held the pillowcase shut. I peeped inside and gasped.

Willits interpreted my gasp as astonishment and I suppose it was; but it was not the sort of astonishment he thought I was experiencing, for in that pillowcase there writhed and twined with each other my one hundred and thirteen baby rattlers and my seventy-four infant copperheads.

Some native shrewdness that I possessed at sixteen and have long since lost made me inquire innocently, "Where did you get them?"

He closed the pillowcase and carefully tied it before answering.

Then he said, "Some dope brought them to the Zoo and Martin gave them to me."

"What for?"

"To plant," he said. "I'm going to plant them on a ledge in the Ramapos."

"Why?"

"I guess you don't know much about snakes, do you, kid? Or about the way Martin operates?" He paused and grinned at me.

"I'm planting them so Martin will have a source of supply for the Snake House — when he needs 'em."

"Oh," I said. "I see."

"Pretty clever, eh?"

"*Very* clever," I said.

Willits did not ask me to accompany him when we got off the train at Suffern and I rapidly vanished from his sight. He did not vanish from mine, however. I instantly became Uncas in *The Last of the Mohicans* and I tracked him from a distance as he climbed the very hill on which I had caught my little darlings and gently placed them on the very ledge where they had been born.

He stood looking down at them benevolently for a few moments; then he vanished. Once he was out of sight I sped to the ledge and — with the exception of a baker's dozen who had crawled into the deeper fissures of the rock — I gathered them all up again: sixty-seven copperheads and one hundred and seven rattlesnakes.

Boiling with rage against injustice — a sentiment that must have had a premature development in my psyche — I caught the train back to Hoboken and the very next Saturday I traveled to Pennsylvania, getting off at a town near Promisedland Lake, and climbed into the hills of Pike County.

There *I* planted the baby serpents on a wooded hillside and watched over them tenderly until they disappeared in the underbrush.

That will teach you, Roland Martin! I said to myself with unutterable satisfaction. That will teach you to lie to *me*! With wings as swift as meditation or the thoughts of lust I had swept to my revenge over *him* — if not over Betsy Martin, his snooty daughter who had had the *chutzpah* to look down her snub nose at *me*.

It was very late when I got back to Riverside Drive, late for *me*, that is, and the sign on the Jersey shore said: THE . . . TIME . . . IS . . . NOW . . . 10:15. MAZOLA.

Actually, it was time itself that avenged me, I suppose. The most recent edition of Roland Martin's *The Snake Book* reveals that its copyright was renewed in 1956 — long after the death of the Curator — "by Betsy Martin."

So, she could not find anyone to marry her — and serve her right! Unless . . . oh *no!* . . . she was a female Schlachter. . .?

Bubo virginianus

IF he said it once he said it a thousand times. Before he died in 1921 of his first and only heart attack at the age of fifty-one he used to say to my mother, Helena, "The day after I die, Lena, you will begin to get telephone calls from men who say they're friends of mine on Wall Street. They'll offer their condolences and tell you that your future and the boys' will be secure if you'll only invest in some stocks they have in mind. *Hang up the phone!*"

Promptly, the day after Nathaniel Leonard died the phone rang and friends of his on Wall Street told my mother how she could take her little nest egg, the thirty thousand dollars in insurance her husband had left, and guarantee her future and the future of my older brother Adrian and me.

She did not hang up. It was my father's fault of course, for he was the one who had taught her to play poker; he was the one who had taught her how to play the races; he was the one whose small killings on The Street had, for a time, brought her marvelous pieces of diamond jewelry cunningly concealed in candy boxes full of chocolate.

My mother therefore became a compulsive (and very bad) poker player. In time she even got to play in nice social games with Arnold Rothstein and Jack "Legs" Diamond whom she loyally described as "perfect gentlemen" even after they had been rubbed out by other gangsters. She played the races *and* the Market and

246

as a natural result of the operation of these dialectical forces she managed to lose at least two-thirds of the insurance money my father had had sense enough not to touch that last week of his life, when he decided he was finally going to be a millionaire by buying cotton — and the bottom fell out of the Market.

By careful management there *was* enough left to send my brother Adrian through medical school and for me to complete my studies at Columbia, and that was all. There is no doubt, however, that our mother also had some sporadic assistance from a mysterious Gentleman Caller whose name was Mr. Krone, who had been around a long time (but only when my father was out of town), and whom I loathed.

I called him The Lobster because he had a bright red face. After my father died he even had the gall to move into an apartment behind us on the same floor. Then I no longer heard the sounds I had listened to all through my boyhood — the muffled arguments in the next bedroom, the dragging of the suitcase out of the closet, the slamming of the outside door as my father left "for good this time," the careful opening of the apartment door early the next morning as he returned with his tail between his legs and set the suitcase on the floor. Then there was muffled weeping and voices were purposefully reduced to whispers.

The sounds I heard after my father died were perhaps happier. I heard muffled conversation, true, but lots of giggling. I heard my mother whisper, "Be *care*ful . . . they're *asleep!*" My brother Adrian might have been asleep but I was not. I never slept. I was an owl. A great horned owl, perhaps.

Then there would be more giggling and the sound of tiptoeing down the hall, the cautious opening of the apartment door; the less-cautious opening of the door to the apartment behind us, louder giggling and — silence.

Sometimes when I woke in the morning and went into my mother's bedroom (she was in the kitchen making breakfast for her two growing sons), I saw — barely concealed behind the window drapes — two small whiskey glasses, side by side, that obviously had been used.

Like my father, Mr. Krone was "a traveling man." He was also a "confirmed" alcoholic (which my father never was). He occasionally tried to cultivate my friendship. He did not succeed. He often called up when he was out of town and on one or two occasions I reached the phone before my mother could and heard his thick and rasping voice say, "'s Lena there? I wanna talka Lena."

Then I would call her, saying contemptuously, "It's *The Lobster.*"

He called one time and I listened to my mother's side of that memorable conversation.

"No, I can't come out tonight. Where are you? . . . No, I *can't* take a cab and come to the hotel . . . What hotel? . . . The *Blackstone*?! Why, that's in *Chicago*! Pull yourself together, please, Herman. How can I take a cab to the Blackstone when I'm in New *York*?! . . . No, I *can't* take a cab! Call me when you're back in town."

He never did come back to town from that particular trip and my mother spent several years vainly trying to find out what had become of him. He had a sister in New York but she hadn't heard from him in years. He simply "vanished into thin air," as my mother said when she was being romantic, or "into an institution to take the Keeley Cure," when she was (occasionally) a realist.

But her relationship with Mr. Krone gave the lie to her later confession that she had often thought of leaving my father because "I never cared for . . . sex. . . ."

Both our parents must have been whacked up in the sex department, for that matter, a fact which was to interest my eventual psychiatrist Dr. Schwarzkopf, who shared my mother's maiden name.

He was fascinated by the tale of my mother and Mr. Krone; by my father's compulsions: washing his hands thirty times a day, bathing and changing his underwear three times a day; tipping his hat to pregnant women on the streets; by the dream my father had had, that I had been kidnapped by "a fiend" and sexually "abused" for a week, then deposited on the doorstep, "a driveling idiot."

To my chagrin, Dr. Schwarzkopf seemed far more interested in my parents' obvious neuroses than he was in mine, but no matter. Certainly he was *most* interested in a conversation my father and I had, walking one Sunday on our invariable visits to his three sisters and one sister-in-law (with boxes of candy or bouquets of roses), when he suddenly said, "What's going on between you and your cousin Cheryl?"

I told him the literal truth. "Nothing" (unfortunately), whereupon he stopped walking right opposite the subway station on 159th and Broadway and looking me straight in the eyes, he said, "If I ever hear that there's anything going on between you and your cousin Cheryl, I'll kill you both — and myself."

But at that time just before his death I was not too much concerned with such steamy matters. I was a college freshman trying desperately to adjust myself to the considerable difference between DeWitt Clinton High School and Columbia and had launched into a course of scientific studies that included biology, zoology and physiology, as preparation for my career as a natural historian-herpetologist.

On the phone with Izzy Stein, who had shared the presidency of the Biology Field Club with me at Clinton, and who was now a premedical student at City College of New York, I compared notes on our respective professors and the courses they were offering.

Owing to the fact that I had majored in biology in high school I was permitted to take college biology and zoology simultaneously. The biology professor, Harry Palmer, earned my immediate dislike even though he was the author of our text. He smiled — continuously — and my instinctive reaction to him was confirmed when I recalled a frequent admonition of my mother: "Never trust a person with a permanent smile."

I was absolutely mad about the zoology prof, Thomas Cameron, a tiny Scot who never smiled at all but who was internationally renowned. He was renowned for having reconstructed, practically single-handedly, the bone fragments of *Pithecanthropus erectus,* Cro-Magnon Man, Peking Man, and Neanderthal Man into lifelike sculptured heads and bodies that were as scientifically accurate as the state of our knowledge in 1920 permitted.

This was not what made him lovable, of course, nor the fact that he was *so* celebrated that when a new femur, scapula or calvarium was found, cables would arrive from, say, the Gobi Desert or from Java and Professor Cameron would take a small handbag, pack it with clean underwear and socks and a set of calipers, and sail forth to examine it.

Nor was it the fact that he was ambidextrous that endeared him to his students. He had a cute habit of drawing an outline on the blackboard with his right hand and simultaneously coloring it in with his left. Students would stamp thunderously on the classroom floor in simultaneous approbation and sarcastic appraisal of this unique accomplishment.

What made Professor Cameron adored and remembered were the hallmarks of any great teacher — he knew his subject, he loved his subject and he loved to teach. He even liked his students, which is more than can be said for ninety percent of those who make a living by tyrannizing students.

Izzy Stein admitted on the phone that none of his profs could compare with Cameron — or even Palmer — and suggested once more that we get together.

I had no greater love for this large and damp young man than I had had in high school — he was a Puritan and a premature stuffed shirt — but I agreed to accompany him one night to a meeting at the Natural History Museum of something called the Linnaean Society.

Obviously it was named after Linnaeus, the celebrated Swedish botanist of the eighteenth century who had not only classified the *flora* and *fauna* of the Scandinavian peninsula (and much of the rest of the world), but who had practically invented the system of scientific nomenclature that is still in use.

In the 1920's no scientific names ever appeared without a parenthetic abbreviation at the end indicating who had first described the species. Thus, for example, the creature that the social scientist H. L. Mencken first described (if he did not actually create it) would be properly named: *Boobus americanus* (Menck.).

Literally thousands of plants and flowers, trees and birds, butterflies and mammals, reptiles, amphibians and insects carried the (Linn.) after their scientific names. The first Linnaean Society, named after the great Swede whose work was so admired that in 1761 he was granted a patent of nobility and was henceforth known as Carl von Linné, was established in London early in the nineteenth century.

Izzy and I were therefore in considerable awe to have been admitted as spectators to the deliberations of this august body and we actually entered the small room on the main floor of the Museum on tiptoe. We were at least half an hour late.

It was not surprising to see Mr. S. Robert Stevenson; he was President of the Audubon Society to whom Izzy had introduced me a year earlier and whose literature had sparked our great crusade to Save the American Eagle! (*Haliaeetus leucocephalus*). But considering how that campaign had fizzled I, for one, was somewhat embarrassed by his presence.

He did not seem to be annoyed, however, but took off his *pince-nez* to look at the newcomers and, having identified us both, smiled and even waved his hand. Izzy confided to me in a loud stage whisper that it was Stevenson himself who had been responsible for our invitation.

There were only eleven members of this prestigious society present, including Mr. Stevenson. To us, most of them seemed to be terribly old but the oldest was probably no more than fifty. One was sound asleep, two were reading documents when the chairman, a fat fellow with a red face, three or four chins and a very long neck cleared his throat to make an announcement.

"We are privileged tonight, gentlemen, to have two young visitors who are interested in our work." He consulted a slip of paper in his hand and said, with slight distaste, "Mr. Isidore Stein?"

Izzy promptly stood and there was a pattering of applause as the assorted graybeards turned around to look at us in the last row of the small room.

"Mr. Julian Leonard?" said the chairman and I rose briefly, was applauded and sat down again.

"Harrumph!" said the chairman. "It is always good to know that younger men are interested in our work and I take this opportunity to thank" — he consulted his paper again — "to thank Mr. S. Robert Stevenson, the distinguished President of the Audubon Society, for inviting these two embryo scientists to our deliberations." He chuckled loudly. Then he personally applauded Mr. Stevenson, who stood, took a bow and sat down again.

Then the chairman said, "This is the point in our monthly meeting which is devoted to the presentation of recent observations in the field.

He craned his neck like a great blue heron (*Ardea herodias*) searching for a likely frog to spear. "Is there . . . anybody . . .?" he said.

There was a considerable pause. Then a man in the front row whose face I could not see and who did not bother to stand, said, "I was in the Rambles in Central Park late this afternoon and observed a Wilson's warbler."

"I saw one too!" Izzy Stein stage whispered in my ear. "Last week."

There was another patter of applause and the man in the front row continued. "Of course, this is rather uncommon, not only for this time of year but in this part of the country."

A tall fellow who looked more like the Egyptian mummy at the Metropolitan Museum of Art than any living human being I had ever seen, stood up and cleared his throat.

"I do not wish to question the distinguished member's observation, but I am inclined to feel that we are *all* too prone, at times, to mistake the immature male yellowthroat for the Wilson."

Then the man in the front row stood up and turned to face his antagonist. He was short and fat.

"Begging the pardon of the distinguished member, I could not *possibly* have mistaken a yellowthroat for a Wilson. In the first place, the black marking was confined to the *crown* of the head — a characteristic of *Wilsonia pusilla*. In the second place, the song was entirely characteristic. I counted the notes: seventeen sharp and very musical chips, dropping slightly in pitch toward the end of the song."

The Antagonist, still standing, said dryly, "I will beg the pardon of my distinguished colleague. I am only seeking to inject a note of caution here. Hasty observation sometimes results in inaccurate identification, or, should I say, wishful thinking. I do *not* accuse my amiable friend of either."

"Thank *you*," said his amiable friend. Both sat down and the Great Blue Heron at the podium said, "Harrumph! Anyone else care to start an argument?"

There was desultory laughter. One member reported hearing (but not seeing) an American bittern near the edge of a pond in Central Park. He gave an imitation of its sound: "Like a creaking pump," he said, "oonck-o-tsoonck."

The Antagonist rose and said, "That cry, of course, is generally heard only on the breeding grounds. Scarcely in the fall. But *again* — I am not contending that the observation was inaccurate." He sat down.

Somebody said, "Maybe the bird *thought* it was on the breeding ground," and everybody laughed.

"In *October*?" said the indefatigable Antagonist. There was more laughter. "*Homo sapiens*, so called," he added, "is the only species that breeds the year around."

I was getting bored. Birds, birds, birds. Who cares about birds? I was interested in reptiles and amphibians. Wasn't there anybody here who shared my interest? There were supposed to be *all* kinds of scientists present, not just bird-watchers.

More rare birds were reported as having been observed in unlikely habitats, when suddenly I found myself on my feet, not knowing what I was doing there and with my heart pounding.

The Great Blue Heron with the four chins harrumphed at me and said, "Our young friend, Mr. . . . . Mr. . . . ."

"Leonard," I said.

"Ah, yes, Mr. Leonard. I think he has an observation to report."

Some of the graybeards turned around to look at me and I knew I *had* to say something and — suddenly — I knew exactly what I was going to say.

"In Van Cortlandt Park last Sunday," I said, "just at dusk." Then I dried up.

"Yes?" said the Great Blue Heron. Mr. S. Robert Stevenson took off his *pince-nez*, the better to focus on me. The Antagonist actually swiveled in his chair and glared.

"*Bubo virgin . . . ianus*" I stammered. "The great horned owl. It was almost dark. I was walking toward the subway station at

242nd Street and had to pass through some second-growth trees."

My panic mounted and I had a hard time finding words. "Something on the ground . . . suddenly moved — maybe a rabbit, I didn't get a good look at it." I paused for breath rather than for effect.

"Then there was a great *whooshing* sound and . . . and the owl came out of nowhere, dropping onto whatever it was that by this time was in the underbrush. There was a squealing sound and with great, slow flaps of its wings the owl rose and flew away with something in its talons."

There was a long silence. I stood there, choking with anxiety.

The Antagonist said, "Are you sure it was *virginianus*, young man?"

"Yes, sir." (Gulp.)

"Are you sure it wasn't the great *gray* owl?"

The fat little man in the front row who had seen the Wilson's warbler in the Rambles stood up, faced the rear of the room and his face became absolutely livid.

"*Now* I have you!" he cried to the Antagonist. "Everybody knows the great gray, *Strix nebulosa*, is not only rare but is *strictly confined* to high altitudes in the Sierra Nevada and the *Rockies*!"

"I was trying to *trap* the young man," said the Antagonist.

"You were *not*!" shouted Wilson's Warbler. "And if you *were*, that is entirely beneath the dignity of a member of a scientific society!"

"Gentlemen, gentlemen!" said the Great Blue Heron with the red face. "Please control yourselves." He focussed his eyes on me and said, "Go right ahead, Mr. . . . ." he consulted his slip of paper and added, "Mr. Stein."

"Leonard," I said. "Julian Leonard." Pause. "I saw its *horns.*"

"Touché!" cried Wilson's Warbler from the front row.

"The long-eared owl, *Asio otus*, can easily be mistaken for *Bubo*," said the Antagonist.

"*Bubo's* horns . . . are farther apart," I said.

"Touché!"

"You *saw* its horns?" said the Antagonist.

"Yes, sir," I said calmly.

"At *dusk*?" he said, a patent sneer on his face. "Flying?"

I was silent. I didn't know how to answer that. There *was* no answer. He had me but I was rescued by a genuine graybeard who had not spoken previously.

He rose and said, "Gentlemen . . . uh . . . I am very much impressed . . . uh . . . with the observation of this . . . uh . . . young man and by the splendid way in which he . . . uh . . . handled himself when his observation was called into . . . uh . . . question by our . . . distinguished member, Mr. Pilk."

He looked around the room and nodded his head. Out of deference to his age and his gray beard, I imagine, there was complete silence. Or maybe he was the head of the whole damned Natural History Museum. I wouldn't know.

"This Society," he said, "is . . . uh . . . very much in need of new . . . uh . . . blood. Young blood." He nodded as though agreeing with himself. "Now . . . uh . . . while it may be somewhat irregular, for . . . uh . . . I do not believe we have any . . . uh . . . members as young as these two scientists . . . uh . . . who have honored us with their . . . uh . . . presence here tonight . . . ."

He paused and nodded his head three times, as though he were some species of bird himself. "I am nevertheless . . . uh . . . proposing both of them for membership in the . . . uh . . . Linnaean Society."

"Hear! Hear!" cried Wilson's Warbler.

"Any second to the motion?" said the Great Blue Heron.

"I second the motion," said Mr. S. Robert Stevenson.

"Discussion?" said the Chair.

There was absolute silence. Even the Antagonist was silent but he made a point of sitting down to demonstrate his disapproval.

"All in favor?"

There was a chorus of "Aye!" that was startlingly enthusiastic for this group of Egyptian mummies.

"Opposed?"

Silence.

"So ordered," said the Chair. "Mr. . . . ." he recovered his slip of paper, which this time had found its way to the floor, "Mr. Leonard . . . and, er, Mr. . . . . Stein are duly elected to membership in the Linnaean Society."

"Point of order," said the Antagonist.

"What is your point of order?" said the Chair.

"Do we have a quorum present?"

"I'm sure I don't know," said the Chair. There was scattered applause; he nodded at me and Izzy and we both stood up. When we sat down Izzy turned to me and said, "Did you *really* see it?"

"*Shut up!*" I stage whispered. I was still in a state of panic. My throat was dry and my heart was banging on my ribs. I was wondering whatever had possessed me to say such a thing. I was actually dizzy and did not even notice that the meeting had been adjourned until a tall, dark man with short, stiff hair stood at my side and said, "Congratulations." Then he giggled.

"Thank you," I said.

"I'm Dr. R. Maple Foss," he said. "Curator of Reptiles and Amphibians here at the Museum."

Whereas I had shaken his hand perfunctorily when he offered his congraulations, I now grasped it with both of mine and pumped it vigorously.

"I'm *very* glad to meet you, sir," I said. Words strangled in my throat but I managed, without denigrating the entire ornithological *fauna* of North America, to say, "What I'm *really* interested in is herpetology."

"That so." (A statement, not a question.)

"I've been interested for *years*," I said. "I collect specimens for the Zoo. I hope to make it my career."

"That so," said Dr. R. Maple Foss and giggled. I vigorously shook my head up and down.

"In college?"

"Columbia, sir. Freshman."

"My office is on the top floor," said Dr. Foss. "Drop in some time."

"I'll do that, sir," I said eagerly. "*Thank* you."

"Maybe you can report seeing an Egyptian cobra on the Palisades," he said, and giggled.

•

The Scientific Method

O F course I dropped in at the office of Dr. R. Maple Foss, Curator of Reptiles and Amphibians at the Natural History Museum, less than a week after he invited me to do so. The invitation had been extended at a meeting of the august Linnaean Society, of which I had been elected to membership on the basis of my first scientific report — at the age of sixteen.

I had reported to the assembled graybeard members of that scientific body that I had observed a great horned owl (*Bubo virginianus*) in Van Cortlandt Park one day at dusk; a most unlikely observation, especially when you consider the fact that I had never seen the bird at all.

But my guilty conscience at having put one over on these learned natural historians was at least partly assuaged by my almost instinctive conviction that the end justified the means.

The end was to become a natural scientist myself, specializing in herpetology. If a little horned lie had to be told to gain *entrée* to the inner sanctum of accredited scientists, what difference did it make? I would make up for my boldfaced fabrication by serious and dedicated work in the department of reptiles and amphibians.

At least that was my intention and I was pleased that when I reported to Dr. Foss he did not swing around in his swivel chair and shout, "You LIED when you said you saw *Bubo virginianus* in Van Cortlandt Park!"

Instead he smiled pleasantly and introduced me to his handsome

257

wife, Samantha Roberts, whose name I had seen recently in the magazine *Natural History*, as the author of an article on anthropology.

He also introduced me to his assistant, Mr. Pildyke, and the reason for their presence together, it seems, centered on a microscope on Dr. Foss' desk.

"Take a look," Foss said to me, "it's fascinating!" He giggled and I gazed through the eyepiece and all I could see were my own eyelashes.

"It's the *gastrocnemius* muscle of *Hyla crucifer*," said Dr. Foss. "Enchanting, isn't it?"

I suppose it was and certainly I knew the name of the tiny frog from which he had detached the muscle — it was the spring peeper whose chorusing in early spring made everybody (including me) say it sounded exactly "like sleigh bells."

I nodded my head with a semblance of enthusiasm and after Samantha Roberts and Mr. Pildyke had each taken another look and had withdrawn from Foss' office, he said, "I have a job for you."

That was exactly what I had wanted him to say and I thought immediately in the racing terminology I had heard my father and mother use so often, "They're off!," by which I mean that *I* was off — into my herpetological career.

"How often can you be here?" said Dr. Foss as he escorted me into a room full of boxes, jars and bottles.

"Well, most of my classes at Columbia are over by three o'clock. Some days at one."

"Good," he said. "Come every day you can."

He pointed to a large wooden crate whose lid was loosely nailed down. A hammer rested on it.

"There are about two hundred *Chrysemys picta picta* in that crate," said Dr. Foss and giggled nervously. He pointed to a large bottle and a tray in which there was a huge hypodermic syringe fitted with a long needle.

"There's formaldehyde. Syringe. Get to work."

He started to walk out and I cursed my ignorance as I said, plaintively, "What am I supposed to do?"

"Inject them of course," said Dr. Foss. "Then put them in those empty jars." He pointed to a row of huge glass jars standing on the floor. He left.

Some native intelligence informed me that if you were going to inject a turtle you would have to do it in its soft parts, between the *carapace* and the *plastron* (upper and lower shells, to the layman).

I therefore filled the syringe with formaldehyde, pried the lid off the crate and brought forth one beautiful specimen of *Chrysemys* — the painted turtle.

I stood admiring him: the brilliant yellow spots and lines on his head, the red and black markings on the margins of the *carapace*, the yellow *plastron* itself. He was a handsome brute.

Then, squeamishly, I inserted the hypodermic needle into the soft part between his left hind leg and the shell and pressed on the ring at the end of the plunger.

So great was my naiveté that I was utterly astounded when the turtle uttered a high, whistling sound and promptly gave up the ghost. I laid it on the table and poked it with one finger. It did not move. I turned it on its back; its head and legs lolled out, inert.

Killing the turtle was apparently the object of the injection and I was certain that I did not like it at all. *This* was herpetology?! I thought. This was *murder*!

I was *so* disconcerted by what I had done that I was able to inject no more than seven turtles before I became overcome with melancholy and sat down on a wooden box and stared into space. Two out of three of the poor creatures had whistled as they expired, a feeble and totally ineffectual protest against inexorable fate.

Finally I gathered courage to report to Dr. Foss what I had done — or, rather, had not done — but he had apparently gone for the day and only Mr. Pildyke remained in the office. He looked up at me when I said, "I have to go now. I live 'way uptown," and he nodded.

"I'll do the rest tomorrow," I said, and he looked puzzled but I was still so upset by my first genuine job as a herpetologist that I did not enlighten him.

Nor was I able to come down to the Museum the next day.

The laboratory sessions in biology had been rescheduled and the best I could do for the entire month was to appear for a few hours a day, about twice a week.

It was possible in the months to come, of course, to forget the shameful start of my unpaid career as a herpetologist: injecting turtles. Or at least to become somewhat callous about it. For in biology and zoology — and later in my physiology course — I became inured to what had to be done when you were a serious student of the many forms that life assumes on our planet.

In those laboratory sessions we had to kill and to dissect the common earthworm, the crayfish and the frog. The frog remained alive — if mercifully unconscious — for quite a time, thanks to a dreadful process known as "pithing": with a scalpel you made a small incision just behind the frog's head, then you inserted a wire into its brain (ugh!), effectively destroying that crucial organ.

The poor frog sat motionless upon your desk. It instantly became what our physiology instructor, the celebrated Professor Franz Uhse, called "a reflex animal." It would not move unless it was stimulated: if you poked it, it hopped; if you dropped a mild acid on the inside of its thigh, it scratched its leg; if you dangled a worm in front of its nose, its tongue shot out, grabbed the worm and it swallowed automatically; if you dropped it into tank of water it would swim. But if you did nothing to it, it would do nothing. In fact, said Professor Uhse, it would sit calmly there until it died of starvation!

Uhse was a character. The first time he demonstrated to us the phenomenon of the pithed frog we came into the classroom and saw it sitting there under a glass bell jar: *Rana pipiens*, the leopard frog. On the side of the bell jar the witty Professor had stuck a label which read: *Insane Asylum*. Then he explained what he had done to the amphibian.

Decades before anyone ever claimed that smoking "may be hazardous to your health," Professor Uhse lectured his classes on the evils of tobacco, simultaneously pulling out his pipe, filling it and lighting it.

"I am the only vun who can smuk in class," he said. "Tobacco iss a deadly poison."

The students stamped their feet on the floor in sign of disapproval. "If I vish to kill myself, dot iss *my* beezness," he said reasonably. "But I vill not be rezponzible vor *your* doing it."

Even that early in my career I had noticed that there was something odd about people working in the sciences. With the exception of our zoology professor, the magnificent Thomas Cameron, who could draw on the blackboard with both hands at the same time, outlining with one hand and coloring-in with the other, all the men and women I met in the Zoo, the Natural History Museum, at Columbia or "in the field" were odd:

The parade had begun with Aaron Vogelsang, my "snake friend," who had injected this passion for reptiles and amphibians (if not formaldehyde) into my fourteen-year-old life. For here was a grown man at least thirty-one who actually *preferred* to live in a tiny room in the Jewish Orphan Asylum because his mother was its matron; who simultaneously worked in Wall Street and read strange books entitled *Building a Dynamic Personality* and *Selling the Difficult Customer*.

The Curator of Reptiles at the Bronx Zoo, Roland Martin, had a brown mustache, brown socks and brown shoes. He was always in a brown study and he never smiled. In fact his composure was positively ophidian and there is no other living creature that is as composed as a snake — or seems to be.

Dr. R. Maple Foss may have been as tall and handsome as a champion oarsman from Yale or Harvard but he had a nervous giggle that was entirely incompatible with his physical or professional stature. Every creature he collected or studied was a "beast," whether it was a giant leatherback sea turtle (*Dermochelys coriacea*) over eight feet long and weighing fifteen hundred pounds, or a cricket frog (*Acris crepitans*) that was three-quarters of an inch in length and weighed an ounce or two.

His assistant, Mr. Pildyke, I rapidly decided was a pill but that judgment might have been colored by simple jealousy. He was an accredited herpetologist who went on to glory at the Field Museum in Chicago — and to martyrdom when he was spectacularly killed by a boomslang (*Dispholidus typus*), one of the most deadly South African snakes. (Or maybe it was a green mamba — *Dendraspis angusticeps* — I don't remember.)

Then, of course, there had been Dr. Foss' immediate predecessor, Susan Anthony Aldridge, who had been carried from the basement of the Museum in a straitjacket when it was discovered that she was reclassifying the study collection of *reptilia* and *amphibia* that reposed in thousands of jars of formaldehyde — by carefully soaking off the original labels and replacing them with new labels typed with the wrong generic and species names.

Dr. Pike, the Curator of Ichthyology at the Museum, looked exactly like a fish. Dr. Holmes, the Museum's preeminent lepidopterist, while he looked like a woodchuck rather than a butterfly or moth, was strange in other ways: he brought a round tin of one hundred Lord Salisbury cigarettes to work with him every morning and lit one from another. He was more than slightly mad, for when I met him he had already spent a year reclassifying the butterfly and moth collection, which comprised several million specimens. He told me with bitterness that was certainly more than skin-deep that "a lepidopterist is a man who takes butterflies out of one case and pins them into another." (He gave them their right names, I think.)

Later I met an anthropologist at the Museum named Herbert Heinz, who was known to his colleagues as "57 Varieties" (he was a scion of the wealthy pickle family), but who insisted on being called Uncle Herbie, and our biology professor at Columbia, Harry Palmer, was another case in point.

We were required of course to study from his textbook brilliantly called *Biology*. That was bad enough and even my stockbroker father pointed out to me in his cynical businessman way that there was no doubt the professor had "made a good thing" out of that arrangement.

What was worse was the fact that he had a permanent smile. He smiled *all* the time, even when his face was in repose, which is a considerable achievement if you've ever tried to do it. My mother had warned my brother Adrian and me: "Never trust a person with a permanent smile." (I've always wondered whom she was thinking about. It could *not* have been my father.)

I did not really need her warning; it was enough to watch Professor Palmer and his ichthyological smile to get shivers down your spine.

This puzzled me. Why should a smile have such an odd effect on people? — even a permanent smile? The smile I watched for every day when I came home from college or the Museum never had such an effect on me.

I used to look across the courtyard toward the maid's room opposite mine and sooner or later she would appear: the Polish (or Russian or Lithuanian) servant girl who liked to undress partially in front of her window and then, pretending to suddenly notice me, would coyly draw down the shade and peek around it and smile her Lithuanian smile.

That woman drove me mad at sixteen. I tried to seduce her by holding up dollar bills one at a time. I even held up a five-dollar bill and she smiled and pulled down the shade. I confronted her in the hallway one day when she was going out in her coat and round red patent-leather hat and grabbed her hand and begged her to let me visit her that very day. She smiled, said something in a foreign language and ran down the staircase instead of waiting for the elevator.

Of course it never occurred to me that of all the natural scientists I knew at that time, whether accredited or hopeful, *I* was the most peculiar. Those things have to be pointed out to you — and sometimes in the most painful ways.

But there *must* be a relationship between absorption in the sciences and total otherworldliness. Ten years after the events recorded here I met a man in his thirties who was said to have invented the photoelectric cell. Like Aaron Vogelsang, he too lived with his mother — but in the same apartment.

He came into New York on the train one day and arriving in Grand Central Station he rushed into a phone booth and called a mutual friend who was a sculptor.

"Waldo," he said breathlessly, "I met a man on the train coming down from Schenectady who said that artists . . . uh . . . use . . . uh . . . naked models! Is that *true?*"

"Sure," said Waldo, a small man who used his eighty-five-pound wife as a model for the powerful imitation-Maillol females he liked to carve.

"Gee whiz!" said the inventor. But if you think *that* is unworldly, consider the fact that this authentic genius not only lived with his mother, he also gave her his entire salary — and she gave him five dollars a week for his lunch and carfare. He told my friend Waldo that the giant corporation for which he had invented the photoelectric cell was "wonderful! They gave me a bonus of five thousand dollars! Imagine that!"

True, this was in the depths of the Depression but Waldo pointed out to him that the company stood to make something like sixty trillion dollars on his exclusive, patented-by-them invention and he could not see the point. Five thousand dollars was a lot of money; it was as much as he made in two *years*!

But I led a sheltered life myself. My obsessions swung between the study of biology, zoology and physiology and a determination to get that girl with the red patent-leather hat into bed with me.

I was not disconcerted more than momentarily that day in the hallway by the discovery that she had one front tooth missing. Her smile was just as provocative without the tooth and her physiology — I was determined to study it as nobody had ever studied it before.

Frustrated by her rejection, however gentle and polite — and by her intermittent coquettishness — there was nothing for me to do except to engage in what my father called "self-abuse," to steal pornographic books from the secret shelves of a bookstore on Forty-seventh Street, read them in bed at night and develop day and night dreams that would have fazed Casanova.

I collected dirty jokes and limericks — and memorized them. I shocked the pants off a fellow student in the biology lab one afternoon by showing him a slide under my microscope that — instead of swarming with *paramecia,* known cutely as the slipper animalcule —was alive with enormously energetic *spermatozoa* — mine of course.

It must have been that very afternoon when I had gone to the toilet to collect the sperm that I wrote one of the poorest jingles I had ever collected on the marble wall of that retreat:

> *Jack and Jill went up the hill*
> *To fetch a pail of water.*
> *Jill came down with a two-dollar bill.*
> *Do you think they went for water?*

We came, eventually, to the study of the nervous and digestive systems of the earthworm (*Lumbricus terrestris*) and there is no doubt that both the digestive and nervous system of this very useful beast would fascinate anyone who was in the right frame of mind.

But we studied that damned *Lumbricus* for an entire month and I was getting bored with it. They had to be dissected under water — a saline solution floated on top of a layer of beeswax that coated a pan. Big as they were (night crawlers were the variety studied) their dissection took enormous care and their outer skin, once incised, had to be pinned back to the beeswax with long pins in order to expose the creature's plumbing. It was not an edifying sight.

At the end of that month when we were about to start on the musculature of the crayfish (*Cambarus diogenes*) and Professor Barry Palmer had lectured on the subject, smiling from ear to ear, he said, "Oh, will Mr. Leonard please see me after class?"

Much as I disliked him, Professor Palmer apparently liked *me*. He never failed to remark — monotonously — on the fact that my brother Adrian had preceded me in his class four years earlier and "if you do as well as Adrian, you will do very well indeed." This of course endeared him to me further.

This time he said, "How is Adrian?"

"Fine."

"In medical school, I imagine?"

"Yes. P. & S."

"Come to my office, Julian," said Professor Palmer. "I have a problem I'd like to discuss — if you have the time."

This interested me and so I went willingly. He even took my left arm and held it walking down the hall.

"I've been looking at your work on *Lumbricus* and it's excellent. *Very* good anatomical drawing, by the way."

"Thank you, sir."

"I hear you're working at the Natural History Museum after classes?"

"Whenever I can," I said.

By this time we had reached his office and he took out a key and opened it and indicated that I was to enter first. I wondered what problem such a permanently smiling man could have, so successful a man, decades of whose students had to study from his text, *Biology*.

"Please sit down," he said. I sat.

He sat behind his desk and looked at me and smiled. He smiled like mad at me and it grew somewhat disconcerting.

"Tell me," he said casually, "what would you think of a person who wrote dirty poems on toilet walls."

Innocently, I said, "Not much."

"The sort of thing you would expect from . . . uh . . . *truck* drivers, isn't it?"

"Yes," I said as a horrid thought rose slowly but inexorably into my mind. (Had I been as wise then as Professor Palmer *should* have been, I would have said, "No. Truck drivers have more sexual outlets than students; they don't *have* to write on walls.")

Professor Palmer took a slip of paper from his desk and read aloud:

> "Jack and Jill went up the hill
> To fetch a pail of water.
> Jill came down with a two-dollar bill.
> Do you think they went for water?"

He smiled at me and my scurrying mind said to me, He doesn't know *you* wrote it. He *couldn't* know you wrote it. *How* could he know you wrote it?

"What do you think of *that?*" he smiled.

"Disgusting," I said with considerable aplomb and saw him nod. "Besides, it's *very* bad verse."

He leaned slightly forward and dropped the piece of paper on his desk.

"Then why did you write it on the wall of the lavatory?"

I was silent. I was silent for quite a long time. While I was somewhat frightened I was far more interested in how he had discovered the identity of the culprit than I was in the fact that I was caught. I figured correctly that I did not stand a chance of denying it and so I didn't deny it. Instead, I said, "I don't know."

As though he were reading my mind and he might very well have been doing exactly that, Professor Palmer said, "I suppose you wonder how I found you out."

I smiled in a sickly manner, myself.

"You want to be a scientist," he said. "You even show certain gifts along that line. To be a scientist," he said — and it could have been Aaron Vogelsang speaking — "you have to use the scientific method. You have to engage in a great deal of patient and tedious observation, experimentation, comparison and study. And you have to use controls."

He cleared his throat as he did so often in the classroom and smiled his automatic built-in smile.

"There are exactly four hundred and thirty-five students who use the lavatories in this building. Students of biology, zoology, physiology, botany, chemistry and physics."

He was staring at me as though I were some weird specimen myself, a fixed smile on his hateful face.

"In the last month all of them have had to submit written work — in the form of reports, theses, term papers."

"You read them *all*!" I blurted out, astonishment flooding me from head to foot.

"I scanned them all. And *you*," he said with his diabolical smile, "are blessed with a very distinctive and characteristic hand-writing."

I knew that was true. I was consciously remodeling my hand-writing on that of a professor of comparative literature who amazed me in more than one way — but that is another story that is scarce-ly germane to biology, zoology or physiology, although it might be germane to psychology at that.

"You will report to the Dean," said Professor Palmer, his smile as fixed and sharklike as ever. "I don't know what view he will take of the matter. To *me*," he said, that smile sinking into my very flesh and blood and bones, "it would be a matter for expulsion."

I must have sat there transfixed for he finally said, "You may go now, Mr. Leonard. I spoke to the Dean and he is expecting you."

As I rose to leave, still enchanted — in the worst sense of the word — by the Palmer Smile, some lines were running through my head that had been intoned in his spectacular baritone by Professor Spinner of comparative literature:

> *O villain, villain, smiling, damned villain!*
> *My tables, meet it is I set it down,*
> *That one may smile, and smile, and be a villain.*
>   . . .

The Serpent Was More Subtil

DEAN Francis A. Falcon of Columbia College did not seem terribly upset by my having written a dirty poem on the wall of the toilet in the science building. "I disagree with Professor Palmer," he said, "that this is a matter for expulsion, although I know he takes a very serious view of such matters. What made you do such a thing?"

Honestly I said, "I don't know, sir." After all, in those days I had not had the benefit (?) of two years with a psychiatrist which came three decades later.

"I don't know how much you think about these things," the good Dean said. (I *loved* his name: somehow it fitted in with my passion for natural science even though birds didn't mean as much to me as reptiles and amphibians.) By "these things," of course, Dean Falcon meant *one* thing — sex.

"You would be well advised," he said, "to divert some of your energies into studies and athletics."

I had already done that. Frustrated by the fact that my desire to be a member of the swimming team (on which my older brother Adrian had been a "star" four years earlier) had been balked because *everyone* who tried out could outswim me from the start, I had gone out for — and been accepted by — the fencing squad.

The team was trained by a fascinating little Irishman no more than five feet three inches tall who insisted on speaking French. But even here, my crescent interest in matters sexual could not be completely sublimated. (A sword — as well as a snake — is a symbol, no?)

It was not so much that Coach Fitzpatrick always yelled, *"La famille! La famille!"* when a member of the squad accidentally came close to the Coach's genitals with his foil, *épée* or sabre. (He dropped his own weapon histrionically and covered *la famille* with both his hands.)

It was the fact that Coach Fitzpatrick was fifty years old, had married for the first time — a girl of twenty-five — and had just become a father.

This gave the members of the fencing squad great "pause," to borrow a phrase from Hamlet's soliloquy. There were all kinds of steamy and jealous speculations about Joe Fitzpatrick's prowess on the matrimonial mattress which were, no doubt, closely related to the fact that he could (and did) take on the entire fencing squad one at a time, and reduce them all to a state of physiological impotency: their knees quaking, their blades falling from their hands, their hearts pounding and their breathing labored to the point of suffocation.

"I *am* on the fencing squad, sir," I said.

"Well, good for you," said Dean Falcon and looked speculatively at me. I knew exactly what he was going to say and when he said it I suppose I nodded (inside my head).

"Your brother Adrian made a very good record when he was here." His kindly face assumed a distinctly avuncular expression. "I understand you boys have recently lost your father."

I nodded physically this time.

"*He* would have wanted you to make as good a record as Adrian, don't you think?"

I nodded again.

Then Dean Falcon stood up and smiled and put one hand on my shoulder. "*You* know better than to do such things, Julian. You won't do it again."

"No, sir," I said and he nodded and I left.

Professor Harry Palmer could not have been too pleased to see me return to his class but he smiled his permanent smile anyhow and to hell with *him*, I thought. He had been overruled by a *really* intelligent man, Dean Francis Falcon.

That was actually the second time I had been threatened with expulsion from a school and I suddenly recalled the first: I had been enrolled in the first junior high school in New York City and had refused to sing *solo* in music class because my voice was changing.

That time the music teacher, Herr Professor Schwanz, had not merely sent me but had *taken* me to the Principal and demanded my expulsion but the Principal, also a *really* intelligent man, had not taken such a serious view of the matter either.

Relieved of the threat of disgrace I could now try to concentrate on my college work and my unpaid afternoon job as a herpetologist-in-training at the Natural History Museum, where I worked directly under the supervision of the Curator, Dr. R. Maple Foss.

The post certainly allowed for a lot of free time, as it consisted mostly of odd jobs. During that free time, when I could resist wandering around the Museum and visiting Dr. Pike, the ichthyologist who looked like a fish, Dr. Holmes, the lepidopterist who looked like a woodchuck or watching the arcane activities of Dr. Foss and his (paid) assistant, Mr. Pildyke, I did odd jobs and dreamed of future eminence in the field.

What form that eminence would assume was difficult to imagine. The late Edward Drinker Cope had already classified all the crocodilians, lizards and snakes of North America. The late Susan Anthony Aldridge, Dr. Foss' immediate predecessor, had classified all the frogs, toads and salamanders, and Dr. Foss and Mr. Pildyke were *re*classifying them all (reptiles *and* amphibians) all over again in collaboration.

I could and did dream of writing brilliant scientific articles for *Natural History*, the official Museum magazine; or for the bulletin of the Linnaean Society whose monthly meetings I occasionally attended at night on the main floor and whose elderly members I had foxed into electing me to membership by falsely reporting that I had seen a great horned owl (*Bubo virginianus*) in Van Cortlandt Park.

But I preferred to dream about making my brilliant contributions to *Copeia*, the monthly publication of the Society of American Herpetologists which owed its title to Cope himself.

I was reading the latest issue of that small recondite publication one afternoon in my office — a storeroom jammed with bottles, jars and boxes — when Dr. Maple Foss materialized and said, "You know Mr. Herbert Heinz of Anthropology."

It was a statement rather than a question and I nodded quickly. Who did *not* know that scion of the great pickle family who was referred to (but never to his face) as "57 Varieties"?

"Go see him," said Dr. Foss and dematerialized.

I walked down the hall to Mr. Heinz's office and threaded my way among the long tables covered with dusty skulls, *femurs*, pelvic girdles and assorted jawbones, *tibiae* and *fibulae* (with an occasional *scapula, ilium, ischium* or *pubis)* until I saw him at his roll-top desk.

He stood and when he stood he was an awsome sight for he was at least six feet five inches tall. He was also bald and had a booming voice.

"How do you do, young man?" he said, extending an enormous hand which I had no option but to grasp, knowing in advance that he would crush my digits as he had the first time we met.

"Sit down," he said and sat in his swivel chair.

I sat.

"Call me Uncle Herbie," he said.

"Yes, sir."

"Dr. Foss has recommended you for a summer job."

"Thank you, sir."

"Call *me* Uncle Herbie," he said, "but thank Dr. Foss. He has a high opinion of your abilities."

"Thank you, Uncle Herbie," I said, somewhat confused.

"You may or may not know," he said, "that in Palisades Interstate Park there is a chain of lakes and on those lakes there are seventeen camps of the Boy Scouts of America."

He paused and scrutinized me, then continued. "We also have a trailside museum, of which I am the director. We will need a naturalist for the summer and Dr. Foss has recommended you."

I was stunned, but not too severely because I really felt I deserved such a post and had been wondering why it had taken so long for my abilities to be recognized.

"The camps and the museum open on July one," said Uncle Herbie. "You will be there then. We will have a large collection of living reptiles, amphibians and mammals, which we borrow every summer from the Zoo. From Roland Martin — you know him."

"Yes, sir."

"It will be your responsibility to care for all these animals: feed them, see that their cages are kept clean, that they remain healthy."

I gulped. This was being a *Naturalist*?

Uncle Herbie continued. "You will have other duties, of course. You will lecture regularly at the museum and at the seventeen Boy Scout camps — on reptiles and amphibians, on mammals, birds and insects. For purposes of these lectures you will utilize the specimens — both living and mounted — at the Trailside Museum as well as lantern slides which will be provided. How do you like the idea?"

"Wonderful!" I said with genuine enthusiasm.

"The job is for July and August and you will of course get transportation, board and room and fifty dollars."

"A month?"

"For two months. Dr. Foss will have certain assignments for you, as well. Report to him on that. Do you agree to the terms of employment?"

"Of course," I said, then added shrewdly, "thank you, Uncle Herbie."

He stood. "Good boy!" he said heartily. "We'll get along." I suffered my digits to be crushed again by his monstrous paw and reported back to Dr. Foss.

"Aside from learning everything you can about herpetological fauna of the Park, he said, giggling nervously, "I will set you to *one* single task."

He brought out a Geodetic Survey map of Palisades Interstate Park and pointed at it with a pencil he took out of his vest pocket.

"In this area of the Park," he said, "the spotted salamander *Ambystoma maculatum*, is common." He moved his pencil about four inches. "In this area, where the habitat is identical — note that, it is *identical* — you will not find one single *Ambystoma.*

He looked up at me and said, "I want you to find out why this situation obtains."

Holy Mackerel! I thought – a *real* scientific assignment! *That* would be the subject of my first paper for *Copeia!* The title immediately sprang to mind: "Notes on the Ecology and Distribution of *Ambystoma maculatum* in Palisades Interstate Park."

I could hardly wait to get to work. My brother Adrian, a sophomore now at the College of Physicians & Surgeons, said he was delighted with my job. He patted me on the back, asked if I had a headache and laughed.

That was a private joke. When he had been a freshman at P & S and I had complained of a headache one evening, he had given me a capsule saying it was the best thing known.

Innocently, I had taken it and when I went to the toilet an hour or so later I had urinated a brilliant *blue!* Ah, these medical students and their merry pranks! Like putting a well-preserved finger or ear in your pocket or bringing home the top of a skull *(Calvarium)* complete with patches of skin and hair and boiling it on the kitchen stove for hours – to make a gleaming white ashtray.

Even my mother Lena was, or pretended to be, pleased by my summer job, "though it certainly doesn't pay much, does it?"

"Does *that* matter?" I demanded angrily. "Is that *all* that counts – the money?"

"No," she said, "but it helps."

What she meant was, having lost so much of the insurance money my father had left playing poker, the Stock Market and the horses, at least I would not cost her anything that summer.

M oney was the least of my problems as I dug into my job at the Trailside Museum on July one. It was located on the shore of one of a chain of three lakes, somewhat west of Haverstraw and north of Ramapo, where I used to catch rattlesnakes for the Zoo.

It was an impressive little building and when I arrived I found that I had an office on which there was a neatly lettered sign that read:

> JULIAN LEONARD
> Naturalist

I also found Uncle Herbie dressed in full regalia – as a scoutmaster! Considering the fact that he was well over six feet tall, the sight of the man with his bald head, his hairy legs like tree trunks sticking out of shorts, was awe-inspiring.

That sign on the door: I did not recognize at the time that it was probably intended more to enhance the prestige of the Trailside Museum than mine. I took it as my due and installed myself in the office, arranged things to suit my convenience and sat in the swivel chair and lit a Lucky Strike. (*Julian Leonard*, I thought, Member: Audubon Society, Linnaean Society. Donor: New York Zoological Society. Staff member: Herpetological Department, Natural History Museum. Staff Naturalist: Trailside Museum, Palisades Interstate Park.)

Later that day I met other members of the staff — the camp doctor, Fletcher; his assistant, who was not even a medical student and who said his name was Doug; a pair of young kids named Bob and Harold who drove the garbage boat. (The boat did not *bring* garbage to the seventeen Boy Scout camps and the museum; it hauled it away to some distant point.)

When each of these fellow employees introduced himself, I identified myself as, "Julian Leonard. I'm the *Naturalist* here."

If they looked at me askance I did not notice it, but I did notice that they were not too friendly and what the hell? Who wanted to be friendly with garbage-boat chauffeurs or a medical assistant who wasn't even studying to be a doctor? *My* colleagues were the doctor himself and the Director of the Museum, loudmouthed and overpowering Call-Me-Uncle-Herbie Heinz. Ridiculous as he was, he was at least an anthropologist.

The routine at the summer museum was rapidly established. There were several outdoor cages covered with wire screening in which we had some timber rattlesnakes, a pine snake, a king snake *(Lampropeltis getulus getulus)*, a large number of enormous bullfrogs *(Rana catesbeiana)* and assorted turtles.

The first week there was a minor calamity: Somehow or other the king snake got into the cage with the rattlers, constricted three of them to death and had swallowed half of one before I appeared on the scene. (They are immune to the venom of the pit vipers.)

The first month the rattlers themselves developed an infection of the mouth. We had no veterinarian and veterinarians are notoriously ignorant about snakes anyhow, so I devised my own treatment and — to my astonishment — it worked. Every morning I took them out of their cage one at a time and swabbed out their mouths and throats with a tincture of potassium permanganate.

Scouts from various of the camps and even park rangers brought in new specimens almost every day. One ranger brought a mother raccoon (*Procyon lotor*) and her baby. One scout brought in an infant skunk (*Mephitis mephitis*) he had found on the road. It was helpless and obviously ill and a cursory examination by the museum's Naturalist revealed that it was infested with intestinal worms. I bought some worm medicine from a pet shop in Tuxedo Park. It had been concocted for dogs, of course, but it worked perfectly. In no time at all the worms were gone and the baby skunk was feeding from a nursing bottle.

Cute as it was, I preferred the baby raccoon but it was difficult to separate it from its mother. I succeeded, however, by trapping the mother under a large wooden box one day when she was teaching her infant how to kill and eat a bullfrog I had provided.

The little 'coon had grabbed the bullfrog by its left hind leg and was being dragged all over the cage when I got its mother under the box, freed the baby from its enormous prey and made it my personal pet.

I bought a small dog collar for it and a leash and in less than two days it was following me all over the place, sitting up and begging for food and generally making itself adorable to every visitor to the museum.

But these activities were the whipped cream on the stale cake of my job. Almost every night the garbage boat came for me and either Bob or Harold ferried me — unwillingly, it seemed to me — to one of the Boy Scout camps on one of the three lakes. (We made little or no conversation.)

There I gave a lecture, either with live snakes or lantern slides, to campfire meetings of the Scouts in what was, I am certain, a vain effort to interest them in and educate them about the *flora* and *fauna* of the eastern United States.

They were a captive audience but they were generally well-behaved. There were always two or three exhibitionists who wanted to handle the larger nonvenomous serpents and show off with them.

The only really interesting lecture of the summer was the one I gave at a *Girl* Scout camp about ten miles away where it was possible for the girls to observe the living snakes and it was possible for me to observe the living girls.

I was tortured at seventeen by fantasies about *Homo sapiens* ♀ (as who is not?) but there seemed no opportunity to put these daydreams into practice. Doug, the nonmedical student assistant to Dr. Fletcher, had already staked out what he called "a juicy piece of neck" at the family camp where visiting parents of the Scouts could stay for a weekend or a week at a time.

Her name was Frances Foyle and she was known as The Sweetheart of the Family Camp, perhaps because she was willing to give a juicy piece of neck to others, as well as to Doug. I did not see her until I was tempted one day to swim the length of the three lakes — a distance of seven miles.

What possessed me to attempt such a feat of stamina I have never known, but with one of the pimply kids who waited table for the staff rowing a boat alongside I accomplished this absurdity after something like five hours in the water, arriving at the family camp dock just before dusk in a state of complete collapse.

Well, I was not *so* exhausted that I did not notice Frances Foyle who was dallying on the dock with Doug and was wearing a one-piece bathing suit that was so scant and so tight that she was making quite a display — not only of her breasts and buttocks but also of her *mons veneris* and even her *labia majora*. All these primary and secondary sexual characteristics were very well developed and provided a fascinating spectacle for the minutes I clung to the pier before I could gather the strength to haul myself out of the water.

Doug introduced me to Frances who batted her eyes at me and, in turn, introduced me to Gladys Fillmore, a girl her age whom she described as "my friend."

Reluctantly I turned my gaze on Gladys who did not possess

*any*where the sort of curves that Frances displayed in her groin alone, but I reluctantly tried to create a fantasy about *her*, knowing Frances Sweetheart was "spoken for."

I had dinner with these girls and Doug at the family camp (it was Sunday), and even took Gladys out walking in the night, trying to develop out of her expressed admiration for my swimming accomplishments some amorous parallel. I failed. I was relieved that I had failed, for I was unable to develop any real excitement in myself. She was a stringy specimen of *sapiens* ♀ and I had already developed tremendous admiration for girls who were built like girls instead of boys; a fetish that has lasted all my life.

Doug and I paddled a canoe back to the staff camp late that night after I had waited an additional hour or so after Gladys went to bed while he got his piece of neck, but I was less disturbed by my self-willed failure with Gladys than I was by a remark made by the kid who had rowed the boat for me that day.

"Julian," he had said, keeping abreast of me as I stroked wearily through the water wishing I had never started on this ordeal, "do you know what the guys around the camp call you?"

I lifted my head and said, "No, what?" and turned over on my back for a few minutes.

"They call you *Jew* Leonard." He paused. "Are you a Jew?"

"Sure," I said.

"Gee whiz!" he said. I wondered why. What was so astonishing about *that*?

I was a Jew because my father had told me I was a Jew and I should be "proud of it." He never told me why, but later research developed considerable grounds for admiring the Jews, if not the accidental fact that I was one of them.

I have often wondered *why* I was a Jew since no member of my family since my paternal grandfather died in 1907 had ever practiced the religion, spoken a word of Hebrew (or even Yiddish) or observed the many cultural customs of my people.

If you reject, as you must, such concepts as "blood" or "racial memory," the only answer to the question must lie in the fact that you are a Jew because your ancestors were Jews. "Racial" or even national characteristics? Ridiculous. There was an I-Cash-Clothes

Man who regularly cruised our block who was a type-specimen Irishman: red hair, blue eyes, broad upper lip, snub nose — until he opened his mouth.

Since I didn't even "look like" one I was doubly aggrieved by the evidence Pimple-Face had given me of the existence of anti-Semitism in the camp. By swiftly ticking off each member of the staff I realized I was the only one of that wandering tribe who are even said to be ancestors of the Irish — which may account for the I-Cash-Clothes Man, too.

Perhaps *that* was the reason that Harold and Bob, the garbage-boat drivers, were so cool to me. Doug was friendly enough but maybe he had been forced into it by my sudden appearance at the family camp that afternoon.

I gave up speculation about this piece of disturbing information because I was too busy. I had received a telegram from Dr. R. Maple Foss that read:

NEED 100 BUFO FOWLERI BY END OF WEEK.
SHIP BY FREIGHT. URGENT. FOSS.

I spent the next three nights till early dawn hunting Fowler's toad by flashlight and was able to find only twenty-seven of the beasts. All the rest were the common American toad *(Bufo americanus)* and I became quite frustrated. If Dr. Foss had asked for one hundred *americanus*, I was convinced, I would have turned up nothing but *fowleri*. (And what was he going to do with them, anyhow, anesthetize and pickle them in formaldehyde?)

In addition to becoming frustrated I caught a cold. This cold — which seems characteristic with me — rapidly developed into influenza and I went to bed the fourth night in the staff camp, which was about half a mile down the road from the museum, with a fever of 102° Fahrenheit.

Dr. Fletcher had supplied me with aspirin and the kitchen gave me a large jar of orange juice but, alone in my tent, I had a hard time falling asleep. I was alternately shivering and sweating, tossing and turning, groaning out loud, coughing and sneezing, my nose running like a faucet.

My conscience was also bothering me about those *fowleri*. What would R. Maple Foss think of a naturalist he had sent into the field as an accredited representative not only of his personal department, but of the Natural History Museum itself, who could not turn up a measly hundred *fowleri* on demand?

What was worse, what would he think of a scientist — I had suddenly remembered the "*one* single task" he had set me — who had not only determined why the spotted salamander could be found in one area of the park, whereas — a few miles off — not a specimen could be found on identical terrain, but who had even failed to give any thought to the problem?

It was too late to do anything about Fowler's toad since the deadline for shipping them had passed, but that feverish night I determined that the moment I was on my feet again I would get to work immediately trying to explain the uneven distribution of *Ambystoma maculatum*. I would not only determine why this situation "obtains," as Foss had put it, but I would document it with chapter and verse.

Then I would be ready — there was only one more month of the job ahead — to write *two* papers for *Copeia*. The Museum itself would publish them: *Notes on the Ecology & Distribution of Ambystoma*, etc., and a more ambitious work: *The Herpetological Fauna of Palisades Interstate Park*.

These papers would be received with such acclaim that I would immediately be offered a paid position on the Museum staff, and I would also be hard put to decide whether to finish my college education through the Bachelor and Master of Science degrees (*and* the Ph.D.) or go to work immediately.

I could foresee long arguments, not only with my mother but with my brother Adrian who was now the "head of the family" with considerable control over what was left of the family non-fortune, and whose arguments would therefore be more persuasive. For it *could* be that I would not receive a large enough salary at the Museum and would need some supplementary income.

Finally, I must have fallen asleep for I can remember my dream: I was wading in a deep pit that was literally alive with *Thamnophis sirtalis*, the common garter snake, but there wasn't a *Bufo*, whether *americanus* or *fowleri*, in sight. I wondered about that. I began to pick the garter snakes up and then I put them down. I started to count them but lost count after one hundred and seventeen when suddenly one of them turned into a king cobra (*Naja hannah*). Then it turned into a brilliantly patterned gaboon viper (*Bitis gabonica*) and then into an asp — the type of beast that finished Cleopatra and which was not an asp at all but was probably an Egyptian cobra (*Naje haje*). Cleopatra herself appeared, *holding* the asp. She was naked except for a round red patent-leather hat, and she had an enormous "Jewish" (really Hittite) nose.

How Cleopatra got into this dream I would not know unless there is some connection between her and Frances Foyle and her luxurious *pudenda*. If so, this would argue that the Freudian analysts *have* something when they insist that a snake is a snake is a penis symbol.

I awoke hearing voices and sat up in the dark, only to find myself grasped and held tightly. I opened my mouth to yell and a gag was placed in it and tied behind my head. I struggled violently and was promptly tied by my arms, legs and waist to the cot on which I was lying. I lay strapped and bound and, to my horror, felt the cot being lifted and carried out of the tent!

Uncle Herbie slept in a tent not twenty feet away and I wondered where he was. Then it occurred to me that perhaps *he* too was a member of this hazing party and I immediately had another reason for disliking him.

Several pairs of feet could be heard now, crunching down the dirt road that led from the staff camp to the road that ran along the lake. Incongruously, I suddenly understood why Cleopatra had been wearing that red patent-leather hat: It was that Slavic servant girl who lived across the courtyard from us in New York, the one who liked to undress partially in front of her window and then, pretending to suddenly notice me, would coyly pull down her shade. *She* wore a red patent-leather hat. Her curves were also something like Frances Foyle's, only more voluptuous.

Not a word was spoken by the group carrying me on my litter (like Cleopatra!) until suddenly the sound of crunching on the dirt road changed into the unmistakable sound of feet moving on a wooden pier over water.

My God! I thought, invoking the Jehovah in whom I had never believed, this was not a hazing — this was a *lynching*! They were going to throw me, cot and all, into the lake! *Why!?* WHY?! I would have screamed if my mouth had been free but I could do nothing but struggle feebly against my bonds and listen to the hammering of my heart in its rib cage.

A hand suddenly touched my forehead; then it was withdrawn and inserted into my pajama jacket. A voice spoke, not unkindly, saying, "He's got a bad fever."

I recognized that voice — it belonged to Doug, the medical assistant to Dr. Fletcher. The cot was set down roughly on the pier. I heard other voices, none of which I could recognize, speaking in what was apparently a muted conference.

Then the cot and I were heaved up into the air again and we retraced our steps back to the main road and turned (to the right, I could feel it) down the road. There was total silence as we marched along the road for what seemed a very long time and my mind was racing like mad, trying to anticipate what was coming next.

From the distance, the time and the sound — again of wood planking underfoot — I figured we had come into the Trailside Museum itself. The men carrying me were breathing hard as they set the cot down on the floor. I could hear them breathing on all sides.

Then there were voices. They said strange, disjointed things but everything they said cut me to the heart.

"Jew bastard." (Pimple-Face had been right!)

"*That's* not important."

"Let's piss on him."

There was silence and some liquid was poured onto my face and head. I knew almost immediately that it was not urine; it smelled like rancid water and I guessed that it came from the jars of botanical specimens that stood on the shelves in the room that opened off the front door.

"Swim, Jewboy, *swim!*" said a voice.

"Great swimmer, ain't he?"

"Show-off."

"No, no," another voice said with heavy sarcasm, *"not* a show-off. He's Julian Leonard — *Naturalist!*"

"Jew Leonard."

"Lay off the Jew stuff," said that recognizable voice — Doug's. *"That's* not important. What's important, he's a prick."

"Circumsized prick."

"Cut it out!" said Doug. I was beginning to love him. I got the distinct feeling that he was trying to protect me even if I was a prick.

The blindfold was not taken off but the gag was taken out of my mouth as someone said, "Maybe he's got something to say." (Before they *kill* me!?)

"Yes," I gasped, feeling thoroughly ashamed in advance of what I knew I was going to say.

"Say it, prick."

"I'm sorry."

"What're you sorry for, prick?"

"That I — that I've been . . . a prick. Arrogant —"

"Arrogant!" a voice said. "Big words he uses!"

"Why not? He's a *college* boy."

"I'm sorry," I said. "It won't happen again."

"It better not."

I felt my head grasped and lifted, felt a pair of clippers cutting uneven patterns through what my mother used to call my "natural marcel wave."

Then some liquid that was at first cool was applied to my head and face. Later, it burned. I felt someone untying the knots that bound me to the cot and I heard feet running on the wooden floor. The door slammed. There was silence.

I lay there a few minutes until I felt certain there was nobody else around, then I tore the blindfold from my eyes, got off the bed shivering from head to foot and groped my way into my un-locked office: *Jew* Leonard — *Naturalist.* I lit the light.

They had cut paths through my hair. My face and scalp were painted with iodine and I spent the next hour and a half cutting off the rest of my hair with a pair of scissors and trying to wash off the iodine with alcohol. It burned.

Leaving the cot where it stood I wrapped the blanket around my shoulders and walked barefoot back to the staff camp. Passing the point of land that reached into the lake, I saw a small campfire and heard laughing voices. I kept on walking, entered a large unoccupied tent next to Uncle Herbie's and lay down on an empty cot and tried to sleep till dawn.

The next day I wore a cap to breakfast, lunch and supper but nobody commented on it and nobody ever said a word to me about that night during the entire month of August. I hitched a ride into Tuxedo Park the day after and had a barber clip off the rest of my hair and I wore the cap when I had to appear in public, either at the museum or at the Boy Scout camps at night to give lectures.

If anything, my introspective qualities were intensified by this experience and I utilized the opportunity that ostracism gave me to stick to my office, where I began work on my report: *The Herpetological Fauna of Palisades Interstate Park*.

It ran to thirty pages double-spaced and covered every single "beast" that could be found in the Park, its habitat, an accurate description of its behavior, markings and color variations — whether I had personally seen a specimen of the breed, or not.

I remember distinctly one paragraph about the water snake *(Natrix sipedon sipedon)*:

> *You will generally find* Natrix *basking in the sun on flat rocks by the shores of streams or lakes, or lying on fallen logs. Its body is heavy and comes to a pointed tail, and when startled it invariably seeks the water, sliding voluptuously into it like a stream of heavy lubricating oil.*

When August was over I packed my suitcase, tucking my contribution to *Copeia* carefully inside, and took a bus from Tuxedo Park. Nobody saw me off and even Uncle Herbie, when I left the museum, gave me no more than a perfunctory handshake.

What do *I* care? I said to myself, watching the landscape rotate about the bus as we traveled down the western shore of the Hudson River. *That* was no job for a scientist, a naturalist, a herpetologist. I had been a *zoo* keeper, cleaning out the cages, lecturing to dumbell Boy Scouts who didn't want to learn anything anyhow, associating with dumb clucks like Doug and Bob and Harold, the garbage-boat chauffeurs who were the leaders of that dreadful night of fear and shame.

Uncle Herbie must have known about it and even approved of what they were going to do. Well, nuts to *him*, too, the overgown Boy Scout in his shorts and hiking boots. Anthropologist! What kind of anthropolgist was *he*? He had a job at the Natural History Museum because his family were pickle millionaires — no other reason.

My mother was astonished by my appearance and asked why I had clipped my "beautiful hair" so short. "Because I *felt* like it," I said, but my brother Adrian the medical student looked at me shrewdly and said nothing.

The week before classes began for what would be my junior year at Columbia I reported to Dr. R. Maple Foss at the Museum and proudly laid my report on his desk. He glanced at it and said, "Good. I'll read it later."

He said nothing for a week and then called me into his office, reached into a compartment of his rolltop desk and fished out a manuscript.

"I've read this thing," he said, emphasizing the last word ever so slightly. He opened it to a page he had turned down and glanced up at me, then down at the page and started to read:

" 'Its body is heavy and comes to a pointed tail, and when startled it invariably seeks the water, sliding *volooptuously* into it like a stream of heavy lubricating oil.' "

There was a contemptuous expression on his face as he said, "You haven't told me anything about the beasts of that area that I didn't know. You call that a piece of scientific work? That's *poetry*."

I said nothing and he handed me the manuscript. "Another thing: I wired you to send me a hundred *Bufo fowleri* and you only sent twenty-seven.

"I couldn't *find* any more."

"Another thing. I sent you up there *specifically* to determine why *Ambysoma maculatum* is so unevenly distributed in the Park and that piece of *literature* of yours —" he waved one hand at me and my manuscript — "doesn't even *mention* the problem, let alone solve it. Maybe you just don't have a scientific *mind*."

Then he softened the blow and said, "You can get out into the field next summer and work up some more data." He turned back to his desk, dismissing me.

I *hated* him! Who the hell did he think he was, anyhow? How did *he* get into the Museum in the first place? Because his *wife*, another so-called anthropologist, was *Society*? How does he expect a kid of seventeen-going-on-eighteen to solve a scientific problem like that when he's been worrying about it for years and can't solve it *himself*?

Depressed beyond measure, I decided to go home; then I decided not to. I walked up the stairs from the top floor into the attic of the Museum — an enormous series of rooms that held a peculiar fascination for me.

There were all kinds of marvelous things in the attic and for some reason or other, exploring there invariably had a soothing effect on me. There were things there was no room to exhibit on the floors below, or they were duplicates. There was a slab of Jurrasic stone in which a fossil *Pterodactyl*, the flying reptile, had been embedded for all eternity. There were surplus dinosaurs of one species or another, mounted or only partly mounted.

Invariably there was the carcass of some small mammal that was being skeletonized. It lay in a wooden box and swarms of Sexton (sometimes called burying) beetles (*Necrophorus americanus*) were hard at work devouring it. Those that were not gorging themselves were merrily copulating, thus maintaining the balance of nature on two levels of activity at the same time.

I watched the beetles working on what was some sort of carnivore for a few minutes. "Everybody's doing it," the song went; except *me*, I thought. What was the speech Professor Spinner of Comparative Literature was so fond of quoting, practically smacking his lips over it?

The wren goes to't, and the small gilded fly
Does lecher in my sight.
Let copulation thrive. . . !

King Lear, no? Yes. *Literature*, Foss had said contemptuously. *Poetry*! he had sneered, and what is wrong with *that*? Had he never read any of the works of William Beebe, whom he would undoubtedly call a "popularizer" of natural history but who was an accredited scientist if ever there was one? He, too, wrote like a poet and he was responsible for a series of monographs on the pheasant as well as the book on the Galapagos Islands he was preparing and from which he had read at the Linnaean Society not so long ago.

Through a doorway I noticed that there was a partially reconstructed *Stegosaurus* in the room and I started through the doorway to inspect it.

I failed to notice that the space between the room in which I had been watching the Sexton beetles and the one in which the *Stegosaurus* was being put together was nothing but a flat pane of opaque glass.

I was thinking, Maybe I *am* a poet; maybe I *should* write literature, as I felt myself sinking through the floor and instinctively threw up my arms to shield my face.

When I came to consciousness again I was lying on a wooden table on the floor below and an ambulance surgeon dressed in white was examining me and what seemed to be the entire staff of the Natural History Museum was standing around, looking.

Above my head I could see the broken pane through which I had fallen; it was a good forty feet away! Somebody was saying, "If he hadn't hit that steel storage case on the way down —"

Foss was saying, "Is he all right, doctor? Will he be all right?"

"Nothing broken," said the ambulance surgeon. He was bandaging the palm of my right hand, which had apparently been cut by the glass.

"You sure you shouldn't take him to the hospital?"

"I'm sure," said the man in white, slightly annoyed by the question.

"Good *Christ*!" said Dr. R. Maple Foss. "What a *mess*!"

As I was riding home in the taxicab they had called for me, un-accompanied and somewhat shaky, it occurred to me that in that sentence Foss had pronounced an obituary over my scientific ca-reer. I knew I would never return to the Museum again. I knew that I did not really want to be a natural scientist at all. I wanted to be a writer.

Words were already running through my mind and arranging themselves in orderly patterns, even rhythmic patterns. What was the name of that Slavic servant girl across the courtyard with the red patent-leather hat? Well, what difference does it make? Call her Elena.

> *Elena, thy beauty is to me*
> *Like those Nicaean barks of yore . . .*

No, no! my mind said. That's somebody else. That's Edgar Allan Poe! Call her Natasha. The lines began again:

> *Natasha, do not draw thy shade tonight,*
> *But let me gaze my full upon thy form,*
> *Let mine eyes but dazzle with the light*
> *Your beauty sheds upon the . . . da da dorm. . . .*

What rhymes with *form*? Patience, I said to myself, the words will come.

Publishing History
Solo Flight and *The Serpent Was More Subtil*

Redbird, *transition*, Paris, February 1929
Only We Are Barren, *Hound & Horn*, New York, July 1931
    Reprinted, Edward J. O'Brien, *Best Short Stories*, 1931
Horizon, *Criterion*, London, July 1931
    Reprinted, O'Brien, 1932
A Little Walk, *Story*, Vienna, June 1932
    Reprinted, O'Brien, 1933
    Reprinted, Uzzell, *Short Story Hits*, 1932
    Reprinted, Gott-Behnke, *Preface to College Prose,* 1935
Pet Crow, *Scribners* magazine, New York, September 1932
Bare Grain, Brooklyn *Sunday Eagle magazine*, N.Y. Nov. 19, 1933
Deer, *Scribners* magazine, New York, July 1933
No Final Word, *Story*, New York, November 1933
    Reprinted, O'Brien, 1934
A Night Call, *Story*, New York, October 1934
Profession of Pain, *Esquire*, Chicago, May 1935
A Personal Issue, *Scribners* magazine, June 1936
    Reprinted, O. Henry Memorial Volume, 1936
Sam's Woman, Brooklyn *Sunday Eagle magazine*, New York, Feb. 25, 1934
Solo Flight, *New Masses*, New York, January 24, 1939
Soldier! Soldier!, *New Masses,* Oct. 3, 1939
    Translated, *Das Magazin*, Berlin, G.D.R., July 1962
My Brother, My Son, *Story*, New York, January-February 1940
    Translated, Berlin, 1955 & 1957 in German and English editions of *The American Century,* Edited by Maxim Lieber, Leipzig, G.D.R.

Man with Wings, *Esquire*, Chicago, June 1940
Call It Love, *New Masses,* New York, January 7, 1941
    Translated, *Das Magazin*, Berlin, G.D.R., March 1963

Susan Aldridge, *Requiescat, American Dialog*, New York, Nov.–
    Dec., 1966
    Translated, *Das Magazin*, Berlin, G.D.R., June 1967

(With the exception of the last story, above, all of *The Serpent
Was More Subtil* is being published here for the first time.)